Janet Evanovich's novels are:

"Suspenseful."—*Los Angeles Times*

"Terrific."—*San Francisco Chronicle*

"Irresistible."—*Kirkus Reviews*

"Thrilling."—*The Midwest Book Review*

"Hilariously funny."—*USA Today*

"A blast of fresh air."—*The Washington Post*

"Inventive and fast-paced."—*San Diego Union-Tribune*

"Superb."—*Detroit Free Press*

FEARLESS FOURTEEN

&

FINGER LICKIN' FIFTEEN

TWO NOVELS IN ONE

JANET EVANOVICH

St. Martin's Paperbacks

Published in the United States by St. Martin's Paperbacks, an imprint of St. Martin's Publishing Group.

FEARLESS FOURTEEN & FINGER LICKIN' FIFTEEN: FEARLESS FOURTEEN copyright © 2008 by Evanovich, Inc. and FINGER LICKIN' FIFTEEN copyright © 2009 by Evanovich, Inc.

All rights reserved.

For information, address St. Martin's Publishing Group, 120 Broadway, New York, NY 10271.

www.stmartins.com

ISBN: 978-1-250-62079-8

Our books may be purchased in bulk for promotional, educational, or business use. Please contact your local bookseller or the Macmillan Corporate and Premium Sales Department at 1-800-221-7945, ext. 5442, or by email at MacmillanSpecialMarkets@macmillan.com.

Printed in the United States of America

St. Martin's Paperbacks edition 2020

10 9 8 7 6 5 4 3 2 1

FEARLESS
FOURTEEN

Woohoo!
To Team Evanovich:
Alex, Peter, and SuperJen

*Thanks to Sandy Sherwood
for suggesting the title for this book*

Chapter

ONE

In my mind, my kitchen is filled with crackers and cheese, roast chicken leftovers, farm fresh eggs, and coffee beans ready to grind. The reality is that I keep my Smith & Wesson in the cookie jar, my Oreos in the microwave, a jar of peanut butter and hamster food in the over-the-counter cupboard, and I have beer and olives in the refrigerator. I used to have a birthday cake in the freezer for emergencies, but I ate it.

Truth is, I would dearly love to be a domestic goddess, but the birthday cake keeps getting eaten. I mean, you buy it, and you eat it, right? And then where are you? No birthday cake. Ditto cheese and crackers and eggs and the roast chicken leftovers (which were from my mother). The coffee beans are light-years away. I don't own a grinder. I guess I could buy *two* birthday cakes, but I'm afraid I'd eat both.

My name is Stephanie Plum, and in my defense I'd like to say that I have bread and milk on my shopping list, and I don't have any communicable diseases. I'm five feet, seven inches. My hair is brown and shoulder length and naturally curly. My eyes are blue. My teeth are mostly straight. My manicure was pretty good three days ago, and my shape is okay. I work as a bond enforcement agent for my cousin Vinnie, and today I was standing in Loretta Rizzi's kitchen, thinking not only was Loretta ahead of me in the kitchen-needs-a-makeover race, but she made me look like a piker in the Loose Cannon Club.

It was eight in the morning, and Loretta was wearing a long, pink flannel nightgown and holding a gun to her head.

"I'm gonna shoot myself," Loretta said. "Not that it would matter to you, because you get your money dead or alive, right?"

"Technically, that's true," I told her. "But dead is a pain in the tuchus. There's paperwork."

A lot of the people Vinnie bonds out are from my Chambersburg neighborhood in Trenton, New Jersey. Loretta Rizzi was one of those people. I went to school with Loretta. She's a year older than me, and she left high school early to have a baby. Now she was wanted for armed robbery, and she was about to blow her brains out.

Vinnie had posted Loretta's bond, and Loretta had failed to show for her court appearance, so I was dispatched to drag her back to jail. And as luck would have it, I walked in at a bad moment and interrupted her suicide.

"I just wanted a drink," Loretta said.

"Yeah, but you held up a liquor store. Most people would have gone to a bar."

"I didn't have any money, and it was hot, and I needed a Tom Collins." A tear rolled down Loretta's cheek. "I've been thirsty lately," she said.

Loretta is a half a head shorter than me. She has curly black hair and a body kept toned by hefting serving trays for catered affairs at the firehouse. She hasn't changed much since high school. A few crinkle lines around her eyes. A little harder set to her mouth.

She's Italian-American and related to half the Burg, including my off-and-on boyfriend, Joe Morelli.

"This was your first offense. And you didn't shoot anyone. Probably you'll get off with a hand-slap," I told Loretta.

"I had my period," she said. "I wasn't thinking right."

Loretta lives in a rented row house on the edge of the Burg. She has two bedrooms, one bath, a scrubbed-clean, crackerbox kitchen, and a living room filled with secondhand furniture. Hard to make ends meet when you're a single mother without a high school diploma.

The back door swung open and my sidekick, Lula, stuck her head in. "What's going on in here? I'm tired of waiting in the car. I thought this was gonna be a quick pickup, and then we were going for breakfast."

Lula is a former 'ho, turned bonds office file clerk and wheelman. She's a plus-size black woman who likes to squash herself into too small clothes featuring animal print and spandex. Lula's cup runneth over from head to toe.

"Loretta is having a bad morning," I said.

Lula checked Loretta out. "I can see that. She's still in her nightie."

"Notice anything else?" I asked Lula.

"You mean like she's tryin' to style her hair with a Smith & Wesson?"

"I don't want to go to jail," Loretta said.

"It's not so bad," Lula told her. "If you can get them to send you to the workhouse, you'll get dental."

"I'm a disgrace," Loretta said.

Lula shifted her weight on her spike-heeled Manolo knock-offs. "You be more of a disgrace if you pull that trigger. You'll have a big hole in your head, and your mother won't be able to have an open-casket viewing. And who's going to clean up the mess it'll make in your kitchen?"

"I have an insurance policy," Loretta said. "If I kill myself, my son, Mario, will be able to manage until he can get a job. If I go to jail, he'll be on his own without any money."

"Insurance policies don't pay out on suicides," Lula said.

"Oh crap! Is that true?" Loretta asked me.

"Yeah. Anyway, I don't know why you're worried about that. You have a big family. Someone will take care of Mario."

"It's not that easy. My mother is in rehab from when she had the stroke. She can't take him. And my brother, Dom, can't take him. He just got out of jail three days ago. He's on probation."

"What about your sister?"

"My sister's got her hands full with her own kids. Her rat turd husband left her for some pre-puberty lap dancer."

"There must be someone who can babysit for you," Lula said to Loretta.

"Everyone's got their own thing going. And I don't want to leave Mario with just anybody. He's very sensitive . . . and artistic."

I counted back and placed her kid in his early teens. Loretta had never married, and so far as I know, she'd never fingered a father for him.

"Maybe you could take him," Loretta said to me.

"*What?* No. No, no, no, no."

"Just until I can make bail. And then I'll try to find someone more permanent."

"If I take you in now, Vinnie can bond you out right away."

"Yeah, but if something goes wrong, I need someone to pick Mario up after school."

"What can go wrong?"

"I don't know. A mother worries about these things. Promise you'll pick him up if I'm still in jail. He gets out at two-thirty."

"She'll do it," Lula said to Loretta. "Just put the gun down and go get dressed so we can get this over and done. I need coffee. I need one of those extra-greasy breakfast sandwiches. I gotta clog my arteries on account of otherwise the blood rushes around too fast and I might get a dizzy spell."

Lula was sprawled on the brown Naugahyde couch hugging the wall in the bonds office, and Vinnie's office manager, Connie Rosolli, was at her desk. Connie and the desk had been strategically placed in front of Vinnie's inner-office door with the hope it would discourage pissed-off pimps, bookies, and other assorted lowlifes from rushing in and strangling Vinnie.

"What do you mean she isn't bonded out?" I asked Connie, my voice rising to an octave normally only heard from Minnie Mouse.

"She has no money to secure the bond. And no assets."

"That's impossible. Everyone has assets. What about her mother? Her brother? She must have a hundred cousins living in a ten-mile radius."

"She's working on it, but right now she has nothing. Bupkus. Nada. So Vinnie's waiting on her."

"Yeah, and it's almost two-thirty," Lula said. "You better go get her kid like you promised."

Connie swiveled her head toward me and her eyebrows went up to her hairline. "You promised to take care of Mario?"

"I said I'd pick him up if Loretta wasn't bonded out in time. I didn't know there'd be an issue with her bond."

"Oh boy," Connie said. "Good luck with that one."

"Loretta said he was sensitive and artistic."

"I don't know about the sensitive part, but his art is limited to spray paint. He's probably defaced half of Trenton. Loretta has to pick him up from school because they won't let him on a school bus."

I hiked my bag onto my shoulder. "I'm just driving him home. That was the deal."

"There might be some gray area in the deal," Lula said. "You might've said you'd take care of him. And anyways, you can't dump him in an empty house. You get child services after you for doin' that."

"Well, what the heck am I supposed to do with him?"

Lula and Connie did *I don't know* shoulder shrugs.

"Maybe I can sign for Loretta's bond," I said to Connie.

"I don't think that'll fly," Connie said. "You're the only person I know who has fewer assets than Loretta."

"Great." I huffed out of the office and rammed myself into my latest P.O.S. car. It was a Nissan Sentra that used to be silver but was now mostly rust. It had doughnut-size wheels, a Jaguar hood ornament, and a bobble-head Tony Stewart doll in the back window. I like Tony Stewart a lot, but seeing his head jiggling around in my rearview mirror doesn't do much for me. Unfortunately, he was stuck on with Crazy Glue and nothing short of dismantling the car was going to get him out of my life.

Loretta had given me a photo of Mario and a pickup location. I cruised to a spot where a group of kids were shuffling around, looking for their rides. Easy to spot Mario. He resembled Morelli when Morelli was his age. Wavy black hair and slim build. Some facial similarities, although Morelli has always been movie star handsome and Mario was a little short of movie star. Of course, I might have been distracted by the multiple silver rings piercing his eyebrows, ears, and nose. He was wearing black-and-white Converse sneakers, stovepipe jeans with a chain belt, a black T-shirt with Japanese characters, and a black denim jacket.

Morelli had been an early bloomer. He grew up fast and hard. His dad was a mean drunk, and Morelli got good with his hands as a kid. He could use them in a fight, and he could use them to coax girls out of their clothes. The first time Morelli and I played doctor, I was five years old, and he was seven. He's periodically repeated the performance, and lately we seem to be a couple. He's a cop now, and against all odds, he's mostly lost the anger he had growing up. He inherited a nice little house from his Aunt Rose and has become domestic enough to own a dog and a toaster. He hasn't as yet reached the crockpot, toilet seat down, live plant in the kitchen level of domesticity.

Mario looked like a *late* bloomer. He was short for his age and had "desperate geek" written all over him.

I got out of my car and walked to the group of kids. "Mario Rizzi?"

"Who wants to know?"

"I do," I said. "Your mother can't pick you up today. I promised her I'd bring you home."

This produced some moronic comments and snickers from Mario's idiot friends.

"The name is Zook," Mario said to me. "I don't answer to Mario."

I rolled my eyes, grabbed Zook by the strap on his backpack, and towed him to my car.

"This is a piece of shit," he said, hands dangling at his sides, taking the car in.

"And?"

He shrugged and wrenched the door open. "Just saying."

I drove the short distance to the bonds office and pulled to the curb.

"What's this?" he asked.

"Your mother's been returned to lockup because she failed to show for her court appearance. She can't make her bail, and I can't take you home to an empty house, so I'm parking you in the bonds office until I can find a better place for you."

"No."

"What do you mean *no*? *No* isn't an option."

"I'm not getting out of the car."

"I'm a bounty hunter. I could rough you up or shoot you or something if you don't get out of the car."

"I don't think so. I'm just a kid. Juvie would be all over your ass. And your eye is twitching."

I hauled my cell phone out of my bag and dialed Morelli. "Help," I said.

"Now what?"

"You remember your cousin Loretta's kid, Mario?"

"Vaguely."

"I've got him in my car, and he refuses to leave."

"Possession is nine-tenths of the law."

Zook was slouched down, watching me from the corner of his eye. Arms crossed over his chest. Sullen. I blew out a sigh and told Morelli the deal with Loretta.

"I'm off at four," Morelli said. "If Loretta isn't bonded out by then, I'll take the kid off your hands. In the meantime, he's all yours, Cupcake."

I disconnected and dialed Lula.

"Yeah?" Lula said.

"I'm outside, and I have Loretta's kid in the car."

Lula's face appeared in the front window to the bonds office. "I see you and the kid. What's going on?"

"He won't get out of the car," I said. "I thought you might help persuade him."

"Sure," Lula said. "I could persuade the hell out of him."

The bonds office door opened, and Lula swung her ass over to my car and yanked the door open.

"What's up?" Lula said to the kid.

Zook didn't answer. Still pouting.

"I'm here to escort you out of the car," Lula said, leaning in, filling the doorframe with her red hair extensions and acres of chocolate-colored boob barely contained in a low scoop neck zebra-stripe sweater.

Zook focused on Lula's gold tooth with the diamond chip, and below that what seemed like a quarter mile of cleavage, and his eyes almost fell out of his head. "Cripes," he said, kind of croaky-voiced, shrinking back into his seat, fumbling to get out of his seat belt.

"I got a way with men," Lula said to me.

"He's not a man," I told her. "He's just a kid."

"Am too a man," he said. "Want me to prove it?"

"No," Lula and I said in unison.

"What's this?" Connie wanted to know when the three of us walked into the bonds office.

"I need to leave Mario someplace for an hour while I hop over to Rangeman."

"I *told* you my name is Zook! And what's Rangeman?"

"I work with a guy named Ranger, and Rangeman is the security company he owns."

"Are you the Zook that writes his name all over town?" Lula asked him. "And what kind of name is that anyway?"

"It's my Minionfire name."

"What's a Minionfire?"

"Are you kidding me? You don't know Minionfire? *Minionfire*'s only the world's most popular, most powerful, totally awesome, badass difficult game. Don't tell me you've never heard of the Nation of Minionfire?"

"In my neighborhood, we only got the nation of Bloods, Crips, and Islam. Maybe a few Baptists, but they don't hardly count anymore," Lula said.

Zook took his laptop out of his backpack. "I can hook up here, right?"

"Don't you have homework?" Connie asked him.

"I did my homework in detention. I gotta check on Moondog. He's a griefer, and he's massing the wood elves."

That caught Lula's attention. "Are these wood elves the same as Santa's elves?"

"Wood elves are evil, and they can only be stopped by a third-level Blybold Wizard like Zook."

"You don't look like no Blybold Wizard," Lula said. "You look like a kid that's drilled too many holes in hisself. You keep doing that, and stuff's gonna start leaking out."

Zook's hand unconsciously went to his ear with the six piercings. "Chicks dig it."

"Yeah," Lula said, "they probably all want to borrow your earrings."

"Getting back to the problem at hand," I said, "I need to park Mario, or Zook, or whoever the heck he is. Ranger wants to talk to me about working a job for him."

"Oh boy," Lula said.

"A *real* job," I told her.

"Sure," Lula said. "I knew that. What kind of job?"

"I don't know."

"Oh boy," Lula said.

Carlos Manoso is my age, but his life experience is worlds away. He's of Cuban heritage and has family in Newark and Miami. He's dark-skinned, dark-eyed, and his hair is dark brown and currently cut too short for a ponytail but long enough to fall across his forehead when he's sleeping or otherwise occupied in bed. He's got a lot of muscle in all the right places and a killer smile that is rarely seen. His street name is Ranger, a leftover from his time in Special Forces.

When I started working for Vincent Plum Bail Bonds, Ranger was doing mostly bounty hunter work and was my mentor. He's now co-owner of a security company with branches in Boston, Atlanta, and Miami. He wears only black, he smells like Bulgari Green shower gel, he's extremely private, and he eats healthy food. I'd be tempted to say he isn't a lot of fun, but he has his moments. And on those rare occasions when we've been intimate . . . *WOW*.

Rangeman Security is on a side street in center city Trenton. It's housed in an inconspicuous seven-story brick building, the name visible only on a small plaque above the door buzzer. The seventh floor is Ranger's private apartment. Two more floors are dedicated to housing Rangeman employees, one floor is occupied by the property manager and his wife, Ella, the fifth floor is control central, and the remaining two floors are conference rooms, first-floor reception, and private offices. There are two levels below ground and I've never gotten the personal tour, but I imagine dungeons and armories and Ranger's personal tailor toiling away.

I key-fobbed my way into the underground garage and parked next to Ranger's black Porsche Turbo. I took the elevator to the fifth floor, waved hello to the guys at the monitoring stations, and walked across the room to Ranger's office. The door was open, and Ranger was at his desk, talking on a headset. His eyes went to me, he wrapped up his conversation and removed the headset.

"Babe," he said.

Babe covered a lot of ground with Ranger. It could be good, bad, amused, or filled with desire. Today it was hello.

I sat in the chair across from his desk. "What's up?"

"I need a date," Ranger said.

"Is date synonymous with sex?"

"No. It's synonymous with business, but I could throw some sex in as a bonus if you're interested."

This got a smile from me. I wasn't interested for a bunch of complicated reasons, not the least of which was Joe Morelli. Still, it was nice to know the offer was on the table. "What's the business?"

"I've been asked to provide security for Brenda."

"*The* Brenda? The singer?"

"Yes. She'll be in town for three days doing a concert, some media, and a charity fund-raiser. I'm supposed to keep her dry and drug-free and out of harm's way. If I assign one of my men to her, she'll eat him alive and spit him out in front of the press. So I'm taking the watch, and I need someone riding shotgun."

"What about Tank?"

Tank is Ranger's next in command, and he's the guy Ranger trusts to watch his back. Tank's called Tank because that's what he is. He's seven feet of muscle packed into a six-foot, four-inch, no-neck body. Tank is also Lula's current boyfriend.

"Brenda's management team has requested security be invisible at public functions, and it's hard to hide Tank," Ranger said. "Tank and Hal will work shifts standing guard at Brenda's hotel. When she's at large, we'll take over. She can pass us off as traveling companions, and you can go into the ladies' room with her and make sure she doesn't test-drive mushrooms."

"Doesn't she have her own bodyguard?"

"He slipped and broke his ankle getting off the plane last night. They've shipped him back to California."

"I'm surprised you're taking this on."

"I'm doing it as a favor for Lew Pepper, the concert promoter." Ranger passed a sheet of paper to me. "This is Brenda's public appearance schedule. We need to be at her hotel a half hour ahead. And we're on call. If she leaves her room, we're there."

I looked at the schedule and chewed on my lower lip. Morelli wasn't going to be happy to have me spending this much time with Ranger. And Brenda was a car crash. Like Cher and Madonna, she didn't use a last name. Just Brenda. She was sixty-one years old. She'd been married eight times. She could crack walnuts with her ass muscles. And she was rumored to be mean as a snake. I couldn't remember her last album, but I knew she had a cabaret act going. Babysitting Brenda had "nightmare" written all over it.

"Babe," Ranger said, reading my thoughts. "I don't ask a lot of favors."

I blew out a sigh, folded the paper, and put it in my jeans pocket. "Looks like the fund-raiser is tonight. Meet and greet at five-thirty. I'll meet you in her hotel lobby at five."

Zook was in the land of Minionfire when I rolled into the bonds office. Connie was working on the computer at her desk, and Lula was packing up, getting ready to leave.

"I gotta get home and beautify," Lula said. "Tank's coming over tonight. This here's the third time this week I'll see him. I think this is getting serious. I wouldn't be surprised if he was gonna pop the question."

"What question are you thinking about?" Connie asked.

"The big question. The *M* question. He probably would already have asked the *M* question, except he's so shy. I been thinking I might help him along with it. Make it easy on him. Maybe I need to get him liquored up first, so he's nice and relaxed. And maybe I'll stop at the jewelry district on the way home and get an engagement ring, so he don't have to do a lot of shopping. You know how men hate shopping."

"How're we doing with Loretta's bond?" I asked Connie.

Connie slid a glance at Zook, bent over his laptop, and then looked back at me. The silent communication was *no luck so far*. Hard to get someone to post a couple thousand dollars in bond when the last person to post bond for Loretta ended up forfeiting their money.

Lula had her bag on her shoulder and her car keys in her hand. "What'd Ranger want with you?"

"He's running security for Brenda for the next three days, and he wants me to ride shotgun."

Morelli lived halfway between my apartment at the edge of Trenton proper and my parents' house in the Burg. It was a modest two-story row house on a quiet street in a stable blue-collar neighborhood. Living room, dining room, kitchen, and powder room on the first floor. Three small bedrooms and bath upstairs. So far as I know, he'd never eaten in the dining room. Morelli ate breakfast at the small table in the kitchen, lunch at the sink, and dinner in front of the television in the living room. There was a single-car garage at the back of the property, accessible by a rutted alley, but Morelli almost always parked his SUV at the curb in front of the house. The backyard was narrow and strictly utilitarian, only used by Morelli's dog, Bob.

I parked and looked over at Zook. "You know Joe Morelli, right?"

"Wrong."

"You're related."

"That's what I hear." Zook studied the house. "I thought it would be bigger. It's all my uncle talks about since he got out of prison. He said it was supposed to go to him, but Morelli swindled him out of it."

"Hard to believe of Morelli," I said.

"I thought he was supposed to be the big, bad, tough cop and lady-killer. What's he want with this dorkopolis?"

In the beginning, I struggled with that one, too. I saw Morelli in a cool condo with a big-screen television and a kick-ass sound system and maybe a pin-ball machine in his living room. Turns out Morelli was tired of sailing that ship. Morelli went into Rose's house with an open mind, and the house and Morelli took stock of each other and adapted. The house gave up some of its stuffiness, and Morelli dialed down his wild side.

I pulled the key from the ignition, got out of the car, and walked to the front door with Zook trailing after me.

"This is so lame," Zook said, dragging his feet. "I can't believe my mother tried to rob a stupid booze shack."

I didn't know what to say to him. I didn't want to make out like armed robbery was okay, but at the same time, I didn't want to be gloom and doom. "Sometimes good people do dumb things," I said. "If you hang in there with your mom, it'll all work out . . . eventually. Step back when I open the door, or Morelli's dog will knock you over."

I unlocked the door, and there was a *woof* and the sound of dog feet galloping toward us from the kitchen. Bob appeared, ears flapping, tongue out, slobber fly-ing in all directions. He hurtled past us, leaped off the small porch, went straight to the nearest tree, and lifted his leg.

Zook went wide-eyed. "What kind of dog is he?"

"We're not sure, but we think he's mostly Golden Retriever. His name is Bob."

Bob peed for what seemed like half an hour and trotted back into the house. I closed the door after him and checked the time. Four o'clock. Morelli's shift ended at four. It would take him thirty minutes to drive home. I had to be dressed and at the hotel by five. The hotel was thirty minutes from my apartment at this time of night. It wasn't going to work.

Zook looked around Morelli's living room. "Can I go wireless here?"

"I don't know. Morelli's computer is upstairs in his office, but I've seen him work down here as well."

Zook pulled his laptop out of his backpack. "I'll figure it out."

"That's great, because I have to go. Morelli should be home any minute now. I'm going to trust you to stay here and wait for him and not get into trouble."

"Sure," Zook said.

I called Morelli on his cell. "Where are you?"

"I just turned onto Hamilton."

"We're at your house. Unfortunately, I have a job at five, and I have to go home first to change, so I'm going to leave Zook here alone for a few minutes."

"Who's Zook?"

"You'll see. And just a suggestion, but you might want to put the Kojak light on the top of your car and step on the gas."

Chapter

I live in a one-bedroom, one-bath unit on the second floor of a no-frills, three-story, redbrick apartment building. There's a small lobby with a small unreliable elevator. The front entrance looks out on a busy street filled with small businesses. The rear exit backs up to a tenant parking lot. My bedroom and living room windows look out at the parking lot. Lucky me, because this is the quiet side, except at five A.M. on Mondays and Thursdays, when the Dumpster gets emptied. I share my apartment with a hamster named Rex.

I rocked to a stop in the lot, bolted from the car, bypassed the elevator, and took the stairs two at a time. I ran down the hall and rammed my key into my front door. I yelled *hello* to Rex on my way to the bedroom. No time for extended pleasantries.

Ten minutes later, I was out the door in black heels and my little black suit with a white tank top under the jacket. I'd spruced up my makeup and fluffed out my hair, and I'd dropped my Smith & Wesson into my purse. The gun wasn't loaded, and I didn't have time to hunt for bullets, but if I had to whack someone in the head with my purse, it was nicely weighted.

I took a call from Morelli while I unlocked my car.

"I just walked into my house, and the kid is wearing a black satin cape, he only answers to the name Zook, and he seems obsessed with someone named Moondog."

"Order a pizza and go with it," I told him.

I was five minutes late when I pulled into hotel parking. This wouldn't be an issue if I was meeting anyone other than Ranger. Ranger has many good qualities. Patience isn't one of them.

I ran through the parking garage, slid to a stop when I got to the hotel lobby, adjusted my skirt, and crossed to where Ranger was standing. He was wearing black slacks, black blazer, and a black dress shirt with a black tie. The black tie had a black stripe. If *GQ* ran an issue on contract killers, he'd make the cover.

"Nice," I said to him.

"Playing the role," Ranger said.

I followed him to the third floor and the only suite in the hotel. Tank was in front of the suite door, arms crossed, feet at parade rest. He was dressed in the usual Rangeman black T-shirt and cargo pants, with a gun at his hip.

"Any problems?" Ranger asked.

"No," Tank replied. "She's been inside since I came on duty."

"We'll take it from here," Ranger said.

I watched Tank walk to the elevator and thought about Lula out shopping for an engagement ring. I could sort of see Tank and Lula engaged, but the mental image of them settling into married life went right to the top of the bizarrometer.

Ranger rapped on Brenda's door and waited. He rapped a second time.

"Maybe she's in the bathroom," I said.

Ranger took a pass card from his pocket, inserted

it in the lock, and opened the door. "See if you can find her."

I tiptoed into the entrance foyer and looked into the living room area. "Hello," I called.

A young woman popped out of the bedroom. She was slim, and her face was pinched and had the hungry, haunted look of someone who'd recently quit smoking. Her short dark hair was pushed behind her ears in a non-style. She was wearing a skirt and a cardigan and flat shoes. She didn't look happy. "Yes?" she asked.

"Security," I told her. "We're here to escort Brenda."

"She's getting dressed."

"Honestly," Brenda yelled from the bedroom. "I don't know *why* I have to do these *things*."

Brenda was Kentucky born and raised. Her voice was country, and her style was ballsy. From what I read in the tabloids, at sixty-one she was on a slippery slope as an aging star. And she wasn't going down gracefully.

"It's a charity event," the young woman said. "It's a goodwill gesture. We're trying to erase the image of you running over that cameraman last month."

"It was an accident."

"You ran over his foot, and then you put your car in reverse and knocked him down!"

"I got confused. For crissake, get off my case. Who do you work for anyway? I want a glass of wine. Where's my wine? I specifically requested that the cooler be stocked with New Zealand sauvignon blanc. I *must* have my blanc!"

I looked at my watch. "Are you responsible for getting her there on time?" I asked Ranger.

"I'm responsible for getting her there alive."

"I'm responsible for getting her there on time," the dark-haired woman said. "I'm Nancy Kolen. I'm the press secretary assigned to this trip. I work for Brenda's record company."

"I have *nothing to wear*," Brenda said. "What am I supposed to wear? Honestly, why am I always surrounded by amateurs? Is it too much to ask to have a stylist here? Where's my stylist? First no blanc, and now no stylist. How am I supposed to work under these conditions?"

Nancy Kolen disappeared into the bedroom, and ten minutes later, Brenda swished out, followed by Nancy.

Brenda was slim and toned and spray-tanned to something resembling orange mud. She had big boobs, lots of curly auburn hair tipped with blond, and her lips looked like they'd been inflated with an air hose.

She was wearing a red knit strapless tube dress that could double for skin, four-inch spike-heeled shoes, and a white sheared mink jacket. She looked like Santa's senior off-season 'ho.

Ranger was standing pressed against my back, and I could feel him smile when Brenda entered the room. I gave him an elbow to the ribs, and he exhaled on a barely audible bark of laughter.

"Look at who we got here," Brenda said, eyeing Ranger. "I swear, you are so hot, I could just eat you up. Sugar, I gotta get me some of you."

Ranger's smile was still in place. Hard to tell if he was enjoying himself or being polite.

"Stephanie and I are providing security," he said.

"Do you have a name?"

"Ranger."

"Like the Long Ranger?" Brenda asked.

There was a moment's pause while I debated correcting Brenda, but truth is, we all knew exactly what she was asking. Finally, Ranger stepped forward and opened the suite door.

"Like an Army Ranger," he said.

Brenda slithered through the door, rubbing against Ranger in the process. "I hear Army guys have big guns."

Nancy and I did some eye-rolling, and Ranger remained pleasantly impassive.

I was the last to leave the room. "I've seen your gun," I whispered to Ranger. "Would you like me to tell her about it?"

"Not necessary, but we could discuss it over a glass of wine later."

Nancy took the lead and punched the elevator button. The doors opened, we stepped in, and Brenda moved close to Ranger. "So, Hot Cakes, are you with me for the night?"

"Stephanie and I will be with you until you return to your hotel room," Ranger said.

"Sometimes I need my bodyguards to spend the *entire* night with me," Brenda said to Ranger.

This produced more eye-rolling from Nancy and me and more passive pleasantness from Ranger. The doors opened, and we moved into the crush of people in the lobby. Nancy led the way, and I followed Nancy, with Brenda sandwiched between Ranger and me. We cut a swath through the crowd to the meet-and-greet room. Once we were inside the room and the door was closed behind us, the atmosphere became much more calm. These were patrons of the charity, and they'd paid a huge amount of money to have a private audience with Brenda. She accepted a champagne flute, drained it, and reached for a second.

"This isn't so bad," I said to Ranger. "It's not like someone is shooting at her. And so far, she hasn't totally exposed herself. You got groped in the elevator, but you're probably used to that."

"Yeah," Ranger said. "It happens a lot."

A forty-something woman approached Brenda.

"What is this?" the woman asked, pointing to Brenda's jacket.

"A jacket?"

"What *kind* of jacket?"

"What kind do you think it is?"

"I think it's mink."

"Bingo," Brenda said.

"You have a lot of nerve," the woman said. "Was this done as a deliberate insult?"

"Sweetheart," Brenda said, "when I insult someone they *know* they've been insulted."

Nancy's eyes grew to the size of goose eggs, and she frantically thumbed through her event schedule. "Oh crap!" she said. "Oh *shit*."

I looked over her shoulder and read down the clipboard. THURSDAY'S EVENT WILL BENEFIT THE HUMANE TREATMENT OF ANIMALS.

The woman narrowed her eyes at Brenda. "Take that offensive jacket off immediately."

"Bite me," Brenda said. "And what's your problem, anyway?"

"Do you have any idea how many little minks it took to make that jacket?"

"Oh puhleeze," Brenda said. "Don't give me that tree-hugger crap. Look, if it's an issue for you, just think of it as Russian weasel."

The woman snatched a glass of red wine from a waiter, dumped it on Brenda's jacket, and Brenda tossed her champagne in the woman's face. Ranger reached for Brenda, but Brenda already had her hands around the woman's throat. There was a lot of kicking and shrieking of obscenities, and by the time Ranger got the women separated, Brenda's boobs had popped out of her dress and the skirt had ridden up to her waist. Ranger dispassionately yanked the dress up over Brenda's breasts and pulled the skirt down over her ass, apologized to the other woman, and dragged Brenda out of the room and into the lobby. Nancy and I rushed after Ranger and Brenda, and we all jumped into the elevator.

Nancy crossed *meet and greet* off her schedule. "One down," she said. "We have ten minutes before the dinner."

Ranger and I elected not to sit at the head table with Brenda. We took a position on the wall toward the front of the room, so we could better see if anyone was rushing at Brenda with a glass of red wine.

Brenda had changed into a black satin bustier, tight jeans studded with rhinestones, and she had an animal-friendly black cashmere wrap draped over her shoulders.

My cell phone vibrated, and I looked at the screen. It was Morelli calling. "I need to take this," I said to Ranger. "I'm going to step outside for a moment."

I found a quiet corridor and dialed Morelli.

"How's it going?" I asked Morelli.

"I don't know. He hasn't stopped playing since I got home. He can play and eat at the same time. I think he took the computer into the bathroom with him. It's kind of creepy. You're coming back here tonight, right?"

"Um . . ."

"Let me rephrase that. *What time* are you coming back here?"

"Hard to say. I'm running security for Brenda."

"*The* Brenda?"

"Yeah. I'm working with Ranger."

There was a full sixty seconds of silence where I suspected Morelli was staring down at his shoe, getting a grip. Morelli thought Ranger was a dangerous guy from multiple points of view. And Morelli was right.

"Don't you want to hear about Brenda?" I asked him.

"No. I don't care about Brenda. I care about you. I don't like you working with Ranger."

"It's just for a couple days."

"I'm out of the house at six tomorrow morning. You need to be here to make sure Picasso doesn't spray paint the dog again."

"Zook painted Bob?"

"He did it before I got home. He said he had to protect Bob from the griefer. He pulls anything like that again, and I'm going to make the griefer look like the Tooth Fairy."

Ranger was leaning against the wall, arms crossed over his chest, calmly watching the room when I returned.

"Did I miss anything fun?" I asked him.

He made a small side-to-side movement with his head. "No."

"Brenda is waving her glass around."

"I told the wait staff not to give her a refill, and she's feeling neglected."

"Hey!" Brenda called to a passing waiter. "Hell-*O*!"

The waiter scurried away, and Brenda waved the glass at another guy. Brenda lapped at the empty glass and waggled her tongue at the waiter. A red scald rose from his collar to the roots of his hair, and he ran for the kitchen.

A waiter carrying plates of food passed behind Brenda, and in the blink of an eye, Brenda had the guy by his nuts. The waiter stopped in mid-stride, tray aloft, mouth open. I couldn't hear Brenda from where I stood, but I could read her lips.

"I need a drinky-poo," Brenda said to the waiter. "Nod your head if you understand."

The waiter nodded his head, and Brenda released him.

"I have to give her credit," I said to Ranger. "She knows how to get a man's attention."

An hour later, we escorted Brenda to her room.

"I want to party," Brenda said in the elevator. "Isn't there a party somewhere?"

Ranger stayed stoic, saying nothing, and I followed his lead. If Brenda had been sober, she would have been hard to control. As it was, her eyes were unfocused, and her attention span was short. The elevator doors opened, Brenda lurched out, walked into a potted plant, and got knocked on her ass.

"Whoops," Brenda said. "Where'd that come from?"

Ranger scooped her up and pointed her in the right direction. She tried to grab him, and he jumped away.

"You need to take point on this," Ranger said to me. "If she grabs me one more time, I'm going to have to shoot her."

I linked arms with Brenda and walked her down the hall to her suite. I opened the door and maneuvered her inside. I herded her into the bedroom, and she crawled into bed fully clothed.

I turned the light off in the bedroom and joined Ranger in the living room. He locked the liquor cabinet, pocketed the key, and we left the suite.

"Tank has the night off, and Hal doesn't come on until midnight," Ranger said. "I'll stand guard until then."

"I'll stand with you," I said. "Just in case Brenda comes out and attacks you and you're tempted to shoot her."

Chapter
THREE

Hal was one of the younger guys on Ranger's team. He was big and blond and blushed when embarrassed. He was over-muscled and looked a little prehistoric. He showed up ten minutes early.

"Call me if there's a problem," Ranger said, giving Hal the room key. "Don't go into the suite alone. If you need to enter and can't wait for me, get hotel security to go in with you."

Hal nodded. "Yessir."

Ranger walked me to the parking garage, gave me a friendly kiss goodnight that sent a flutter of emotion through me that I'd rather not name, and watched me drive away.

I got back to Morelli's house a little after midnight. Morelli's porch light was on and a nightlight was burning in the hall leading to the stairs. The rest of the house was dark. I unlocked the front door and stepped inside. The house was quiet. Everyone was asleep, including Bob Dog. I didn't need light to find my way around Morelli's house. I spent a decent amount of time there, and it was almost identical to the house where I grew up. I made my way into the kitchen and checked the fridge for leftovers, hitting the jackpot with pepperoni pizza.

I put the pizza box on the counter, and the cellar door crashed open next to me. A stocky guy jumped out, ran for the back door, and instantly was gone into the dark night. I was too startled to scream, too freaked to move. After a second or two, my heart resumed beating and brain function kicked in.

"What the—" I said to the empty kitchen.

I heard footsteps on the stairs, and Morelli sauntered into the kitchen. He was wearing a T-shirt and boxers, and his hair was tousled.

"I thought I heard you come in," he said. "How was Brenda? And why is the back door open?"

I was breathless. "Some guy . . . some guy charged out of your basement and ran out the back door."

"Yeah, right."

I had my hand over my heart in an effort to keep it from jumping out of my chest. "I'm serious!"

Morelli went to the door and looked outside. "I don't see anyone."

"He ran away!"

Morelli closed and locked the door. "Someone actually was in my cellar?"

"He scared the bejeezus out of me."

"Anyone we know?"

"It was dark. He was chunky. Dressed in dark clothes. I didn't see his face. It happened so fast, I didn't get a good look."

"Hair?"

"He was wearing a knit hat. I couldn't see his hair."

Morelli opened a kitchen drawer, removed a gun, and stepped to the cellar door.

"Wait," I said, "maybe we should call the police."

"Cupcake, I *am* the police."

"Yes, but you're *my* police, and I don't want you to get shot."

"I'm not going to get shot. Stay here in the kitchen."

No problem with that. I had no desire to follow Morelli into his spooky basement.

Morelli flipped the light switch and padded barefoot down the stairs. He stood for a moment, looking around, and returned to the kitchen.

"I can't imagine why anyone would be in my basement," he said. "There's nothing down there. Just the furnace and the water heater."

"Sometimes people have offices or playrooms down there," I said. "Maybe he was looking for something to steal."

"My laptop is on the table. He didn't take it. He left the Xbox and television in the living room."

I took a piece of pizza from the box and tried to get it to my mouth, but my hand was still shaking. "Maybe he didn't get to it. Maybe he started downstairs, and I scared him off."

Morelli dialed dispatch and reported the break-in. "Ask someone to do a couple drive-bys and keep their eyes open," he said.

Bob trotted into the kitchen and stood looking at the pizza box. He couldn't hear a burglar break into the house, but wave a piece of pizza around and he was there. Pink and green fluorescent paint glowed in the dark on Bob's back.

"The label on the spray paint said it would wash off with water. I'll hose him down tomorrow," Morelli said.

I fed Bob my crust, and Bob smiled and wagged his tail.

Morelli draped an arm across my shoulders. "There's a way you could make me look that happy."

"Someone just broke into your house. How can you think about sex?"

"I always think about sex."

"Mario is in the guest room!"

"Yeah, you'd have to try to control yourself and not make a lot of noise."

"He's just a kid. You need to set a good example."

"Which means what?"

"The couch. Zook's in the guest room, and you wanted me to spend the night, so I assumed you'd sleep on the couch."

"You assumed wrong."

"We're not married."

"No, but we're old. There are different rules when you get old," Morelli said.

"I'm not old."

"Not to me, but to Zook anyone over twenty is old."

"Okay, that does it. I'm going home. I'll be back tomorrow morning at the crack of dawn."

"Oh for crissake," Morelli said. "I'll sleep on the friggin' couch. There's a sleeping bag in my office. Throw it down with a pillow."

I opened my eyes and squinted at the clock. The room was dark, but the glowing blue digital readout told me it was five in the morning. And the sound of a drawer being opened and closed told me I wasn't alone. I reached for the bedside lamp, switched it on, and stared at Morelli. His hair was damp from the shower, he was freshly shaved, and he was naked.

"What's going on?" I asked him.

"I need clothes."

No kidding. "I would have gotten them for you. What if Mario sees you walking around naked in my room?"

"First, it's not *your* room. It's *my* room. Second, I doubt he'd be shocked. You have to stop worrying about Zook. Third, he's asleep."

"Did you sleep okay?"

"No. The couch sucks."

Morelli was dressing in his usual uniform of jeans and T-shirt while he was talking. If the occasion dictated, Morelli sometimes wore slacks and a dress shirt, but Morelli avoided suits. He looked like an Atlantic City pit boss in a suit. And no one could keep a straight face at Morelli in khakis. Morelli was as far from preppy as a guy could get.

He sat on the bed, laced his shoes, leaned over me and nuzzled my neck. "I like when you're all warm and soft from sleep." He looked down at the shoes he'd just laced and thought for a moment. "These could come off."

"Tempting." *Really* tempting. "Will you be late for work if you take your shoes off?"

"Yeah. Don't care. If the choice was a promotion and raise or *doing* you and getting fired, there'd be no contest."

"The power of testosterone."

"I thought it was love, but you could be right . . . it could be testosterone," Morelli said. "Not that it matters, because bottom line is . . . *I want you bad*."

I had the T-shirt halfway over his head. "Take your shoes off . . . *fast*," I told him.

There were scuffling sounds in the hall and a timid knock on the bedroom door. "Anybody home?" Zook asked.

Morelli flopped spread-eagle onto the bed. "Crap."

"Uno momento," I called to Zook.

"I'm not sure what I'm supposed to do," Zook said from the other side of the door. "Should I go downstairs and look for cereal?"

"Yeah," Morelli said. "Just prowl through the cupboards. Stephanie will be down in a couple minutes."

I was already out of bed and searching for clothes. I went with one of Morelli's T-shirts and a pair of his sweats. I stayed over from time to time, but I didn't leave a lot of things at his house. Some underwear, socks, an extra pair of running shoes, some unmentionable personal products.

Zook had a box of Frosted Flakes in his hand when I walked into the kitchen. "My favorite," I said to him.

"Do you live here?"

"Sometimes."

"So you could be my, what . . . aunt-in-sin?"

"It's my understanding that Morelli's some sort of distant *cousin,* so technically . . . I wouldn't be an aunt of any sort."

I took a carton of milk from the refrigerator and set out a couple bowls. Morelli waltzed in and got coffee brewing.

"You're up early," Morelli said to Zook. "When do you have to be at school?"

"Not until eight, but I didn't know how long it would take to walk."

"You're not walking," Morelli said. "Stephanie's taking you to school, and she's going to watch you go through the door."

"Dude, that's so untrusting," Zook said.

"Yeah, deal with it."

Bob was sitting, tail wagging, looking at the cereal box. I knew Morelli had already walked and fed Bob, but that was meaningless in the world of Bob. Bob was the bottomless pit when it came to food. Bob was also the poster dog for canine graffiti art. I looked more closely and realized the pink and green swirls outlined in black on his back spelled out *Zook*.

"Pretty cool, hunh?" Zook said.

Morelli cut his eyes to Zook. "It's not cool. You painted my dog."

"Yeah, dude. He's awesome. And totally arcane."

"What's arcane mean?" I asked.

"Magical."

I thought I saw some steam starting to wisp out of Morelli's ears and off the top of his head.

"Why don't you grab a doughnut and some coffee on the way to work," I said to Morelli. "I'll take care of everything here."

Morelli blew out a sigh and felt his pockets for Rolaids. "I have to run anyway. Early morning meeting. See you tonight." He gave me a quick kiss and left the house.

When I heard the door close, I turned on Zook. "What the heck were you thinking? You don't go around painting a man's dog without his permission. You don't even do it *with* his permission. It's rude and insensitive and . . . wrong!"

I was yelling and waving my arms, and Zook was calmly pouring milk on his cereal.

I leaned palms on the table and got into his face. "Are you listening?"

Zook looked up at me. "What?"

"I'm yelling at you."

"I didn't notice. It sounded like dinner at my grandma's house."

Okay, I could relate to that. "Did you paint anything other than Bob?"

"I sort of painted the garage."

I went to the back door and stared out at the garage. It looked a lot like Bob. *Zook* in bright pink and green, outlined in black. Magical designs swirled around the name. It was glowing in the semi-dark.

"Has Morelli seen this?"

"I don't think so. He didn't say anything."

"You need to lose the paint before he gets home."

"But it represents the power of Zook! It's my portal."

"What do you mean it's your portal?"

"Okay, so it's not a portal, but it could be someday."

"You're not serious."

"That's the way it happens in the game."

"This isn't the game."

"Yeah, but Zook likes to keep in the zone."

I squelched a major mental head slap. It could be worse, I told myself. He could be spending his day surfing porn sites.

I was still at the back door, and it occurred to me that I wasn't seeing any sign of forced entry from last night. I went to the front door and checked out the lock and the doorjamb. No forced entry there, either. I went window to window. All locked and intact. Hard to believe Morelli hadn't locked the back door. That meant either someone let the intruder in, the intruder was good with locks, or he had a key.

"Did you let anyone into the house yesterday?" I asked Zook.

"The pizza delivery guy."

"He didn't go into the cellar and stay there, did he?"

"No. He left in his pizza car."

I sat at the little kitchen table with Zook and ate a bowl of cereal and drank my coffee. I had a bad feeling about the guy in the cellar. And I didn't know what to do about Zook. He was pushing his cereal around in his bowl, letting it get sogged up with milk. He was frowning and chewing on his lip.

"What?" I asked him.

"Nothing."

"It's something. What is it?"

"It's my stupid mother, sitting in that stupid jail."

"You're worried about her," I said.

"It's all her own stupid fault. She robbed a stupid liquor store. I mean, it wasn't even a bank. A bank, I could see. That could be lots of money. My uncle robbed a bank and they never found the money, and now he's out and he's gonna be on easy street. But my dumb mother robbed a liquor store, and all she took was a bottle of gin! And now my stupid relatives won't even bail her out."

"Connie's working on it. Hopefully, we'll find a way to get your mom out today. In the meantime, Morelli will look in on her and make sure she's okay."

"I don't ever want to grow up. Growing up sucks. People do stupid things."

"Growing up isn't so bad," I told him. "What do you want to do when you get out of school?"

He kept his eyes glued to his bloated cereal. "You'll think it's dopey."

"And?"

"I want to be an engineer and design roller coasters."

I was dumbstruck. "*Wow*. That's fantastic."

"Yeah, except I'll never get into college because my grades suck, and we have no money."

"So fix your grades and go to a state school. That's what I did. You could even try for a scholarship."

Morelli called on my cell phone.

"Tell Zook, or whoever the hell he is today, that his mom says *hello*. She isn't happy, but she's managing."

"Thanks. I'll pass it on. Any information on last night?"

"You mean the break-in? No. No other disturbances in the neighborhood."

Chapter
FOUR

Connie was at her desk when I walked into the office. I dumped my shoulder bag on the couch and cut my eyes to Vinnie's inner sanctum. The door was closed.

"He's not here," Connie said. "He's at a bail bonds conference in Shreveport."

"What's happening with Loretta Rizzi?"

"Not a damn thing. It's pathetic," Connie said. "No one wants to take a chance on her."

"You could bond her out on her own recognizance."

"Vinnie would kill me."

"He wouldn't have to know."

"Vinnie knows everything. He has this office bugged."

"I thought you debugged it."

"He keeps hiding new ones."

"I have to get Loretta out. Morelli and I aren't ready for parenthood. If I was going to target one of her relatives, who would be my top choice?"

"Her brother. He's got a stash somewhere. He stole nine million dollars, and it was never recovered."

"Do you have an address?"

"He's staying at his mother's house on Conway Street."

"I know the house."

"You might want to take Lula. Word is he's unstable."

"Where *is* Lula?"

"Late. Like always."

I caught a flash of red in my peripheral vision and Lula swept through the front door. Her hair was still fire-engine red, and her sweater, skirt, and shoes matched her hair.

"Speak of the devil," Connie said.

"I ain't no devil," Lula said. "I'm respectable, mostly. I'm an engaged woman. I got a ring and everything. I told you I had a feeling."

She held her hand out, and we looked at her ring.

"Wow, that's a big diamond," Connie said. "Is it real?"

"Sure it's real," Lula said. "I got it in the diamond district on Eighth and Remington."

"That's the projects," Connie said.

"Yeah. Scootch Brown runs that corner. He said this was a real good ring. He gave me a good price on it."

"So it was okay with Tank that you bought the ring?"

"Tank got a real important job," Lula said. "He don't necessarily have time to go shopping for shit like this."

"Does he know he's engaged?"

"Of course he knows," Lula said. "It was real romantic, too. He came over, and we always get right to it, if you know what I mean. So anyway, we got that out of the way, and then Tank fell asleep and I put the ring on. And then when Tank woke up, I told him how happy I was, and how he was such a sweetie. And then I celebrated by making him feel real good, and after that he fell asleep again."

"Congratulations," I said to Lula. "When's the wedding?"

"I haven't decided that. June might be nice."

"That's next month."

"Yeah," Lula said. "You think it's too far away? I don't like long engagements."

"You can't go wrong with June," Connie said. "Everyone wants to get married in June."

"That's what I figure," Lula said. "I always wanted to be a June bride, but I don't want one of them schmaltzy weddings with the big white gown and all. I just want to get married real quiet." She looked at me. "What about you? Did you have a big schmaltzy wedding?"

"Yeah. And then I had an even bigger divorce."

"I remember the divorce," Connie said. "It was spectacular. It was a real accomplishment, since you'd only been married about fifteen minutes." She handed a file over to me. "This guy just came in. Failed to appear for his court appearance. Not a big bond, but it shouldn't be hard to find him. He lives with his brother in a row house on Vine Street."

"What's the charge?"

"Indecent exposure."

"That sounds like fun," Lula said. "I might have to help you with that one."

I read through the bond document. "He's eighty-one."

"Now that I think about it," Lula said, "I got a lot to do. I might not have time to round up some eighty-one-year-old naked guy."

"I'm sure he's not *always* naked," I said to Lula. "He probably just forgot to close the barn door."

"Okay, I'll go with you, but I don't want to get involved with no eighty-year-old doodles, you see what I'm saying?"

"Before I forget, Mary Ann Falattio is having a purse party tonight," Connie said. "Are you interested?"

Mary Ann Falattio's husband, Danny, hijacked trucks for the Trenton Mob, and from time to time, Mary Ann supplemented her household budget by tapping into the merchandise stored in her garage. "What's she got?" I asked Connie.

"She said Danny got a load of Louis Vuitton last night. Picked them up at Port Newark."

"I'm in," Lula said. "I could use a new bag. She just get bags or did she get shoes, too?"

"I don't know," Connie said. "It was a message on my machine."

I shoved the new file into my pocket. "I'm working tonight. Brenda's having dinner with the mayor. If she passes out early enough, I'll stop by."

There was still rush-hour traffic clogging Hamilton when Lula and I left the bonds office. The sky was as blue as it gets in Jersey, and the air was warm enough that I could unzip my sweatshirt.

Lula walked half a block to my parked car and stopped short, eyes bugged, mouth open. "Holy cow."

Zook was written over the entire car in black and scarlet and gold, surrounded by swirling flames edged in metallic green.

"He did it when I took a shower this morning. He said it would wash off," I told Lula.

"Too bad. It's a real improvement on this hunk of junk car."

"It's supposed to protect me from the griefer."

"You can never have too much protection," Lula said.

We buckled in and I drove the short distance to Conway Street.

"I'll just be a minute," I told Lula. "I need to talk to Dominic Rizzi."

"Holler if you need help. I hear he's a nut case."

Alma Rizzi's small front yard was bare of landscaping, with the exception of a plaster statue of the Virgin Mary. The Virgin and the weather-beaten gray clapboard house behind it were stoic. They'd seen it all. Good times and bad.

I knocked on the front door and Dom answered. He was about five-feet-nine, with a barrel chest and a head like a melon. He was a couple years older than Loretta, and a lot of pounds heavier. He looked like Friar Tuck with road rage.

"Stephanie Plum," he said. "You got a lot of nerve coming here. First you put my kid sister in jail, and then you kidnap my nephew. If I wasn't on probation, I'd shoot you."

"I didn't kidnap Mario. Loretta made me promise to take him. And if you'd bail her out, he could go back home instead of living with Morelli and me."

Dom went goggle-eyed. "Mario is living with Joe Morelli? That bastard has my nephew?"

"Yeah."

"In his house?"

"Yeah."

Dom was just about vibrating in front of me, hands fisted, neck cords bulging, spit foaming at the corners of his mouth, face purple.

"Sonovabitch. Sonovabitch. I'm gonna kill that snake Morelli. I swear to God, I'm gonna kill him. I'm gonna cut off his head. That's what you do to a snake."

Yikes. "Yeah, but not when you're on probation, right?"

"Fuck probation. He deserves to die. First he got my kid sister pregnant. And then he took Rose's house. And now he's got Mario."

"Whoa, wait up a minute. What do you mean he got Loretta pregnant?"

"It's obvious," Dom said. "Take a look at the kid. Recognize anyone?"

"Loretta and Joe are vaguely related. It's not shocking that there'd be a family resemblance."

"It's more than a family resemblance. Besides, I caught them in the act. They were doing it in my old man's garage. Nine months later, Mario popped out of the oven. That piece of shit Morelli. I should have killed him then."

I was stunned. I'd seen the resemblance, but this had never crossed my mind. Morelli had been pretty wild in high school and his early twenties. He hadn't been my favorite person, and I was willing to believe a lot of bad things about him. This went beyond what I would have expected. Hard to believe he'd have a romantic relationship with Loretta and then walk away from her and the baby.

"I know Morelli had a Casanova reputation in high school, but this is out of character," I said to Dom. "Family and friends were always important to Morelli."

"He ruined my kid sister's life. She was smart. She always got the good grades. She could have been something, but she had to quit high school. And now she's in jail. This is *his* fault. He stole her future, just like he stole mine. You tell the sonovabitch to live in fear. You tell him to watch his back, because I'm gonna chop the head off the snake. And you tell him to stay far away from my nephew," Rizzi said, eyes narrowed.

"If you'd post the security for the bond on Loretta . . ."

"I'm living in my mother's house. Does that say something? Like maybe I haven't got a cent? No job. No money. No goddamn house."

"I thought you might have some cash laying around."

"What are you, fucking deaf? I have nothing."

"Okay then. Good talking to you. Let me know if you find some money. Just give me a ringy dingy."

I turned and practically ran back to the car. He was friggin' scary. And I couldn't believe I told him to give me a ringy dingy! Where did that come from?

Lula was eyebrows up when I slid behind the wheel. "Well, how'd that go?" she asked.

"Could have been better."

"He gonna bond Loretta out?"

"Nope."

"Sounded to me like he was yelling about something."

"Yep."

"You want to talk about it?"

"Nope." What on earth was I supposed to say? He saw Morelli boinking Loretta and getting her pregnant? I could barely *think* it, much less *repeat* it.

"Hunh," Lula said. "I was gonna make you my maid of honor, but I might have to rethink that if you're gonna go all secret on me."

"I thought you were going to have a quiet wedding."

"Yeah, but you gotta have a maid of honor. It's a rule."

Vine Street ran off Broad and was at the edge of the Burg. I cruised along, checking off the numbers of the row houses.

"What's this guy's name?" Lula wanted to know.

"Andy Gimp."

"That's a terrible name. That's a strike against you right from the start."

"He's eighty-one. I imagine he's used to it." I pulled to the curb and parked. "Showtime."

"I hope not," Lula said. "I finally got me some good stuff. I don't want to ruin my mental image. I don't want some old wrinkled wanger burned into my cornea when what I want to remember is Tank and the big boys."

I took a business card and a small can of pepper

spray out of my purse and rammed them into my jeans pocket. "Big boys?"

"Yeah, you know . . . the fuzzy lumpkins, the storm troopers, the beef balls."

I covered my ears with my hands. "I get it!" I stepped onto the small cement front porch and rang the bell. A little old man with wispy gray hair and skin like a Shar-Pei answered.

"Andy Gimp?" I asked.

"Nope. I'm Bernie. Andy's my older brother," the man said. "Come on in. Andy's watching television."

"I got a bad feeling about this," Lula said. "If this is the younger brother, what the heck does the older one look like?"

"Hey, Andy," Bernie called out. "You got company. You got a couple hot ones."

I followed Bernie into the living room and imme- diately spotted Andy. He was slouched into a broken- down overstuffed chair facing the television. He was wearing a white dress shirt buttoned to the neck and black socks and black shoes, and that was it. No pants. He looked like a bag of bones with skin cancer. He was milk-white skin and red splotches everywhere. And I mean *everywhere*. There was a lot of nose and a lot of ears, and gonads hanging low between his knobby knees.

"Come on in," he said, gesturing with big boney hands. "What can I do you for?"

"I knew it," Lula said. "I knew it. I knew it. I knew it. This here's gonna haunt me forever. This is what I got to look forward to after a hundred years of mar- riage. This here's what happens to outdoor plumbing when a man gets old. I don't know if I can go through with the wedding."

"Age don't got nothing to do with it," Bernie said. "He's always looked like that."

"You're not wearing any pants," I said to Andy Gimp.

"Don't like them. Never wear them."

"Fine by me," I said, "but you didn't show up for your court appearance."

"Are you sure?"

"Yep."

"I had it marked on my calendar," Andy said. "Bernie, where's the calendar?"

"Lost it," Bernie said.

"They say I didn't show up for my court appearance."

Bernie shrugged. "So what? They'll give you another one."

Andy was on his feet, looking for the calendar. He walked body bent, arms akimbo, feet planted wide for balance, his nuts practically dragging on the floor.

"I know it's here somewhere," he said, shuffling through magazines on the coffee table, rifling through a pile of newspapers on the floor.

"I'm feelin' faint," Lula said. "If he bends over one more time, I'm gonna pass out. I can't stop lookin'. It's a train wreck. It's like the end of the universe. You know, when you get sucked into that thing. What do you call it?"

"Black hole?"

"Yeah, that's it. It's like staring into the black hole."

Andy was distracted by the calendar hunt, so I gave my business card to Bernie and introduced myself.

"Lula and I need to take Andy to the courthouse so he can reinstate his bail bond," I told Bernie. "Can you get him to put some pants on?"

"He don't own none," Bernie said. "And I'm not loaning him any of mine. You don't know where he's been sitting."

"Hell, I'll buy him some pants if he'll stop bending over," Lula said.

"Won't do no good," Bernie said. "He won't wear them. He made up his mind."

Since I've had this job, I've hauled in a naked, greased-up fat guy, a half-naked homie, and a naked old pervert, and I've worked with a little naked guy who thought he was a leprechaun. A geriatric nudist wasn't going to slow me down.

"Get a jacket," I said to Andy. "We're going downtown."

"I'm not wearing pants," he said.

"Not my problem."

I walked him out of the house and settled him onto a newspaper on my backseat.

"The desk sergeant is gonna love this," Lula said.

An hour later, Andy was in line at the courthouse, waiting to see the judge, and Lula and I were back on Hamilton Avenue, coming up to Tasty Pastry.

"Pull over!" Lula said. "I want to go into the bakery. I gotta look at wedding cakes, and I wouldn't mind getting an éclair to settle my stomach. I think I got wedding jitters."

I thought that was a great idea. I didn't have wedding jitters, but I had guy-in-basement jitters, and Loretta jitters, and Joe Morelli fatherhood jitters. I might need *three* éclairs.

I parked the Sentra, and Lula and I marched into the bakery. Betty Kuharchek was behind the counter, setting out a cookie display. Betty is an apple dumpling woman who has worked at Tasty Pastry forever. If you pass her on the street, there's the lingering scent of powdered sugar icing.

"I'm gonna be a June bride and I need to consider some wedding cakes," Lula said to Betty. "I like the one in the window with the three tiers and the big white roses with the green leaves, but before I get down to business, I need an éclair."

"Me, too," I said to Betty. "I need three."

"*Three?*" Lula said. "I'm the one with the wedding jitters, and you're trumping me on éclairs. What's with that?"

"I have Zook and Loretta jitters."

"That don't seem like three-éclair jitters to me," Lula said. "That's barely a single éclair. That might be a half a éclair. Maybe I need more éclairs." She looked over at Betty. "You might want to put a couple more éclairs in that box."

Betty boxed up six éclairs and handed them over. "What kind of cake are you thinking about?" Betty asked. "Chocolate, vanilla, carrot cake, rum cake, chocolate chip, spice, banana? And then you get to choose the filling between the layers. Lemon pudding, chocolate mousse, whipped cream, coconut cream, tropical fruit filling?"

"I like all them cakes," Lula said. "The part I want to talk about is the bride and groom. The little people on top the cake have to be right. Tank and me are darker than the little people you got displayed. And we're more . . . full-bodied. You see what I'm saying?"

The door to the bakery opened and Morelli sauntered in, draped an arm around my shoulders, and gave me a friendly kiss just above my ear. "Saw your car parked at the curb," he said. "Nice paint job."

"Protects me from Moondog."

"One less thing for me to worry about," Morelli said.

I took the box of éclairs and went outside to talk. I opened the box and offered it to Morelli. "Hungry?"

Morelli's eyes went beyond the box to my T-shirt and traveled south. "Yeah," he said.

"Right now, I'm only offering éclairs."

Morelli blew out a sigh and took one. I did the same, and we stood in the sun with our backs to the building and ate our éclairs.

"I had a disturbing conversation with Dominic Rizzi," I said to Morelli. "His contention is that not only did you steal his Aunt Rose's house out from under him, but that you're Mario's father."

"That's ridiculous," Morelli said.

"Dom claims he caught you in the act with Loretta in her father's garage, and nine months later Mario was born."

Morelli chewed slowly and thought about it. "I went through a lot of women back then. I don't remember all of them."

"Seems to me you'd remember having sex with your cousin."

"To begin with, Loretta's not exactly part of the family tree. It's more like she's in the forest."

"What the heck is that supposed to mean?"

"I don't know. It's like we're forty-third cousins or something." He finished eating and took a paper napkin from me. "I guess I have some vague recollection of a skirmish in the garage, but I don't recall doing it with Loretta."

"Then who was in the garage with you?"

"I don't know," Morelli said. "It was dark." He looked at the éclair box. "Can I have another one?"

"No."

"You're mad."

"Of course I'm mad. How could you have been so irresponsible? God, you were such a . . . *pig*."

"That's not exactly a secret," Morelli said. "Everyone knew I was a pig. *You* knew I was a pig."

"There's more bad news," I told him.

"Terrific. What is it?"

"Dominic has decided you should die, and he's going to kill you."

"I need to have a talk with Loretta. And then I'll talk to Dom. See if I can get him interested in solving his mental health issues." He gave me a kiss on my forehead. "Gotta go. Are you working tonight?"

"Yes. Brenda has a press conference this afternoon and dinner with the mayor tonight."

"Will you be able to pick Zook up after school?"

"If I can't, I'll get someone else to do it. And I'm going to leave him with my parents this afternoon, if Loretta isn't bonded out. Dom is too irrational about you. I don't want to make things worse by putting his nephew in your house." And what went unsaid was that I was still spooked by the guy in the basement. Morelli's house didn't feel secure.

Morelli opened the driver's side door to his SUV and clumps of dog hair tumbled out and drifted off on a breeze. "Be careful tonight," he said.

"No problem. Brenda isn't dangerous."

Morelli angled himself behind the wheel. "I was thinking of Ranger."

Lula bustled out of the store, and we watched Morelli drive off. "That man is *fine,*" Lula said, taking an éclair from the box. "I get a rush just looking at him."

I glanced over at her.

"Well, hell," she said. "I'm engaged. I'm not *dead.*"

Chapter
FIVE

I was back in my black suit and black heels. In an effort to compete with Brenda, I'd added an extra swipe of mascara and I'd run a brush through my hair. If I'd had an extra hour and a half, I could have done a lot better.

I reached the hotel five minutes late, and Tank was still on duty in front of Brenda's door.

"Ranger's at a meeting with hotel security," Tank said. "I'll stay with you until he gets here."

Spending time with Tank was always excrutiating, because for the most part Tank didn't talk. Ranger didn't talk a lot, either, but he said a lot with his eyes and his touch. I'd reached a level of comfort with Ranger. Ranger looked at ease and in control when he was with me. Tank looked like he wanted to bolt and run.

"So," I said to Tank, doing some mental knuckle-cracking, searching for an icebreaker. "Congratulations."

"What?"

"On your engagement."

"Oh jeez," Tank said, his upper lip breaking out in a sweat. "You know about it?"

"Lula told me."

"What did she say? Did she say how it happened? You know, how I proposed?"

"She said it was very romantic."

Tank did a grimace. "Listen, can I talk to you real confidential? I mean, Ranger trusts you, and he doesn't trust *anyone,* so maybe I can trust you, too, right?"

"Sure."

"I don't remember proposing. I guess I was so nervous, I blanked out or something. I don't even remember buying the ring! All I remember is I fell asleep, and when I woke up, I was engaged. Lula was wearing the ring, and she was all excited."

Oh boy. "I guess the important thing is that you're happy about it," I told him. "You *are* happy, aren't you?"

"I don't know. I'm confused. You won't tell Ranger, will you? He'll laugh his ass off."

"Ranger laughs?"

"He laughs on the inside."

"You're going to have to tell Ranger sooner or later," I said to Tank.

"Why?"

"Because you'll get married and . . ."

"Married! We just got engaged."

"That's usually followed by marriage."

Tank's eyes were blank and his face went gray under the brown. He staggered back, went down to one knee, and crashed to the floor in a faint.

The elevator doors opened, and Ranger stepped out and spied Tank stretched out on the carpet.

"Fainted," I said.

Ranger walked to Tank and stood hands on hips, staring down at him. "Tank doesn't faint. I've been in firefights with him. He's a rock."

"Well, the rock fainted."

Ranger toed him, and Tank moaned a little and opened his eyes.

"Why did he faint?"

"I can't tell you."

Ranger cut his eyes to me. "Excuse me?"

"I promised."

Ranger gave Tank another nudge with his foot. Actually, it was almost a kick.

"I do," Tank said. "No, wait, I don't. I do. I don't." He shook his head, his vision cleared, and he looked up at Ranger. "Crap."

"You fainted," I told Tank.

"I did not," Tank said. "That's a lie."

Ranger grabbed Tank by the shirt and pulled him to his feet. No small task, since Tank had about fifty pounds on Ranger.

"Talk," Ranger said to Tank.

Tank looked at me.

"You might as well," I said to Tank. "He'll find out anyway. He always does."

"I'm engaged," Tank said. "I guess it's to get married."

Ranger didn't move for a beat. "Engaged," he finally said. "And you think it's to get married?"

Tank nodded his head.

"And your fiancée?"

"Lula," Tank said.

Ranger rocked back on his heels, grinning. "No wonder you fainted."

"You gotta help me," Tank said.

"No way I'm getting involved in this. You're on your own." Ranger glanced at the door to Brenda's suite. "Any word from the diva?"

"Haven't seen her all day," Tank said. "The PR person is in there."

Ranger checked his watch and rapped on the door. Nothing happened, so he rapped again, and Nancy answered. "Five minutes," Ranger said.

Ten minutes later, Ranger opened the door with his

key card, and we walked in on Brenda. She was in a hotel bathrobe, and she was talking on the phone.

"I'm in the middle of something," she said to Ranger.

"We need to leave," Ranger said.

"Be a good boy or mommy will spank you," Brenda said to Ranger.

Ranger yanked the phone cord out of the wall, and the little plastic clip popped off and flew across the room.

Brenda looked Ranger over. "Very masterful," she said. "I like your style."

Hard to tell if it was sarcasm, or if Brenda was feeling like she wouldn't mind wearing Ranger's handcuffs. I was going with some of both.

Ranger looked at Nancy. "Does she have clothes?"

Nancy had a bunch of dresses draped over her arm. "We're working on it."

"Work on it faster," Ranger said.

I could hear muffled voices and scuffling sounds in the hall. There was a loud thud, someone shrieked, and that led to more voices all talking at once.

Ranger opened the door, and we looked out at Tank. He was surrounded by women carrying signs protesting Brenda and breast augmentation. Tank had one of the signs in one hand and a woman by the back of her jacket in the other. The woman's feet weren't touching the ground.

"What's going on?" Ranger asked Tank.

"They wanted to get in to see Brenda, but I wouldn't let them, and then this one hit me with her sign," Tank said.

"That's assault," Ranger said to the woman. "We could have you arrested."

The woman looked at Ranger and sucked in some air.

"Put her down," Ranger said to Tank, "and return

her sign." He faced the rest of the women. "You can't protest here. You have to return to the lobby. You can have your demonstration down there. Brenda will be walking through in a couple minutes."

The women turned and got into the elevator and disappeared.

Ranger punched hotel security into his cell phone. "We have protestors in the elevator, heading for the lobby," he said. "I want them escorted out of the hotel."

"You're sneaky," I said to Ranger.

Ranger ushered me back into the suite. "Something to remember."

Brenda had crammed herself into a low-cut black sweater and tight black jeans. The sweater gave a first-rate display of her spectacularly augmented breasts. Truth is, for a moment I was just a teensy jealous. I was half her age, and I was worried that even on a good day, I didn't look as sexy as Brenda. She was wearing strappy heels and long, dangly diamond earrings that caught the light when she moved.

"What was that all about?" she asked.

"More animal cruelty protestors in the hall," I said. "They're gone." I thought this was easier than explaining about the breast augmentation issue.

"Honestly, I don't know what their problem is! It's not like I'm torturing puppies. It was a friggin' mink coat. Those minks were born to be coats. Has anyone ever explained that to them?" She turned and pointed her finger at Nancy. "I want *you* to talk to them. It's your job to make things run smoothly and effortlessly for me. This is all your fault."

"I'm getting a migraine," Nancy whispered to me. "I might have to skip the press conference."

"A migraine isn't going to get you out of this," I told her. "If you died, I'd drag your cold, dead body to that press conference. If I have to go . . . you have to go."

* * *

The Women Against Augmentation were MIA when we walked into the lobby with Brenda. A few die-hard fans were milling around, clumped together behind the potted plants, but we swished through before they realized Brenda was in their space. Ranger was wasting no time moving her to the large conference room at the opposite end of the hotel. Nancy was practically running in an attempt to keep ahead of him as he towed Brenda, his hand wrapped around her wrist, partially to hurry her along, partially to keep her from grabbing him. I was last in line, guarding the rear.

The conference room was filled with media when we arrived. A small, raised stage had been set in place. It held two chairs and a table with a vase of flowers and two handheld microphones. Brenda took a chair and Lew Pepper, the concert promoter who had hired Ranger, took the other. Pepper looked over at Ranger, and Ranger deadpanned a cold-eyed stare, extended his index finger at Lew, thumb up to simulate a gun, and pulled the trigger. Lew laughed but looked nervous and pointed to the first reporter up.

A small man with gray hair tied back in a ponytail and wearing a lumpy sports coat of no specific color stood. "I'm from the Princeton paper, and I'd like to know if you feel the lyrics to your latest album are relevant in today's culture."

"They weren't even relevant when I *made* the album," she said. "I always try to avoid content in my songs."

A woman from a Hunterdon County weekly asked Brenda if she liked horses.

"Sure," Brenda said. "Doesn't everyone?"

That was followed by a guy who looked like he'd been kicked around the block a few times, recently.

"I'm from the Newark paper, and I'd like to know what the gate is on this concert."

"Not as big as your booze bill," Brenda said.

Everyone laughed. These people all knew one another. This was a conference for local newsmen. Brenda was a big deal in Trenton, but New York wouldn't cross the river for her. But then, New York didn't cross the river for anyone.

Halfway through the interview, a guy from the Asbury Park paper stood and said he'd heard a rumor that Brenda was being harassed by a stalker who had unsuccessfully tried to kidnap her. Was that issue being addressed while she was in Trenton?

"Absolutely," Lew Pepper said. "No one's going to kidnap Brenda while she's in Trenton. All stalkers are going to have to be content with buying an album."

Everyone laughed but Ranger. Ranger was watching the room.

"Is it being addressed?" I asked him.

"He's in the third row. Pudgy guy. White hair. Black-rimmed glasses. In his forties."

"Why don't you have him ejected? Isn't there a restraining order against him?"

"Yes, but I'd rather have him where I can see him."

A reporter for one of the Trenton papers got the nod. He looked mid-twenties. Probably fresh out of college. He was slim and dressed in an oversize shirt and khaki slacks.

"Brenda," he said, "my grandfather has been a huge fan ever since he first heard you perform when he was in college. Do you expect to see much of that early fan base here at your concert in Trenton?"

"Cripes," Brenda said. "Your grandfather? How old *are* you? You look like the last guy I dated."

Nancy jumped out of her chair. "And that concludes our press conference. Thank you all for coming."

Ranger helped Brenda off the stage and handed her a can of soda and a cookie from the refreshment table set out for the press.

"Keeping her hands occupied?" I asked him.

"Trying."

He put his hand to Brenda's back and guided her through the crowd. I watched for the stalker guy and put myself between him and Brenda when he moved toward her.

"Are you her bodyguard?" the stalker asked.

"I'm part of the security team."

"I gotta talk to her."

"No can do," I said.

"You don't understand. It's critical. I had a new vision."

I moved closer to Ranger, closing the gap, and followed him into the elevator. The doors closed and Brenda's stalker was out of my life, stuck in the lobby with the rest of the crazies.

Brenda drank some soda and nibbled the cookie. "Where am I again?"

"Trenton."

She did an exaggerated eye roll. "I *hate* Trenton. It's dreary and provincial. Why can't I be in New York or Paris?"

"No one wanted you there," Nancy said. "We could only get you a gig in Trenton."

"That's ridiculous," Brenda said. "It's your incompetence that has me stuck here. Why do I always get the incompetent assistants?"

Tank was in the hall when we stepped out of the elevator. He was back to silent mode after spilling his guts about his engagement. I thought he probably wouldn't speak to me again for another four or five years. We lured Nancy and Brenda into the suite with the promise of room service and closed the door after them.

"Tank and I can take it for the rest of the afternoon," Ranger said. "I'd like you back here at six-thirty. The dinner is at seven. It's formal. Black tie."

"Formal! You never told me the dinner was formal. I haven't got anything to wear."

He gave me a credit card. "Take the corporate card. Get whatever you need."

My eyes went wide. "It's not that easy! Do you have any idea how hard it is to find the right gown? And then I have to accessorize. Shoes and a purse and jewelry."

"Babe," Ranger said.

Zook was waiting when I rolled to a stop in front of his school. He was with the same odd assortment of friends, and they all applauded when they saw my car.

He slid onto the passenger seat, dropped his backpack between his legs, and buckled up. "I guess my mom's still in the slammer," he said on a sigh.

"I'm sorry."

"I feel sort of stupid that I can't help her."

"Yeah," I said. "Me, too."

My cell phone rang with a number I didn't recognize on the display.

"It's your new best friend, Dom," he said. "I'm watching you, but you'll never find me, so don't bother to look around. Just act like everything is normal. I don't want to freak the kid."

"Okay, what's up?"

"Just making sure you're not taking him back to Morelli's house. You take him back to Morelli's house, and I'm gonna have to kill you along with Morelli."

"Have you thought about getting help? Maybe seeing a doctor?"

"I don't need help. I know what I'm doing. You're the one who's gonna need help if you don't take good care of the kid."

And he disconnected.

This was a family beyond dysfunction. Dom's mother was probably the sanest of them all, and she was being fed pureed peas.

I pulled away from the school and hooked a left. Zook turned in his seat and looked out the back window.

"Who's the guy following you?" he asked.

I looked in my rearview mirror. White car right on my bumper. Might be a Taurus. That probably meant it was a rental, since no one actually buys a white Taurus. My first thought was Dom. I stopped for a light and got a glimpse of the driver. White hair. Pasty complexion. Large, framed, black plastic Buddy Holly glasses. Definitely not Dom. It was the stalker. Must have followed me from the hotel garage. Just what I needed, one more nut to add to my collection.

"Hang on," I said to Zook. "I'm going to get rid of him."

I have a routine that I do in the Burg when I want to lose a tail. It involves a lot of cornering and rocketing down alleys, and it always works. It was especially easy this time, because the stalker was clearly an amateur. I lost him halfway through my drill.

"Cool," Zook said. "That was excellent. Do you know that guy?"

"He's a Brenda stalker. I don't know why he attached himself to me."

I rolled through the Burg and parked in front of my parents' house.

"I have to work tonight, so I'm leaving you with my parents," I told Zook.

"What about Morelli?"

"I thought we'd test-drive this arrangement. Variety can be good, right?"

My Grandma Mazur had the door open before we

even got to the front porch. Grandma was dressed in her favorite lavender slacks, white tennis shoes, and flowered shirt. Her gray hair was freshly set in rows of curls, her nails were painted to match her slacks. She'd been a beauty in her time, but a lot of her had shrunk and sagged. This went unnoticed by Grandma, who seemed to get younger in spirit as her body aged.

"Who do we have here?" she wanted to know.

"This is Mario Rizzi, Loretta's son. Everyone calls him Zook."

"Zook," Grandma said. "That's a pip of a name. I wish I had a name like that." She took a closer look at him. "You got a awful lot of holes in you. How do you sleep with all those rings attached to your head? Don't it bother you when you roll over?"

"You get used to it," Zook said.

"You remind me of someone," Grandma said. "Stephanie, who does he look like?"

I gnawed on my lower lip. "Gee, I don't know."

Grandma snapped her fingers. "I know who it is. It's Morelli! He's the spitting image of Joseph when he was Zook's age."

"They're very, very distant cousins," I said.

Zook peeked into the living room. "This house has high speed Internet, right?"

"Sure, we got cable," Grandma said. "We're not in the Stone Age here. I blog and everything."

"I have to go," I said to Zook. "Don't paint anything. Moondog doesn't stand a chance against Grandma."

I left my parents' house and drove the short distance to Morelli's house to let Bob out to tinkle. I parked and let myself in through the front door. The house was quiet. No Bob feet galloping to greet me.

"Bob!" I yelled. "Yoohoo! Want to go out?"

Nothing. I walked through the dining room to the kitchen. Still no sign of Bob. I looked out the window over the sink and saw Bob sitting in the sun in Morelli's little backyard. Bob was wearing his collar but no leash. Morelli wasn't around. I opened the back door, and Bob rushed in, tail wagging, all smiley face.

I wasn't nearly so happy as Bob. I had creepy crawlies, plus the willies. I took Bob's leash off the kitchen counter, snapped it onto Bob's collar, and walked him straight through the house to the front door, out the door to my car.

I loaded Bob into the back of the Sentra and I called Morelli.

"I stopped by to let Bob out to tinkle, and he was sitting in your backyard," I said. "Did you let him out?"

"No. You were the last one out of the house."

"Bob was sleeping in your bed when I left. And I know your kitchen door was locked, because I remember checking it, but it was unlocked when I got here just now."

"Does it look like anything is missing? Any sign of forced entry?"

"I didn't hang around long enough to find out. I've got Bob in my car, and I'm dropping him at my mom's. You need to go home and walk through the house, and please don't do it alone, like a big, stupid, macho cop. Two break-ins in a row is too much of a coincidence. Something is going on here."

Chapter
SIX

It had taken me longer than I would have thought to get clothes for the dinner. I had Ranger's credit card, with a limit high enough to buy a house, but I couldn't spend beyond my own comfort zone. And then there were Ranger's rules, which he hadn't articulated but I knew existed. He'd want me in black, and he'd want me to wear something that would allow me to move about unnoticed.

I'd done a decent job, with the possible exception of the skirt. And lucky for Ranger, I'd run out of time before I got around to accessorizing at Tiffany's.

I hiked my skirt up over my knees so I wouldn't catch my heel in my hem, and I ran through the parking lot to the hotel. I was ten minutes late. I was wearing a white silk camisole under a short black satin jacket and a simple floor-length black skirt with a slit up the front that stopped a couple inches short of slut.

I barreled through the lobby and was sideswiped by the stalker. He reached out for me, and I slapped his hand away.

"I have to talk to you," he said.

"Go away," I told him, on the run for the elevator. "I'm late."

"It's important. It's about Brenda. I had another vision. There was a big pizza . . ."

I rushed into an open elevator, he tried to follow me, and I gave him a two-handed shove that sent him out of the elevator and onto his ass. The elevator doors closed and I checked my hair and makeup in the shiny gold door trim.

Ranger and Hal were in the hall when I stepped out. The shift had changed, and Tank was either getting ready to face Lula, or else he was at the airport, heading for South America and points unknown.

Ranger was wearing a perfectly fitted black tux, black shirt, black-on-black striped silk tie. I've seen him in SWAT black fatigues, black T-shirt and jeans, black slacks and jacket, and I've seen him naked. He always looks great, but Ranger in a tux was a heartstopper. *Almost* as good as Ranger naked. Almost, because nothing was better than Ranger naked.

I returned the credit card, and he pocketed it with a smile. "Nice," he said, eyes fixed on the slit in the front of my skirt.

It was one of those moments that if Hal hadn't been present, we might have torn each other's clothes off right there in the hall.

Ranger knocked on the door, and Nancy answered.

"How long?" Ranger asked.

"Hard to say. She's undecided on gowns."

"I'm going to knock again in ten minutes, and she'll go to the dinner in whatever she's got on."

"Jeez," Nancy said. And she closed the door.

"Boy, you're tough," I told Ranger.

"It was a desperate, hollow threat."

Ten minutes to the second, the door opened, and Brenda flounced out in a very low-cut, skintight, iridescent white gown trimmed in long, fluffy white feathers.

The feathers fluttered from her shoulders and the lower half of her skirt. I couldn't imagine what sort of bird had grown the fabulous feathers, but I suspected there were a lot of them running around bare-skinned.

"Wow," I said.

Brenda wiggled so the feathers would swirl around her. "It's from the Ginger Rogers collection."

No shit.

She sidled up to Ranger. "I'm not wearing panties. The dress is too tight. I thought you'd want to know."

"Eeuw," I said.

Brenda looked at me. "You have a problem with that?"

"Too much information."

Hal looked like he'd swallowed his tongue. Nancy took a large bottle of Advil from her purse, tapped out two pills, and popped them into her mouth. Ranger picked feathers off his black tux. The Ginger collection was molting.

We marched the bird-woman through the lobby to the waiting motorcade. Downy feather remnants drifted like dust motes on air currents in our wake, and a blizzard of feathers whirled across the floor. A handful of fans and a few members of the press took pictures, and Brenda posed and smiled and flapped around.

I felt heavy breathing on the back of my neck and turned to see the stalker hovering in my personal space.

"You're breathing on me," I said to him.

"I thought if I got close enough I might be able to send you a mental message. It was an experiment."

"It failed. Go away."

"You don't understand. It's critical that I talk to you."

"No, *you* don't understand. It's critical that you go away, because if you keep bothering me, that Latino guy in the tux is going to throw you out a third-story window."

Ranger looked over at me, and the stalker backed up into a luggage cart.

Brenda moved toward the limo, and we all climbed in after her. Nancy and I sat in the seat facing backwards, and that left the seat next to Brenda for Ranger. He picked a feather out of his mouth and looked across at me and smiled. I pressed my knees together, but no matter what I did with my legs, from where he sat there was a direct line of sight up my skirt.

Ranger walked me to my car in the parking lot. It was a little after midnight and Brenda was in her room, with Hal standing guard.

"That had to be the longest night in the history of the world," Ranger said. "I was captured by Colombian rebels and tortured for three days, and it was better than that dinner." He brushed feathers off his sleeve. "I don't know whether to have this cleaned or just throw it away."

"You look like you wrestled a big chicken."

He looked at my jacket and skirt. "Why aren't you covered with feathers?"

"I stayed away from Brenda."

"I didn't have that luxury," Ranger said.

"Yeah, I noticed. She was *all over you*."

He took his jacket off in an effort to distance himself from the feathers, but he had feathers stuck to his shirt. "I don't usually have that problem. Most women are afraid of me."

"Maybe she's not smart enough to be afraid of you."

"More likely, she knows I'm no match for her," Ranger said.

* * *

Ranger had offered the use of his bed, but I didn't think that was a good idea. I'd checked on Zook, and he was with my parents, sleeping in my old bedroom. I had my own apartment, but that held little appeal tonight. Truth is, I missed Morelli. I cruised by his house and the porch light was on, so I parked and went to the door. Locked. I tried my key. Wouldn't work. He'd changed the locks. That was a relief. I rang the bell and waited. I heard the dog feet first, clattering down the wood stairs. Moments later, Morelli opened the door. He was in socks and jeans and a T-shirt. His eyes were soft and sleepy and his hair was more unruly than usual.

"I was hoping you'd come back tonight," he said. "I tried to wait up, but I fell asleep halfway through *Letterman*."

He pulled me into the foyer and kissed me. "Did they feed you at the dinner? Do you need something to eat?"

"I'm starving."

"Me, too. I want French toast."

Morelli got the fry pan out and started it heating while I whipped eggs and soaked the bread. We sat at his kitchen table, and between the three of us, we went through almost a loaf of bread and a bottle of fake maple syrup.

I pushed back in my chair. "I see you've had your locks changed."

"Probably I should have done it sooner. I never bothered when I moved into the house. For all I know, Rose could have given keys out to half the Burg."

"So what was the deal with Bob in the backyard today?"

"I don't know," Morelli said, "but I'm not happy. I don't like people breaking into my house, and I especially don't like them messing with my dog. I went all through the house, and I couldn't see where anything was taken. It occurred to me that someone might have been dropping off rather than picking up, so I had a crew go through looking for bombs, drugs, and bugs. Nothing was found."

"I wish I could tell you more about the guy last night, but he caught me by surprise, and he was moving fast."

"Do you remember hearing a car take off?"

"No. My heart was beating so hard all I could hear was my own blood pressure. What's happening with Loretta and Zook?"

"I thought it was best to leave Zook with your parents. Loretta is still in jail."

"Have you had a chance to talk to her about the garage event?"

"No. Too many people listening. No privacy in jail. I'll wait until she's out."

Okay, I knew I shouldn't be concerned. To begin with, Morelli had way too much testosterone as a kid, but he wasn't really a bad person. And besides that, he's an amazing guy now. He's smart and responsible and honorable and loving. And it wouldn't matter if he had a son. It would feel weird, but it wouldn't matter. Having thought through all this, I was still a little freaked out.

"So what's your take on it?" I asked him, morbid curiosity winning out over trust and sensitivity. "Do you think it's possible that you're Zook's father?"

"I guess anything is possible, considering my hit-and-run lifestyle back then," Morelli said, "but I can't see me doing it with Loretta. And I think Loretta would have come to me for help by now. Besides, I always used condoms. Even in high school."

"You didn't with me."

Morelli grinned. "You were different."

"We were lucky I didn't get pregnant."

"Maybe," Morelli said. "Maybe not. If you'd gotten pregnant, we'd be married now. It would all have been much more simple."

Morelli was gone when I woke up. Bob was in bed with me, and a note was attached to his collar.

Feed Bob and walk him and remember to take a blue plastic bag. Mr. Gorvich (the grouch next door) is complaining. Love you, Joe.

   PS—make sure Zook gets to school.
   PPS—there's a new house key for you on the kitchen table.

I stumbled into the bathroom, took a shower, and dressed for the day as a Rangeman employee. I dragged Bob out of bed, down to the kitchen, and fed him. Then I dragged him outside to go for a walk. I ignored Morelli's instructions and let Bob poop to his heart's content on everyone's lawns. I know it was irresponsible of me, but I wasn't up to bagging poop first thing in the morning.

I dropped my new house key into my purse and drove the short distance to my parents' house.

My mother's house always smells wonderful. Apple pie, roast turkey with stuffing, chocolate chip cookies, marinara sauce. Never air freshener. Air freshener was for sissies and slackards. My mother's house announced the day's menu. This morning, it was bacon and coffee and home fries with onion and green pepper.

Everyone was at the kitchen table when I walked in. My mother was manning the stove, frying the potatoes. My grandmother was at the table with Zook. Zook was dressed for school in his usual Gothic black getup. Grandma was a carbon copy, except for the piercings. Black jeans, black boots, black T-shirt with WARRIOR written in gold-and-red flames across her chest. Big chunky chain belt and a wooden cross on a chain around her neck. She looked like the Grandma from Hell.

"Nice outfit," I said to her. "What's the occasion?"

"I'm going online as soon as I'm done with breakfast," she said. "I'm gonna lay waste to the griefer."

I looked over at my mother and she made a gesture like she was going to hang herself.

"What's a griefer?" I asked. I'd heard Zook use the term, but I didn't actually know what it meant. I also knew Moondog was a griefer, but I didn't know what a Moondog was, either.

"A griefer's a snert," Grandma said. "A cheese player. A twink."

I nodded. "That makes it all clear."

"A cyberbully," Zook said. "I got your grandmother playing *Minionfire* last night, and Moondog terminated your grandma's PC. That's a player character. Had him take a dirt nap. Man, your grandma was really pissed."

My mother clanked the fry pan against the burner, and we all jumped.

"Excuse me," Zook said. "I meant she was . . . angry. Anyway, she was able to regen, and now she's rolling."

"Yeah," Grandma said. "I'm a newbie, so my PC runs at a pretty low level, but I've got some überelves camping for me. They're evil, but they're bitchin'."

"Where'd you get the clothes?" I asked her.

"Harriet Gotler took me shopping after we paid our respects to Warren Kruzi. He had an early viewing. And I'm not Grandma no more," she said. "I'm Scorch."

"Scorch?"

"Yep, 'cause I'm hot. Get it? Scorch."

My mother was eyeing the cabinet alongside the stove where she kept the liquor.

"It's sort of early in the day," I told her.

She blew out a sigh and shook the potato pan. She brought it to the table and dumped the home fries into a bowl. She had eggs going in another fry pan, and she divided them up on everyone's plates.

My stomach was filled with eggs and potatoes, Zook was at school, and I wasn't scheduled to meet with Ranger until eleven. I had a stack of skips to find, but nothing recent and nothing that interested me. For lack of something better to do, I stopped at the office.

Lula was on the couch, wading through a stack of bride magazines, marking pages with little red sticky tabs.

I looked over at Connie, and Connie did an eye roll.

"I saw that," Lula said. "Don't you do an eye roll about me. I gotta consider my options. I gotta keep an open mind. Tank could be real disappointed if he don't see me in a long white dress. And what about his mama? She could be expecting a wrist corsage. I gotta consider flowers. I don't want to get started on the wrong foot with his mama."

It was hard to imagine Tank having a mama. Much less one who would wear a wrist corsage.

"You said you didn't want a big wedding," I said to Lula.

"Yeah, but looking at the cake got the ball rolling."

"Have you talked to Tank about any of this?"

"No. I didn't see him last night. He called up and said he had one of them stomach viruses."

"Sometimes men don't like elaborate weddings," I

said to Lula. Especially when they don't want to get married.

"That better not be Tank," Lula said, "on account of I'm starting to get into this wedding shit. And anyways, after all the things I do for him, the least he could do is marry me in a church and all."

"You do lots of things for Tank?"

"Well, I might in the future," Lula said.

My mother's ring tone went off on my cell phone.

"There's a strange man here, and he's looking for you," my mother said. "I told him you weren't here, but he won't go away."

"Does he have white hair and big black glasses?"

"Yes."

"I'll be right there."

"Me, too," Lula said. "Where we going? Who has white hair and glasses?"

Chapter

There were three cars lined up at the curb in front of my parents' house. The white Taurus was one of them.

"I never seen a real stalker before," Lula said. "I'm looking forward to this."

I parked in the driveway and slid from behind the wheel. "Let me do the talking. I don't want to make a big deal over this. And I especially don't want to freak my mother out."

"Sure," Lula said. "I understand that. My lips are sealed."

"And don't shoot him or gas him or fry his hair with your stun gun."

"You got a lot of rules," Lula said.

"He's harmless."

"That's what those stalkers want you to believe, and then *wham*—they get naked pictures of you and put them on the Internet."

"You have personal experience?"

"No, but I heard. Well, okay, maybe a little experience. But not with a stalker."

My mother was at the door waiting for me. "How do you attract these strange men?" my mother asked. "They're never normal."

"He's a stalker," Lula said. "He might even be dangerous."

I turned and looked at Lula. "What about the sealed lips?"

"I forgot. I got carried away."

"He's confused," I said to my mother. "I just need to talk to him. Where is he?"

"He's in the kitchen. I have a full house today. Your grandmother is in the dining room with Betty Greenblat and Ruth Szuch. They're all insane. They each have a computer, and they're playing that game. They don't even take bathroom breaks. I think they're all wearing Depends. They said they're ganging up on the griefer. They don't like being disturbed, so you have to sneak past them."

My mother, Lula, and I tiptoed past Grandma, Betty, and Ruth. They were all dressed like Zook, and they were all hunched over their computers.

"We got a bad snert here, girls," Betty said. "Let's kick ass."

"This looks like the *Queen of the Damned* costume party at the Shady Rest Nursing Home," Lula whispered to me. "Is this what the golden years looks like?"

"I heard that," Ruth said. "The golden years are for pussies. We went straight to brass."

The stalker was in the kitchen stirring a pot of chili. He did a big smile when he saw me. "Surprise," he said.

"So you're the stalker," Lula said, looking him over. "I thought you'd be nastier. You're kind of a disappointment."

"Yeah," he said, "I'm not any good at this. I can't get anyone to pay attention to me."

"You gotta look assertive if you want people to hear

you," Lula said. "You gotta talk with authority. You gotta walk the walk and use the language. You see what I'm saying?"

"I guess so. I guess I could try that." He stiffened his spine and pointed his finger at me. "Listen, bitch . . ."

My mother gave him a whack on the head with her wooden spoon. "Behave yourself."

"Don't you have anything better to do?" I asked him. "Don't you have a job?"

"I'm currently between positions. I had a job, but then I had the dream, and I had to give the job up so I could follow Brenda around."

"Okay, now we're getting somewhere," Lula said. "This is about a dream?"

"I told all this to the police and the judge and the psychiatrist," the stalker said.

"Then you should have the story down good," Lula said. "Tell it to me."

"Three years ago, I was struck by lightning in the Wal-Mart parking lot. All my hair fell out, and when it grew back, it was this white color. And I was sort of psychic. Like sometimes people glow and I can see their aura."

"Oh yeah? What's my aura?" Lula wanted to know.

"I'm not seeing one right now."

"Hunh," Lula said. "Some psychic. Can't even see my aura. I bet I have a hell of a aura, too."

"Wait a minute. I think I'm starting to see one. It's . . . red."

"That's a powerful color," Lula said.

"Anyway, sometimes I have these vision dreams that I'm pretty sure mean something. And I started having them about Brenda. And I got this feeling that I was supposed to be protecting her. You know, like staying close by for when I got a vision of danger."

"What's this vision of danger look like?" Lula asked him.

"It's . . . um, a pizza."

"Say what?"

"It's a *big* pizza. It's symbolic. See, there's Brenda, and there's this big pizza she's running away from."

"Maybe you're the pizza," Lula said.

"Or maybe the danger is that she'll get fat if she eats the big pizza," I said.

He shook his head. "No, this is an evil pizza. It's none of those things."

"And you told this to the psychiatrist and he still let you run around loose?" Lula said.

"I'm not considered dangerous," he said. "Just annoying."

"Here's the deal," I said to him. "I promise to keep my eyes open for the big pizza, if you'll go away."

"How about if I just keep a distance?"

"Sure. But it has to be out of sight."

"Okay. And I'll let you know right away if I get any more messages."

"Deal," I said.

I walked him out of the kitchen, past Grandma and the ladies, and into the hall. I watched him leave, and then I locked and bolted the front door.

When I got back to the kitchen, my mother had the spray bottle of bleach in hand and she was disinfecting the counters and the stalker's chair. "Marion Zajak's daughter doesn't have stalkers. Catherine Bargalowski's daughter doesn't have stalkers. Why do I have to be the one with the daughter who has stalkers? Isn't it enough that my mother kills griefers? I mean, what kind of a woman kills griefers? Can she go to jail for that? Am I an accomplice?"

Grandma came into the kitchen. "That no-good son

of a peach basket ganked me. I had my bitches here and I still got ganked."

"You didn't kill the griefer, did you?" my mother asked.

"No. Aren't you listening? He *ganked* me."

My mother and I had no clue what happened when someone got ganked, but it didn't sound good.

"Thank heaven," my mother said. And she made the sign of the cross.

"I got big news," Lula said, flashing the ring. "Notice anything new?"

"Wow, that's a pip of a ring," Grandma said.

"I'm engaged to my big sweet potato, Tank," Lula said. "I'm thinking of a June wedding."

"You can't go wrong with a June wedding," Grandma said. "Do you have the hall?"

"No," Lula said. "I only just got started."

"What about flowers?" Grandma asked.

"I was thinking little pink sweetheart roses."

"You could put them on the cake, too. Only make them out of icing," Grandma said. "And then you need table decorations, and what color were you gonna use for bridesmaids?"

"Pink," Lula said. "Everything could be pink, like the roses. It could be my theme. I read in one of the magazines the best weddings have themes."

"They're more memorable that way," Grandma said.

Lula's eyes got wide. "I just got the best idea. We could put Tank in a pink tuxedo."

"I've never seen a groom in a pink tuxedo," Grandma said. "It might make the news. You could be on television."

"It would look real good with his skin tone," Lula said. "We might have to get it made special, though. I should get started right away."

I wasn't a Tank expert, but I was pretty sure he'd

drive his car off a bridge before he'd be seen in a pink tuxedo.

"I'm going back online, and I'm gonna get my chameleon going," Grandma said. "I might even raise my sneak level and go invisible. I got a feeling about the griefer. There's something familiar about him."

Connie called on my cell. "Good news," she said. "Dom just bailed Loretta out. He got their mother to use her house as collateral."

"I thought her mother was in rehab."

"She is. I didn't look too hard at the signature. Here's the problem. I can't leave the office, and I need someone to spring Loretta and drive her home. Dom won't go anywhere near the jail."

Chapter
EIGHT

"I just want to go home and take a shower and get into clean clothes," Loretta said. "And for the rest of my life, I don't want to ever see a Tom Collins."

I turned down her street, and a block away we could see the disaster. There was a mound of furniture and assorted junk at the curb in front of her house.

"Shit," Loretta said. "It's that bastard slum lord who owns my house. He's evicted me."

I parked and looked at Loretta's front door. It had a board nailed across it and an eviction notice tacked to the board.

"You had to know this was coming," I said to Loretta.

"I was behind on my rent, but I was hoping he'd give me another month. We're coming into wedding season, and the firehouse is booked solid with showers and receptions. I could have caught up this month."

She wrenched the passenger-side door open and got out and stood staring at all her worldly possessions.

"Is this everything?" I asked her.

"Yeah," she said. "Pathetic, isn't it? Most of the big furniture pieces, like the beds and the couch, came with the rental."

"You need to get this trucked out of here. There's

not that much. You could haul it in a pickup and store
it in your mom's garage."

"I don't have a phone," she said. "My phone went
dead in jail."

I gave her my phone, and she called Dom.

Forty minutes later, Dom rolled in driving a rat-
tletrap truck. He pulled to the curb, and I took off. I
didn't want another confrontation with crazy Dom,
and I was due at the hotel at eleven. I was wearing
black slacks and black boots, a stretchy white T-shirt,
and a fitted black leather jacket. I was ready to represent Rangeman.

Tank was on guard in front of Brenda's suite when I
stepped out of the elevator. I tried to imagine him in a
pink tuxedo, but the picture wouldn't come together.

"How's it going?" I asked him.

"Good," he said.

"No trouble with Brenda?"

"No."

So much for conversation.

At precisely eleven o'clock, Ranger arrived, walked
straight to Brenda's door, and knocked.

Nancy opened the door a crack and looked out at
Ranger.

"The car is here," Ranger said.

Nancy grimaced. "She can't get her eyelashes on."

"And?"

"She can't do television without eyelashes."

Ranger looked over at me. "You want to step in here
and translate?"

"*False* eyelashes," I told him. "Doesn't the station
have someone doing makeup?" I asked Nancy.

"No. Budget cuts. We have hair and makeup coming in from New York for the concert, but there was a

scheduling screwup and they won't arrive in time for this television show."

"Good grief," I said. "This isn't rocket science." I pushed past Nancy and found Brenda in the bathroom, fiddling with her hair. She was wearing a white stretch wraparound shirt that tied in the front and showed a lot of cleavage and a lot of skin between the bottom of the shirt and the top of her jeans. She had her hair in two ponytails. She looked like Daisy Duke.

I looked at the mess of makeup spread out on the bathroom counter. She had individual lashes, which would take an hour to get on, and she had strip lashes, which any idiot could glue to her lids in ten seconds.

"I can do this," I told her. "We'll go with the strip lashes. You don't have time for the individuals."

"Are you a professional?" she asked.

"Even better. I'm from the Burg. I was putting lashes on my Barbie doll when I was seven. Close your eyes."

I glued the lashes to her eyes and swiped on liquid eyeliner. I looked at my watch. Ten minutes late. Could be worse.

We maneuvered Brenda through the lobby to a side exit, where three black Rangeman SUVs idled. Ranger, Nancy, Brenda, and I got into the middle car, and we all cruised off into traffic.

I was in the backseat, and I was thinking I should be sort of excited to be part of Brenda's entourage. After all, she was a star. And she was going to be on television. And I was going to be a backstage insider for the concert. That's a big deal, right? Problem was, she didn't look like a star up close. She looked like she sold real estate to people with more money than brains.

It was a short ride to the station. We signed in at the front desk and followed an intern through a maze of shabby corridors to the green room, which turned out to be painted tan. Some pastries and fruit and coffee had been set out. There were some dog-eared magazines on a side table. The upholstered couch and chairs were leather and slightly shabby. The carpet was the color of dirt.

We all took a seat and watched the television set that was tuned to the station. This was midday news and the anchors and guests were wearing conservative suits. Brenda looked like she was ready to get raffled off at a hoedown.

"How do I look?" Brenda asked Nancy. "Do I look okay? Is my hair okay?" She reached in and rearranged her breasts. "Are the girls okay?"

"Remember to plug the concert tonight," Nancy said. "We need to sell tickets."

The producer popped in with the soundman, and they hooked a mic to Brenda and led her away.

"I don't have to do this," Nancy said. "I could get lots of good jobs. I could sell shoes at Macy's, or I could clean kennel cages."

Ranger was on his cell phone, conducting business. His eyes were on me, but his thoughts were elsewhere. Nancy and I, smelling disaster, nervously scarfed down doughnuts.

A man and a woman were anchoring the news. They talked a little about the concert, and they introduced Brenda. And then Brenda was suddenly onstage, in a chair next to the female anchor. Brenda's legs were demurely crossed and her bulging breasts looked like polished marble. She was all smiles and white teeth and sparkling eyes. Brenda was stunning. Something happened between Brenda and the camera. Even the whole Daisy Duke thing was working.

Nancy had her fingers in her ears and her eyes squinched shut. "Tell me when it's over."

"It's good," I told her. "You have to see this. She's beautiful."

Nancy opened one eye. "Really?"

"It's magic," I said to her.

"I just love it here," Brenda said to the anchor. "I'm in Trenton, right?"

The anchors laughed. Brenda was adorable.

"Everyone is wondering about your love life," the anchor said. "There's a rumor that you're engaged . . . again."

Brenda clapped her hands over her eyes. "Good Lord," she said. "No way!"

She took her hands away and a feathery black object dropped onto her cheek.

Nancy leaned forward. "What *is* that?"

Brenda's eyes crossed as she focused on the thing on her face, and hysteria jolted her out of her chair. "Spider," she shrieked, jumping around, slapping at her face. "Spider, *spider*!"

Nancy and I were mouths open, eyes wide, watching the television. Even Ranger turned his attention from his phone call to the show.

A stagehand rushed onto the set, tackled Brenda, and dragged her back to her chair.

"What was that?" Brenda asked. "Is it gone? Is it dead?"

One of the anchors picked the thing off the floor and looked at it. "It's a strip of eyelashes."

Brenda blinked and put a finger to her eye. "Oh shit!"

Nancy's face went white. "She just said *shit* on television. And if that isn't awful enough, she looks ridiculous. She's only got lashes on one eye."

"It's not my bad," I said. "I swear. She rubbed her eyes! Everyone knows you don't rub your eyes when you've got lashes glued on!"

"I wouldn't worry about it," Ranger said. "No one looks at her eyes."

Five minutes later, Brenda stormed into the room. "That was so hideous," she said, teeth clenched. "My eyelash fell off. Did you see it? I thought it was a spider." She looked around the room, finally finding me. "You!" she said, pointing her finger. "This is all your fault. You're the one who glued the eyelash. You said you knew what you were doing, but obviously that was a lie."

"You rubbed your eye. The eyelash would have been fine if you hadn't rubbed your eye."

"I'm leaving now," Brenda said, head high. "And I don't want this horrible liar in my car. Does everybody understand that?"

"She's part of your security detail, and she's going in your car," Ranger said.

"Then I'm not going."

"No problem," I said. "I'll ride in one of the other cars, and we'll sort this out later." Hallelujah! With any luck, I'd get fired.

Ranger's men stayed with the cars at the hotel's side entrance. Ranger, Nancy, and Brenda had taken the elevator to Brenda's floor. And I was waiting in the lobby. Ranger's orders. Hard to tell what would happen next, but I suspected I wouldn't be seeing the concert.

I saw the stalker coming at me from across the room. He was smiling and waving like we were old friends.

"Hi," he said. "Remember me?"

"Of course, I remember you. You're the stalker."

"I just wanted to tell you everything seems to be okay, cosmically speaking."

"Good to know."

"I saw Brenda on television this morning. She did

fabulous. And the eyelash bit was funny. Tell her I liked the eyelash bit."

"Okeydokey. I'll pass it on."

The elevator binged, Ranger stepped out, and the stalker scurried away. Ranger crossed over to me, his eyes on the stalker, who was now hiding behind a big potted plant.

"Is he bothering you?" Ranger asked.

"No. He's harmless."

"Let me know if that changes. Tank is on hall duty. Nancy is in the suite with Brenda. You're off the hook for a couple hours, but you need to be back here to get Brenda to her sound check at four. They'll run through the show, and then Brenda will stay there for makeup and wardrobe. Don't let her out of your sight. I won't be able to go to the sound check, so you're in charge until I get there."

"*What?* You aren't serious! I was counting on being fired."

"Why would I fire you?"

"The eyelash."

"Babe, you've gotta do a lot better than that to get fired."

"I can't get Brenda to the sound check. She hates me. She won't listen to me."

"You'll figure it out," Ranger said. "I have to go. I'll see you tonight."

I blew out a sigh and hiked to my car. Easy to find it these days with *Zook* written in Day-Glo paint all over it. I drove to the office and parked at the curb.

Lula was on the phone when I walked into the office. "What do you think about having fireworks go off after the ceremony?" she asked me. "It's part of the package if you have the reception at the VFW hall. They ring the church bells, and then they shoot off fireworks."

"I guess that could be fun," I said.

"Yeah, we'll consider the fireworks," Lula said into the phone. "And maybe while the fireworks are going off, you could serve some of them pigs in a blanket. I love them little things." She listened for another minute and disconnected. "That went real good," she said. "They had a cancellation on a baby shower, and I was able to sneak in."

"Isn't all this going to come to a lot of money?" I asked her. "The gown, the cake, the flowers, the hall, the pigs in a blanket, the fireworks?"

"A wedding is priceless. A girl only gets married once."

"Not the girls in this room," Connie said. "Have you thought about a prenup?"

Lula's eyes widened. "A prenup? You think I need one?"

"He could end up getting your Firebird."

"No way! Not my Firebird."

"And what about your house?"

"I just rent an apartment. I own the couch, though. He better not try to take my couch or my TV."

"You need a lawyer," Connie said.

Lula took a pad out of her purse. "I'll put it on my list. Now that I'm getting married, I'm more detail-oriented. I'm keeping track of things in my pad."

"How's the Brenda job going?" Connie asked. "What's she like?"

"She's just like she is on television, but she's prettier on television. I need someone to help me get her to a sound check at four. Any takers?"

"Is there money in it?" Lula asked.

"Yeah. You'll be on Ranger's payroll."

"I never been on Ranger's payroll before," Lula said. "I'll do it."

"If you represent Ranger, you have to be dressed in black. I'll meet you in the hotel lobby at three-thirty."

"That don't hardly give me any time," Lula said. "I gotta get home to my apartment and change my makeup if I'm wearing black. And then I got wardrobe decisions to make."

"You have hours."

"Yeah, but this here's important. I'm gonna be mingling with all them entertainment people. This could be my big break. I could get discovered."

Lula left, but I stayed at the office and did some phone work on a couple skips. At three-fifteen, I swiped on some mascara and lipgloss and headed out. At three-thirty, I was in the lobby, waiting for Lula. I didn't see Brenda's stalker, but I knew he was somewhere nearby.

Lula barreled into the lobby through the front door and motored across the floor. She was in black heels and black stockings and a short, totally sequined, tight black skirt. Her boobs were overflowing out of a black satin bustier, and she had it all topped off with a black satin tuxedo jacket. Her hair was Budweiser red. I suspected she was also wearing a Glock at the small of her back, under the jacket.

"Hey, girlfriend," she said. "Let's rock and roll."

"Brenda might not be too happy to see me," I said to Lula in the elevator. "She had a makeup malfunction on television, and at first glance, it might have seemed to be my fault."

"Are you talking about the eyelash fiasco? Connie and me almost wet our pants."

The elevator doors opened at Brenda's floor, and I looked out at Tank, standing halfway down the hall in front of the suite.

"It's my sweetie!" Lula shrieked, taking off at a run on the stiletto heels.

Tank froze, deer in the headlights. Except with Tank, it was more like rhino in the headlights. Lula grabbed Tank and gave him a kiss, and Tank broke out in a sweat.

"Ranger bailed on the sound check," I told Tank, "so I brought Lula to help out."

Tank almost smiled. He knew Ranger would have a seizure at the thought of Lula working for him.

"I'm all dressed in Rangeman colors," Lula said to Tank.

"Yeah," Tank said. "You look fine."

"And I've been working on our wedding all day," Lula told him. "I've got all the details worked out, so you don't have to worry about anything. I know you want the whole big deal with the fireworks and me in a veil and a gown with a big long train and all, so I've got it all goin' on. And all you gotta do is go for a fitting for your tuxedo."

The sweat was dripping off Tank's chin onto his T-shirt. "Tuxedo?" he said. "Fireworks?"

"And lots of pigs in a blanket. You like pigs in a blanket, right?"

"Yeah," Tank said.

"Then it's all settled," Lula told him.

"I got it covered here," I said to Tank. "Maybe you want to take a break."

Tank nodded but didn't move.

"You aren't going to faint again, are you?" I asked him.

"Tank don't faint," Lula said. "Look at how big he is. He got a circulation system like a steam engine."

I knocked on Brenda's door and Nancy answered.

"Uh-oh," she said when she saw me.

"Ranger is busy," I told her. "Lula and I are here to take Brenda to the sound check."

Nancy looked at Lula and gasped.

"Who's there?" Brenda called from the bedroom. "Is it Mr. Hard Ass?"

I pushed my way into the suite. "Mr. Hard Ass is busy. It's the eyelash expert and her sidekick, Lula. The cars are downstairs, waiting."

Brenda power-walked out of the bedroom. "I am *not* going with you. You destroyed my good reputation. I have an image to uphold. I was a beauty queen. I was America's Sweetheart. I've gone platinum."

"And I was a 'ho," Lula said. "What's that got to do with the price of beans?"

Brenda's eyebrows raised up an inch. "Were you really a 'ho? I've never met a real 'ho before."

"Probably you did," Lula said. "There's lots of 'hos out there, but we look just like regular people."

Brenda and I stared at Lula for a couple beats. Lula didn't nearly look like a regular person.

"So let's get a move on," Lula said. "I don't want to miss nothing on this sound check."

We moved out of the room, into the hall, and hustled into the elevator. We dropped to the lobby, started across the floor, and Brenda spotted the stalker.

"There's Gary," she said. "He's not supposed to be here. I had a restraining order put on him. He should be home with his mother. Ever since he got hit by that lightning, he hasn't been right."

"You know him?"

"He's my cousin. Before the lightning hit him, he had brown hair. Can you imagine that?"

"He said I had a red aura," Lula said.

"You go on home," Brenda yelled across the room to Gary. "I'll get the police after you if I see you again."

"Watch out for the pizza," Gary yelled back.

We climbed into one of the black SUVs and my cell phone rang.

"Where are you?" Zook asked.

"I'm in a car," I said. "Where are you?"

"I'm at school, waiting for someone to pick me up."

"Your mother got bonded out this morning. She was supposed to pick you up."

"She isn't here."

"Okay, stay right there, and I'll get back to you."

I dialed Dom.

"What?" Dom said.

"I'm looking for Loretta."

"She went to get the kid."

"He just called me. He's on the street, waiting."

"She left an hour ago," he said. "Maybe she went to the store or something."

I couldn't see Loretta doing that. She would have been anxious to see her son. She would have gone to the store after she picked him up.

"Oh shit!" Dom said, panic-voiced. "I gotta go." And he hung up.

I redialed. No answer. I called Morelli.

"Something's not right," I said to him. "I can't locate Loretta."

"Do you think she skipped again?"

"I don't know what I think, but I have a bad feeling in my stomach. I got a call from Zook. She never picked him up. I called Dom, and he said she left an hour ago. Someone has to get Zook."

"Dom?"

"He hung up on me, and I can't get him back."

"Then I guess *you* have to get Zook."

"I can't get Zook. I'm working. You have to get him."

"I can't get him. I'm in the middle of something."

"What?"

"Baseball. You know I play ball with the guys every Thursday."

I rolled my eyes so severely I almost fell off my seat. "Please help me out here," I said. "He's your . . . cousin."

"Okay," Morelli said. "But only because you said *please.*"

The SUVs wound their way into the arena back lot, and we off-loaded at the door. The lot held the semis that haul the staging and sound equipment, two band buses, a bunch of cop cars, and a SAT TV truck.

"This is just about the most exciting thing I've ever done," Lula said. "This is better than when Grandma Mazur burned the funeral home down. There were TV trucks from all over the place covering that."

A woman who looked like a Nancy clone led us through the maze of cinderblock corridors to the area set aside for costume changes and makeup. Twenty to thirty people milled around a couple tables of catered food. Electrical cables snaked along the floor, and the whole deal felt like the circus was in town.

Brenda's arrival prompted a flurry of activity. The stage manager, the bandleader, the makeup wrangler, the hairdresser, and the wardrobe specialist clustered around her. I followed Ranger's instructions and kept Brenda in sight, but I did it from a distance. Brenda was suddenly the consummate professional. She answered questions, she made decisions, she followed instructions. People drifted away from the food to do their jobs, and Lula, Nancy, and I waited backstage while everyone walked through the show.

"This here's what I should be doing," Lula said. "I always wanted to be a supermodel, but now I see I should be a singer. I've been doing gigs with Sally Sweet, but it don't showcase my talent. I need to be out there on that stage with a whole bunch of half-naked men dancing behind me."

I gnawed on my lip a little.

"What?" Lula said.

"Nothing."

"Yessir, there's something."

"You can't sing."

"Yeah, but I look real good, and if the band plays loud enough, it don't matter. I think I could be a real star."

My phone rang and I stepped into the corridor to talk.

"I got Zook and I left him with your mother," Morelli said. "Then I rode around the neighborhood looking for Loretta's car. I found it three blocks from her mother's house. No Loretta, but her purse was on the passenger seat and there was blood on the steering wheel and door."

I put my hand to the wall to steady myself. "How much blood?"

"Not a lot. I'm guessing she was wrestled out of the car."

"And what about Dom?"

"Vanished."

"Now what?"

"I have a crime scene guy here, examining the car. And I put out an informal request to look for Loretta and Dom. The mother's house wasn't locked, so I'm going back there to snoop around. How's it going with you?"

"Could be worse."

The sound check lasted an hour. When it was over, the Nancy clone fetched us back to the dressing rooms and Lula, Nancy, and I mooched food while Brenda settled into a director's chair and the makeup wrangler started working on her. An hour later, the makeup thing was still going on and the hair guy had Brenda's hair rolled up in curlers the size of soup cans.

"You're eating a lot of doughnuts," Lula said to me. "Something bothering you?"

"I'm worried about Loretta. She's disappeared."

"That was fast."

I told Lula about the car.

"That's ugly," Lula said. "I don't like the way that sounds."

My mother's number popped up on my cell screen. It was my Grandma Mazur.

"We're on to the griefer," Grandma yelled into the phone. "We got him on the run. We're moving the operation to Morelli's house, so the griefer can't track us."

"Why would he track you?"

"Griefers are like that," Grandma said. "And anyway, we're driving your mother nuts."

Chapter
NINE

I had arranged for three comped tickets to be left at will call for Morelli, Zook, and Grandma. I thought it would help to take Zook's mind off his mom. Morelli phoned at seven to tell me they were in the building and so far, no word on Loretta.

"After the show, I'm bringing Zook back to my house," Morelli said. "He's persona non grata with your mother. He spray-painted his name on your mother's sidewalk and front door, and then your grandmother spray-painted *Scorch* on everything, including your parents' ninety-two-year-old neighbor, Mrs. Ciak. They said it was to throw the griefer off."

"You need to talk to Zook. He needs a father figure."

"I know *nothing* about being a father."

"You're good with Bob. Just pretend he's Bob. Remember when Bob ate all your furniture? How did you get Bob to stop?"

"I didn't. He still eats the furniture. He has me trained to live with it."

"You're just a big softy," I said to Morelli.

"Don't tell anyone, okay? I don't want that to get around. I have to go. I can't let Zook wander away from me. I'm afraid he'll redecorate the men's room."

Ranger strolled in at ten after seven.

"Where were you?" I asked him.

"Meetings with house security and checking the building." He glanced across the hall to Lula, who was taking pointers from the makeup lady. "I understand I have a new employee."

"I needed someone to help persuade Brenda to come with me."

"Looks like it worked."

"How's Tank doing?"

"He's confused. If this goes on much longer, I might have to kill Lula."

"You're kidding, right?"

Ranger didn't answer.

"Right?" I asked him again.

He hooked an arm around my neck, pulled me to him, and kissed me on the top of my head. "I'm kidding. But it *is* tempting."

"So what's going on out there? Bomb threats? Animal rights activists? Stalkers? Women against boobs?"

"No bomb threats. All the other crazies are in full force. Never have a rock concert on a full moon."

"How were ticket sales?"

"She sold out. Not a lot to do in Trenton this week. And Brenda still has a lot of fans. Mostly your parents' generation."

Truth is, I liked Brenda's music. She had a brassy way of combining country and rock, and she could really belt it out when she wanted. At least, that was true of her last album, but that was a bunch of years ago. I suspected that, in spite of all her efforts, she wasn't capturing the kids. And the kids were the ones who spent money on music. The kids bought sex, and Brenda was good, but she wasn't sexy to a sixteen-year-old. Even the Stones were struggling with that . . . and they were *the Stones*!

Brenda spotted Ranger and blew him a kiss.

"Sorry," I said to Ranger, "you can't kill her, either."

"I'm getting nervous," Brenda said. "I'm gonna throw up. I need a drink. I need a pill. Somebody get me something."

"You'll be fine," Nancy told her.

"I *need* a *pill*."

"Last time you took a pill before a performance, you fell off the stage."

"Yes, but it was a *lot* of pills on that occasion."

Lula stood hands on hips. "You don't need no pills," she said. "You're a professional. Get a grip on yourself."

"You don't know what it's like," Brenda said. "I had a chili dog for dinner. Suppose I fart?"

"You're in Trenton. No one would notice a fart," Lula said.

After the concert, we immediately hustled Brenda off the stage, through the maze of corridors, out the door to the secure lot.

"I was hot," Brenda said. "I remembered all the words to the songs. And I didn't knock any of the dancers down."

"You were great," Nancy said. "The concert was fabulous."

We wedged Brenda into the SUV's backseat between Ranger and me. Nancy and Lula were behind us. We rolled out of the lot with a police escort. We didn't need the police, but the concert promoter wanted the flashing lights.

"So what about it?" Brenda asked Ranger.

"No," Ranger said.

"I swear, you aren't any fun at all. What's the deal with you? I know you aren't gay. You aren't nice enough to be gay."

The caravan pulled up to the front entrance of the

hotel and photographers rushed out to take pictures. Local television was inside, plus a handful of journalists. And scattered in the mix were random fans and special-interest protestors hoping to get a spot on the evening news. Ranger got out first, then Brenda, and then the rest of us. Brenda posed for photos and made her way through the big glass doors into the lobby. The local anchor was waiting for an interview. Brenda stepped up to the anchor, and the circle of fans and photographers closed in.

"We need space," the anchor said.

"I'm on it," Lula told her. "You people better back up, or I'm gonna sit on you. Oops, did I step on your foot with my high heels? 'Scuse me. Sorry I got you with my elbow. Coming back. *Beep, beep, beep.* I got a gun . . . you better listen to me."

"Do you really have a gun?" the anchor asked.

"Sure I got a gun. What kind of half-assed security would I be without a gun? 'Course, I'm just moonlighting here for a friend. Stephanie and me are mostly bounty hunters. And I sing with a band. You might want to have me on your show sometime. I got moves." Lula snapped her fingers and stuck out a hip. *"Woo!"* she said.

Ranger had me by the back of my jacket. "Get her out of here before she tells them she works for me. I'll get Hal to help me with Brenda."

I parked in front of Morelli's house, and Morelli pulled in behind me.

"That was great," Zook said. "Everyone at school's gonna be way jealous. And Joe used the Kojak light to get us through traffic."

Morelli opened the front door, and Bob bounced out at us. He ran to a patch of wilted grass, tinkled, and ran back inside the house.

I followed Bob through the house to the kitchen. I gave Bob a dog biscuit, and I looked in the freezer for ice cream. Hooray! A new tub of chocolate.

Morelli and I sat at the little kitchen table and ate our ice cream. Zook took his into the living room and went online.

"Do you think he should be online at this hour?" I asked Morelli. "It's a school night."

"When I was his age, I was stealing cars at this time of the night, and you were sneaking out your parents' bathroom window."

"Yeah, but we're on the other side now. We're supposed to be smarter than Zook."

"I just spent half a day with him, and I'm not sure I'm smarter. And I'm not sure I feel comfortable being on the other side. It's like I fast-forwarded my life by fifteen years."

"He's not here," Zook said from the living room.

"Who?" I asked.

"The griefer. Moondog. He's always here, but now he's not."

"Maybe you and Grandma scared him off."

The doorbell rang, and Morelli and I did raised eyebrows. It was late for someone to be visiting.

Morelli went to the door, and I trailed behind. With the way things were going, it could be Dom or Loretta or a cop with bad news.

Morelli opened the door, and we both gaped at the guy on the porch. He was my age and just under six feet tall, with shoulder-length, light brown hair, parted in the middle. He was slim and pale, dressed in baggy jeans and a *Fruits Basket* T-shirt.

"I'm looking for Zook," he said.

I switched the porch light on and stared out at him. "Mooner?"

He squinted back at me. "Stephanie Plum?" He

turned his attention to Morelli. "And the dude! Whoa, this is too heavy. What's going on? You aren't Zook, are you?"

I'd gone to high school with Walter MoonMan Dunphy. MoonMan was the class stoner and voted most likely to get adopted by a little old lady. He drifted in and out of people's lives, happy to get the occasional bowl of ice cream or cat kibble. He used to live with two other losers on Grant Street, but last I heard he'd moved back home with his mother.

"*I'm* Zook," Mario said from the couch.

Mooner looked in at him. "The little dude is Zook. I can dig it. It's always a little dude."

"Who are you?" Zook asked.

"I'm Moondog."

"No way!"

"Way, man," Mooner said. "I hacked this address. I wanted to see what you looked like. Man, you're harsh. I was having a good run, and you rained on my parade. You and Scorch. I'm, like, all bummed now."

"It's not like we finished you off," Zook said.

"Dude, it was only a matter of time. And Scorch is an animal. Scorch comes on, and I can smell sulfur."

"So, you're the griefer," Morelli said. "How'd that happen?"

Mooner shrugged. "Destiny, dude."

"What are you going to do now?" Zook asked Mooner. "You still have a powerful PC."

"Yeah, but not as powerful as yours. You could go all the way. You could be the Mega Mage of wizards. You could rule Minionfire."

"Do you really think so?"

"Yeah, but you'd have to make a deal with the wood elves."

"I don't like the wood elves."

"They're okay. They're misunderstood."

"Maybe we could form an alliance, and then *you* could deal with the wood elves," Zook said.

"An alliance would be cool," Mooner said. "We'd need an awesome name . . . like the Legion of Q."

"What's Q?" Zook asked.

"It's everything. It's the big Q. It's, like . . . wind, man."

Mooner dragged his backpack in from the front porch and took his laptop out. "I'll send a pigeon to the king of the wood elves."

"You're going to need a drug test before you run an alliance from my house," Morelli said to Mooner.

"Hey, I'm clean. Swear to God. You gotta be sharp to be a griefer of my magnitude."

We let Mooner send a pigeon, and then we kicked him out, and we all went to bed.

I was so relieved to be off the Brenda job that I fell asleep instantly and slept like the dead. I didn't wake up until Morelli kissed me good-bye the next morning.

"I set the alarm," he said. "You can't oversleep today. You have to get Zook off to school."

I listened to his tread on the stairs and heard the front door open and close. And then two shots from a high-powered rifle shattered the early morning quiet. I flew out of bed and ran to the window. Morelli's SUV was still at the curb, but I didn't see Morelli. I grabbed some clothes off the floor, rammed myself into them, and ran to the stairs. I was halfway down the stairs when I realized Morelli was back in the house, in the foyer, talking on his cell phone.

"What the heck was that?" I asked him. "Are you okay?"

Morelli slid his phone into his pocket. "Yeah, I'm okay. That was crazy Dom. I saw him. He stepped right out where I could see him and opened fire on me!

I don't know if he's a lousy shot or if he just meant to scare me. Anyway, he fired two rounds and took off. I called it in to dispatch. If he stays in that same car, there's a good chance someone will pick him up."

I looked up the stairs. No sign of Zook.

"I guess the Legion of Q isn't bothered by gunfire," Morelli said. "He probably sleeps wearing earbuds hooked to his computer so he can listen for the wood elves."

I dropped Zook off at school and went home to my apartment. I gave Rex fresh water, a bowl of hamster crunchies, and a potato chip. He rushed out of his soup can, twitched his whiskers at me, stuffed the potato chip into his cheek pouch, and scurried back into his soup can. It's easy to have a decent relationship with a hamster. So little is required.

I took a shower and changed into clean clothes. No more Rangeman black. That job was done. I was about to get a pot of coffee going when Connie called.

"You need to come to the office," she said. "We have a situation."

"What does that mean? What's a situation?"

"You have to see for yourself."

I locked up my apartment and went down to the lot to the Zook car. I checked the sky. No clouds. That meant no rain. The paint wouldn't get washed away again today. When I picked Zook up from school, I was going to make him wash my car. And then I'd have him scrub my mom's door and sidewalk.

Ten minutes later, I cruised by the office. Lula's Firebird was parked curbside behind a black stretch limo and a TV news van. Just keep driving, I told myself. This smells like Brenda.

I was two blocks away when my phone rang.

"We saw you drive by," Connie said.

"Maybe it wasn't me."

"How many cars have *Zook* written all over them?"

"I couldn't find a parking place."

"There's lots of parking. Lula's outside waiting for you to turn around. If you don't turn around, she's going to get in her car and come after you."

"I'm pretty sure I could lose her."

"I wouldn't count on it. She's really motivated."

I hung up, hooked a U-turn, and parked in front of the limo.

Lula came running. "Hurry up!" she yelled at me. "Everybody's inside waiting for you!"

She was dressed entirely in black leather. High-heeled stiletto boots, short black leather skirt, black leather bustier, and a black leather bomber jacket that had CRIME BUSTERS stitched in gold on the back. If you were a guy and you ordered a dominatrix by the pound, Lula would be a wet dream come true.

I got out of the Zookmobile and followed Lula into the office. Brenda was there with her hair teased up. She was dressed in tight black leather pants and a black leather vest. Nothing under the vest but Brenda. Nancy was with her, plus a man and a woman I didn't know. A camera crew sat slouched on the couch, their equipment at their feet.

"What's up?" I asked, not actually wanting to hear the answer.

"This is Mark Bird and his producer, Jenny Walen," Nancy said. "Some suit at Fox was watching the local feed last night and got the brilliant idea of teaming Brenda up with you and Lula on a bust for a Sunday-night special. Mark is going to run point with it."

I put my finger to my eye to stop the twitching. "Don't we already have enough bounty hunter shows on television?"

"Not with Brenda," Mark said. "I think we could

really get ratings with this. It would be a cross between *Dog the Bounty Hunter* and Paris Hilton's *The Simple Life*."

Eeek!

"Trouble is, you're not dressed the part," Lula said to me. "You gotta be in black leather."

"I'm not wearing black leather," I told her. "And you shouldn't, either. You look like an S&M ad."

"This is bounty hunter clothes," Lula said. "All the bounty hunters on television wear clothes like this."

I pressed my finger harder against my eyeball. "First off, no real bond enforcer dresses like that. It's like announcing, *Here comes the bounty hunter.* And second, my mother would have a heart attack if she saw me in that getup."

"Yeah, but you're always giving your mother a heart attack," Lula said. "And anyways, you haven't seen the best part. They had jackets made for us. And they got the show's name on the back and our names on the front. It's like we're Charlie's Angels."

"For crissake," Brenda said to me. "You're a bounty hunter. Buy into the stereotype and get it over with. And here's something to consider. I'm getting a crack at reality TV, and I'll kick your ass from here to kingdom come if you screw it up for me."

"I think you should ask Ranger to do this," I said to Nancy. "He'd be a better partner for Brenda."

"We already asked him, and he turned it down," Brenda said.

"This isn't a good idea," I said to Connie.

"They called Vinnie last night, and *he* thinks it's a great idea. It's out of my hands."

"Can I discuss this with you in private?" Lula said to me. "Would you step into my office behind the building for a moment?"

I followed Lula past the bank of file cabinets and

through the storeroom to the back door. We stepped outside and stood on the small patch of blacktop that was allocated as emergency parking . . . an emergency usually being when someone is trying to collect money from Vinnie and he doesn't want his car to be seen in front of the agency.

"This here's my big opportunity," Lula said. "I could get discovered. I could have my own reality TV show with Brenda. Even my horoscope said I was gonna look to new horizons today."

"This is a disastrous idea! Think about it. We're like Lucy and Ethel out there. We never know what the heck we're doing. And now we're going to drag Brenda around with us? And it's going to be documented. Remember when that mop fell out of the closet and you thought it was a snake? Do you want that picture to go into a million homes?"

"Maybe not that picture."

"And what about the time you fell in the grave and couldn't get out and freaked?"

"Yeah, but anyone would have. I figure we just have to pick a good bust. Like the old naked guy would have been okay."

"You can't put an old naked guy on national television. Anyway, we already brought him in."

"Connie said she had something we could use. And besides being my big break, they're gonna pay us."

That caught my attention because I needed a new car . . . bad. "How much?"

"A couple thousand. And they thought we'd only have to do two days of filming."

"Okay, I'll do it, but I'm not dressing in black leather."

"You're gonna be sorry. You're gonna look like a amateur. You're not gonna fit in with Brenda and me. You should at least wear the jacket."

"Fine. I'll wear the jacket."

Lula hustled back inside. "We're ready to roll. We just cleared our schedule for you. And Stephanie's all excited about wearing the jacket."

"What have you got?" I asked Connie.

"Susan Stitch. Just came in. She had a fight with her boyfriend and tried to leave, but he climbed onto the roof of her SUV and wouldn't get off, so she drove him to Princeton. Actually, she didn't quite make Princeton. The police finally stopped her on Route 1 about a half mile from the interchange."

"Jeez," I said. "Was he hurt?"

"Not from the ride, but he sort of flew off the car when Susan stopped short, and then she kind of ran over him."

"Kind of?"

"He tried to scramble to his feet, but she gunned the car and clipped him in the leg."

"She sounds dangerous," Lula said. "We want to make sure we're packin'."

"*No!* No packing," I said. "No packing *anything*. This is a domestic disturbance."

"Sure. I know that," Lula said.

"Why did she miss her court date?" I asked Connie. "Did you call her?"

"She said she forgot, and she said she was sorry. So it should be an easy pickup. She lives on Bing Street in North Trenton. It's a small apartment building. She's in apartment 212."

"You see," I said to Lula. "She's sorry. We don't want to overreact with this woman."

"This sounds like it's going to be boring," Brenda said. "I think we should hunt down a rapist or something."

"Gee, sorry," I said. "There aren't any of those around right now, right, Connie?"

"Yeah, we already caught all the rapists."

"We gotta have a plan for the takedown," Lula said. "Do you have your cuffs ready?" she asked Brenda.

"Cuffs?"

"You gotta have handcuffs," Lula said. "How're you gonna do a takedown without handcuffs?"

Brenda glared at Nancy. "Dammit, why don't I have handcuffs?"

Nancy was head down, thumbing through the pages on her clipboard. "Wardrobe didn't list handcuffs."

"Isn't it bad enough I haven't got a gun?" Brenda said. "Just because little Miss Goody Two Shoes Stephanie Plum doesn't have the stomach for it. Doesn't want to stress out the disturbed woman who ran over her boyfriend."

"You ran over a cameraman," Nancy said to Brenda.

"He deserved it," Brenda said. "The sonovabitch."

"I always got a gun," Lula said. "I got a big one."

"This just isn't going to work," Brenda said. "How are we supposed to look like bounty hunters if we don't go in with guns drawn? This is *very* disappointing. My fans will be expecting action. They're going to want to hear me say, *Freeze! We're bounty hunters.*"

"She got a point," Lula said.

"Yes, but here's the problem," I said. "Television bounty hunters do that sort of thing, but I'm not a television bounty hunter. I'm a real-life bond-enforcement agent. So here's how it's going to happen. I'm going to knock on Susan's door and hand her my card and explain who we are. Then I'm going to ask her to come downtown with us so she can get rebonded."

"Hunh," Lula said. "I guess you could do it that way, but it's not gonna get ratings."

"Humor me," I said. "Brenda can go to a studio and do voice-overs, and no one will know the difference."

"That might work," Lula said to Brenda.

"Freeze, suckah," Brenda said in a crouch position, pretending she had a gun.

"That's pretty good," Lula told her. "You should have your own show. You could do *CSI: Brenda*."

I took the paperwork from Connie and shrugged into my jacket. It was almost eighty degrees outside, and I was going to sweat like a pig in this thing.

"Here's the way it works," the sound guy said. "I'm going to wire you all, and I've also wired the Firebird. We'll be able to hear everything, so switch yourself off if you need to use the bathroom. We've also got a lipstick cam in the Firebird, and we'll be filming from the van. When you enter the lady's house, Jeff will follow you with the minicam."

"What if she doesn't want to be filmed?" I asked.

"Everyone wants to be filmed," the sound guy said. "Just start singing the 'Bad Boys' theme song."

We trudged outside, Lula got behind the wheel, Brenda got in next to her, and I climbed into the back. Brenda and Lula were in full view of the lipstick cam mounted above the driver's side door. The camera didn't cover the backseat. Fine by me. My hair didn't look all that great, and my cleavage couldn't nearly measure up.

Lula drove across town to North Trenton and turned down Bing Street. The film crew van was right behind us. We parked in the apartment building lot, and we all got out. I thought we looked like one of those Publishers Clearing House commercials. The only thing missing was the big check and a bunch of balloons.

I led the parade into the building and up one flight of stairs. The building wasn't fancy, but it was clean and the paint looked new. There were six apartments on the second floor.

"Now, remember," I said to Brenda and Lula. "Let me do the talking."

"I should be the one to do the talking," Brenda said. "I'm the star."

"And I'm almost a star," Lula said. "What about me? I need to get a chance to talk."

"Yes," I said. "But I'm the one who signed her name to the contract to apprehend. I'm the one who gets sued if there's a screwup."

"Okay," Lula said. "That sounds fair."

"I can live with it," Brenda said.

According to my paperwork, Susan Stitch was twenty-six years old, unmarried, and worked nights as a bartender at the Holiday Inn. She had no priors. And she lived alone.

I rang the bell and a young woman answered the door. Shoulder-length brown hair, brown eyes, slim. Susan Stitch. She looked just like her booking photo. I introduced myself and gave her my card.

"I'm here to bring you to the courthouse so you can get rebonded," I told her. And that was partially true. The part I neglected to mention was that she would have to go through the arrest process again and that it wasn't a given she would be released.

She looked over my shoulder at the cameraman and sound guy and Brenda and Lula. "Who are all these people?"

"This is your lucky day," Lula said. "You been selected to be arrested by Brenda. And these are the guys who follow her around and take pictures."

"Freeze, bitch," Brenda said.

Susan squinted at Brenda. "Omigod! Is it really you?"

"Yep," Brenda said. "In the flesh."

"Omigod. *Omigod!*" Susan said. "I've got goose

bumps. The lady at the bonds office didn't tell me. I would have worn something different. Omigod, you have to come in so I can get my camera. No one's going to believe this."

Susan ran off to get her camera, and we all shuffled into her small apartment.

Her furniture looked a lot like mine. Inexpensive and without personality. Neither of us was a nest-builder. I always had good intentions of buying throw pillows and arranging pictures in frames and maybe getting a houseplant, but somehow it never happened.

"Hey," Lula yelled into the bedroom at Susan. "Did you really give your boyfriend a ride on the roof rack?"

Susan came in with her camera. "He's *not* my boyfriend. He *used* to be my boyfriend, but he's a total jerk. I'm just sorry all I got was his leg. If he hadn't gotten up so fast, I would have run over him like he was a speed bump." She focused the camera and took everyone's picture. "Now one of me with Brenda," she said, handing the camera to Lula. "This is so cool."

"Why'd your boyfriend jump on the car?" Lula wanted to know. "Guess he didn't want you to go?"

"Had nothing to do with me. It was that I took Carl. He just wanted his precious Carl."

"Isn't that tragic," Brenda said. "You have a little boy. A split is always so hard on the children."

"Actually, Carl's a monkey," Susan said.

Lula snapped her head around. "He isn't here, is he? Nothing personal, but I hate monkeys."

"I have him in the bathroom. He gets excited when strangers come into the apartment."

"I have to see this," Brenda said, crossing to the closed bathroom door. "What kind of monkey is it?"

"Don't open the door!" Susan said.

Too late. Brenda yanked the door open, and the monkey launched himself out at her and draped himself over her head.

Everyone in the room went rigid and sucked air.

Brenda rolled her eyes, trying to see through her skull. "What the heck?"

"Hee, hee, hee," Carl said. And he reached down and pinched Brenda's nose . . . hard.

Brenda slapped his hand away, and Carl shrieked and hunkered down, digging into Brenda's scalp with his monkey fingers and toes. All you could see was monkey tail and brown monkey fur sticking out of Brenda's rat's nest hair.

"Uh-oh," Lula said. "I never seen a monkey hump before, but I could swear Carl's in love."

"Somebody do something, for crissake," Brenda yelled. "Get him off me! Kill him. Get him a damn banana!"

It was the spider all over again, times fifty. The difference was that this time Brenda's freak-out was justified. If I had a monkey humping my head, I'd be freaked, too.

"Don't slap at him," Susan said. "You'll make him mad."

Lula had her gun out. "Hold still, and I'll nail the nasty little bugger."

The sound guy reached for Carl, and Carl latched on to his arm and bit his hand.

"Yow! Shit!" the sound guy said. "Shoot him. *Shoot him.*" He whipped his arm out, and Carl flew off into space, hit the wall, and bounced off like a tennis ball. And he kept bouncing. Onto the table, to the chandelier, to the couch, to an end table, to the television.

Carl rocketed around the room, shrieking and chattering and baring his teeth. His eyes were black and glittery and bugged out of his head, and he was spraying monkey spit.

"It's a *demon* monkey!" Lula yelled. "Get a priest."

"I'm out of here," the cameraman said. "Life's too short."

The sound guy was already in the hall, and Brenda was at the stairs.

"Wait for me," Lula said, pounding after them.

If I didn't catch up, they'd leave without me. They'd drive away and never look back.

"Turn yourself in," I said to Susan. "Sorry about the monkey."

I sprinted across the lot and got to the Firebird just as Lula put the key into the ignition. I hurled myself into the backseat, and we took off with the camera crew truck right on our ass.

"What the hell was that?" Brenda wanted to know.

Lula gave the Firebird gas. "She said don't open the door, but would you listen? Heck, no. You had to go open the door. What were you thinking?"

"I wanted to see the monkey. Did she say the monkey was rabid? No. Did she say the monkey was on crack? No. I assumed it was a pet. Its name was Carl."

"Right there, it tells you something," Lula said. "Carls are always crazy. You never trust anyone named Carl or Steve."

"That's ridiculous," Brenda said. "Do you have any other theories on names?"

"Yeah. It's been my experience that guys named Ralph only got one good nut."

I was sitting behind Brenda, and her hair was Wild Woman of Borneo, with a couple chunks obviously chewed off by the monkey.

"Is my hair all right?" Brenda asked. "Do I need to comb it or something?" She patted the top of her head. "What's this sticky stuff?"

At the very best, I thought it was monkey spit.

"Jeez," I said. "I don't know. I think it might be your gel or something. Probably you want to wait until you get to a ladies' room to comb it."

Chapter

TEN

Mark Bird and his producer were waiting for us at the office. The producer gasped when Brenda walked through the door. "H-h-how'd it go?" she asked, her attention caught on Brenda's hair.

"This bounty hunter thing is harder than I thought," Brenda said. "I need a ladies' room."

"There's a powder room straight back," Connie said. "It'll be on your right."

Brenda sashayed off to the powder room, and we all stayed mute until the door closed.

"What the heck happened to her?" Connie asked.

"Monkey," Lula said. "Bugger humped her head."

The sound guy was grinning wide. "We looked at the footage in the truck on the way here. It's great!"

"You couldn't possibly use it," I said to him.

"It would be a crime not to," he said. "It's gold."

Connie looked to me. "I assume there was no capture."

I took my cell phone out and punched Morelli's number in. "Your assumption is correct."

Morelli answered with a grunt.

"What's new?" I asked him.

"Nothing worth talking about. I caught a double homicide this morning and haven't been able to do anything about Dom or Loretta. Larry Skid is working Loretta. So far, no one's spotted Dom."

"Larry Skid is an idiot."

"Yeah. My description for him would be sack of shit. I've got to go. You're picking the kid up today, right?"

"Right."

I disconnected and fished around in my bag, looking for my keys. "I have to talk to some people," I said to Connie. "I'll get back to Susan Stitch later. Her monkey needs alone time."

"Where you going?" Lula wanted to know. "I might have to go with you. I don't want to be here when Ms. Monkey Hair comes out of the bathroom."

Ten minutes later, we were in front of Dom's mother's house. I knew Morelli had done a search, but I didn't think it would hurt for me to take a look, too. I knocked on the front door. No answer. I turned the knob and the door swung open. We stepped inside and listened.

"All I hear is the refrigerator," Lula said.

The interior of the house was dark and fussy. Lots of candy dishes and figurines and vases filled with plastic flowers. The dining room table was covered with a lace tablecloth.

"What are we looking for?" Lula wanted to know.

"Clues."

"Good thing I asked. I thought it might have been elephants."

I prowled through the kitchen, and it looked to me like Dom had cleared out in a hurry. There were dirty dishes in the sink and a fry pan on the stove. The refrigerator held the usual staples. Yesterday's paper was open on the small kitchen table. A cup of cold coffee was beside the paper. A cardboard box containing cereal, jars of soup, and canned food was on the floor next to the sink. I was guessing this came from Loretta's stash. There were more cardboard boxes upstairs in a spare bedroom. They were labeled "clothes" and "bathroom." The master bedroom was untouched, the bed neatly made. A second bedroom was a disaster. Linens rumpled into a mess in the middle of the bed. Drawers open with clothes everywhere. Either Dom was a slob or else the room had been tossed.

I checked the garage. No cars. Loretta's possessions neatly stacked in a corner.

"What'd we learn here?" Lula wanted to know.

"Not much. Loretta moved in and then disappeared. Dom made an unplanned departure. Hard to tell how many people have searched the house. I'm guessing at least three . . . Morelli and me and someone else."

The limo and the film crew van were gone when I returned to the office.

"Guess it's safe to park," Lula said. "Looks like everyone went away."

Not everyone. Gary-the-Stalker was sitting on the curb in front of the bonds office. He stood when I got out of the Sentra and walked over to me.

"Brenda went back to the hotel," I told him.

"I know. I saw her leave. I thought I'd have better luck talking to you."

"I'm not working security for her anymore."

"Yeah, but you talk to her."

"Actually, no."

"I had a dream that she was sitting on a toilet in the southbound lane of Route 1."

"Un-hunh?"

"I thought someone needed to know."

"Why?"

"Just in case," he said.

"Anything else?"

"No. That's it."

"Okay, then," I said. "Thanks."

My phone rang and a strange number popped onto the screen.

"Is this Stephanie Plum?" a man asked.

"Yeah," I said, recognizing the voice. "Is this the Mooner?"

"Affirmative. It's the Moonster, the Moondog, the MoonMan. I'm here at the house, looking for Zoo-karama, but he isn't here."

"He's in school."

"School! Far out."

"Anything else?"

"Here's the thing. It was real late when we were done playing last night, and I think I might have left my computer in the house, because I don't seem to have it with me. So I was wondering if you could, like, let me into the house."

"Sure," I said. "I'm at the bonds office. I'll be right there."

Morelli's house is minutes from the bonds office. It was close to noon, and there was no traffic. No kids playing. No dogs barking. Only Mooner sitting on the small porch, patiently waiting for me.

I unlocked the door, and Bob galloped over to us. Bob stuck his snoot into Mooner's crotch and took a sniff.

"Whoa," Mooner said. "He remembers me. Cool."

We pushed past Bob and found the computer exactly where Mooner had left it, on the coffee table.

"When's the little dude get out of school?" Mooner asked.

"Two-thirty."

Mooner flopped onto the couch.

"What are you doing?" I asked him.

"Waiting."

I decided some time ago that Mooner fell into the

pet category. He was like a stray cat that showed up on your doorstep and stayed for a few days and then wandered off. He was amusing in small doses, fairly harmless, and for the most part, housebroken.

I left Mooner on the couch and went to the kitchen to check out the contents of Morelli's refrigerator. It was noon, and as long as I was there, I figured I might as well eat. If I'd been in my house, I would have made a peanut butter sandwich, but this was Morelli's house and he was a meat guy, so I found deli-sliced ham and roast beef and Swiss cheese. I made a sandwich for me and a sandwich for Mooner, and I dragged a big bag of potato chips out of the cupboard. I put it all on the small kitchen table and called Mooner in.

"Thanks, Mom," Mooner said, sitting down, dumping some chips onto his plate. "This is, like, excellent."

I ate half a sandwich, and I realized Bob was at the table, and he was holding a man's shoe in his mouth. It was a scuffed brown lace-up shoe, and I didn't recognize it as Morelli's. I looked under the table at Mooner's feet. Both of them were stuffed into beat-up sneakers.

"Where'd Bob get the shoe?" I asked.

"He brought it up from the basement," Mooner said. "The door's open."

I turned and looked behind me and, sure enough, the basement door was open. I got up and cautiously peeked down the stairs. "Hello?" I called. No one answered. I took the carving knife out of the butcher-block knife caddy, switched the light on in the basement, and carefully crept down the stairs and looked around.

"What's down there?" Mooner wanted to know.

"Furnace, water heater, and a dead guy."

"Bad juju," Mooner said.

The dead guy was spread-eagle on his back, eyes wide open, hole in the middle of his forehead, lots of

blood pooling under him, wearing only one shoe. I
didn't recognize him. He looked like he came out of
central casting for a *Sopranos* episode.

I took a moment to decide if I was going to throw
up or faint or evacuate my bowels. None of those
things seemed to be going on, so I stumbled up to the
kitchen, closed the basement door behind me, and dialed Morelli.

"There's a d-d-dead guy in your b-b-basement," I
told him.

Silence.

"Did you hear me?" I asked, working hard to control the shaking in my voice.

"I know this is stupid, but it sounded like you said
there was a dead guy in my basement."

"Shot in the f-f-forehead. Bob took his shoe and
won't give it b-b-back."

"Have you called the police?"

"Just you."

"You know what would be good?" Mooner said
when I hung up. "Coleslaw. I don't suppose you have
any coleslaw?"

"No."

"Just thought I'd ask."

"Aren't you bothered by the fact that someone was
killed in Morelli's basement?" I asked Mooner.

"Do I know him?"

"I don't know. Do you want to take a look?"

Mooner stood and ambled down the stairs. Moments later, he strolled back into the kitchen and took
a handful of chips. "Don't know him," he said, finishing his sandwich, eating his chips.

I wasn't nearly so calm. I don't like dead people, and
I especially hated that someone was killed in Morelli's house. It felt unclean and scary and like the house
had been violated.

* * *

Mooner had taken a lawn chair from Morelli's back-yard and set it on the sidewalk in front of Morelli's house, so he could watch the homicide show in comfort. He had a can of soda in one hand and the potato chip bag in the other, and he was kicked back. There were several squad cars parked at angles on the street, plus the medical examiner's meat wagon and a couple other assorted cop cars. A clump of uniforms stood by the meat wagon, talking and laughing. Morelli was on his porch, the front door to his house open behind him. He was talking to Rich Spanner, another homicide cop. Spanner had obviously caught the case. I knew him on a superficial level. He was an okay guy. He was a couple years older than Morelli and built like a barrel.

Just minutes ago, they'd carried the victim out in a zippered bag and stuffed him into the ME's truck. The crime lab guy was still inside, working.

I was leaning against my car, not wanting to be in the middle of all the police activity inside the house. Rich Spanner and Morelli concluded their conversation. Spanner left, and Morelli walked over to me.

"This is a frigging nightmare," Morelli said.

"Did you know the dead guy?"

He shook his head. "Not personally. His name is Allen Gratelli. The address on his license was Law-renceville. Spanner ran him through the system, and he has no priors. He worked for the cable company."

"So what's his connection to you?"

"Don't know. Was he the guy who ran out of the basement the other night?"

"Could have been. Seemed like the right size, but I couldn't be sure. I don't recognize the name. Did Spanner know him?"

"No. No one knows him. He's nobody."

"Well, somebody knows him, because they killed him in your basement."

"Let's review my life," Morelli said. "I have crazy Dom shooting at me because he thinks I stole this house out from under him. I have his nephew living with me. I'm not sure why, except that he looks a little like me, and the kid's mother is missing. And in the last three days, I've had my house broken into twice and a guy killed in my basement. Did I miss anything?"

"Does Mooner count?"

"No."

"Do you suppose there's a connection between all those people?" I asked him.

"Yeah, I do. And I think it's all related to the bank job. We know that four men participated in the robbery. Dom took the fall and the other three men were never identified, and the money was never recovered. I'm guessing when we dig around a little, we'll find out Dom knew Allen Gratelli."

"And maybe Gratelli was involved in the robbery."

"It would explain the hole in his head," Morelli said.

"And maybe the money is hidden in your house!"

"It was a lot of money. They hauled it off in a van. More likely, a key or a clue to the location is hidden in the house."

"We need to comb through the house."

"Little by little, I've been making this house my own, and I've gotten rid of a bunch of things that belonged to Rose. A lot of the clutter has been tossed."

"Yes, but a lot of it is still here. You never throw a key away. You still have your locker key from high school. If you found a key, you'd put it in one of your junk drawers." I looked at my watch. "I have to get Zook. When I come back we'll start looking."

Chapter

Zook settled himself onto the passenger seat and stared down at his shoes.

"Problems in school?" I asked him.

"No."

"Well?"

He bit into his lower lip.

"Your mom hasn't turned up in any of the local hospitals," I told him. "That's a good sign."

"Or the morgue."

"Yeah, or the morgue," I said.

"Maybe she took off."

"She wouldn't take off without you. She loves you."

"Thanks," Zook said. "Do you think she's okay?"

"Yes. I do."

I ran into the deli on the way home and picked up lunch meat and chips and ice cream sandwiches. Marion Fitz was working checkout.

"I hear you found a dead guy in Morelli's basement," she said. "Is this Virginia baked ham or the low sodium?"

"Virginia baked."

"I heard it was Allen Gratelli."

"That's what I'm told."

"Wasn't he dating Loretta Rizzi?"

Bang. Direct hit to my brain. "I don't know," I said. "Was he?"

"His truck's been in front of her house a lot. Maybe she just had cable problems."

I carried my bag out to my car, tossed it onto the backseat, and got behind the wheel. Zook was hooked into his iPod, waiting for me.

"Was your mom dating a guy named Allen Gratelli?" I asked him.

"He's Uncle Dom's friend. He'd come over sometimes to see if we were doing okay. I thought he was sort of a jerk. Sometimes it was like he was trying to put moves on my mom, but she always made a joke about it."

"I ran into him today."

"Lucky you."

"He was in Morelli's basement. Someone shot him."

Zook's eyes went wide. "Get out. Was he hurt bad?"

"Yes."

"How bad?"

"Real bad."

I suspect if I was relaying this information to a fourteen-year-old girl, she would be sad at this point. She'd be remembering pets and relatives and stuffed animals that had been injured, and the tragedies would be commingled in the frontal lobe of her brain. Zook, being a boy, thought it was cool.

"Oh man," Zook said. "Is he dead?"

"Yes."

Zook was leaning forward, straining against his seatbelt. "Who shot him?"

"I don't know. He was dead when I found him."

"What did he look like?"

"He looked dead. Bullet hole in the middle of his forehead."

"Whoa. That's amazing. Is he still there?"

"No. They moved him out."

Zook slumped back. "Darn. I miss all the good stuff."

"Did your Uncle Dom ever say anything about the money? Like where it was hidden?"

"No. He just kept saying he was going to be living the high life."

"Did he have other friends besides Allen Gratelli?"

"I guess, but I don't know any. Allen was the only one who came around after Uncle Dom went to prison. And Allen just started to come around a couple months ago."

The police were gone when I returned to Morelli's house. Only Mooner in the lawn chair and a single van from an emergency cleaning service suggested something unusual had just occurred.

"Zookamundo," Mooner said. "Been waiting for you, man. We gotta convene with the wood elves."

"Did you see the dead guy?" Zook asked.

"Yeah. He was real dead," Mooner said. "Pooped in his pants and everything."

"Awesome," Zook said.

I left Mooner and Zook in the living room with the ice cream sandwiches and the wood elves, and I went to the kitchen to help Morelli. He was methodically going through drawers, extracting keys and odd scraps of paper. The basement door was open, and the smell of bleach and pine-scented detergent drifted up the stairs.

"Zook tells me Allen Gratelli was friends with Dom," I said to Morelli. "Shazam."

Morelli grinned and wrapped an arm around me. "I'm going to get you naked tonight and make you say *shazam* again."

I knew that wasn't an empty promise. "Having any luck here?" I asked him.

"I've got a pile of renegade keys, and I now know the problem with our plan. It's not enough to find a key. You have to know where it goes."

My cell phone rang, and I answered to Connie.

"I have Brenda back with the film crew," Connie said. "They want more footage."

"Are you kidding me? They want more monkey?"

"No. They want a different takedown."

"We screwed up a simple domestic disturbance. Where do we go from there?"

"How about Loretta? She's disappeared, right? That's a violation of her bond agreement."

"I can't find Loretta. I have no place to look. I have no clue."

"Just lead them around. Make something up. At least no one will shoot at you. And there won't be any monkeys," Connie said.

I hung up and looked at Morelli. "Connie wants me to find Loretta."

"Good," Morelli said. "I want you to find Loretta, too. Loretta probably knows what's going on. She might even know where the money is located."

"I don't know where to begin."

"There were four men involved in the robbery. Go on the assumption that Allen Gratelli was one of the men and find the other two. I'm guessing one of them has Loretta."

"Why aren't *you* looking for Loretta?"

"I'm babysitting her kid. And it seems to me it's more dangerous to stay in this house than to be on the streets. So I'm staying here, and you're hitting the streets."

"Okay, fine, terrific, I'll go find Loretta, but you're going to owe me."

"Shazam," Morelli said.

* * *

The bonds office looked like it was holding a casting call for *'Ho Bounty Hunters*. Lula and Brenda were there, dressed in their leathers, plus Nancy, Mark Bird, and his producer and the camera crew.

"I can't drag everyone around with me," I told them. "I need to talk to people, and the camera crew is intimidating. They're going to have to stay in the van."

"Okay," Mark said, "we'll wire you for sound and we'll do re-creations."

"What's this Loretta like?" Brenda wanted to know. "What did she do?"

"She robbed a liquor store," I told her.

"Was she armed?"

"Yeah. She had a lightsaber."

"A what?"

"She had her kid's *Star Wars* lightsaber from Disney World."

"But she got a lot of money, right?" Brenda said.

"Actually, she got a bottle of gin. She needed a Tom Collins."

"Been there, done that," Brenda said.

I took the new paperwork from Connie, plus a profile on Allen Gratelli, and we all piled into Lula's Firebird. Lula drove north on 206, past Rider College, to a neighborhood of modest houses. She wound down a couple streets and stopped at a house with a lot of cars parked in the driveway. This was Gratelli's house and it looked like people were arriving to give their condolences. Problem was, according to Connie's computer check, Gratelli lived alone. He was divorced, no children. His parents were deceased. He had two brothers and one sister.

Lula parked on the street, and we walked to the house. The front door was open, and I could hear people yelling at one another inside.

"Knock, knock," I said, peeking into the house.

Two men were shoving each other around, a guy in a cable uniform was ransacking a chest in the hall, and a woman was yelling at the two men.

"You dumb shit," the woman said to one of the men. "Who cares if he slept with your wife? Your wife is a slut. Everyone's slept with your wife. Stop being a jerk and go look for the stupid directions."

"What directions?" I asked her.

Her head snapped around, and she took in Lula and Brenda and me. "Cripes," she said. "It's the rod squad. I knew Allen was a sicko, but this is ridiculous."

Lula stiffened her spine. "Say what?"

"You heard he was dead, right? And now you're here on the scavenger hunt? Well, back off, because I was here first," the woman said.

I corralled Lula and Brenda and pulled them aside. "Cozy up to the guy in the cable uniform and find out what he's looking for."

The woman made a disgusted gesture at the men and flounced off to the kitchen. I tagged along and watched her open and close drawers.

"Are you his sister?" I asked the woman.

"Yeah."

"I'm sorry," I said. "This must be a terrible time for you."

"We weren't close." She cut her eyes to me. "Have you known Allen long?"

"Long enough."

"I guess men talk when you're, you know, doing things."

"Mmm."

"Like what did he say?" she asked me.

"Uh, mostly he gave instructions."

"Really? What sort of instructions? Did he say where it was located?"

"No. I knew where it was located. He mostly said

hit me harder. And then *ouch* and *yow* and that sort of thing."

"I don't mean *those* instructions. I mean, did he tell you where the money is hidden?"

"Oh. No."

"Allen was such an idiot. I can't believe he got himself shot. What was he thinking?"

"Do you know who shot him?"

"I imagine it was someone looking for the money, just like him. Probably crazy Dominic Rizzi."

"This is the money from the robbery, right?"

"I guess. He just kept talking about the money he was going to get when Dom got out of jail. And then Dom got out and nobody could find the money. And then last night, Allen said he had directions and today he's dead. I figure I'm next of kin and the money is mine. I just need to find the directions. Me and my two remaining moron brothers."

"Doesn't it bother you that Allen was probably killed over the money and you could get killed, too?"

"Do you have any idea how much money we're talking about?"

"A lot?"

"More than a lot. We're talking a shitload."

"What if you don't find the directions here?"

"I guess I just start digging around the death house. I figure Dom gave the money to his crazy old Aunt Rose, and she hid it somewhere. And then she died before Dom got out of prison."

I left the kitchen, gathered up Lula and Brenda, and herded them outside.

"What did you find out?" I asked them.

"He worked with the dead guy," Lula said. "And the dead guy was always talking about the money he was gonna get when Rizzi got out of prison. And so this jerk-off figured now that the dead guy is dead, he was gonna come look for the money."

"That's it?"

"Yeah."

"Did you get his name?"

"Morty Dill. He was all taken with Brenda here. He would have told us anything."

"He reminded me of my fifth husband," Brenda said. "Sort of cute the way he kept calling me *darlin'*."

"I know all about you from *Star* magazine," Lula said. "I thought your fifth husband was that English guy who got caught with his pants down in the movie theater. You're thinking of your sixth husband, who was the country singer. Kenny Bold."

"Are you sure?"

"There was the guy you married right out of high school. The plumber. Then there was the ice skater who turned out to be gay. The third guy was a stock car driver. Then you remarried the plumber, but that only lasted a couple weeks. And then the English guy."

"You're right," Brenda said. "I'd forgotten about the second marriage to the plumber."

A black Mercedes sedan with tinted windows cruised down the street, stopped in front of the house for a moment, and sped away.

"Guess he don't like a crowd," Lula said. "My opinion is, people gonna be coming out of the woodwork to get that robbery money."

"Morty said Allen had directions to the money," Brenda said. "Morty was looking for the directions."

I looked back at the house. "I suppose we should join in the hunt. Or at least we should wait around to see if anyone finds the directions."

An hour later, everyone cleared out. The house had

been searched from top to bottom and the result was a big zero.

"I'm not going to get an Emmy on this episode," Brenda said. "This is a huge yawn."

"You'd get an Emmy if we found the directions," I told her. "Let's just think about this a little. Supposedly, Allen Gratelli had directions to the money, and next thing, he was dead in Morelli's basement. So, if the directions weren't on him, and they aren't in his house . . . where would they be?"

"In his car," Lula said.

"I don't remember seeing his car. It wasn't parked in front of Morelli's house."

"If I was doing B&E on a cop's house, I wouldn't park in front of it," Lula said. "When we break into someplace we always park around the corner."

Chapter
TWELVE

A half hour later, we were back in Morelli's neighborhood. According to Connie's research, Gratelli drove a silver Camry. Lula motored around the block and, sure enough, there was Gratelli's car, parked around the corner, a block away. Lula pulled in behind it, and we all got out and looked into the Camry. There was a briefcase on the backseat. The cameraman panned across the car and went in for a close-up.

"There it is," Brenda whispered into her mic. "There's the briefcase with the directions to millions of stolen dollars."

We tried the doors. Locked.

"No problemo," Lula said. She opened her trunk and removed a slim metal tool. She rammed the tool into the doorframe and popped the lock. "It's not like I steal cars or anything," Lula said, "but a girl needs to be prepared. A girl's gotta have skills, you see what I'm saying?"

I took the briefcase from the car and set it on the hood. It was a Samsonite hardside attaché case. The kind gorillas can jump on and not make a dent. I released the two locks and everyone crowded close together, excited to see if the directions were inside. I lifted the lid and . . . *Bang!*

Blue dye exploded out of the attaché case.

No one moved. No one spoke. No one blinked. We all just stood there, dripping blue dye.

"What happened?" Brenda wanted to know. "Am I okay? Was it a bomb?"

I looked at the dye on my hands and shirt. "Gratelli booby-trapped his briefcase."

"He's lucky he's dead," Lula said. "I'm wearing leather. Somebody's gotta be responsible for this dry-cleaning bill."

The cameraman looked at his blue lens. "I'm done for the day."

I closed the attaché case and snatched it off the hood of Gratelli's car. "I'm taking this with me. I'll give it to Morelli to check out."

"It's in my hair, isn't it?" Brenda asked. "I feel so funky." She looked down at herself. "I have blue boobies."

Lula carefully eased herself into the Firebird and drove away. Brenda and the camera crew took off in the van. And I walked to Morelli's house.

Mooner answered the door. "Far out," he said. "Off the chain."

I had no idea what "off the chain" meant, and I didn't care. I was blue. I walked through the living room, and Zook never looked up from the computer screen. I got to the kitchen, where Morelli was stirring a pot of spaghetti sauce, and I dropped the attaché case onto the kitchen table.

Morelli gaped at me with the spoon in his hand. "What the hell happened to you?"

"Booby-trapped attaché case."

"Have you seen yourself?"

"No. Is it bad?"

"How do you feel about blue?"

I stepped into the powder room, switched the light

on, and stifled a sob. Blue hair, blue eyebrows, blue eyelashes, blue lips, blue face. I soaked a hand towel and dabbed at my cheek. Nothing happened.

Morelli was behind me, smiling. "You look like a Smurf. I think I'm getting turned on."

"Everything turns you on."

"Not everything. Remember the time you fell off the fire escape and rolled in the dog diarrhea?"

"I took the briefcase out of Gratelli's car. There's a chance it contains directions for finding the money from the robbery."

Morelli went to the attaché case and flipped the locks. "Guess I don't have to worry about a dye bomb," he said. He raised the lid and looked inside. Everything was soaked in blue dye.

"Gratelli didn't get the memo telling him to put his important papers in plastic pouches," Morelli said. "If there were directions in here, they're gone."

I got a spoon out of the silverware drawer and tasted the spaghetti sauce. "Yum," I said.

"It needs to simmer," Morelli said. "I like to let the sausage soak in the gravy. It's for tomorrow. We're supposed to have dinner at your parents' house tonight."

I put the spoon in the dishwasher. "I bet I know where the money is hidden. I bet it's in your basement."

"I've looked in the basement."

"I bet it's buried. I bet it's under your floor."

"That floor is poured concrete."

"And?"

Morelli partially covered his sauce. "I'm not going to take a jackhammer to my basement floor."

We trooped downstairs and stared at the floor. It had just been professionally steam-cleaned to remove the bloodstains.

"This is an old house," I said. "The floor down here looks pretty new."

"I had it put in two years ago. It used to be dirt."

"Omigod!"

"I'm going to forget we had this conversation," Morelli said. "I don't care if there's a fortune buried here. It's not like the money would be mine. It's bank money."

"The bank would be happy to see it."

"The bank would think it was a pain in the ass. They've already collected the insurance."

"What about the insurance company?"

"Screw the insurance company," Morelli said.

"You would let nine million dollars sit under this concrete?"

"Yeah." He toed the concrete. "I like my floor. The guys did a good job on it. It's nice and smooth."

"If we got married, and you died, I'd have this floor up before your body got cold."

"As long as you don't slit my throat while I'm sleeping." He looked down at me. "You wouldn't, would you?"

"Not for money."

A half hour later, I was fresh out of the shower and I was still blue. I got dressed in a clean T-shirt and a pair of Morelli's sweats, and I padded downstairs.

"Help," I said to Morelli.

"I have some turpentine in the garage," he said. "Maybe that'll work."

He opened his back door to go to the garage, and there were two people digging in his yard. They looked up and saw Morelli and took off, leaving their shovels behind.

"Anyone you know?" Morelli asked me.

"Nope."

My cell phone rang. It was Grandma Mazur, and she was excited. "I just saw you on television," she said. "You were on the early evening news. They were doing a report on the murder in Morelli's basement and they said it was believed it was tied to that bank robbery that happened years ago. And then there was this part where Brenda found a briefcase in the dead man's car and it had directions about where the money was buried. And some lady said she was pretty sure Dominic Rizzi gave the money to his Aunt Rose and Rose hid it somewhere before she died. Just think— Morelli could have hidden treasure in his backyard!"

I glanced out the kitchen window at the hole the two diggers had started. "And they said all that on television?"

"Yep. It was a pip of a report."

I hung up and passed the news on to Morelli.

"There might be money buried in my basement," Morelli said. "But I'm pretty sure the only thing anyone is going to find in my yard has been left there by Bob."

Morelli jogged across his backyard to his garage and returned with a small can of turpentine. We dabbed it on my hand and rubbed and nothing happened.

"I'll call the crime lab and see if they have a suggestion," Morelli said.

The doorbell rang and Mooner answered. "It's some dude named Gary," Mooner yelled at me. "He says he's a stalker."

I went to the door, and Gary tried hard not to notice I was blue. He looked at his feet, and he looked above my head, and he cleared his throat.

"It's okay," I said. "I know I'm blue."

"It caught me by surprise," he said. "I didn't want to seem rude."

"Just so you know, Brenda is blue, too."

"Is this some art thing?"

"No. It was an accident. What's up?"

"I had the toilet dream again, only this time a bull came charging down the southbound lane, right at Brenda."

"Jeez. What happened then?"

"I woke up." His attention shifted to Mooner and Zook. "Are they playing *Minionfire*? What's their PC?"

"Zook and Moondog."

"Are you kidding me? They're famous. Zook is like a god. He's a Blybold Wizard."

Gary inched his way in and stood behind the couch, watching over Zook's shoulder. "Feel the power," Gary said. "The dragon's coming. There he is! There he is! Go arcane."

Zook turned and looked at him. "How did you know the dragon was coming?"

"Ever since I got hit by lightning, things happen in my head before they happen on the screen. It's like I'm a step ahead of cable, and I'm way faster than dial-up."

"Whoa," Zook and Mooner said, eyes glued to Gary.

Zook looked over at me. "You're blue."

"It's a long story."

"Who's your PC?" Mooner asked Gary.

"I haven't got one. I just lurk. I thought it wasn't fair for me to play with the lightning advantage."

"Far out," Mooner said. "A dude with honor."

Morelli ambled in. "We need to go to your parents' now." He checked out Gary. "Is this the stalker?"

Gary extended his hand. "Pleased to meet you," he said to Morelli.

"Everyone sign off," I said. "We're going to my parents' house for dinner."

* * *

My grandmother opened the door, and we all marched in. Zook, Mooner, Gary, Morelli, me, and Bob.

"You better set more plates," Grandma yelled to my mother in the kitchen. "We got a group."

My father was in the living room, dozing in front of the television. He picked his head up and looked at everyone standing in the foyer. He mumbled something that sounded a little like *friggin' mutants* and went back to napping.

Bob bounced around, doing his happy dance.

"Isn't he something," Grandma said. She patted his head, and Bob took off for the kitchen.

A moment later, my mother shrieked, and Bob bounded out of the kitchen and streaked through the dining room with a ham firmly clenched in his mouth. He skidded to a stop in front of my father and dropped the ham.

My grandmother ran in and scooped the ham up off the floor. "Thirty-second rule in effect," my grandmother said, returning the ham to the kitchen. There was the sound of water running, and moments later, my grandmother reappeared with the ham on a plate. "Dinner's ready," she said. "Everyone sit."

We dragged extra chairs to the table, and I shuffled plates and silverware around. Bob took his place under the table, ever on guard for food to fall out of someone's mouth onto the rug.

My mother brought in creamed corn, green beans with bacon, and mashed potatoes. She got to the table, looked at me, and her mouth dropped open.

"Booby-trapped attaché case," I said. "No big deal."

She set the side dishes on the table and made the sign of the cross. "Dear God," she said. And she returned to the kitchen. I heard the cabinet door creak open and moments later, my mother returned with a glass of whiskey.

"Isn't this nice," my grandmother said. "It feels like a party. We even got the stalker here."

My mother tossed some whiskey down her throat.

"Stalker?" my father said, mashed potato bowl in hand.

"Yep," Grandma said. "He's a genuine stalker. He's even got a restraining order against him."

My father considered that for a beat and went back to filling his plate. Clearly, he didn't find a stalker to be especially interesting. Now, if Gary had been a cross-dresser, my father would have had something to work with.

"So how's the treasure hunt going?" Grandma asked Morelli. "Did you find all that money yet?"

This got everyone's attention.

My mother had a grip on her whiskey glass. "What money?"

"I guess I'm the only one who watches television," Grandma said. "The early news ran a piece on the dead guy in Morelli's basement."

"Why don't I know about this?" my mother asked.

"I guess I forgot to tell you, being that I was so busy answering all the phone calls," Grandma said.

"You didn't kill him, did you?" my mother asked me.

"No! I just discovered the body."

"The dead guy's name was Allen Gratelli," Grandma said. "Stephanie broke into his car and found his suitcase, and that's how she got blue. And it turns out Allen Gratelli and Dominic Rizzi were friends, and the television reporter said Allen Gratelli was in Morelli's basement looking for all that money that was never recovered from the robbery. Nine million dollars, and Joseph's Aunt Rose, rest in peace, hid it somewhere and now everyone's looking for it."

"Sweet," Mooner said. "You could get high-def TiVo with nine million dollars."

"I could get a lawyer for my mom," Zook said.

"I could get a sports car," Grandma said.

"You don't have a driver's license," my mother told her.

"I could get a driver," Grandma said. "A hot one."

My father had his head down, shoveling in ham. My father would like to see the hot driver deliver Grandma Mazur to the old people's home in Hamilton Township.

"Maybe I could find the money," Gary said. "I could divine it."

"Dude," Mooner said. "That would be awesome. Can you, like, really do that?"

"I found a chicken salad sandwich once. I found it in my sock drawer," Gary said.

"Badass," Mooner said. "Wicked cool."

"What are you doing now?" Grandma asked Mooner. "Are you still involved in the pharmaceutical industry?"

"I mostly gave that up. I was getting stiff competition from the Russians. I've been reviewing my options, and I thought I might open a Japanese teahouse. Either that or a nudie bar."

My father picked his head up. "Don't you need money to open a nudie bar?"

"Yeah, dude, isn't that a bummer? Where's the justice? I mean, where's the incentive for the little businessman?"

"I think you should open a nudie bar for women," Grandma said. "There's lots of bars for men where they can see naked women, but there's no place us women can go to see ding dongs."

"I dig it," Mooner said. "You want private parts parity. Far out."

My mother chugged the rest of her whiskey.

Morelli was slouched back in his chair, taking it all

in. He draped an arm across my shoulders and whispered into my ear. "Do women really want to see ding dongs?"

"Yeah," I said, "as long as they don't have to touch them."

"Is it sexual?"

"No. Morbid curiosity."

"How about mine?" he asked.

"Yours is definitely sexual . . . and touchable."

He nuzzled my neck. "Can we go home now?"

"No!"

"Why not?"

"We haven't had dessert. And besides, I feel funny shazaming with Zook in the house."

"We could shazam in the garage."

"I don't think so."

"The SUV?"

"No!"

"I'm becoming more motivated to find Loretta," Morelli said.

Chapter
THIRTEEN

It was a little after eight when Morelli pulled to the curb in front of his house. A small crowd was gathered on the sidewalk, watching two men dig in Morelli's tiny front yard. Morelli got out of his car and joined the onlookers.

"Excuse me," Morelli said to the guys digging. "What are you doing?"

"Digging," the one guy said.

"This is private property," Morelli said.

"What?"

"Private property."

"I think there's something about digging," the guy said. "Like people only own the top of the property."

"I think you're wrong," Morelli said.

The guy kept digging. "And why would I give a rat's ass what you think?"

"Because I own this house, and if you don't stop digging, I'm going to have you arrested for destruction of personal property."

"Look at me—I'm so scared," the guy said. "Call the cops. Call the cops on me."

Morelli badged him. "I am the cops."

The guy looked at Morelli's badge. "Oh. Sorry."

Everyone dispersed after that, and Morelli, Zook,

Mooner, Gary, and I trooped into the house. Morelli walked straight through and swore when he looked out his back window. His backyard was filled with people digging, and his garage door was open.

"This is unbelievable," Morelli said.

"Dude," Mooner said. "You should sell tickets. Like, it would be a hundred dollars to dig for a half hour. We could be, like, rich, dude."

Morelli walked out his back door, unholstered his gun, fired a shot into the ground, and the diggers scattered like roaches when the light goes on. He crossed the yard to his garage and returned with a roll of yellow crime scene tape.

"Do you think that's going to help?" I asked him.

"It's worth a try."

Ten minutes later, Morelli's entire property was behind the yellow tape. Zook, Mooner, and Gary were in the living room making deals with the wood elves, and Morelli and I were sitting out on the back stoop, watching Bob sniff around the holes in his yard.

"I'm going to have to jackhammer my basement," Morelli said. "This isn't going to stop until we find the money."

"If we found the money, Loretta might even turn up."

"I wouldn't count on it. I think Dom did the time and figured he didn't owe his partners anything. Problem was, for whatever reason, Dom couldn't put his hands on the money right away."

"Maybe because it was buried in Rose's basement and you came along and inherited the house and poured concrete down there."

"Yeah. And it keeps getting worse. Dom's nephew is living in this house, so he can't just blow it up, and thanks to the early news, half of Trenton is on a nine-million-dollar scavenger hunt."

"And Loretta?"

"I'm guessing Loretta is being held hostage by one or both of the partners until Dom forks over the money. I'd feel a lot better if we could get to her before the money is found. There's no guarantee she won't be disposed of the instant she's no longer useful."

"We need to get Dom," I said. "He can take us to the other two partners."

"Any ideas?"

"I'm sure he's worried about his nephew. He hates the thought that Zook is with you. Plus, he wants him away from this house. And maybe he's thinking there's a possibility that whoever has Loretta will decide to hedge his bets and snatch Zook, too. So I think Dom isn't far away. I think he's keeping his eye on the house and on Zook. He's only been out of jail for a week, and he doesn't have a job. We know he hasn't got a lot of money."

"He has a gun," Morelli said.

"True. And a car."

"The car he was driving belongs to his mother. We found it abandoned."

"Where's he sleeping? Is he sneaking back into his mother's house?"

"No. We've been doing random checks," Morelli said.

"It's warm enough to sleep outdoors. Just another street person if he migrated downtown."

"Yes, but he has a rifle. It would make him conspicuous if he carried it with him."

Bob was digging in one of the holes. He had his head below ground level and dirt was flying between his hind legs.

"I think Dom's in the neighborhood, waiting for a chance to get into the house," I said. "So maybe we can set a trap. Make it look like no one's home, but you could be in a closet or something, waiting to jump out and capture Dom."

"Gee, that sounds like lots of fun."

"You have a better plan?"

Morelli blew out a sigh. "No."

Morelli woke me up out of a sound sleep. "Did you hear that?" he whispered.

"I was sleeping. I didn't hear anything."

"Shush," he said. "Listen."

It was warm and the windows were open. The white gauzy curtain still left from Aunt Rose moved on a gentle breeze.

"There," he said. "Did you hear it?"

"It sounds like someone's digging."

"What does it take to discourage these idiots?"

"I don't know, but I don't care if they're digging. Go back to sleep."

"I can't go to sleep," Morelli said. "This is making me nuts."

He rolled out of bed and moved toward the door.

"Where are you going?"

"I'm going to shoot the digger."

"That's not a good idea. Not to mention, you're naked."

"The digger won't care. He'll be concentrating on his bullet hole."

"You needed a new lawn anyway," I said to him. "Think of this as soil preparation."

He found a pair of boxers and pulled them on. "How's this? Does this meet your dress code for shooting trespassers?"

I dragged myself out of bed and grabbed some clothes off the floor. "Let's at least see who's out there before you shoot them. If we're lucky, it'll be Dom. Do you have a flashlight?"

"In the kitchen."

We padded downstairs and tiptoed through the dark house. I found the flashlight, and Morelli had his Glock in hand. We stood in the pitch-black kitchen and looked out the window. Someone was clearly digging in the backyard, but it was too dark to see much of anything.

"Okay," Morelli said. "On the count of three, I'm going to open the door, and you shine the flashlight on this bastard. One, two . . . three!"

Morelli yanked the back door open, and I hit the button on the flashlight and caught the digger in the act.

"Good God," Morelli said.

It was Grandma Mazur.

"Howdy," Grandma said. "Hope I didn't wake you."

"Of course you woke us," I said. "It's two in the morning. What the heck are you doing?"

"I felt lucky," Grandma said.

"I don't think the money is buried in the backyard," Morelli told her.

"That's okay," she said. "I still feel lucky. It isn't every day I get to see a man in his underwear."

"How did you get here?" I asked her.

"I drove the Buick."

"You're not supposed to drive," I told her.

"I'm old. I've got rights," she said.

That could be true, but Grandma Mazur was the worst driver ever. She knew only one speed. Foot to the floor.

"I'll drive Grandma home," I said to Morelli.

I dropped Grandma off at the door and locked the Buick up in my father's garage. Morelli was waiting curbside in the SUV when I got to the front of my parents' house. I slid onto the passenger seat and looked over at him. He was only wearing the boxers.

"I thought you might have changed your mind about the SUV," Morelli said.

I checked out his underwear, which was imprinted with pictures of bunnies. "Where did you get those shorts?" I asked.

"Wal-Mart. They came in a pack."

I blew out a sigh. Morelli was irresistible in his bunny boxers. "I haven't changed my mind about the SUV, but I've changed my mind about your bedroom."

Morelli is at his best on a Saturday morning. His body temperature is a little higher and his blood pressure is a little lower than on a Monday. Everything about him is a little softer, a little more sensual. He was at the kitchen table in faded navy sweatpants and a matching sweatshirt that had the sleeves cut short. I suspected he was commando under the sweatpants. He'd showered, but he hadn't shaved, and he looked like he could give a dead woman an orgasm.

He glanced up from his paper and smiled at me. "Shazam."

I smiled back at him. It had been a multiple shazam morning.

I sipped my coffee. "What's going on today?"

"I'm getting someone to demo the basement floor. And I'm going door-to-door looking for Dom. I think you're right. He's nearby."

It was a little after eight, and Zook was still sleeping. Mooner and Gary hadn't yet appeared on Morelli's front doorstep. The sound of car doors slamming shut and people talking carried in from Morelli's backyard.

"It's Saturday morning," Morelli said. "Don't these people take a day off?"

I peeked out the window. "Brenda is in the yard with the film crew."

Morelli took his coffee to the door and stepped out.

"Hell-o!" Brenda said, eyeballing Morelli. "You are *hot*. Hold me back!"

Morelli turned and looked at me. "Is she for real?"

"Yes. And you want to keep arm's distance, or she'll give you a pat-down."

"You're trespassing on private property," Morelli said. "And you've ignored the crime scene tape."

"We didn't ignore it," the cameraman said. "We got a real good shot of it."

Brenda was in another black leather outfit. She was wearing four-inch spike-heeled shoes, and her hair and her face and her chest were blue. She had a handheld mic, and she was having a hard time navigating because her heels were sinking into the freshly dug dirt. She climbed onto a dirt mound and looked down into the hole. The cameraman focused on Brenda.

"Here we are at Aunt Rose's house," Brenda said to the camera. "And as you can see, digging for the stolen money has already begun."

"Excuse me," Morelli said. "You're going to have to leave."

Brenda stumbled over to Morelli with the mic. "Are you by any chance the handsome owner of the property—"

"That's it," Morelli said. "I've had enough."

He set his coffee cup on the stoop, reached over the railing, grabbed the garden hose, and turned it on Brenda and the cameraman.

Brenda hit high C at the first blast of water. "Eeeeeee!" she shrieked. "Dammit, shit, sonovabitch!"

The dirt instantly turned to mud, and Brenda lost her footing and went down. The sound guy rushed in to help, and he went down, too.

"Maybe you want to turn the hose off," I said to Morelli.

Brenda had one shoe on and one shoe in her hand. "What *is* your *problem*?" she yelled at Morelli. "Do you know who I am? I'm *Brenda*. I'm doing the news here, and the news is *sacred,* for cripe's sake. You can't turn the hose on the news, you moron!"

Morelli shut the water off and retrieved his coffee cup. "This is going to be another one of those days," he said.

We backed into the house, closed and locked the door, and pulled all the shades down.

Morelli stood in the middle of his kitchen. "I hate this," he said. "I hate bringing this shit into my home."

"We need to find Dom."

Morelli nodded agreement. "I'm going to change my clothes and canvass the neighborhood."

"We'll split it in half."

Morelli smiled down at me. "Nice offer, Cupcake, but you're blue. You'll scare the crap out of everyone."

"I forgot."

"Stay here with Zook. Keep people out of my yard. Get me some estimates on jackhammer rentals."

Morelli went upstairs, and I crept to the window and looked out. No Brenda. No cameraman. No film crew van. I went to the front of the house. No one was there, either. Good deal.

Bob was sleeping in a patch of sun in the living room. He was still spray-painted. He didn't seem to care. While I was standing, looking out the window, Lula's red Firebird slid to a stop in front of Morelli's house. Lula hoisted herself out of the car and marched to Morelli's front door.

"Hey," I said, opening the door to her. "What's up?"

"I need you to help me with my prenup. I got a lawyer appointment this afternoon, and I gotta have this ready."

"I don't know anything about prenups."

"You just gotta help me make out my list. I'm supposed to list all my assets. And then Tank lists all his assets. And we got what we got."

"So Tank is doing this, too?"

"I left a message on his phone. I said if you got any-thing you want to keep, you better list it out or I could get it in case of divorce. Not that I intend to get a di-vorce, but I guess you never know, right?"

"Right."

"Do you think Tank and me would ever get di-vorced?"

"I'm still struggling with you and Tank getting *mar-ried*."

"Hunh," Lula said. "Anyways, I got this list. You want to hear it?"

"Sure."

"I got a television, a DVD player, a cable box." Lula cut her eyes to me. "I hate those cable fuckers."

"Everybody hates them."

"I got my Firebird, my Glock, a fur coat that's al-most mink, a clock radio, a whip."

"Wait a minute. You have a whip?"

"Don't everyone?"

"I don't have a whip."

"Hunh."

"What do you do with the whip? What does it look like? Is it one of those long black ones like Zorro uses?"

"No," Lula said. "It's the kind a jockey uses. It's for bad boys."

"Eeuw."

"Okay, if you're gonna be squeamish about it, I'll skip over my collection of professional experience en-hancement tools. I never used the whip anyway. It went with a Halloween outfit."

Morelli came down the stairs in jeans and running shoes, and a sweatshirt over a T-shirt.

"What's up?" he said to Lula. "I see you're a mem-ber of the Blue Girl Group."

"Blue isn't my best color," Lula said.

Morelli grabbed me and kissed me and went off to do his cop thing.

"He looks like he got some last night," Lula said. "Where's he going?"

"He thinks Dom is somewhere in the neighborhood. He's going to look around."

"How come you're not helping him?"

"I'm blue."

"Oh yeah, I forgot. I'm starting to get used to it."

"And someone has to stay here with Zook. I don't want to leave him in the house alone."

"I could babysit him," Lula said. "I'm taking the morning to put my prenup in order. I could just as leave do it here."

"I'd really like to go back to my apartment and check on Rex and get some clothes."

"Go for it," Lula said.

I ran upstairs and knocked on Zook's door.

"Yeah?" he said. A moment later, he was at the door, looking almost awake.

"I have to go back to my apartment for an hour or so. Morelli is working, so Lula is going to stay here with you."

"No way! She scares the crap out of me."

"You'll be fine as long as you don't tell her she's fat. And you might want to avoid mentioning the blue dye."

"I'm not going out of my room."

"That would be okay, too."

I grabbed my purse and ran downstairs. "Don't let anyone dig in the yard," I told Lula. "Morelli takes it personally. And Zook is a good kid, but it would be great if he didn't paint anything."

"I'm on it. You can count on me. Do you think I should list shoes in the prenup?"

"Do you and Tank wear the same size?"

"No."

"Then probably your shoes are safe."

My apartment isn't that far from Morelli's house. Too far to walk but fast to drive. I parked the Zook car, bypassed the elevator for the stairs, and let myself into my apartment. I tapped on Rex's cage, and he peeked out at me. I dropped a baby carrot and a piece of cheese into his food dish and gave him fresh water. I stuffed clean jeans and a couple shirts into a tote bag. I didn't need much. Just enough to get me through a couple more days while we straightened out the Zook arrangements.

I took one last look at myself in my bathroom mirror. I wanted to believe that the blue was fading, but truth is, it wasn't. I was hideously blue. I was like Dom . . . conspicuous. A bunch of people were looking for Dom, and Dom didn't want to be found. And Dom didn't have the luxury of taking off for Rio. Dom had to hang close. Dom had his own agenda.

So let's step into Dom's shoes. I'm ultra-recognizable, and I'm confined to a small area. How would I move around? In disguise or at night. Second problem, I have no money. So either I mooch from someone I trust or else I hold up a convenience store. I'm going to guess he's mooching.

I called Connie. "Would you run a personal history on Dom for me?"

"What do you want to know?"

"Where was he living when he was sent to prison?"

"That's easy. He owned a house on Vine Street. When he was sentenced, his wife divorced him and got the house. So far as I know, she's still living there and has remarried."

I got the house number from Connie and hung up. I'd forgotten about the ex-wife. This was great. Ex-wives loved ratting on their ex-husbands.

* * *

The Vine Street house was a small single-family cape with a detached single-car garage. It had a green Subaru sitting in the driveway.

I parked and knocked on the front door. A woman answered and gasped when she saw me.

"Sorry," I said. "I know I'm blue. I had an accident with some dye."

"I know who you are," she said. "You're Stephanie Plum. There was a piece on you on the late news last night. They said you were involved in the robbery treasure hunt, and you and Brenda got sprayed with blue dye. Do you really know Brenda?"

"Yes."

"What's she like?"

"She's like Brenda. Could I ask you some questions about Dom?"

"Sure, but I don't know much about him anymore. I haven't seen him since he got out."

"I'm interested in the guys he used to hang with."

"Mostly they were from his old neighborhood. Victor Raguzzo, Benny Stoli, Jelly Kantner. And the guy who was shot. Allen Gratelli. Allen and Dom worked together."

"Did you think any of those guys pulled the job with him?"

"I could see Allen doing it. Victor, Benny, and Jelly, no."

"Dom's hiding out somewhere. Do you have any ideas?"

"He's not with his mom?"

"No."

"Jelly would be dumb enough to take him in. Or maybe he's still seeing Peggy Bargaloski. That's why I divorced him. I found out he was spending a *lot* of time at Peggy's house."

I gave her my card and told her to call me if she saw Dom.

I drove around the corner, pulled to the curb, and got addresses from Connie. Jelly was living in a second-floor apartment two blocks from Dom's mother's house. Peggy was in Cleveland.

I wanted to do a drive-by on Jelly's house, but I was too obvious in the Zook car. There was a car wash minutes away on the corner of Hammond and Baker, but I didn't want to put up with the car wash crew and their comments on my blueness. I know that's chickenshit of me. What can I say? I'm blue, and I'm feeling fragile.

I drove back to Morelli's house, thinking I'd check on Lula and trade my Zookmobile for Morelli's SUV. I let myself into the house and couldn't find anyone. Mooner's laptop was on the coffee table beside Zook's, but there was no Mooner or Zook. I walked to the back of the house and looked out. Mooner and Zook were digging in the backyard with Bob. Lula was standing guard with her gun drawn. A small crowd had formed on the perimeter of the crime scene tape. Gary was sitting on the stoop, watching.

"What the heck is this?" I asked Lula.

"We figured it wouldn't hurt to look. There's still some undisturbed ground here. And if we find it, we'll share it with Morelli."

"Are you insane? If you find it, you'll hand it over to the authorities! You're looking for stolen money."

"Hunh," Lula said. "You sure got a stick up your ass. When did you get so play-by-the-book?"

"I've always been play-by-the-book. *You're* the one who doesn't play by the book."

"Well, I knew it was one of us."

"Anyway, I don't think the money is buried in the backyard."

"Me, either," Gary said. "I'm not seeing anything. I told them it was a waste of time, but no one would listen."

"Yeah, but you might be a nut," Lula said.

"Hey," I yelled at Zook and Mooner. "Stop digging. The money isn't in the backyard."

A murmur went up from the people pressed against the crime scene tape. Two of them had shovels.

"It isn't in the front yard, either," I told everyone. "Go home!"

Mooner, Zook, Bob, Gary, Lula, and I left the yard and huddled in the kitchen. I gave everyone an ice cream sandwich, except Bob. Bob got a slice of ham.

"How come you think the money isn't in the yard?" Lula wanted to know.

"People wouldn't be breaking into Morelli's house if the money was in the yard. The only people digging in the yard are idiots who saw Brenda on television."

Lula peeled the wrapper off her ice cream. "So you think the money's in the house?"

"I'm not sure there *is* any money. I suspect it was here at one time, but Dom was in prison for almost ten years, and there were a lot of changes. Rose died. Morelli moved into the house. Things were thrown away. Rooms were renovated. For all we know, Rose could have found the money and given it to the church."

"I don't think so," Gary said. "I'm getting a sharp pain in my forehead."

"It's the ice cream," I told him. "You're getting a brain freeze." I herded everyone into the living room and found some Saturday morning cartoons on television. "I need to go out again, but I'll be back by noon."

I found the keys to Morelli's car and left my keys in their place. I drove to Jelly's house and idled across the street. It was a small two-story house that had been converted into two apartments. There was only one front door, so I assumed the owner had made a small foyer with two inner doors. I looked up to the second floor. Four windows going across. The shades had been raised on all four windows. It would be easier to snoop if Jelly lived on the ground floor. I drove around the block. Sometimes older neighborhoods in Trenton have alleys intersecting the blocks. This block wasn't divided by an alley. I parked around the corner, walked to Jelly's house, and tried the front door. Ordinarily, if you look like you belong somewhere, no one pays attention. Unfortunately, I was blue, and I looked like I belonged in some distant galaxy.

The front door was unlocked, so I stepped inside. Just as I'd thought, there was a small foyer. The door to my left led to the ground-floor apartment. The door directly in front of me led upstairs. I rang the bell. No answer. I rang again. Nothing. I tried the doorknob. Locked. I looked under the mat. No key. I felt the top of the doorjamb. Eureka . . . a key. I plugged the key into the lock, the door clicked open, and I stepped inside. I closed the door and stood listening, hearing nothing but quiet.

I crept up the stairs and cautiously peeked into the apartment. Living room with a galley kitchen at one end. A small hall leading to a bedroom and a bathroom. Dirty dishes in the sink. A cereal box on the counter. A pillow on the couch in front of the small television. An open half-empty bag of chips on the coffee table. I moved to the bathroom. Not clean. Two toothbrushes. Two razors. Towels on the floor. Toilet lid up. Ick. The door was open to the bedroom. Bed unmade. Sheets looked like they'd been on there since Christmas. Socks and underwear on the floor. Top bureau drawer open. Big mess.

I thought there was a good chance Dom was crashing here. I was tempted to do a more thorough search, but I wasn't sure what it would produce. And the longer I lingered, the better my chance of getting caught in the act. I decided to sneak out and do a background search on Jelly and turn the whole mess over to Morelli.

I walked out of the bedroom into the short hallway, and I heard the door open and close at the foot of the stairs. Instant panic! I was trapped. I wasn't in a position where I felt I could successfully detain Dom, and I didn't want to blow his cover and have him run. I did a ten-second imitation of a cat on roller skates. I pulled myself together, scurried into the bedroom, and dove under the bed.

The reality of hiding under a bed is that it's uncomfortable, it's terrifying, and you feel like an idiot. I inched to the middle, so there was less chance I'd be seen, and I tried to breathe quietly.

There were two sets of footsteps on the stairs and then there was a moment of quiet, and I knew they were in the living room.

"Nobody home," a male voice said. Not Dom's.

"Yeah, but I know he was here. I can smell him."

The second voice was also male. And again, not Dom's.

"Look around. Maybe he left something laying out that would tell us something."

"He wouldn't do that. He's living with Jelly. He's not going to let Jelly see anything."

"Look around anyway. People are stupid. They do stupid things. And maybe if we stay here long enough, he'll come home, and we can persuade him to talk to us."

"We've got his sister on ice. How much more persuading can we do? Personally, I don't think he knows where the money is."

"For crissake, just look! Would it kill you to look?"

Holy crap. Dom's partners. And I was stuck under the bed. I went cold inside. I could feel everything liquefying in my intestines. How does this happen to me? How do I get myself into these situations? I heard them rummaging through the living room and kitchen. They came into the bedroom, and my heart rate picked up.

"These guys are such slobs," one of them said. "It's like two pigs living in their own slop."

"You should talk. I've been in your apartment and it isn't that great."

"Wait until I get my hands on the money, and you'll see great. I'll be out of that shit-hole apartment. I'll be cruising the islands in my boat. Did I ever show you a picture of my boat?"

"Only about a million times."

They were walking around the bed, and I could see their shoes and the bottoms of their slacks. The one guy was wearing scuffed brown tie shoes, worn down at the heel, and tan slacks with cuffs. The other was in jeans and beat-up CAT boots with a gash in the toe. They went through the bureau drawers and rifled the single drawer in the bedside chest.

"There's nothing here," the one guy said. "What do you want to do now?"

"I don't feel like waiting. I got stuff to do. My wife's on my ass."

"I wouldn't know about that."

"Yeah, no one would marry you."

"Lots of women would marry me."

"Oh yeah? Who?"

"Lots of women. And I'm not paying through the nose for a woman I'm not even getting anything from."

They left the bedroom, and moments later, I heard them on the stairs. The door opened and closed, and the apartment was quiet. I didn't know what to do. I was afraid to crawl out from under the bed. I was pretty sure they were no longer in the apartment, but what if I was wrong? I waited a couple minutes more and slithered to the edge, where I had a better view. I held my breath and listened. I carefully looked around. Now or never, I thought. I belly-crawled out, got to my feet, and forced myself to creep down the hall to the living room. I almost keeled over with relief when no one was there. I hurried to the foyer at the bottom of the stairs and hesitated. If the two bad guys saw me leave, they might think I was coming from the downstairs apartment. Unless they watched the evening news. Then they'd know who I was because I was *blue*.

I locked the door, placed the key on the top of the doorjamb, opened the front door a crack, and looked out. No one standing there with a gun in his hand. No black mafia staff cars with tinted windows lined up at the curb. I casually walked away from the house, down the block to the corner, around the corner, and angled myself behind the wheel of Morelli's SUV. I two-handed the key into the ignition and pulled away from the curb with a white-knuckle grip on the wheel. Okay, so I was a little freaked, but I hadn't messed my pants. That was pretty good, right?

By the time I got to Morelli's house, I'd calmed down a little but not entirely. It was almost noon and Morelli was sitting on his front step with Bob. I plunked myself down next to him, he put his arm around me, and I collapsed into him.

"Either you like me a lot, or you've had a bad morning," Morelli said.

"It's both. I did some legwork and ended up at Jelly Kantner's apartment."

"*At* his apartment or *in* his apartment?"

"In."

"Were you *invited* in?"

"No, but I also wasn't told to stay out."

"Nobody home," Morelli said.

"Mmm. Anyway, it was obvious someone was staying with Jelly, and it wasn't a woman."

"You think it was Dom?"

"Yes. And I wasn't the only one to reach that conclusion, because just as I was about to leave, two guys showed up."

I felt Morelli tense against me and go silent for a beat. "You told them you were the maid?"

"I didn't tell them anything. I was under the bed."

"This is why our relationship is stressful," Morelli said.

"I think they were Dom's two remaining partners. They were looking for him because they wanted the money. And they have Loretta. They're holding her hostage, but so far Dom hasn't come through."

"Did you get to see them? Do you have names?"

"No names. One is married and one isn't. One of them lives in an apartment. One was wearing beat-up CAT boots and jeans, and the other was wearing tan slacks with cuffs and brown shoes. I couldn't see more than that."

What I didn't say was that the voice on the single guy sounded familiar. It had a slight rasp, like a smoker. And there wasn't a lot of inflection. I couldn't associate a name or face with the voice. I just felt like I'd heard it before.

"I'll bring Bob in and then I'll go to Jelly's and wait for Dom," Morelli said. "Where's Zook?"

"Zook's in the house with Lula."

"I got back about ten minutes ago, and Lula's car was here, but no one was in the house."

"Did you look in the backyard?"

"Yeah," Morelli said. "No one's in the backyard. It's wall-to-wall mud. I think if I keep turning the hose on it no one will dig there."

"That's weird," I said, "because I could swear I hear digging."

Morelli listened. "It doesn't sound like digging. It's more like drilling and . . . oh shit."

"What?"

Morelli was on his feet. "That's a jackhammer."

I followed Morelli to the kitchen and down the cellar stairs. Mooner was wailing away at the concrete floor with a pickax, and Lula had a jackhammer propped against her belly. She gave the jackhammer a blast of juice, and I was afraid her breasts were going to break loose from their moorings and knock her out. Gary and Zook were in a corner, mesmerized by the spectacle.

"This is my basement floor," Morelli yelled. "You can't just go into a man's house and jackhammer his floor!"

Lula jiggled to a stop. "Well, *excuse* me. It's not like we weren't gonna share the money with you."

"There's no sharing," Morelli said. "The money was stolen."

"It was over ten years ago," Lula said. "Isn't there some kind of time limit and then it's finders keepers losers weepers?"

"No," Morelli said. "Where'd you get the jackhammer?"

"I sort of borrowed it."

"Oh great," he said. "A hot jackhammer."

"It's a Saturday. You can borrow these things on a Saturday," Lula said.

"This is a lot of floor to demo," Morelli said. "And after we demo the floor, we still don't know where to dig."

"Guess that's why there were directions," Lula said. "Probably it was like a treasure map. Seven paces north and two paces west and the treasure is buried under the piece of floor with the X marked on it."

"I thought you had an appointment with your lawyer," I said to Lula.

"Yeah, I guess I better get going." She turned to Morelli. "You want me to come back and jackhammer some more when I'm done with the lawyer?"

"No," Morelli said. "But I appreciate the offer."

"So, like, now what?" Mooner asked Morelli. "This is majorly disappointing. I was counting on some moola, man. Like, being a griefer doesn't pay a lot, you know what I mean? And a man has needs, right? Like, what happens when I have a craving for a Big Mo candy bar or a crab puff?"

"Here's a deal," Morelli said. "I could use some security in the house. Suppose I pay you guys to protect the house. That means you have to keep people from digging in my yard, pickaxing my basement, spray-painting my dog . . ."

"Whoa, cool," Mooner said. "And how about the Zookduder and me? Can we do those things?"

"No," Morelli said. "You have to protect the house from everyone, including yourselves."

"How much?" Zook asked.

"Five dollars a day."

"No way," Zook said.

"Ten."

"Twenty," Zook said. "Apiece."

"Ten," Morelli said. "Apiece."

"Take it, dude," Mooner said to Zook. "It's a cool gig."

"Me, too?" Gary asked.

"Yeah, you, too," Morelli said.

"Should we be, like, packing heat, or something?" Mooner wanted to know.

"No!" Morelli said. "If someone comes to the house, you politely tell them to go away. If they won't go away, you call me."

"Gotcha," Mooner said.

"Looks like we're done in the basement," I said. "Everyone upstairs for lunch."

Gary had been quietly standing in his corner. "I think it might be here," he said.

Everyone looked at him.

"I feel like I have a vision coming, but it's still in the back of my head. Sometimes it's like that. It's like brain constipation."

"Oh man, I hate when I get that," Mooner said.

"Maybe lunch will help," I said to Gary.

Gary didn't budge from the corner. "I think I should stay here."

I made sandwiches for Zook, Mooner, Morelli, Bob, and me, and I brought Gary's sandwich down to the basement.

"How's it going?" I said to him. "Anything coming through?"

"I had sort of a tingle before, but it went away."

"Okeydokey. Shout out if you need anything."

Lula left, and Mooner and Zook checked in on Minionfire.

"I'm going to get my cousin Mooch over here to finish the basement," Morelli said. "Part of it's torn up. I might as well finish the job."

Mooch owned a small construction company. He

specialized in renovation, and fitting people into cement overcoats. His Yellow Pages ad read Mooch Morelli, demo and disposal.

"Can you trust Mooch to let you know if he finds the money?" I asked Morelli.

"I'll keep my eye on him."

"What about Dom?"

"You can watch for Dom," Morelli said. "Stake out Jelly's apartment and call me if Dom shows up."

Chapter

FOURTEEN

Four hours later, I was still watching for Dom. My ass was asleep, and I had to tinkle. I got Jelly's phone number from Connie and tried calling him. No one answered, so I called Morelli.

"What's new?" I said to Morelli.

"Mooch and his guy Tiny have gone through two six-packs and have destroyed almost my entire basement. I think they only have maybe four or five more bottles of work left to do."

"What did they find?"

"Dirt."

"Are they going to dig up the dirt?"

"No. They're wasted. Mooch is lucky he hasn't jackhammered his foot."

"I need a bathroom break."

"No activity?"

"None. It looks to me like no one's even in the bottom half of the house."

"I'd take your place, but I'm afraid to leave Mooch alone with the kids."

"Afraid he'll plant them in the cellar?"

"No. I'm afraid he'll share my remaining beer with them."

So I had a dilemma. I had to tinkle. *Bad.* And I had

no one to relieve me. I could drive around and look for a gas station or convenience store with a bathroom, but that could take time. Or I could run across the street and use Jelly's bathroom. If I used Jelly's bathroom, I ran the risk of getting trapped again. Not to mention contracting a disease.

I did a mental coin toss, and Jelly's bathroom won. I pulled the key out of the ignition, shoved it into my pocket, and crossed the street. I let myself into the apartment, went straight to the bathroom, and lined the seat with toilet paper. Even with the toilet paper, I tried to be careful not to touch anything. This wasn't a bathroom that inspired confidence, and better safe than sorry. I was about to squat when I heard a crash and a sizzle, and an explosion rocked the building. I yanked my pants up and ran out of the bathroom. I got to the hall and saw a wall of flames race around Jelly's living room, creating an instant inferno. No way to get to the stairs. I ran back to the bedroom and slammed the door shut. I shoved the window up and crawled out. I hung by my hands, took a deep breath, closed my eyes, and let go. My feet hit first and then I was flat on my back with the wind knocked out of me.

I dragged myself to my feet and took a couple deep breaths. This wasn't good. I didn't want to be found here. I limped through the house's little backyard and half climbed, half fell over the split-rail wood fence, into his neighbor's yard. I crept between houses and came out on the street behind Jelly's.

A big black glob of smoke rose above the housetops, into the sky. Two police cruisers raced past me, and I could see the flashing lights of a fire truck farther down the street. I walked around the block and stood by Morelli's SUV, across the street and two houses down. My face felt flushed from the heat of the fire, and the realization that I could have died on the toilet.

My back ached and my arm was scratched and bleeding. I was having a hard time breathing, and I could feel tears collecting in my throat and behind my eyes. I managed to get into the SUV, but I was paralyzed by the horror and unable to drive. Jelly's house was completely engulfed in flames. Firemen were spraying water on neighboring houses and the fire didn't seem to be spreading. Thank goodness for that.

Emergency vehicles clogged the street. Fire trucks, cop cars, EMS trucks. Even if I was capable, I couldn't leave. One by one, the surplus trucks began moving out. I waited for my opportunity, and then I left, too.

Morelli, Mooch, and Tiny were in the kitchen, drinking coffee and eating sandwiches, when I walked in.

"We need to talk," I said to Morelli.

Morelli looked at my scraped arm. "Are you okay?"

"Marginally. Somebody blew up Jelly's house while I was in his bathroom."

Everyone went slack-jawed and stared at me.

"I was staking it out, and I had to go," I told them.

"Jeez," Mooch said. "Blowing up a house is serious stuff. Not in Trenton, but in most places."

Morelli paled. "You couldn't find a gas station? You actually broke into his house to use his bathroom?"

"It seemed easier. Until the house blew up."

"Was anyone hurt?"

"I don't think so. I think the downstairs apartment was unoccupied. And I was alone upstairs. It must have been a firebomb shot into the front window. I heard the glass shatter, and then the explosion, and then everything was in flames. I was able to escape by dropping from the bedroom window."

"Why were you watching Jelly?" Mooch asked.

"I was watching for Dom," I told him. "It's possible Dom's been bunking with Jelly."

"Do you have any ideas about Dom's partners?" Morelli asked Mooch.

"There's been some talk lately about Stanley Zero. The fourth partner is a big mystery."

The name sounded familiar, but I couldn't place him. "Who's Stanley Zero?"

"Football player," Morelli said. "He was a couple years ahead of us. Probably in Dom's class. Not good enough to make pro and too dumb to get into college."

"He's in construction," Mooch said. "He does framing for Premier Homes. He's been working for them for years."

"Why is he suddenly linked to the robbery?" I asked.

"I don't know," Mooch said. "Hard to say how these things start going around. A guy shoots his mouth off in a bar, or talks to a girl, and next thing it's public."

I looked at the cellar door. "Is Gary still down there?"

"No. He went home," Morelli said.

"Kentucky?"

"No. Home here in Trenton. I'm not sure where that is. He said he had a headache. I imagine it was from listening to the jackhammer."

"I got a headache, too," Tiny said.

Morelli took the SUV keys from me. "I'm going to take Mooch and Tiny home. They can come back for the truck tomorrow. We need to finish carting the concrete chunks out anyway."

Tiny was about a thousand pounds. I had no idea how Morelli was going to get him into the SUV, and if he did succeed, I had a mental image of the tires going flat.

"We're out of food," I said to Morelli. "You need to stop on the way home and get something for supper."

"This is getting expensive," Morelli said. "I'm paying protection money to three guys so they don't destroy my home, *and* I'm feeding them. Plus, I've now got Mooch and Tiny on the payroll."

"I had Connie run a check on Jelly," I told Morelli. "He's driving an orange Corolla. I have the plate number, but I don't think you need it. How many orange Corollas are there in Trenton?"

"I'll watch for it," Morelli said, herding Mooch and Tiny through the house and out the door.

Miraculously, Morelli got Tiny into the SUV and the tires didn't buckle. I watched them drive away, and I called Ranger. I wanted information on Stanley Zero, and Connie only worked a half day on Saturday.

"Babe," Ranger said.

"I need information on Stanley Zero. Place of residence, car, anything personal . . . like friends, wife, whatever."

"How do you want it? Can I e-mail it to you?"

"No. I'm at Morelli's house. I don't have my computer."

"I can send it to Morelli."

"That would work. How's Tank doing?"

"He's distracted."

"Why doesn't he just break it off?"

"The man is confused," Ranger said. "Sometimes it's difficult to tell what you want to do with a woman."

"Are you speaking about yourself?"

"No. I know exactly what I want to do."

I knew what he wanted to do, too.

"Is there anything else you need from me?" Ranger asked.

"Not right now."

"There will come a time," Ranger said. "Let me know when." And he disconnected.

I opened the freezer and stuck my head in to cool off. If there'd been any more innuendo in that conversation, I could have fried an egg on my forehead.

Ranger was a successful bounty hunter because he was exceptionally intuitive and doggedly aggressive. And that was also his description as a lover.

I removed my head from the freezer, and I brought an ice cream sandwich out with me. Morelli's computer was upstairs in his office. I was eating the last of the ice cream, so I sneaked past Mooner and Zook and tiptoed up the stairs.

Ranger's office was ultra modern and very high tech. Polished glass, stainless steel, and black onyx surfaces with black leather chairs. It was dust and clutter free. The computer and phone system was state of the art and there was a plasma television on one wall.

Morelli's office was a mess. A red plastic milk crate held his baseball mitt, bat, and some tennis balls he'd collected for Bob. Stacks of dog-eared files hunkered in corners and against the wall. Smaller stacks of books he'd been given as presents or he thought he might like to read but never seemed to get to were tucked between the files. A dead houseplant on a small table by the window. Coffee cup rings everywhere. A yard sale desk and chair. Running shoes that had seen better days, kicked off under the desk and forgotten. And his computer, which was a nice new MacBook Pro. Plus a DeskJet printer.

I turned the computer on and brought up Morelli's mail program. I'm not a computer whiz, but I can do the basics. I knew it wouldn't take Ranger long to run the background check, but I relaxed in Morelli's chair for a moment before checking in. Truth is, I like Morelli's office. Okay, it could be a little cleaner, but it felt warm and comfy, like Morelli.

I could see across the hall into Zook's room. It was a typical teen disaster. Rumpled bed and every piece of clothing he had with him was on the floor. I thought he was doing remarkably well, considering his

mother was missing. I imagined there might be some
tears when he went to bed at night, but during the
day he managed to hold his own. Mooner was helping. Mooner wasn't the world's best role model, but he
kept Zook occupied.

I hit the GET MAIL button and Ranger's file came
up. I printed it out and sat back to read it. Stanley Zero
was married with two kids but not living with them.
He was living alone in a low-rent apartment complex
off Route 1. He worked for Premier Homes. I already
knew that. So maybe he was Work Boots, and he was
the partner with the crapola apartment. He'd run up
his credit cards, but he wasn't in collection. He drove a
red F150 truck. Four years old. No prior arrests. His
wife was a nurse. Worked at St. Francis. She was living in a house that was owned jointly by Stanley and
her. Heavily mortgaged. The kids were five and nine.
The typical American family. Except Stanley might
have robbed a bank, blown up a house, and shot a guy
dead.

So I had Stanley Zero, Allen Gratelli, and Dom.
If I could find the common thread, the one thing that
brought them together, I might learn the identity of the
fourth man. Or maybe there was no common thread.
Stanley and Dom had gone to school together. Dom
and Allen had worked together for the cable company.
Maybe Dom was the organizer.

I straightened Morelli's bedroom, made the bed, and
did a superficial cleaning of the bathroom. I peeked
in at Zook's room and decided not to invade his privacy. Stephanie Plum, Ms. Sensitivity and half-assed
housewife.

I heard Bob gallop from the kitchen to the front
door, and I knew Morelli had arrived with food.

"Steph," he yelled. "I'm home."

Ricky Ricardo brings Lucy her dinner.

I met Morelli at the bottom of the stairs and took a grocery bag from him. He handed the other bags over to Zook and Mooner.

"Meatball subs, potato salad, coleslaw for all of us," he said to Zook and Mooner. "The beer is for me."

I took the bag into the kitchen and put the lunch meat, milk, orange juice, and sliced cheese in the fridge. Morelli'd also gotten bread and a cake that said HAPPY BIRTHDAY KEN.

"A birthday cake?" I said to him.

"I know you love birthday cake, and apparently Ken didn't need his."

We brought napkins, plates, silverware, and soda to the living room and Morelli remoted the television on. We crammed ourselves onto the couch and ate our food and watched the early evening news.

"And now we bring you our special report from that special person . . . Brenda," the anchor said.

Brenda popped onto the screen. Her face was blue, she was in full black leather bounty hunter mode, and she was in Morelli's backyard.

"Here we are at Aunt Rose's house," she said. "And as you can see, digging for the stolen money has already begun."

There was a shot of Morelli telling her to leave, and there was a full thirty seconds of Morelli turning the hose on her. The screen went black for a moment, and then Brenda reappeared in dry clothes, free from mud. "Here we are back at Aunt Rose's house," Brenda said. "We aren't going to bother the hot guy who lives here, because he might turn his hose on us again, and while I wouldn't mind seeing his hose in private, I'm not taking any chances in his backyard. As you can see, there's this big dump truck parked behind his garage. I had one of my crew climb up on the truck and look inside, and he said it's getting filled up with chunks of concrete. And even as we speak I can hear the jackhammer working in Aunt Rose's basement." Brenda aimed the microphone at the back of Morelli's house, and there was the faint sound of the jackhammer, which at that distance sounded like a woodpecker. "As you all know, it's been thought the missing nine million dollars was last seen by Aunt Rose, and maybe this new development will bring us closer to all that money. This is Brenda signing off and saying . . . see you soon!"

Zook gave a howl of laughter.

"Dude," Mooner said. "Awesome. Ratings fabuloso."

The next shot was Brenda in the studio sitting opposite the anchor.

"That was an interesting piece of film," the anchor said to her. "I understand you've been an insider on this investigation."

"Yes, I have," Brenda said. "In fact—"

And at that instant, Gary crept up behind Brenda and tapped her on the shoulder.

"I have to talk to you," he said. "I had a headache, so I went to my bedroom to lay down, and I had another one of those dreams. You know, the big pizza dream. Only this time, the pizza was pepperoni and black olives, and it was very disturbing because it could fly! I saw it *flying through the air.*"

Brenda rolled her eyes. "Gary, how many times have I told you to go home? Have you stopped your medication again?"

The anchor was on his feet. "How did he get in here? Who is he?"

"I'm her cousin on our Grammy Mim's side," Gary told him.

The anchor had his hand waving in the air. "Security!"

"You have to beware of the big pizza!" Gary said to Brenda. "It's not an ordinary pizza, and it's out to get you. And it might be when you're sitting on the toilet on Route 1."

"I swear," Brenda said. "You are *such* a *nut*."

Two uniformed guards appeared on the set and the station went to commercial.

"That was primo," Mooner said. "The dude was, like, a real celebrity stalker. And the white hair is a good look for him. Au courant but raging retro. Like totally Warhol."

Morelli cut his eyes to me. "The really scary part of all this is I'm starting to understand Mooner."

"Just think of it as learning a foreign language," I said to Morelli. "Pretend you're visiting the Republic of Moon."

We finished the subs, potato salad, and coleslaw, Mooner sang happy birthday to Ken, and we dug into the cake.

We ate half a cake and the phone rang.

"I'm at the police station bonding out Gary-the-Stalker," Connie said. "Someone needs to take him somewhere and get him to shut up about the big pizza before he gets carted away and shot full of Thorazine. And it's not me, because I'm late for JoAnn Garber's baby shower."

"I'll come get him. How do you want to do this?"

"I'll take him with me, and we'll make the switch at the firehouse," Connie said.

"I'm on it."

I took possession of Gary fifteen minutes later.

"How did you get to the television station?" I asked him.

"I drove. I followed Brenda from her hotel. I tried to talk to her before she got into the car, but she was moving too fast. And then she parked in a special lot at the station, and I couldn't get in. So I had to find a place on the street, and then it wasn't easy getting into the building. I had to climb in through a window in the back."

"Most people would leave a message on Brenda's cell phone."

"I'm not most people."

No kidding.

"And she keeps changing her number," Gary said.

"Because she doesn't want you bothering her?"

"She's very brave. And she doesn't want to impose."

"Has it ever occurred to you that you might be delusional?"

"That's what the psychiatrist said, but I think he's wrong. There's an evil flying pizza out there, and it's got Brenda's name on it."

"I'm assuming your car is still parked on the street."

"Yes."

"I'm going to take you to your car, and then you're going to go home."

"Yes."

"Where is home?"

"Morelli's garage," Gary said.

"Excuse me?"

"I have a little camper that I tow behind my car. I parked it in Morelli's garage yesterday, and it's still there."

"Does Morelli know this?"

"I don't think it ever came up."

We located his car, he followed me to Morelli's house, and we both parked at the curb. I got out and looked at his white Taurus.

"I thought this was a rental," I said to him. "No one *buys* a white Taurus."

"It matches my hair," Gary said. "And it's my zodiac sign."

It made as much sense as anything else in my life. "Have you had dinner?"

"No."

"Prowl through the fridge and make yourself a sandwich. If you're lucky, there's still some birthday cake left."

"Whose birthday?" he asked.

"Ken's."

I brought him into the house, and he settled in with Zook and Mooner, so he could lurk. Morelli was in the kitchen loading the dishwasher.

"I brought Gary back here," I told him. "He's helping out with the wood elves."

"That's a comfort."

"Yeah, I knew you'd be excited. I had Ranger run a check on Stanley Zero. I have the printout upstairs. One of us should take a look at him."

Chapter
FIFTEEN

The phone rang at two in the morning. Morelli came awake first, a bare arm reaching across me to get at the bedside phone. Not the first time he'd gotten a call in the middle of the night.

"Yeah?" he said.

There was a short conversation, and Morelli hung up and flopped back onto his side of the bed.

"You're not going to believe this," he said. "On second thought, it makes perfect sense. That was your friend and mine, supercop Carl Costanza. He's working a shift with Big Dog, and they got a report that there were lights in the cemetery. Turns out it was a bunch of people who all got the idea to dig up Rose. One of them was your Grandma Mazur."

"Is she in jail?"

"No. Everyone ran away when Carl and Big Dog drove up, but your grandmother recognized Carl and told him she needed a ride home."

"Omigod."

"Yeah. Carl said they're bringing her here. She didn't want to get dropped off at your parents' house in a police car because people would talk."

I rolled out of bed, scuffed through the clothes on the floor, and found what I needed.

Zook was in the hall when I opened Morelli's bedroom door. "I heard the call," he said. "Was it about my mom?"

"No. It was about my grandmother. She's having a friend drop her off here, and then I'm going to give her a ride home."

Zook smiled. "I bet she did something bad and she's afraid your mother will ground her."

"Close enough," I said.

I padded downstairs in the dark and looked out the front window. No police car yet. I walked through the house to the kitchen to get a bottle of water and checked on the yard. No one digging, but there was a bar of light under Morelli's garage door. Gary was still up. Or maybe Gary was afraid of the dark. Lucky for Gary there was electric in the garage. Unfortunate for Morelli, since he was paying the bill.

I returned to the living room, and Morelli joined me.

"You didn't have to get up," I said to him.

"No way was I going to miss this."

We saw headlights glide to a stop in front of the house, and we went out to say hello to Carl and Big Dog.

"Here she is," Big Dog said to me, opening the door for Grandma. "Maybe your mother should put a bell around her neck." He looked at Grandma and shook his finger. "No more sneaking out at night. It's dangerous."

"Thanks for the ride," Grandma said. She looked in the car at Carl. "My regards to your mother."

Carl smiled and nodded.

"Thanks," I said to Carl and Big Dog. "I really appreciate this."

"We would have hauled her in, but it was too embarrassing," Big Dog said. "She was the only one we could catch."

Morelli waved them off, and I buckled Grandma into the SUV.

"Where's your shovel?" I asked her.

"I didn't have one. I was just supervising. I went to Elmer Rhiner's viewing and Marion Barker was there with Bitty Kuleza. And Marion said she heard Rose was always saying how she was gonna take her fortune to the grave. And one thing led to another, and it ended up that we thought it would be a good idea to dig Rose up and take a look. So Bitty gave me a ride, and we met Marion and her two grandsons at the cemetery. Her grandsons are real big guys, and they were doing the digging."

"That's crazy!"

"Yeah. I don't know what it is about that money, but it's just got ahold of me. It's a beaut of a mystery."

Morelli drove the short distance and parked in front of my parents' house. We watched Grandma sneak in, and we waited a couple minutes to make sure she didn't sneak back out.

"You should snap me up," Morelli said. "Not many men would marry you after meeting your grandmother. You're lucky to have me."

I looked over at him. "Is that a proposal?"

There was total silence for a couple beats. "I'm not sure. It just popped out."

"Let me know when you're sure."

"Would you say *yes*?" Morelli asked.

"I'm not sure."

"I bet I could convince you it would be a good thing," Morelli said. "How about taking a look at my assets?"

Oh good grief.

It took us about twenty minutes in the alley behind the bonds office to appreciate his assets. When we finally returned to his house, all the lights were blazing and two squad cars were angle-parked at his curb. Morelli slid to a stop, and we hit the sidewalk at a run.

"What's going on?" he said to the cop at the door.

"Your houseguest heard someone break in and called 911."

Zook was standing in the hall, hanging on to Bob's collar. "Right after you left, I heard someone at the back door," Zook said. "Bob heard them, too, and he started barking, and he never barks if it's someone he knows, so I grabbed Bob and brought him into my room, and then I locked my door and called 911. I put all my lights off and looked out the window at the backyard, and just before the first police car showed up, I saw two men run out of the house and across the yard."

"What did they look like?" Morelli asked.

"I don't know. Just average. I couldn't see. It was real dark. But one of them had a shovel."

"You have forced entry on the back door," one of the cops said to Morelli. "And the basement door was open. Other than that, everything seems okay."

After everyone left, Morelli walked through the house, checking windows and doors. He searched the basement, the closets, all nooks and crannies and under the beds.

"Tomorrow we get the alarm system up and running," he said.

Morelli took his cereal bowl and coffee mug to the sink. "I'm going to take a look at Stanley Zero this morning. Do you have any plans?"

"I'm doing laundry."

"That's pretty exciting."

"I'm washing sheets," I told him.

Morelli slid an arm around me and kissed my neck. "I love when you talk about sheets."

Now, here's the thing I like about Morelli. There's a lot of variety to his sexiness. He can be hot, he can be funny, he can be loving, he can be short on time and hungry. This morning, he was playful.

"Would you like to know what I'm going to do to you tonight when you slide between those sheets?" I asked him.

The depth of his eyes instantly changed, and he left playful behind. "Yeah," he said. "I'd like to know."

"You have to wait."

"I'm not good at waiting."

"No kidding!"

Morelli broke out in a wide grin. "Have I just been insulted?"

"Only a little. Did you get the background report on Zero? I left it on your desk."

"Got it. Thanks. Keep your eyes open here."

"You betcha."

Ten minutes after Morelli left, Zook shuffled down the stairs and into the kitchen. He helped himself to a bagel and took it into the living room.

Moments later, Gary was at the back door. "I thought I smelled coffee."

I pointed to the coffeepot. "Help yourself."

He looked at the bag of bagels sitting on the counter.

"Would you like a bagel?" I asked him.

"Yeah! That would be great."

Morelli was going to have to find the nine million and take a cut just to pay his electric and food bills.

Sunday mornings are quiet in the Burg and surrounding communities. The women go to church, and the men take the Sunday paper and sit on the can. I've never understood the attraction of sitting on a toilet, pants at your ankles, newspaper in hand. I could think of a million better places to read the paper. And yet this is a firmly adhered-to Sunday ritual for Burg husbands. My father couldn't imagine a Sunday morning without this quality bathroom experience. Unmarried men seem to be exempt.

After Morelli's car left his neighborhood, there was no more street traffic. No dogs were walked. No kids on skateboards. Just Sunday morning quiet. And that's why it was twice as startling when the brick sailed through Morelli's living room window.

Zook and Gary were on the couch, deep into the world of Minionfire, I was walking though the living room, on my way to collect the laundry, and the glass shattered. We all jumped and there was a collective gasp of surprise.

Jelly's apartment explosion and fire were still fresh in my mind. I looked at the brick, which had a small box attached, and my first thought was *bomb*. I rushed over, picked the brick up, and threw it back outside via the broken window.

Gary and Zook were frozen on the couch, eyes huge, mouths open. I went to the front door and looked out. The brick was just sitting there on Morelli's postage-stamp lawn. The box attached to the brick looked small to be a bomb, but heck, what do I know? I watched it for a couple minutes and cautiously crept out to take a closer look. I was standing there, looking at the brick, when Mooner strolled up and stood next to me.

"Whoa," Mooner said. "That's a brick."

"Yep."

He bent down to see it better. "It's got a box attached to it."

And before I could stop him, he picked it up and shook it to see if the box rattled.

"It's got the dude's name on it," Mooner said.

I craned my neck and read the writing on the box. JOE MORELLI.

"What's it doing sitting here in the yard?" Mooner wanted to know. "There's no mail delivery today. It's a Sunday. Even I know that."

"Someone tossed it through Morelli's window."

"Get the heck out," Mooner said. "Was the window open?"

"No," I told him.

"Get the heck out," he said.

The box was held to the brick with electrician's tape. I took the box upstairs, set it on Morelli's desk, and called Morelli.

"How's it going?" I asked him.

"Not good. I got a call from dispatch. Two gang killings in the projects. I'm on my way there now. I don't know when I'll get home. Sometimes these things take time to sort out. What's up with you?"

"Someone pitched a brick through your living room window. And attached to the brick was a box with your name on it."

"Is this for real?"

"Yep."

"Put the brick and the box in the garage. Don't leave it in the house. Better to blow up the garage than the house."

"Do you think it's a bomb?"

"I think it doesn't hurt to be careful. I'll deal with it when I'm done here," Morelli said. "And I'll call Mooch and get him to replace the glass. And I'll make arrangements to have an alarm system installed."

I disconnected and stared at the box. I was faced with a dilemma. Gary was living in the garage. I didn't want to explode Gary. No big deal, I thought. Just ask Gary to pull his camper out of the garage.

The doorbell chimed, the door opened and closed, and I heard Lula ask for me.

"I'm upstairs," I yelled at her. "Come on up."

Lula was dressed down. Running shoes, black stretch yoga pants, and a black stretch T-shirt that looked like it was going to burst at the seams.

"What's the occasion?" I asked her.

"I went to try some wedding gowns yesterday, and it was a depressing experience. First off, they only had itty-bitty sizes for those skinny bitches. Like us big and beautiful women don't get married? And then they said they were gonna have to charge extra on account of they were gonna have to order so much material. What the heck is that about? It's not like I'm getting a circus tent. So anyway, I decided I'd join a gym. I figure with the money I save on less material, I could pay for the membership."

"That's a terrific idea. I should do something like that. What gym did you join?"

"I didn't exactly join a gym yet. I just got the clothes."

"It's a start," I said to Lula.

"Damn right," Lula said. "What's this package with Morelli's name on it? And why's it on a brick?"

"Someone pitched it through his living room window just now."

"Get the heck out. What are you going to do with it?"

"Morelli wants me to put it in the garage for safe keeping until he gets home later today."

"I don't think that's a good idea." Lula picked the box up and tested its weight. "It could be something important that requires immediate attention. I think you should open this sucker."

"It could be a bomb."

"Okay then, let Gary open it."

I did an eye roll.

"Nothing wrong with that," Lula said. "He's always saying how he knows things. Let's see if he knows it's a bomb. Anyway, it don't look like a bomb."

"It's all wrapped up. How could you tell?"

"Well, if it was a bomb, it would be a little one."

I heard Bob jump off the bed and head down the stairs.

"I need to get the glass cleaned up before Bob steps in it," I told Lula. "Put the box down and look up some gyms in the phone book and we'll check some out."

Five minutes later, I walked back into Morelli's office and found Lula unwrapping the box.

"It's not a bomb," Lula said. "There's a note in here and something all wrapped up." She handed me the note.

"That was addressed to Morelli," I said to her.

"Yeah, but I didn't want him to get hisself all blown up. Besides, I kicked the box around some and nothing happened, so I figured it was safe."

I unfolded the piece of paper and read the printed message.

I know you have the money. Give me the money and I'll give you Loretta. Just so you know I'm serious I'm enclosing a present. Every day I don't get the money you'll get another present. Hang a red scarf in the upstairs window when you want to make a deal.

"I like getting presents," Lula said, "but this one don't smell too good."

I had a bad feeling about this present. I carefully peeled away the tissue paper, and we stared at a pinkie toe with red toenail polish.

"Good pedicure," Lula said.

I clapped a hand over my mouth and told myself I wasn't going to throw up. I was sweating at my hairline and little black dots were floating in front of my eyes. They'd chopped off one of Loretta's toes, and they were going to keep chopping until they got their money.

"Maybe we should give them the money," Lula said.

"We don't have the money," I whispered.

"Oh yeah. I forgot."

"I don't want Zook to see this," I told her. "He's just a kid. He doesn't need this. And I can't stand around and let them chop off Loretta's body parts. We have to find either Loretta or the money."

"And we're gonna do this how?"

"I have a lead."

"Okay," Lula said. "But what about the pinkie toe?"

"It's evidence. I'll put it in the freezer for now."

I'd seen army barracks that were more attractive than Stanley Zero's apartment complex. Hummingbird Hollow consisted of six cement-block, three-story buildings clustered around a large macadam parking lot. As far as I could see, there were no trees, no flowers, no hummingbirds. And the only hollow was an empty, sick feeling in the pit of my stomach. The mailboxes would lead me to believe that there were twenty-four units to each building. Zero lived on the second floor, in unit 2D, with his windows facing the lot. According to my report, he lived alone. I found his truck in the lot, and I checked the plate to make sure.

"He's home," I said to Lula.

We were in Lula's Firebird. It wasn't the best surveillance vehicle, but it was better than my Zook car. Lula slid into a space behind and to the left of the F150.

"Now what?" Lula asked.

"Now we wait."

"I hate to wait. He don't know me. How about if I go up and ring his bell and ask if he wants some Lula? Then I could look around and see if he got Loretta tied up without her toe in his closet."

"They don't have Loretta here," I said. "It's not private enough. You can probably hear everything through these walls. I'm hoping he'll go out and lead us to his partner."

We sat for an hour, looking up into his windows, watching the building's back door. Nothing.

"He might not even be in there," Lula said. "Maybe someone came and picked him up, and we'll sit here 'til the cows come home."

"Then we'll check out the car that drops him off, and maybe that car will belong to the partner."

"You sure you don't want me to go up there and poke around?" Lula asked.

I cut my eyes to her. "You're not going to give up, are you?"

"I should have brought my bride magazines to read. I got nothing to do here. I sit here much longer, I'm gonna get that thing they were talking about on the morning show . . . restless leg syndrome."

"Okay already, go see if he's home."

Lula marched across the lot and into the building. Five minutes later, she was back at the car.

"Nobody home," Lula said. "I tried the door, but it was locked."

"That doesn't usually stop you."

"I fiddled with the lock a little, but I couldn't get anything to work. Too bad, because this here's a good opportunity to snoop."

I called Ranger. "I'm watching an apartment off Route 1, and I'd like to get in but it's locked up tight."

"I'll send Slick."

I gave Ranger the address, and Lula and I waited with slightly elevated heart rates. Breaking and entering was always tense. Especially since it was a crapshoot if Lula could squeeze under a bed. A shiny black Rangeman SUV pulled into the lot and Slick got out and went into the building. He was out of uniform, dressed in jeans and a baggy shirt. Wouldn't be good if he was seen picking a lock in Rangeman black. Five minutes later, he walked through the door, looked my way, and nodded. He got into the Rangeman SUV, and drove away.

"Rock and roll," Lula said.

We took the stairs to the second floor and went directly to Zero's apartment. I turned the knob, and the door opened. We stepped inside and closed the door.

"Hello," I called out.

No one answered.

We were standing in an area that was living room, dining room. Beyond was the kitchen and a hall that would lead to the bedrooms. The furniture was old and collected for comfort with no thought to design. Empty beer cans and Styrofoam coffee cups with days-old coffee still in the bottom were left on end tables. A couple newspapers had been tossed to the floor. Mud had been tracked onto the rug. Not that it mattered. The rug looked like it hadn't been vacuumed in a long, long time. Maybe never.

We glanced at the kitchen and moved into the hall. It was a one-bedroom, one-bath apartment, and the bedroom door was open. Lula and I looked through the open door and froze. There was a man on the floor, toes up, eyes open, bullet hole in the middle of his head. Dead.

"I *hate* when we find dead people," Lula said. "Dead people give me the heebie-jeebies. I'm not doing this no more if we keep finding dead people. And I'm getting out of here. I'm not staying in no room with a guy with a hole in his head."

Don't panic, I told myself. Take it one step at a time. I followed Lula back to the living room, did some deep breathing, and punched Morelli's number into my cell phone.

"Talk," Morelli said.

"I found another dead guy."

"You want to run that by me again?"

"Lula and I decided we'd talk to Stanley Zero, so we knocked on his door, and the door swung open, and we found a dead guy in the bedroom."

There was a moment of silence, and I knew Morelli was either popping Rolaids or counting to ten. Probably both. "The door swung open when you touched it," he finally said.

"Yeah." No need to go into details on how the door got unlocked, right? I mean, he didn't ask how it got unlocked.

"Where are you now?"

"In the living room," I told him.

"Anything else I need to know before I call this in?"

"Nope. That's the whole enchilada."

I disconnected and noticed Lula had her keys in her hand.

"Are you going somewhere?" I asked Lula.

"I figure you don't need me anymore, so I thought I'd go home. I got things to do. I gotta think about a honeymoon. And this place is gonna be swarming with cops, and I hate cops. Except for Morelli. Morelli is fine."

"If you leave, I have no way to get home."

"What about Morelli? What about Ranger? What about calling a cab?"

"What about waiting in your car in the parking lot?" I said to her.

"I guess I could do that."

She hotfooted it out of the apartment, and I thought there was a twenty percent chance she'd be in the lot when I was ready to go home. Not that Lula was unreliable, more that her cop phobia overrode her best intentions.

I figured I had five to ten minutes before the first cop showed up, so I told myself to get over the dead guy and think about rescuing Loretta. I did a quick run through the kitchen, being careful not to leave prints. I found leftover fast-food chicken and expired milk in the refrigerator, and dots of blue mold on the bread that was sitting on the counter. Not enough mold to slow down a big, tough construction guy from Trenton. No scraps of paper lying around with a phone number or address.

I walked back into the bedroom, and as best I could, I avoided looking at the body. A pair of beat-up CAT boots had been kicked off beside the bed, and a framed photograph of a large powerboat was propped on the dresser. I'd found the third partner's apartment. And probably the guy on the floor was the third partner, since he was in socks. I guess I could have seen if the boots fit, but I didn't want to know who he was that bad. Let the police figure it out.

There were clothes all over the place. Hard to tell if the apartment had been tossed, since Zero wasn't the world's best housekeeper. I went through all pockets, omitting the ones attached to the dead guy, and I looked through drawers. I did a fast bathroom check.

I looked out the bedroom window and saw the first police car angle to a stop in the lot. He'd come in without a siren, probably at Morelli's suggestion. A second squad car followed. Eddie Gazarra got out of the second squad car. That was a relief. We'd grown up together and he'd married my cousin, Shirley the Whiner. Eddie wouldn't come at me with a suspicious, hostile attitude, and that would make my life much more pleasant.

I stepped out of the apartment and waited in the hall. I got an eye roll from Gazarra when he walked out of the elevator, and then concern.

"Are you okay?" he asked.

"Yes. The door was open when I got here. He was dead on the floor in the bedroom. No one else was here. I assume it's Stanley Zero, but I don't know for sure."

Gazarra went about securing the crime scene, and a couple minutes later, Rich Spanner showed up.

"We have to stop meeting like this," Spanner said to me. "People are gonna talk." He entered the apartment, checked out the body, and returned to the hall. "What do you think?"

"I think he's got one too many holes in his forehead."

"Yeah," Spanner said. "I noticed that. I also noticed he reminds me a lot of the dead guy in Morelli's basement."

"Because of the hole in his head?"

"Mmm. And because you found him."

"It's getting old."

"I bet," Spanner said.

I repeated my mostly true story for Spanner. The ME slipped past us, followed by two paramedics and a forensic photographer.

"Do you have anything else you want to share?" Spanner asked.

I shook my head. "No. Do you think that's Stanley Zero on the floor?"

Spanner moved into the doorway. "Hey, Gazarra, you have a tentative ID?"

"Looks like Stanley Zero. We got a driver's license here. He matches the photo, except for the hole in his head."

Chapter

I was shocked to find Lula still in the lot.

"What are you doing here?" I asked her.

"Waiting for you."

"It's been over an hour and you're still here."

"I have stuff to ask you. I want to know about the honeymoon. I'm thinking Paris or Tahiti."

"Can you afford that?"

"Don't the groom pay?"

"Can Tank afford that?"

"He better," Lula said. "I don't come cheap."

"I thought the groom planned the honeymoon."

"That was in the Dark Ages. And besides, Tank's busy. He don't got a lot of time for that stuff. He's gotta watch Ranger's ass."

"If it was me, I'd go to Paris," I told her. "Better shopping, and it's a shorter plane ride. Italy would be good, too, if you're interested in handbags and shoes."

"I never thought of Italy, but that's a good idea. I could always use a new handbag."

"Why do you want to get married?" I asked Lula.

"I don't know. It just sort of popped into my head. And then one thing led to another, and before I knew it, I was at the lawyer drawing up my prenup. I guess it was one of those snowball things. You don't think

I'm rushing into it, do you? I could postpone it to July, but I got a good deal on the hall for the reception. I'd have to give the hall up. And the fireworks wouldn't be the same. This way, I get the jump on July Fourth." Lula cranked her car over. "Where we going now?"

"Back to Morelli's house. I should make sure Zook is okay."

Everything looked status quo at Morelli's. It was early afternoon, but there was no activity. The crime scene tape was in place. No gawkers present. Lula pulled to the curb, took the key out of the ignition, and there was a sound like a grenade getting launched, and then *thud,* something hit the passenger-side door.

"What the bejeezus was that?" Lula yelled. "Incoming! We're under attack. Call SWAT. No, wait a minute. I hate those SWAT guys."

Mooner waved at me from Morelli's small front porch. "Sorry," he said. "My bad."

I got out and examined the car door. There was a dent in it, and something was splattered from one end to the other. I cautiously touched it with my finger.

"Potato?" I asked Mooner.

"Yep. Yukon Gold."

Lula was around the car and next to me, and there was a frightening amount of white showing in her eyes. The whole eyeball was about the size of a tennis ball. "My baby!" she yelled. "My Firebird! Who did this? Who made this mess on my Firebird?" The big eyes narrowed, her face scrunched up, and she took a closer look, her nose just about touching the potato splatter. "Is this a dent? This better not be a dent I'm seeing."

"I didn't recognize you," Mooner said. "Good thing I was all out of Russet. Russet is, like, atomic."

Zook and Gary were standing behind Mooner.

"We've been guarding the house," Zook said. "Mooner is so cool. He knows all about homegrown security. He knows how to make potato cannons."

Mooner tapped the top of his head. "No grass growing here."

"What's a potato cannon?" Lula wanted to know.

"All you need is PVC pipe and hairspray and a lighter," Zook said. "And you can shoot *anything* out of it. You can shoot eggs and apples and tomatoes."

"See, that's the thing about a potato cannon," Mooner said. "You can stuff anything into it. You could shoot monkey shit out of a potato cannon. All you gotta do is find a monkey."

"I know where there's a monkey," Lula said.

"Whoa," Mooner said. "Far out. You want to go get some shit?"

Great. Just what I need. Mooner shooting monkey shit at passing motorists.

"It's illegal to shoot monkey shit on a Sunday," I told him. "Have you had lunch?"

Zook was grinning. "We didn't *eat* lunch. We *launched* lunch."

"I got a deductable, and I don't know if I'm covered for potatoes," Lula said, her eyes still narrowed.

I was having a hard time getting worked up over the dent in Lula's Firebird. I had bigger fish to fry. I had a pinky toe in Morelli's freezer. And tomorrow I'd have *two* toes if I didn't hang a scarf in the upstairs window.

"Everyone inside," I said. "You stay out here too long, and some new griefer will take over."

"We're not playing *Minionfire* anymore," Zook said. "We're in charge of homegrown security now. We got weapons to make and posts to man. We're keeping the integrity of the crime scene. We're protecting the house."

"Yeah, but what about the back?" Lula asked. "You can't see the back from here."

"Dude, she's right," Mooner said. "Man your potato cannon. Secure the yard!"

Mooner, Zook, and Gary ran inside. Lula and I followed at a slightly slower pace.

"You got a loony bin," Lula said to me.

Mooner was already at the living room window when we walked into the room. He was holding a two-foot section of white PVC pipe that had a smaller pipe glued toward the base.

"Lieutenant Zook," he said into a two-way attached to his shirt. "Are you in position?"

"Yessir, Captain," Zook answered from the kitchen.

"Munitions Expert Gary, are you ready?"

"Yessir," Gary said.

Gary was in the dining room, halfway between Mooner and Zook. He was wearing a utility belt that carried a can of hairspray and a grill lighter. And he was holding a basket of potatoes. Tucked into the potato basket was a large bag of M&Ms and a large order of fast-food fries still in the cardboard container.

"What's with the M&Ms and the fries?" Lula wanted to know.

"It's in case we need a shotgun."

"Makes sense," Lula said. And she turned and looked at me and made the crazy signal with her finger going around alongside her head.

Zook's voice whispered over the two-way. "I got a bandit at two o'clock. I need a partial baked."

Gary ran into the kitchen and handed Zook a potato. Zook dropped it into his PVC pipe and rammed it down. Gary sprayed hairspray into the pipe and jumped back. Zook pointed the spud gun out the door and *phoonf!* Zook got knocked on his ass from the kick, and the potato rocketed out of the pipe and caught the digger in the back of his leg. The guy went down like a house of cards and rolled around yelping. He got up and half limped, half ran out of the yard.

I was dumbstruck. I didn't know whether to burst out laughing or be truly horrified.

Zook got to his feet. "We only use raw potatoes on cars and stuff. We use half-baked on poachers. It leaves a good bruise, but it isn't lethal. We tried using eggs, but the gun kept misfiring."

I called Morelli and got his voice mail. "Just checking in," I said. "And by the way, no reason to get alarmed, but do you have personal liability insurance tacked on to your homeowner's?"

Lula had her head stuck in the refrigerator. "Where's the fried chicken? You gotta have fried chicken on Sunday."

"I want to talk to Stanley Zero's almost-ex-wife," I said to Lula. "We can stop at Cluck-in-a-Bucket on the way."

"Why do you want to talk to his ex?"

"I had good luck with Dom's ex. I thought it wouldn't hurt to try Zero's."

Lula looked at Gary, standing in the dining room. "You think we should leave the homegrown idiots alone?"

I was between a rock and a hard place. I didn't trust the three potato heads to make the right decision on *anything,* but I was panicked over Loretta's fingers and toes.

"You stay here," I said to Lula. "I'll have a little conversation with Zero's wife, and I'll stop at Cluck-in-a-Bucket on the way home."

"You aren't going to be long, are you? I don't have a lot of patience when it comes to fried chicken."

"An hour, tops."

"Okay," Lula said. "I guess I could last. I want a

large bucket of extra spicy, extra crispy fried chicken. I want a order of biscuits with gravy and some coleslaw."

"I thought you were trying to lose weight."

"Yeah, but I don't want to waste away to nothing. And anyway, everyone knows you don't gain weight on Sunday. Sunday's a free day."

Lisa Zero lived in a nice little house in Hamilton Township. The nine-year-old answered the door and Lisa immediately showed up behind him. She was wearing makeup and a skirt, and I guessed she'd gone to church this morning. She was a couple inches shorter than me and a couple pounds heavier. Her eyes were red, as if she'd been crying. I supposed she'd heard about Stanley.

I introduced myself and apologized for being blue and for intruding.

"It's okay," she said. "Let's step outside. I don't want the kids to hear. I haven't told them yet. Stanley was an asshole, but he was still their father."

"Did you know he was involved in the bank robbery?"

"I suspected. Not at the time, but the last couple years he started drinking too much and he'd say things. I guess you're after the money."

I shook my head. "No. I'm looking for the fourth partner."

"I'm afraid I can't help you there. Stanley never said anything about the partners. He only talked about the money. How when Dom got out, they could put it all together, and they'd all be rich."

"Put it all together?"

"Yeah, I don't know what he meant by that, but I got the feeling there was a map or something. Or maybe a bank account in all their names. Like they each had a piece of a puzzle. I didn't figure I'd ever see it, so I didn't pay close attention. He'd drink, and then he'd get real talky, and then he'd get mean."

"I'm sorry."

"It's okay. I got the house, and we're moving ahead with our lives."

"Do you know a guy named Allen Gratelli?"

"No."

"But you knew Dom."

"Not really. I only knew him from the newspaper articles when he robbed the bank, and then when Stanley started talking about him."

"You must have been surprised to learn Stanley was mixed up in a bank robbery."

"Stanley was always mixed up in something. He was always looking for easy money. One time, he held up a convenience store and stole lottery tickets. *Hello.* Like they couldn't figure that one out if he won?"

I gave Lisa Zero my card and told her to call if she thought of anything helpful. I wound my way through her subdivision, hit Klockner, and drove on autopilot to Cluck-in-a-Bucket. I parked in the lot, under the big rotating chicken. I stuffed a couple twenties into my jeans pocket and got out of the Zook car.

Cluck-in-a-Bucket is a zoo on Sunday. It's the lunch of choice for the lazy, the fat, the salt-starved, the emotionally injured, the families on budgets, the cholesterol-deprived, and the remaining ten percent of the population who just want a piece of chicken.

The tables and booths were filled and there were lines in front of all the registers at the counter. Clucky Chicken was making balloon chickens for the kids and handing out coupons for Clucky Apple Pies. I went to the end of a line and zoned out. No one seemed to notice I was blue.

I was thinking about Lisa Zero and her comment about the puzzle pieces. Suppose Dom was the one who hid the money, and to make sure it was still intact when he got out of prison, he didn't tell his partners the exact location. But maybe it was a concern that Dom might not make it through his term, so each partner got a piece of the treasure map. No. That didn't work. They could put their pieces together any time they wanted and cut Dom out. Okay, suppose a fifth person, like Aunt Rose, hid the money? And then she gave each of the partners a piece of the map. I shuffled forward in the chicken line, still thinking about the map. The fifth-person theory didn't totally hold up, either. The partners were ruthless. They were killing one another off and mutilating Loretta. They would have gotten the money location out of Rose.

I absentmindedly looked around as I took another step forward. Two people in front of me. Three lined up behind. There were five registers working. I was in the line farthest from the door. I looked over and saw a stocky guy push in. Big head, balding, curly black hair. Unibrow. Looked like he slept in his clothes. Dom.

I had nothing on me to help subdue him. Stun gun, pepper spray, cuffs were in my purse in the car. He was bigger and meaner than me, and I had no legal reason to apprehend. I moved out of line, keeping my eye on him, trying to be invisible. My plan was to work my way around to the door and try to follow him when he left.

Dom was rumbling around, looking for the shortest line. My line moved forward, Dom elbowed his way over and spotted me. Our eyes locked for a moment, and Dom whirled around and shoved his way to the door. His effort was misconstrued as line-breaking, and this was an unfortunate thing, since line-breaking doesn't go down well in Jersey.

"Asshole," some woman said, giving him a hard shot to the kidney.

Dom instinctively turned on her and coldcocked

her with a punch to the forehead. The woman went down to the ground and the rest was pandemonium. I dove for Dom and missed him by inches. Mothers were grabbing for their children and dropping food. Clucky Chicken was in the mix, waving his wings, trying to keep his footing. I slid on mashed potatoes and took Clucky down with me. A pack of people piled on top of us.

"I hate this lousy job," Clucky said, kicking people off him. "This is the third time this has happened this month."

I was on hands and knees, and I saw Brenda and her crew at the door. Brenda had a mic in her hand and the camera guy was filming.

"This is Brenda reporting from Cluck-in-a-Bucket," Brenda said. "Bringing you a live update on the latest developments in the hunt for the missing nine million dollars. We're here to interview Stephanie Plum."

I dragged myself to my feet and picked mashed potatoes out of my hair. I was drenched with soda and covered with gravy. I looked around, but I didn't see Dom.

"So," Brenda said, pointing the mic at me, "are you making any progress at locating the money?"

"How did you find me?" I asked her.

"We were driving by and saw the Zook car in the parking lot."

Great. The Zook car.

"No comment," I said, easing my way past the film crew.

"Jeez," Brenda said. "Give me a break here. I'm trying to get something going. Do you have any idea what it's like for a sixty-one-year-old woman in show business? The only parts you can get are witches and grandmothers."

"What about the stage show?"

"The stage show sucks. I'm playing Trenton, for crying out loud! All the men in the act are gay and all the women are forty years younger than me. Okay, I know I don't look my age, but I'm busting my ass on maintenance. I don't know how much longer I can keep this up before I need more work."

"What kind of work?"

"All kinds of work. My facelift is eight years old. I've got two years, tops, and then the warranty runs out. The implants are shifting in my breasts, and these young guys I'm fucking are killing me. I'm going to need a vagina transplant."

"Maybe you should consider a man more your own age."

"Have you ever seen a man my age naked? It's frightening. It's like everything has stretched. And then you do the deed with him and it's like fucking Rubberman. And halfway through, you're wondering what the heck that noise is and you realize he's fallen asleep and he's snoring. You have to have football playing on television to keep him awake."

"Sometimes Joe watches football after."

"Joe. Is that the Italian Stallion who turned the hose on me?"

"Yep."

"No offense, but I wouldn't mind doing him."

"No offense taken. Almost everyone wants to do him." I looked down at my shirt. The gravy was congealing. "I need to get home and change my shirt."

"Well, there you have it from Stephanie Plum," Brenda said to the camera. "It looks like the money is still up for grabs, folks."

I hurried to my car, rammed myself behind the wheel, and motored off. Depressing news about sixty-one-year-old men. Probably it didn't apply to Morelli and Ranger. I called Lula when I was half a block away.

"Don't let anyone shoot vegetables at me," I told her. "I'm about to park in front of the house."

"Copy," Lula said. "Cease all operations," she yelled out.

This wasn't a desirable sign. I was hoping Lula would confiscate weapons, but it sounded like she'd signed on to Star Fleet.

"Where's my chicken?" Lula wanted to know, opening the door to me. "I don't see no bags or buckets. All I see is you wearing dinner."

"It's complicated," I said.

"I bet. Is that my mashed potatoes in your hair?"

"I never got that far. I was in line and there was a riot."

"Yeah, but after the riot you should have tried the drive-through."

Mooner was holding his position at the front window.

"He hasn't shot anyone, has he?" I asked Lula.

"Since you been gone? He lobbed a tomato at an old guy with a shovel. Got him in the head and it was instant salsa. That was about it."

The news van pulled to the curb behind my car.

"Whoa," Mooner said. "It's the news. I hate the news. It's never good."

"I'll get rid of them," Lula said. "Give me the big boy."

Gary ran forward and handed Lula a monster spud gun. It was made from wide bore black pipe and had to be four feet long. Lula opened the door, set the pipe on Mooner's shoulder, Gary dropped a honeydew melon into the pipe, rammed it down, and sprayed it.

"Fire in the hole," Lula yelled, and turned the ignitor knob.

POW! The melon exploded out of the pipe, Lula and Mooner were knocked off their feet, and the melon sailed over the news truck like a cannonball and took the top off a flowering crabapple tree on the other side of the street.

"Did I hit the target?" Lula asked.

"No, but you scared the crap out of them. They're already in the next county."

"I need a sight," Lula said to Mooner. "All us expert marksmen have sights."

"It would be awesome if we had monkey shit," Mooner said.

"Forget the monkey shit," Lula told him. "I'm not getting you no monkey shit. I hate monkeys."

"This isn't a good idea," I said. "Someone's going to get hurt with this stuff. I want it all put away. Put it in the cellar."

"Mooch and some other guy are in the cellar digging," Lula said. "Zook accidentally beaned Mooch with a half-baked when he saw him in the yard, and we might not want to get too close to Mooch until he calms down."

"Then put the spud guns someplace else. Just stop using them."

"Yeah," Lula said, "but what if we see people trespassing? Morelli's paying these men good money to protect his property. You wouldn't want them to be derelict in their duties."

My eye was twitching like mad. I put my finger to it and looked at Lula out of the other eye. "I'm going to take a shower. Use some common sense."

"Sure, I got lots of common sense," Lula said. "You can count on me."

I threw my clothes into the laundry basket in Morelli's room, wrapped myself in his robe, and ran across the hall to the bathroom to take a shower. When I came back to the bedroom with clean hair and body, I found Bob eating my clothes. Couldn't blame him. They smelled like fried chicken and gravy.

I wrestled what was left of the clothes away from Bob and assessed the damage. T-shirt half there. Jeans had chunks missing. Socks and underwear, gone. Not the first time Bob had eaten my underwear, so I knew the drill. Bob would be spending a lot of time in the backyard tomorrow, letting nature take its course.

I got dressed and blasted my hair with the hair dryer. I took a close look at myself in the mirror. The blue was fading. I was now a ghoulish shade of pale. I went back to the bedroom and dialed Morelli.

"Yep," Morelli said.

"Have you got a minute to talk?"

"Thirty seconds, tops. This is a royal mess. Two kids dead. A shooter who is related to a councilman. Two more at large. And the neighborhood is in a state of siege. What's up?"

"You have three lunatics guarding your house, there are a bunch of fortune hunters creeping around your yard, someone sent you Loretta's pinky toe, and Bob ate my underpants."

"Lucky Bob."

"I put the toe in your freezer."

"Shit," Morelli said. "I'm out of Rolaids. Are you sure it was a toe?"

"Either that or a giant garbonzo bean with a toe-nail."

"I'll be home as soon as I can, but it will probably be late tonight."

"Should I report the toe to someone?" I asked him.

"I'll tell Spanner about it. I'm sure it's all related. Gotta go."

I flopped onto the bed and covered my eyes with my hands. The day was grinding on, and I wasn't making any progress. Loretta was suffering somewhere, and I couldn't get to her.

Let's list all this out, I thought. What do I know about the fourth partner? I know he's single. I know what his shoes look like. I might remember his voice. That's it. That's all I know.

No it isn't, I thought. I know more. None of it good. I know he robbed a bank and let his partner take the fall. I know he killed one or more of his partners and blew up a house. I know he has Loretta and is capable of doing most anything to her. I know for sure that he wants the nine million real bad. And either he thinks Morelli has already found the money, or he's decided his best shot is to force Morelli to find it for him. What else do I know? I know Dom is still in the neighborhood.

I carted my half-eaten clothes downstairs and tossed them into the garbage. I ate a bowl of cereal and a banana, and I went into the living room. Zook, Mooner, and Gary were back to the world of Minionfire. The spud guns were lined up along the wall.

Lula was on the phone. "What do you mean he don't want to talk to me? Of course he wants to talk to me. I'm his honey. We're engaged to get married. Did you tell him it was Lula?" She listened for a minute, tapping her toe, looking really pissed off. "You're a big fibber. I've got a mind to come over there and hit you alongside the head. How'd you like that, you little pissant?"

I gave Lula raised eyebrows.

"Hunh," Lula said. "He hung up on me."

"You called him a pissant."

"I just learned that word yesterday. It was on one of them game shows. I bet he don't even know what it means."

"Who were you talking to?"

"Some guy at Rangeman. Hal or Cal or something."

My cell phone rang.

"Babe," Ranger said. "*Do* something with her."

And he disconnected.

I called Ranger back. "No," I said. "And I need information on Jelly Kantner. His apartment got blown up, and I need to find him."

"And I should do this why?"

"Because you like me."

There was a full beat of silence. "I do," Ranger said. "I like you a lot. Sometimes I'm not sure why. Give me a couple minutes."

I slid my phone into my pocket and waited. Five minutes went by and finally Ranger called.

"What do you mean you're not sure why you like me?" I asked him.

"Liking you doesn't seem to be getting me where I want to go."

"Maybe you need to change the destination."

"Maybe," Ranger said. "But not today. I have a personal information report for you on Jelly Kantner, also known as Jay Kantner."

"E-mail Kantner's report to Morelli."

"Ten-four."

I moved to Morelli's office and waited for the e-mail to come in. I printed the report and sat in his chair to read it. Kantner's parents were deceased. He had a sister living in the Burg. She was married with two kids. Kantner had no derogatory information. His credit was good. He'd worked as a maintenance specialist for J. B. Management Associates for ten years. Probably didn't make a lot of money, but his work history was solid. He'd never married.

I called the sister's number and asked for Jelly.

"Jelly," she shouted. "It's a *girl*!"

"Hello?" Jelly said.

"Hey, it's Stephanie Plum."

"Oh no!"

"Don't hang up. I just want to talk to you."

"Okay," Jelly said. Tentative. Not sure if it was a smart thing.

"I'm trying to find Dom," I told him.

"I don't know where he is. He got my apartment blown up. And I haven't seen him since."

"You're friends. You must have some idea where he went."

"We *were* friends. In the past. No more. Not ever again. He took off as soon as I didn't have an apartment. He never even said *thank you* or *gee, I'm sorry*. All he thinks about is himself. He used to be fun, but now he's crazy. All he ever talked about was the money and how he hates Morelli. He blames Morelli for everything. He said Morelli swindled him out of his house and his future. He never said, but I figured the money had to be in that house somewhere. He was obsessed with the stupid house."

"Did he have a map or directions that led to the money?"

"No. He said it was in his head."

"What about Victor or Benny? He used to hang with them. Would they take him in?"

"Are you kidding? Those guys are locked down. Their wives would kick their asses if they had anything to do with Dom."

"Relatives?" I asked him.

"Maybe. He's related to half the Burg. He used to be close to his cousin Bugger, but I don't know about now."

"Bugger Baronni?"

"Yeah, there's only one Bugger."

Thank heavens for that.

Chapter

I left Mooner, Zook, and Gary home alone with detailed instructions. They were to wash my car. They were to stay close to Morelli's house. They were *not* allowed to shoot *anything*. They were to stay away from Mooch.

We were in Lula's Firebird, and Lula was in a mood. "First off, I never got no chicken. And now I'm driving you to check out some guy named Bugger. I don't even want to know how he got that name."

"Sixth grade," I said. "On a class trip to a petting zoo."

"What's he doing now?"

"He's a lawyer."

"Figures," Lula said.

Bugger lived a little north of Trenton, in an affluent neighborhood close to the river. He specialized in messy divorce cases, and the word on him was that everyone took it up the ass when he got involved. Literally and figuratively.

I thought chances were slim that Dom was here, but no stone unturned. Bugger was a relative and sometimes that meant something. As would the possibility of getting cut in on nine million dollars. There was no

Mrs. Bugger. No Mr. Bugger, either. Just Bugger and a big dog named Lover.

Lula drove by the house and gave a low whistle. "This guy does okay."

The house was a redbrick colonial that looked like about ten thousand square feet under roof. It was on a large landscaped lot with a gated drive. Much of the house and yard was obscured by a privacy hedge.

The house was impressive but felt excessively large for one person. I guess you have a big house like that, you get used to living in it, but all I could think of was keeping toilet paper in all those bathrooms.

"What's this guy look like?" Lula wanted to know.

"I only met him once when I was at a party years ago, but I remember him as a slim Dom."

If my life wasn't so complicated, I'd stake out the house. It was as good a place as any for Dom to hide. He'd be relatively safe behind the gates. Bugger obviously had guest rooms and probably had a couple cars. Plus, Bugger had no scruples and loved money. It was a match made in heaven.

"I don't suppose you'd want to do a stakeout for me?" I asked Lula.

"Don't suppose I would," Lula said. "Who you want to stake out?"

"Bugger."

Lula looked up and down the street. "How are you gonna do a stakeout here? Everyone parks their car in their garage. I don't even see any cars in driveways. We're sitting here looking like we're planning a robbery."

She was right. A car parked at the side of the road was painfully obvious.

I had my hand on the door handle. "I'm going to

sneak around in the bushes and look in some windows. You can circle the block and pick me up when I'm done."

"Better you than me," Lula said. "This is one of them snooty neighborhoods, and they probably got all kinds of dogs and alarms and shit like that."

"I've heard rumors about Bugger's dog, and as long as I don't bend over, I think I'll be okay."

I was out of the car and about to cross the street when the gates to Bugger's driveway swung open. A silver Lexus rolled from behind the hedge, through the open gate, and turned left. Only one person in the car. Dom. We locked eyes, and Dom floored it.

I ran around and jumped into the Firebird. "Catch him!"

He had a good head start, but in his panic he turned down a cul-de-sac. Lula angled her car across the road and blocked his exit. He swerved coming at us, jumped the curb, and took out about five thousand dollars' worth of hedge. The house behind it looked like pictures I've seen of Versailles.

The Lexus stalled in the hedge, and Dom wrenched the door open and took off for the faux chateau. I ran flat-out after him and tackled him halfway to the house. He was heavier and stronger than I was, but I was willing to fight dirty. I brought my knee up and rearranged his private parts so that they were halfway into his intestines.

Dom grabbed himself and went into a fetal position. He was sweating and gasping for air, and for a moment I was afraid he might throw up. I removed a gun from him and stood.

"You're out on parole," I told him. "You're not allowed to carry a gun."

He sort of nodded. Still trying to get it together.

"Be a shame to have to shoot you with your own

gun," I said. "So I want you to move nice and slow and not get me excited."

Another nod.

"You need to listen carefully, because this is serious," I said. "Your fourth partner has Loretta."

"I know. I'm trying to help her," Dom said, "but I can't get to the money. If I let Morelli in on it, he'll turn the money back to the bank, and I'm afraid Loretta will be killed, just like Allen."

"And Stanley Zero."

Dom locked eyes with me. "What do you mean?"

"Someone put a bullet in Zero. I found him earlier today."

"Do you know who did it?"

I shook my head. "No. But I'm thinking your fourth partner."

"Bastard," Dom said. "I never felt good about him."

"I need a name."

Dom was on his feet, still holding himself and a little stooped over, but starting to get color back in his face.

"I don't have a name," he said. "He was the inside guy. I never even saw him. Stan brought him in. Said he had a sensitive job and no one could know who he was. I always figured he worked for the bank, because he was able to get information. He had access to files and schedules. Or maybe he was one of those computer hackers."

"How did you get in touch with him?"

"Stan got in touch with him. They were buddies. Stan was friends with *everyone*."

I wanted to get Dom someplace more secure. I wanted him in cuffs and shackles so he couldn't get away. I wanted him talking to Morelli. There was a lot at stake, and I was well aware that I wasn't entirely competent. Problem was, he was talking, and I didn't want to give him pause to reconsider and shut up. So I held my breath and pushed on.

"Obviously, something is hidden in Morelli's basement. What is it?" I asked him.

He pulled his pants waistband out and looked down at himself. I guess making sure they were actually still there. "It's two keys on a keychain. I knew I was spotted at the bank, and I'd be locked away for a while. I saw the camera pan to me before we took it out. I wasn't sure I trusted the guys, so I changed the plan. I was supposed to drive the van to a warehouse where we were going to keep it on ice until the money was safe to use. Instead, I drove it to a garage I knew about. Then I buried the keys to the garage and the truck in Rose's basement. Rose was old, and she'd always promised the house to me. She always told me I was in her will."

"But she was disappointed that you robbed a bank, and she changed her will."

"That would be Morelli's version. My version goes that he sweet-talked her out of the house and screwed me like he screwed my sister."

He'd stopped holding himself, but he was still standing bent and bowlegged. "I'm gonna have cramps for days," he said. "You should register that knee as a lethal weapon."

"It was an accident."

"Yeah, right. And if I stop talking, it's gonna be an accident that you shoot me."

"Let's skip to where you get out of prison."

"That was a real kick in the head. I break into the house and what do I find? Asshole Morelli has poured concrete in the basement. I can't get the friggin' keys. So I tell everybody, but they don't believe me. They think I'm juicing them out of the money. And the truth is, I was thinking about it. I did the time. I figured I deserved extra. I never ratted on anyone."

"And?"

"It just got more and more fucked up. Everybody was hungry for the money and nobody trusted anybody else. And Gratelli thought he was James Bond. He was carrying a gun and planting bugs he bought at the Spy Store and going around at night wearing infrared goggles. This is the guy who pissed his pants as soon as we got into the bank. As a joke, I gave him a map with directions and told him he couldn't show anyone. I said it was top secret and it would take him to the money, but he had to guard it and wait for things to settle down. I told him we'd cut the other guys out and get more for ourselves. It was directions to Starbucks, but Gratelli took it serious. Poor dumb, dead shmuck."

Oh great. I got dyed over directions to Starbucks.

"Anyway, I'm up shit creek because my nephew is now living in Morelli's house, so I don't want to give away that the keys are in Morelli's basement. I'm afraid these sons of bitches will go in there like World War III. So I'm telling them not to get their shorts in a bunch and they get all pissed off and snatch Loretta."

"How did Gratelli get shot?"

"They had Loretta. So I said I would take them to the keys, but they had to go with me, and we had to wait for a time when I knew the house was empty. So the three of us wait until everybody goes out of the house, and then we all go in and troop into the basement, and I show them the nice, new, perfect concrete floor. It's in that corner, I say. Under six inches of concrete that asshole Morelli laid down. And this is sort of the funny part. I mean, it's not really funny, but . . . Anyway, Gratelli is sort of freaking because he has a map in his car that I swear leads to the money, and he knows it doesn't take him here. He knows it takes him to Starbucks. And he actually thinks the keys are hidden somewhere at Starbucks. Stan doesn't know what to make of any of it, but he has plans for the money, and he's tired of the whole thing. And I haven't mentioned this before, but Stan has done the occasional job."

"Job?"

"Wet work."

"Yikes."

"Yeah. So to make an impression, and because Stan has already figured out Gratelli isn't an asset, he pulls his gun and pops Gratelli in the forehead. We both look at the stairs and decide it's too much of a pain in the ass to get Gratelli out of the basement, so we leave. And on the way out, Stan tells me his friend is getting real restless, and if I'm messing with them and this isn't for real, I'm going to look like Gratelli real soon."

"Turned out he was the one who looked like Gratelli."

"I don't know what to make of that. I thought they were tight. I guess when it comes to nine million, things change."

"So where are we now?"

"The keys are in the corner by the water heater. You had the cellar dug up. I'm surprised you didn't find them."

"Morelli had the cement broken up, but he didn't dig through all the dirt."

"You should be looking happy because you know where the keys are," Dom said. "Why don't you look happy?"

"Two men broke into Morelli's house last night while Morelli and I were out. Zook heard them come in the back door and called the police, but it looks like they were in the cellar before leaving."

"That's not good news," Dom said. "And now Stan's dead and the fourth partner is left. But at least he don't know how to find the garage where I stashed the van. He still needs me. So he still needs Loretta to be alive. Otherwise, I'd never deal with the prick."

This was making me feel a little less panicky. We could still bargain for Loretta. We could arrange a hostage swap.

"This is great," I said to Dom. "We can give your partner the money and get Loretta back."

"I don't want Morelli involved. Morelli will never do it. He'll do his cop thing and turn the money in to the bank. He walked away from my sister before, and he'd do it again."

Dom was agitated. He was pacing around. Obviously, his equipment had dropped back into place, and he wasn't feeling so vulnerable. Not the time to argue paternity, I told myself. Let it slide for now. Just find out where he's got the money.

"Okay, we won't involve Morelli," I said. "We'll do it without him. Where's the money?"

"I hate Morelli," Dom said. "I've always hated him. Rotten S.O.B. He's not even bald."

"Excuse me?"

"*Bald!* Go ahead, tell me you didn't notice I'm going bald."

Oh boy. He'd flipped out. Just like that. One minute normal, and the next minute rabid bald guy.

"Maybe you're a little bald on the top," I said, "but it's not unattractive."

"Is Morelli bald?"

"No."

"Damn right he's not bald," Dom said. "He's the golden boy. Has he got hair on his back? On his ass?

Does he have hair on his knuckles? On his toes? No. He's perfect. He's got hair on his *fucking head*."

I thought about Morelli. "Maybe a little on his ass," I said. Hell, he was Italian. It was practically *required* for him to have hair on his ass.

We both paused for a moment, our attention caught by high-pitched whining.

"What's that?" Dom asked.

The whining changed to yelps, and the realization hit us.

"Dogs," Dom said.

The pack rounded the back corner of the house and raced toward us. Five Dobermans with "killer" written all over them.

"Run!" I yelled at Dom.

We had a large expanse of rolling lawn between us and the dogs, and an equally large expanse between us and the road. We took off, and I could hear Dom pounding after me, his breath wheezing through his teeth.

"Shoot 'em!" he was shouting at me. "Shoot the fuckers."

I was running with Dom's gun in my hand, and while a small corner of my panicked, terrified brain wanted to stop the beasts in their tracks, the rest of my brain was seeing them as Snoopy. No way could I shoot them. Probably if they caught us, they wouldn't hurt us, I told myself. But just in case, I was running like hell.

We reached Dom's car with the dogs at our heels. I scrambled onto the car and perched on the roof, and Dom kept running. He crossed the street and disappeared behind another huge mansion-type house. The dogs stayed with me, surrounding the car, barking and snarling.

Lula had been waiting in the Firebird all this time.

She rolled out of the car, pointed her Glock skyward, and fired off a shot. The dogs gave one last yip, turned tail, and ran back to the house.

I climbed down from the Lexus, walked shaky-legged to the Firebird, and collapsed into the passenger seat.

"That was almost it," I told Lula. "I thought for sure I was going to be dog food."

"Where'd you get the gun?"

"I took it from Dom."

I dropped the gun into my purse and sat back with my hand over my heart. "I've gotta join a gym," I said. "I almost died back there."

Chapter
EIGHTEEN

It was almost eleven when Morelli dragged himself through the front door. I'd sent Mooner home. Gary was tucked away in his camper in the garage. Zook was in bed. Bob and I were on the couch pretending we were watching television when really we were just waiting for Morelli.

Morelli gave both of us a kiss on the top of the head and kept going into the kitchen. We followed after him and watched him knock back a beer. He dropped his jacket on the floor and threw his gun on the counter and belched.

"Beer," he said by way of explanation.

"Tough day?"

"Unh."

He took a tub of deli potato salad out of the refrigerator and forked some into his mouth.

"Did you get anything resolved?" I asked.

"It's a process." His gaze went to the small table. "What's with the gun in the plastic bag?"

"Test it out to see if it matches either of the murder weapons."

"Where'd you get it?"

I gave him the short version.

Morelli tossed the empty potato salad container into the trash. "Have you looked in the basement?"

"Yes. Big hole in the corner where the keys were supposedly buried. No keys."

"Good riddance. Let's go to bed."

Morelli was still in the kitchen when I got back from driving Zook to school. Morelli was showered and shaved and looked relatively civilized in a blue button-down shirt and jeans. He had his gun clipped to his belt, the phone cradled against his neck and shoulder, and he was taking notes in a small pad he always carried. I poured myself a second cup of coffee and waited for Morelli to get off the phone.

"You're getting a late start," I said when he disconnected.

"I want to talk to you, and I didn't want to do it until Zook was out of the house. There was a padded envelope stuck under my windshield wiper when I went out this morning. I put the contents in the freezer."

My heart stuttered in my chest.

"I've been talking to Larry Skid and Spanner and the Fed who headed the bank job, and they're going to set up a sting. I doubt Dom will go back to Bugger's house. And it doesn't seem likely he'll get in touch with you, so we're going without him. Hang the scarf in the window and tell the fourth partner you talked to Dom and you know everything. Tell him you want to swap what you know for Loretta. Let the partner suggest how to make the exchange. He'll be less suspicious of a trap if he sets it up. The Feds have a garage in place." Morelli handed me a page from his notebook. "This is the address. Make sure he passes you Loretta before you give him this information."

"Was it another toe?"

"Yeah." He poured coffee into a travel mug, and took two bubble-wrapped packages from the freezer and dropped them into a plastic bag. "I'm taking these in with me, along with the gun. Don't call me on your cell phone if you want to talk about this. Call me on something that's secure." He kissed me and left.

I gave him twenty minutes and hung a red scarf in the window. It was cashmere and had been a Christmas present from Morelli's mom two years ago. He'd never worn it. He wasn't a red scarf kind of guy.

I got a call on my cell phone ten minutes after I hung the scarf.

"Who hung the scarf?" he said.

I recognized the voice. Slight rasp. Flat. "I did," I told him.

"And?"

"I know everything. I had a conversation with Dom yesterday. He wants to make a deal for Loretta."

"Why isn't he talking to me?"

"Afraid, I guess."

"But you're not afraid?"

"I'm not involved like Dom."

"What about Morelli?"

"He's not part of it."

I sat out a full sixty seconds of silence. I suppose he was debating whether to go forward. Or maybe he was waiting to see if I'd get nervous and start blabbering.

"Here's the deal," he finally said. "You tell me where the van is located, and I give you Loretta."

"I need Loretta first."

"Not gonna happen, sweetie."

I hated this guy. I hated his voice. I hated his arrogance and his ability to kill and maim in cold blood. And I hated that he called me sweetie.

"You're going to have to come up with a plan we can both live with," I told him.

"I'm a reasonable guy," he said. "I'll call you back in twenty minutes."

By the time he called, my eye was twitching and my stomach was clenched in a knot. The phone rang and I jumped in my seat. I took a moment to breathe and steady my voice, and I answered the phone.

"The keys are taped to the underside of a bench in front of the train station," he said. "Look for the bus stop with the Nike ad. When you get the keys, you can use them to get the van. After you've secured the van, you can call me. The phone number is in the envelope with the keys. You need to remember two things. If anything goes wrong, I'll kill Loretta. Then I'll kill her son. And then I'll kill you. And don't doubt for a moment that I won't."

"What's the second thing?"

"Be careful not to set off the detonation device."

Oh boy. "Dom didn't tell me about the detonation device."

There was a moment of silence. "Allen booby-trapped the van. Allen loved doing that sort of thing. In this case, it wasn't a bad idea, since none of us could really be trusted. The key is necessary to disarm the mechanism. So, while Dom has always known where the van was located, he had no access to the money without the key. Allen probably could have bypassed his system, but he didn't know the location of the van. Once Zero was convinced he knew where the key was located, he eliminated Allen. And then, of course, I eliminated Zero after we retrieved the keys. Nine million is much better than four and a half. And I'm telling you this so you will be careful when inserting the ignition key, and also so you understand that I'm ruthless."

I didn't respond.

"Well?" he said.

"I'll get the van."

"No police. If you bring the police in on this, I'll know. And it won't be good for Loretta."

"I have to make sure she's okay."

"She's as okay as anyone could be who just had two toes removed, and that's as close as you're going to get to her."

My newly washed car was at the curb. No more Zook decorations. Just rust and faded paint and a bunch of dings and dents. I drove to the office and got there just as Connie was unlocking the door. No sign of Lula. I called Morelli on the office phone, and he called me back from a landline.

"He's left the keys on a bench at the train station. I'm to pick them up and get the van. When I have the van, I'm supposed to call him. His number will be with the keys."

"We can do this," Morelli said. "We have video of the van. We can duplicate it and have it in the garage. Get the keys and I'll get back to you when we're ready."

The door to the bonds office banged open and shut and Lula stormed in.

"I swear," she said. "I have a mind not to get married. That man came to my house stinking drunk last night. I opened the door, and he called me Charlotte. Who the hell is Charlotte? He said it was his mother, but I don't believe it for a minute. And then when I said I wanted to meet his mother, he said she was dead. And I don't think that's true. I think he don't want me to meet his mama."

"We've got a stack of filing," Connie said. "Are you up to filing?"

"I'm up to murder. I'm in a vicious mood. I was ready for a good time, if you know what I mean. And he fell asleep in the bathroom. I thought he was getting ready. You know how sometimes men need to get ready?"

I didn't have that problem. The men in my life were always ready. In fact, I could do with a little less ready.

Connie looked confused by it, too. "Ready for what?" Connie asked.

"Whatever," Lula said. "How the hell do I know what they do in there? Anyway, he's not coming out and he's not coming out, and finally I go in and he's asleep on the floor. So I said to him, *Hey!* And he never even twitched. And then I pushed him around. And that didn't do nothing. So I watched some television and went to bed, and when I got up, he was gone. Good thing, too, because I wasn't happy. I'm not marrying no alcoholic."

I couldn't imagine Tank or Ranger drunk. They were always in control. They ate vegetables. They exercised. They didn't eat butter, and they ate whole wheat bread. What on earth could drive Tank to drink? The answer was clear. The answer was . . . Lula. Big, tough Tank was no match for Lula.

"I have an errand to run," I said. "I'll be back."

The train station wasn't far away, and the bench was easy to find. There was only one with a Nike ad. I illegally parked, ran over, and sat on the bench. I had my choice of feeling around or bending over and looking. Neither was appealing, considering what might be stuck there besides the keys. I went with the looking and had good luck. The keys and the phone number were in an envelope held to the seat with electricians tape. I shoved the envelope into my pocket and motored back to the office. Connie was on the phone and Lula was filing when I walked in.

I sunk into the couch and paged through one of Lula's bride magazines. Connie got off the phone and looked over at me.

JANET EVANOVICH

"Vinnie's coming home on Wednesday, and he's not going to be happy about the number of skips out there," Connie said. "We have a stack of low-money losers that adds up to a lot of money."

I knew she was right. I had a list in my purse. Loretta had been taking precedent over the job.

"Susan Stitch would be a good place to start," Connie said.

"No way," Lula said from behind a file cabinet. "That's the monkey lady. I'm not going back there. I hate monkeys. And I especially hate *that* monkey. That monkey is the spawn of the devil."

"It was Brenda's fault for letting him out of the bathroom," I said. "I'm sure he'll be fine as long as we don't drag Brenda and a film crew along with us."

Truth is, I was nervous about the ransom sting, and I wouldn't have minded a diversion while I waited for Morelli's phone call. I stood and hung my bag on my shoulder.

"I'm off to North Trenton," I said to Connie. I cut my eyes to Lula. "Are you coming with me?"

"I guess I am," Lula said. "Someone's gotta go along and protect your skinny ass."

"You didn't do a lot of protecting yesterday. You sat in the car when I chased down Dom."

"Darn right. I knew there was gonna be dogs. These people got dogs and all kinds of security shit. Did you think of that? No. You chased Dom into that yard, and next thing, there was a pack of killer dogs running after you."

We got out on the sidewalk, and Lula looked at my car. "No more *Zook*," she said. "I thought the *Zook* was an improvement."

"It was too recognizable with *Zook* on it."

"Yeah, Connie and me always knew when you were trying to sneak past the office."

I drove to North Trenton and parked in Susan's lot. We took the stairs, and I knocked on her apartment door. No one answered, but the door eased open.

"Uh-oh," Lula said. "There's always dead bodies inside when this happens." She stuck her head in and sniffed. "I smell monkey," she said.

I rapped on the open door. "Anyone home?" I yelled.

No one answered, but I could hear a television squawking somewhere. I stepped into the apartment and scanned for the monkey. No monkey in sight.

Lula was pressed tight behind me. "I better not get attacked by no monkey," she whispered. "I'm gonna be mad at you if I get a monkey on my head. There was lots of other losers we could have gone after."

The living room and kitchen area was unoccupied. The television was blaring from the bedroom.

"Hello," I yelled again. "Anyone home?"

"Who could hear over that television?" Lula said. "Sounds like one of them music video stations."

We cautiously crept to the bedroom and peeked through the open door. Susan was naked on top of some guy with a cast on his leg, and she was going to town on him, grinding and pounding away in time with the music.

"Oops," I said. "Sorry."

Susan paused for a moment and covered her breasts with her hands. "We made up," she said.

I was telling myself not to look, but my eyes weren't cooperating. "Great, but you still have to get your bond straightened out."

"It was for Carl," she said. "He was unhappy."

"Un-hunh."

I could hear Lula making choking sounds behind me.

"We'll wait in the hall until you're done," I said to Susan.

"Okay," she said. "It never takes long."

"Cripes," the guy said. "What's that supposed to mean?"

Lula and I almost knocked each other over trying to get out of the bedroom.

"I gotta get outta here before I bust from trying not to laugh out loud," she said. "I didn't want to be rude, but I was a 'ho for a bunch of years, and I never seen anyone bouncing around on a wanger like that. That woman still got some anger left in her. He's lucky if she don't bend something and do permanent damage."

Lula was looking at me and not paying attention to what she was doing. She opened the powder room door instead of the front door and Carl lunged out at her and grabbed her face.

"Eeeeee," she squealed. "I got a monkey on my face. Help! Do something."

Carl backflipped off her and ran around the room.

"Get me out of here," Lula said. "Where's the door? Someone open the door!"

She found the door, yanked it open, and Carl scampered out. He ran down the hall, jumped up, and punched the elevator button. The elevator doors opened, Carl leaped inside, and the doors closed.

"I didn't see that," Lula said. "I had nothing to do with it, and I never was here."

I didn't want to go back into the bedroom, so I yelled as loud as I could. "Susan! Your monkey just got into the elevator."

"Oh *yes*!" Susan shouted. "Yes, yes, yes. Yippie-ki-yay, cowboy!"

"I'm gonna pretend she heard," Lula said.

"I did my best to tell her."

Lula nodded in agreement. "Nobody could ask for anything more from you."

The racket was still going on in the bedroom.

"Probably we shouldn't wait for Susan to get done," I said.

"Yeah. I just remembered I got something to do."

We hurried down the stairs and slunk through the lobby to the lot. We didn't see Carl.

"I hope Carl's okay," I said to Lula.

"Carl's probably on his way to stick up a 7-Eleven."

Chapter
NINETEEN

I dropped Lula at the office and went to my apartment to check on Rex. I leaned over his cage and told him about my day so far. He was in his soup can and probably wasn't listening, but I talked to him anyway. I gave him an olive and a corn chip, and I called Susan Stitch.

"Did you find Carl?" I asked her.

"Yep. He escapes like that all the time. He's such a clever little dickens. He was on the first floor visiting with Mrs. Rooney. He likes to play with her beagle."

"Would this be a good time to get rebonded?"

"It's perfect, but you don't have to worry about it. Ron and I are going to the courthouse together. We're meeting his lawyer there, and hopefully this can all be worked out."

"That's great," I said, assuming Ron was the guy with the leg cast and stiffy. "Good luck."

I hung up, and I took a moment to enjoy being in my own space. Morelli's house had ice cream sandwiches, but my apartment was home. My apartment was quiet and sane and was free from überelves and bank robbers.

My cell rang, and I saw on the screen that it was Morelli. I was tempted not to answer, but I knew he'd keep calling until I connected.

"Hola," I said to him.

"Do you have a landline?"

"Yes. I'll get back to you on my kitchen phone."

"Here's the deal," he said when we reconnected. "The address I gave you earlier is actually a storage facility down by the river. The lockers are big. Garage-size. People keep furniture and boats and ATVs in them. It's not a stretch to drive a van into one. It's locker number twenty-four, and it's rigged with a lock that will open with any key. Inside is an exact replica of the van used in the robbery. The key is in the ignition. We've got nine million in dummy money in the back of the van. All you have to do is go along with the deal."

"How am I going to communicate?"

"I'll put a wire on you. Give me twenty minutes."

I put the phone down and went back to talking to Rex.

"I hate this," I said to him. "I don't know if you've noticed, but I'm not the hero type. I wanted to be Wonder Woman when I was a kid. Now that I'm an adult, I think kicking ass leaves a lot to be desired. For one thing, I'm not that good at it. And wearing a wire makes my stomach feel squishy. I'm always afraid I'll get found out, and I'll end up with a bullet in the head like Allen Gratelli."

It was a sobering thought when said out loud.

"Not that it would happen," I said to Rex.

I refilled Rex's water bottle and gave him an extra bowl of hamster food, just in case. And then Rex and I waited in silence in the kitchen for Morelli to arrive.

Ten minutes later, Morelli knocked and opened the door. He had a key.

"I'm not supposed to be doing this," he said. "I'm still working the gang thing, but I didn't want anyone else feeling you up when they taped the wire."

"If something happened to me, you'd take care of Rex, wouldn't you?"

"Nothing's going to happen to you."

"Yes, but if it did."

"If anything happened to you, I'd be so destroyed they'd have to strap me to a bed and feed me through a tube. After five or six years, I might be capable of taking care of Rex. In the interim, you should assign a guardian."

Morelli had his hands under my shirt and supposedly was installing the wire, but his thumb kept tracing a line across the tip of my breast. I was starting to lose focus.

"If you're trying to get my mind off the ransom, it's working," I told him.

"Yeah, sometimes I love my job," he said, giving me a whole-hand fondle. He took a small receiver out of his pocket, put the attached earbud into his ear, and stepped back. "Push the button and switch it on."

I felt along the battery pack and pushed the button. "Testing," I said. "Mary had a little lamb. Yada, yada, yada."

"Perfect," Morelli said. "You're going to be transmitting to the Fed. Unfortunately, he won't be able to talk to you, so you'll have to run with it. If you feel like you're in trouble, do whatever you have to do. It's okay if you abort."

"I'm a little weirded out," I said.

Morelli looked down at me. Serious. "You don't have to do this."

"Yes, I do."

He kissed me on the forehead. "You'll be fine."

I went to the window and watched him cross the lot to his car. He opened the driver's side door, stood for a moment, and then slammed the door shut without getting in. My window was closed, so I couldn't hear what Morelli was saying, but clearly he was talking to himself. He was waving his arms and pacing and his face was getting red. He punched the car and stood hands on hips, starring down at his shoes. I've seen him do this a million times. Getting a grip.

I called him on my cell. "I'll be fine," I told him.

"This really sucks," he said. And he got in his car and drove away.

The storage facility chosen by the Feds was down by the river, off Lamberton Road. I took Hamilton and passed by the bonds office and the hospital. I turned at the junction of South Broad and felt my way around until I hit Lamberton. I was watching my mirror for a tail, but I didn't pick one up. I turned onto a private road leading to a small industrial park, and kept driving until I saw the sign for the storage facility. The facility itself was about a half acre in size and protected by a chain-link fence. The gate to the fence was open. There was a one-room cinderblock building that served as office. So far as I could see, the office was vacant. Beyond the office were rows of storage lockers, each the size of a single-car garage.

I drove down the second row of lockers and stopped at number 24. I got out of my car and looked around. Very quiet. No sign of the fourth partner. No indication of police presence. I had the wire switched on, but I wasn't saying anything.

I walked to the garage door, took a deep breath, and shoved the key in. The door rolled up to reveal a dark maroon Econoline van with Pennsylvania plates.

I looked in the driver's side window. The key was in the ignition, as promised. I wrenched the door open and climbed in. I was feeling calmer now that every-thing was in motion. Piece of cake, I said to myself. Cool as a cucumber. Wonder Woman on board.

I cranked the engine over, backed the van out, put my car in the garage, and rolled the garage door down. I carefully drove the van out of the storage facility, parked on the side of the road, and dialed the number the fourth partner gave me.

"Long time no hear," he said.

"I had things to do. I had to look in on a skip."

"Is that all you had to do?"

"Pretty much."

"What about waiting for the police to set the trap?"

"Nope. Didn't do that."

"I told you I would know. I know everything."

"Not *everything*," I said.

"I know you've got phony money in the back of that phony Econoline. I know you got the van out of a phony garage off Lamberton. I know you're wired. Now, here's the deal. Hang the scarf in the window when you're ready to make a trade without police in-volvement. If I don't see the scarf by noon tomorrow, I'm cutting Loretta's hand off."

"But I don't . . ."

He was gone.

"He knew," I said into the wire. "He knew the whole deal. You need to clean house. He's on the inside."

I retraced my route back to the garage and traded the van for my car. Still no one walking around, but I knew police were planted somewhere. I drove out of the industrial park and went straight to Morelli's house. School was still in session. Just me and Bob at home.

I took the red scarf from the upstairs window

and set it on Morelli's desk. All the way home, I'd been boiling inside, seething mad that this had gotten screwed up. I wanted it over and done. I wanted Loretta to be safe. I was angry at Dom for running away from me, and I was angry at the police that they couldn't manage a secure operation.

I sat in Morelli's chair and forced myself to think. Who is this fourth partner? A cop? A computer whiz? A professional crook? I looked at the red scarf. He wanted it hung from the second-floor window. Why the second floor? Wouldn't it be easier to see it from the *first* floor if you were walking or driving past the house?

I swiveled around and stared out the window. The houses on the opposite side of the street were all two-story, like Morelli's. Easy to see into their bedroom windows from here. The convenient assumption would be that the partner lived in one of these houses, but Morelli had already gone door-to-door in his neighborhood and hadn't found anything odd.

I called Morelli, but got his voice mail. I called my mother, and got my grandmother. She said my mother couldn't come to the phone because she'd taken a pill and fallen asleep after seeing me wrestling with the chicken on *News at Noon*. I called the office and was transferred to Connie's cell. She was at the courthouse trying to help resolve the Susan Stitch mess.

My modus operandi when investigating is, if you have no ideas . . . eat something. It doesn't help to get ideas, but it passes the time. So I trekked downstairs and nuked a tray of mac and cheese.

This got me to feeling very mellow, because it's impossible to stay upset while eating mac and cheese. Here's the positive side, I told myself. You continue to make little inroads on the fourth partner's identity. If you can't find Dom and get your hands on the money, maybe you can find the fourth partner. He's kind of full of himself, and that confidence could be his undoing.

I called Ranger.

"I want to get into Stanley Zero's apartment again," I told him.

"That's a sealed crime scene," Ranger said.

"And?"

"It would be safer if we went in at night."

"I can wait."

"I'll meet you in his apartment parking lot at eleven."

I reached the school just as it was letting out. Zook ambled over to the car with his usual cluster of misfits and pulled the passenger-side door open. He slouched into the seat, dropped his backpack on the floor between his feet, and looked over at me. "The kids at school are talking."

I gave the Sentra some gas and moved into the stream of traffic. "What are they saying?"

"They're saying my mom cut out on me. Like maybe she found the nine million and took off with it."

"They're wrong."

"I sort of wouldn't blame her. That's a lot of money."

"Your mom is okay. She's just not . . . accessible right now."

"What's that mean?"

"I can't tell you, but we're trying to work it all out."

He pushed his backpack around with a foot that seemed way too big for his slim frame. He was like a puppy that hadn't grown up to his feet yet. "I'm not some dumb little kid," he said. "I deserve to know what's going on with my mom."

I turned onto Hamilton and slid a sideways glance at him. He wasn't dumb, and he wasn't a little kid. He was a *big* kid. And he had a point. He needed to know what was going on with his mom.

"You're right," I said. "You deserve to know. But you can't tell anyone. No one at school. Not Mooner. Not Gary. No one."

He nodded his head.

"Three men robbed the bank with your Uncle Dom. Two are dead, and your uncle is in hiding. The fourth partner has your mom and is holding her for ransom. He wants the nine million dollars. Problem is, we don't have it, and we don't know where it's located. The police are involved, and we're making progress at getting your mom back, but you have to be patient."

"That is *so sucky,*" he said.

"You're right," I said on a sigh. "It is totally sucky."

Mooner and Gary were waiting on Morelli's front steps when I pulled to the curb with Zook. They were dressed in Army fatigues, and they stood and saluted when I parked the car.

Zook and I burst out laughing.

"I know they're goofy," I said to Zook, "but I like them. They're in the moment."

I unlocked Morelli's front door, and Bob rushed out and ran around in circles. He did some yelping and grunting, and then he hunched and pooped out my underwear.

"Whoa," Mooner said. "Victoria's Secret colonic, dude. Far out."

Bob ran back into the house the instant he was done, and we all followed. Eventually, I'd come out in rubber gloves and contamination suit and scoop up the deposit, but for now I was walking away from it.

"Where did you get the clothes?" I asked Mooner.

"Army surplus. We got some for the Zookster, too."

"We changed the patches," Gary said. "We made them say 'Homegrown Security.'"

I got everyone settled in the living room with chips and pretzels and sodas. I phoned for pizza. I asked about Zook's homework.

How bizarre was this? It was like running a day-care facility. Makes you wonder, doesn't it? I mean, who am I? I was raised to have traditional values, but I screwed up on my first marriage big-time, I took an odd job, and now I love two men. One is definite husband-and-father material. The other . . . I don't know what to think of the other. And now here I was, doing my "mother cat" impersonation.

The doorbell rang and I went to answer it. I opened the door and didn't bother to hold back the grimace. It was Brenda and her film crew.

"How about it?" she said. "Have you thought of anything?"

"No."

"Make something up. You've got an imagination, right? This is the news. It doesn't have to be real."

"I thought that was the whole purpose of the news . . . to report real stuff."

"Oh puhleeze. You don't actually believe that crap. You think we could get ratings with real stuff? The news people make up entire wars. Listen, all you have to do is find something sexy to say about the money. Like, 'Tall, dark and handsome Morelli was taking a nap, and he woke up and thought he heard a noise in the yard, so he rushed out naked and tackled some guy who was digging with a shovel, and Morelli saw a couple hundred-dollar bills sticking out of the ground.'" Brenda smiled. "See? It's easy."

"I'd like to help you, but I don't think I could pull that off."

"Of course, you can. Look at me. I can do it, and

I'm not that good. I'm just motivated. I've got a three-million-dollar house in Brentwood with a mortgage big enough to choke a horse." She looked at the guys on the couch. "Is that Gary?"

Gary waved at her. "I'm lurking."

"No shit," she said. "What's with the uniform? Did you join the Army?"

"Homegrown Security," Gary said. "I'm a gunnery officer."

"Great," Brenda said. "Perfect. A gunnery officer. That makes me feel real safe."

"Yeah, but you still have to watch out for the pizza," Gary said.

Brenda's face brightened. "Maybe I could do a feature on stalkers. We could film you stalking me," she said to Gary.

"I appreciate the offer, but no, thanks," Gary said. "I haven't got time to stalk right now. I promised the guys I'd lurk, and I'm on standby with Homegrown."

Brenda narrowed her eyes at Mooner. "You stole my stalker."

"No way, the Mooner doesn't steal. He, like, borrows sometimes, but he's got a code. He's protecting his oneness."

"Oneness, my ass," Brenda said. "I could own you like a cheap suit."

"Whoa," Mooner said. "Have you been talking to the wood elves?"

The soundman was standing behind Brenda. "If we don't get film to the studio soon, we'll miss our spot."

"I'm not missing my spot," Brenda said, turning from me and storming off the porch.

I closed the door and peeked out the living room window at her. She was standing over Bob's poo while the cameraman zoomed in for a closer look.

"And here we have a suspicious substance on Joe

Morelli's front lawn," Brenda said into her mic. "It would appear that the dog in this household has been fed a thong. Clearly a case for investigation by . . ." She looked over at the soundman. "Who investigates this shit?"

Chapter

TWENTY

Lula was on my cell phone. "I'm two minutes away," she said. "Be out front. I'm in a consultation for my wedding gown, and I need an opinion. You gotta go back to the bride store with me."

"Okay, but I can't stay away too long. I don't like leaving Zook on his own."

"Don't he have Homegrown Security with him?"

"Yeah, that's part of the problem."

I grabbed my purse, told everyone I'd be back soon and I was on my cell if an emergency arose, and I ran out of the house. The Firebird careened around the corner and slid to a stop in front of me. Lula was behind the wheel in a silky bathrobe.

"I got a hour appointment with these bitches," she said, "and the clock's ticking."

"You're in a bathrobe."

"It took less time than getting back in my clothes."

I fastened my seat belt and we rocketed away. "I thought you were having second thoughts about marrying an alcoholic."

"Yeah, but I had this appointment, and I didn't want to lose it. I might have to wait weeks to get another appointment. I mean, even if I don't marry Tank, chances are good I'll marry someone else someday. Might as well get the gown, I figure."

"You might want to rethink that plan."

"Yeah, it's insane, right? It's that I have momentum. You see what I'm saying? It's all in motion and it don't stop. Turns out, that's how it is with weddings. You just keep getting in deeper and deeper until you want to throw up."

Lula hooked a left, cut across traffic, and zipped into the small parking lot that attached to the bridal salon. We got out and hurried into the showroom.

"You sit down, and I'll put the gown on," Lula said.

I was halfway through a magazine when she rustled out of the dressing room. The gown was brilliant white satin and fit like skin from Lula's ankles to her armpits. It was strapless and had a bustle in the back over her ass and a twelve-foot train that stretched out behind her.

"We like this one because it's so slimming," the saleswoman said. "We think it hugs her curves and is very flattering. She's a lucky lady that we had her size in stock."

"All it needs is some of them crystal beads to make it sparkle," Lula said. "They said they could sew them on."

The gown was slimming because it was two sizes too small and squished in all Lula's fat and pushed it up until there was no more gown. She was spilling out of the top in rolls of Lula. She had cleavage *everywhere* . . . front, back, side.

"It's pretty," I said, "but there seems to be a lot of you oozing over the top. Maybe you should go up a size."

"They don't got this in a bigger size," Lula said. "And anyway, I don't want it too big on account of I'm planning to lose some weight."

I heard something pop and fly off the back of the dress, and the zipper burst open.

"Hunh," Lula said. "This here seems to be shoddy workmanship."

Ten minutes later, Lula dropped me at Morelli's.

"Boy," Lula said. "I dodged that bullet. Those people don't know how to sew."

"You might consider getting married in a dress instead of a gown," I said. "It wouldn't even have to be white."

"And it could be more representative of my outgoing personality," Lula said. "It could be animal print. You know how I'm partial to animal print."

"And it would be practical because you could wear it even if you didn't get married."

"I'm psyched," Lula said. "I'm going to the mall. You want to come?"

"No. Morelli should be getting off his shift right about now and I need to talk to him."

I was in the kitchen, eating pizza, when Morelli rolled in. He helped himself to a piece from the box and went to the refrigerator in search of beer.

"My refrigerator is filled with potatoes," he said, door open, face bathed in refrigerator light. "They're everywhere. I've got potatoes in the egg holder."

"Ammo. I think the beer is behind the half-baked."

He moved some potatoes around and grunted when he found the beer. "Zook's a terrific kid, but I feel displaced. Bad enough Mooner is always here, now we've got Gary. Once, I got up in the middle of the night to get water, and I swear I saw him sitting in a lawn chair in front of my garage."

"Imagine that," I said. "How odd."

"Have you heard from the partner?"

"No. The ball's in our court."

Morelli took a second piece of pizza. "This is bad. Either someone is leaking information or the guy is inside."

"Or maybe he's some genius computer geek that can tap into phones and computers."

Morelli shook his head. "That only happens in the movies. This guy knew about the van and the money. I didn't tell anyone, and Spanner swears he didn't tell anyone. I know the Fed who's running the show, and I can't see him telling anyone."

"What about the sack of shit?"

"Larry Skid? He could leak. And there were some other people working details. Looking at it in retrospect, we should have played it tighter, but there's always all this chain-of-command crap."

"I assume the department is investigating."

"Yes, but there's not much to go on. Truth is, some of this op went through the bureaucracy. The van needed to be requisitioned, the storage facility had to be cleared, yada yada."

I checked to make sure Zook wasn't listening and I lowered my voice. "He said he would cut Loretta's hand off at noon tomorrow if he doesn't have the money."

"He's sick," Morelli said. "He's caught up in the drama. If he was thinking sanely, he'd back off and wait. There's no way he's going to drive away with nine million dollars. It was a good plan when they executed it ten years ago, but it's not a good plan now that the police are involved."

"I suppose he figures he can stay ahead of the game if he can force me to locate the money and drive the van to him without telling anyone."

Morelli cut his eyes to me. "You wouldn't do that, would you?"

"Of course not," I said. And we both knew I would.

Problem was, I had the key but I didn't know what to do with it. And I had no way to reach Dom. I suspected Dom and the fourth partner had the same dilemma. Dom had always talked to Zero and Gratelli.

"I can practically see the wheels turning in your head," Morelli said. "What are you thinking?"

"I'm thinking this is pathetic. There's no communication between the major players here. Dom and I have identical goals right now, but we can't get anything done because I can't get in touch with him."

"Connie couldn't pull up a cell number?"

"No. Nothing for Dom. And the partner has me calling him on Zero's phone. I had Connie run it."

"Let's go obvious," Morelli said. "We think Dom watches the house, so make a sign and hang it in the living room window. 'Have key. Call me.'"

I ran upstairs to Morelli's office and used black magic marker on a piece of computer paper. I brought the sign downstairs and taped it to the window.

"We only have a couple hours of daylight where he can read it," I said to Morelli.

"No problem. I'll hook up a spot."

We moved Zook and Mooner and Gary into the dining room, and Morelli and Bob and I sat in front of the television, waiting for the call.

At ten o'clock, I got a call, but it was from the wrong person.

"You must be kidding," he said.

It was the fourth partner.

"What?"

He sighed into the phone. "You don't have any way of getting in touch with this idiot, either, do you?"

"You mean Dom? No."

"You better hope he sees your sign, because I'm running out of patience."

And he disconnected.

"That was the fourth partner," I told Morelli. "He saw the sign."

At ten-thirty, I had a problem. I didn't know how to get out of the house to meet Ranger without Morelli going postal. Take the coward's way out, I thought. Go out the bathroom window and deal with Morelli when you get home.

I didn't want anyone to think I was kidnapped, so I wrote a message on the toilet lid with my eyeliner pencil. BE BACK SOON. DON'T WORRY. I climbed out the window onto the small overhang that shelters the back stoop. Morelli's house is almost identical to my parents' house, and this was the route I'd used all through high school to sneak out with my friends. I rolled off the edge of the roof and lowered myself down. I felt hands at my waist, and I got an assist from Morelli.

"Dammit," I said to him. "How did you know?"

"I have the windows attached to the new alarm system. It dings when you open them. What are you doing?"

"I'm meeting Ranger, and you don't want any more information than that."

"Wrong." He glanced at his garage. "It looks like the light is on."

"Gary has his camper parked in there."

Morelli was silent for a couple beats. "Notice I'm not yelling," he said to me.

"Yeah, but I think the roots of your hair are smoking."

"How long has Gary been squatting in my garage?"

"A couple days."

Morelli opened the back door for me. "Get in the house."

Fine with me. My car was parked out front. Now I didn't have to walk halfway around the block. "I won't be long," I told Morelli, wasting no time getting through the kitchen and dining room. "Maybe an hour."

Morelli was close behind me. "Is this about Loretta?"

"Yep."

"I'm going with you."

"That's not a good idea."

"Why not?"

"You don't want to know," I told him.

"And Ranger is in on this?"

"He's not *in* on it. I asked him to help me. He has skills I lack."

"Such as?"

"He's good with locks."

"You're right. I don't want to know, but if anything happens to you, I'll go after Ranger, and it won't be pretty."

"Nothing's going to happen." Probably.

I ran to my car and took off. The fourth partner saw the sign, and that meant he was watching the house. I didn't want to be followed, so I wound around in the Burg, looking for headlights behind me. When I felt absolutely safe, I cut across town to Route 1 and headed for Stanley Zero's apartment complex.

Ranger was already there when I pulled into the lot. He was in his black Porsche Turbo, watching the building. I parked next to him, and he got out. He was wearing black jeans and T-shirt and a black windbreaker. Nothing with the Rangeman insignia. He looked at my ghoulish complexion and smiled.

"Long story," I said.

"I know the story. I'm just sorry I missed seeing you before you faded."

We walked to the entrance, and when we got to the door, he draped an arm across my shoulders. We were a couple, home from date night. When Ranger got close to me like this, I could smell his Bulgari shower gel. I've used the same gel, and the scent is fleeting on me. It lingers on Ranger.

Zero's apartment was sealed with yellow crime scene tape. A DO NOT ENTER notice was tacked to the door. Ranger peeled the tape back, used a pick on the lock, and in seconds we were inside. Nothing keeps Ranger out when he wants to get in. I've seen him open a door when a slide bolt was thrown. It's borderline eerie.

We pulled on disposable gloves and methodically moved through the apartment. There were smudges where the crime lab had searched for prints, and marks on the carpet where the body had fallen.

"I'm looking for something that might give me the identity of Dominic Rizzi's fourth partner," I told Ranger.

"Either the killer swept the apartment, or else the crime lab did an unusually thorough evidence collection," Ranger said. "I'm not finding anything. No cell phone, no computer, no address book."

"I had a few minutes to look around after I discovered the body, and I don't remember seeing a computer or phone. I went through all his pockets, with the exception of the clothes he was wearing. I couldn't bring myself to touch the body."

"He was dressed?"

"In jeans and a shirt. His boots were beside the bed."

"They're still there," Ranger said. He walked into the bedroom and picked up one of the boots. "I know it's a cliché, but people really do hide things in their shoes." He removed the padded insert and found a scrap of paper with a phone number on it.

"Damn," I said. "You're good."

Ranger smiled. "That's what they tell me. Do you recognize the number?"

"No, but it's local."

Ranger called his control room and gave them the number. Two minutes later, the answer came back. The number belonged to Alma Rizzi.

So Dom was using his mother's cell phone, and Zero hadn't wanted to share that information with his partner. He didn't trust himself to remember the number, so he hid it in his shoe. This was quite the group of guys.

I dialed the number, but there was no answer.

"Nothing in the other boot," Ranger said. "I think we've done as much as we can here."

We let ourselves out, took the stairs, crossed the small lobby, and walked to our cars.

"Not much of a date," Ranger said.

"Not true. I got a phone number."

He kissed me on the cheek. "You could have gotten more than a phone number."

"I'll take a rain check."

Morelli remoted the television off when I walked into the house. He stood and stretched. "Well?"

"Someone picked Zero's apartment clean."

"You didn't find anything?"

"No."

Our eyes held for a moment, and he didn't ask anything more and I didn't tell. I trusted Morelli, but he was a cop, after all. And the cops didn't have a good track record on this operation.

It was four in the morning, and I was wide awake, trying not to thrash around and disturb Morelli. I couldn't stop thinking about the fourth partner. He was out there, moving through his day as a normal person. This guy who could kill his friends and mutilate a mother. He did his mundane job and talked sports scores while he drank coffee with his friends. And he was watching Morelli's house and monitoring police action. How was he doing that?

When the bedside clock hit five-thirty, I got dressed in jeans and a T-shirt and sneakers. I went downstairs, made coffee, and dialed Dom. Still no answer. I could hear Morelli moving around upstairs. It was a work-day.

I was pacing when he came into the kitchen.

"What's the special occasion?" he asked. "You're never up this early."

"I couldn't sleep. Loretta will lose her hand today if I don't figure this out."

"It's not your fault."

"I know that. I just don't want it to happen."

"Me, either. I'm still on the gang killings, but Spanner's keeping me in the loop. The Feds are nuts that the op got blown. They're on everyone's ass."

"You went door-to-door, right? You talked to all your neighbors?"

"Everyone on the street. I covered three blocks." He poured coffee into a travel mug and capped it. "I have an early meeting. I'll grab a bagel on the way in." He kissed me on the top of my head. "I have to go. Be careful. This guy is a real crazy. Don't piss him off. I'll try to keep in touch."

I fed Bob and hooked him to his leash. "Time for a walk," I told him.

I knew we were missing something, and walking Bob would give me a chance to look around. The fourth partner was close. He saw the sign intended for Dom. He saw the scarf. And he was the one who broke into Morelli's house and got the key. He knew when Morelli and I left the house to take Grandma home.

I walked two blocks in each direction, several times. The guy was so close, I could practically smell him, but I couldn't put my finger on him.

Zook was eating breakfast when I returned. He looked up expectantly.

"Hang in there," I told him.

"She's okay, isn't she?"

"Yes." Alive is okay, right? Worse things in life than missing a toe or two. I tried to give him a reassuring smile, but I'm not sure I totally pulled it off.

I drove Zook to school and rode around Morelli's block. I cruised by his house and looked up at the second-floor windows. They were visible from the street, but I was having a hard time thinking this guy was constantly driving by. He was squirreled away somewhere, and he could see the house.

I kept a gym bag in the back. It held bounty hunter stuff. Cuffs, shackles, stun gun, Cheez Doodles, flashlight, and binoculars. I grabbed the binoculars out of the bag and brought them into the house. I ran up the stairs and trained the glasses on the houses across the street. I looked in all the windows. I looked at the front yards and the cars parked in front of the houses. I looked over the roofs to see if line of sight carried to any houses on the next block.

I put the binoculars down and pressed my fingers to my eyeballs. Think, Stephanie. What are you missing? There has to be something.

I raised the binoculars again and ran them across the housetops. And there it was . . . a camera. It was positioned on the roof, directly across from Morelli. I don't know how I missed it. I suppose I just wasn't looking for it before.

I called Ranger on my cell.

"I need some technical information," I said to him. "Can you mount a camera somewhere, like on a roof, and access it from somewhere else? I mean, do you need wires and things?"

"No. You can transmit wireless. If you're going a distance, you need relays. Or you can bounce it off a satellite."

"Suppose you want to run it all day, day after day. You'd need a power source, right?"

"Yes. If it was on a roof, you could tie into the house's electric. It would be easy if the house had a dish."

I used the phone in Morelli's office to call him.

"What," he whispered into his phone.

"I've got it."

"I'm in a meeting," he said. "Is this important?"

"Didn't you hear me? *I've got it.* I know how the fourth partner saw the scarf and the sign, and I know how he saw us leave the house to take Grandma home. There's a camera on the roof of the house across from you."

"Are you sure?"

"I'm looking at it through binoculars. Do you know the people who live across from you? Would they put a camera on their roof?"

"Mr. and Mrs. Geary live across from me. They're nice, but they're about a hundred and ten. I can't imagine why they'd have a camera on their roof. I'm stuck in this meeting, but I'll send Spanner over with a tech."

I was cracking my knuckles now because in a couple hours Loretta would lose her hand. I was calling Alma Rizzi's phone every fifteen minutes and no one was answering. The sign was in Morelli's window. Nothing happening with that. The red scarf was on

Morelli's desk. I had no reason to hang it in the window.

I looked up, and Mooner was in the doorway.

"The door was unlocked, so I figured you were open for business," Mooner said.

I had my hand over my heart. "You took me by surprise. Next time, yell when you come into the house."

"I was projecting my aura, but you might have been too distracted to catch it. Probably you were struggling with the feng shui in this room. Major bummer on that one." He looked across the hall. "Where's Zooka-mundo?"

"School."

"Again?"

"Five days a week."

"Whoa. He must be serious about it."

"Have you had breakfast?"

"No. We were all out of Cap'n Crunch. I have my standards, you know. I was hoping the dude had some."

We trekked downstairs, I pawed through Morelli's cupboard, found a half-empty box of Cap'n Crunch, and gave it to Mooner. I brewed a new pot of coffee and turned to see Gary at the back door. I opened the door and Gary came in.

"How long have you been standing there?" I asked him.

"I just got here. I had a dream you were making coffee."

"You dreamed correct," I told him. "Help yourself."

I went to the living room and looked out the window, and Mooner and Gary followed me.

"What are we looking at?" Mooner wanted to know.

"I'm waiting for one of Morelli's partners to show up."

"Cool," Mooner said, sharing the box of Crunch with Gary.

Spanner finally arrived in a blue Fairlane.

"Bummer," Mooner said. "No lights."

"He's not a uniform," I told Mooner. "I have to talk to him. You stay here."

"Homegrown Security on the job," Mooner said. "You can count on Gary and me."

If you knew where to look, you could see the camera from the street. I positioned Spanner as far back as he could go in Morelli's small yard and handed him my binoculars.

"I see it," Spanner said. "It looks like a camera all right."

We walked across the street and Spanner knocked on the Gearys' front door. The door was answered by a little old man still in his pajamas. Spanner introduced himself and asked about the camera.

"You have a camera on your roof," Spanner said.

"What?" Mr. Geary asked.

"A camera."

"Where?"

"On your roof."

Mr. Geary looked confused. "Where's the camera?"

"I'd like permission to take a look at it," Spanner said.

"What do you want to look at?" Mr. Geary asked.

"The camera."

I looked at my watch. This could take a while.

Spanner had it figured out, too. He jumped in with the bottom line. "Okay, thanks," Spanner said to Geary. "Appreciate you letting us take a look at the camera. I'm going to send a tech up there."

"Sure," Mr. Geary said. "Always happy to help the police."

"I need to run," Spanner said to me. "I'm going

to send someone to get the camera. In the meantime, you might want to close your curtains when you get undressed."

Getting caught undressing was the least of my problems. I was counting down to dismemberment. I watched Spanner drive away, and I spotted the news van parked at the end of the block. Brenda was hovering. I couldn't blame her. I understood her problem, and I might have done the same thing. She was trying to make a job for herself. Still, it was annoying.

I paced in the living room, watching for the tech to come get the camera. To pass the time, I called Alma Rizzi's cell phone. And Dom picked up.

"What?" he said.

"Dom?"

"Who's this?"

"It's Stephanie. Don't hang up! I have to talk to you about Loretta."

"What about her?"

"Your partner has amputated two of her toes and sent them here. If I don't give him the garage location by noon, he's going to cut her hand off."

I could hear Dom suck in some breath. "Jesus," he said.

"Morelli isn't involved in this," I told Dom. "It's just me negotiating with your partner, and he's desperate. He wants the money."

"I don't even care about the money anymore," Dom said. "I just want this over. And I want to be the one to talk to him. I want to hear his voice. I want to make sure he isn't going to hurt Loretta anymore."

I didn't trust Dom to keep it together. He wasn't exactly smart, and he wasn't emotionally stable.

"We can call him together," I said. "I can put him on speakerphone, so you can listen, but please let me do the talking. I don't want this screwed up."

"Yeah. You're right. I'd probably screw it up. I want to kill the bastard. I want to rip his eyes out. I want to cut his balls off and shove them down his throat."

"Probably you should do the anger management course that was offered to you," I said to Dom.

"Fuck that. That shit is for pussies. Give me ten minutes. I gotta get a car."

I disconnected Dom, and saw a crime scene van park in front of the Gearys' house. The tech off-loaded a folding ladder, set it against the house, and climbed to the roof.

"You guys stay here," I told Mooner and Gary. "I want to talk to the tech."

I waited on the sidewalk while the tech unbolted the camera and put it in a large evidence bag. He climbed down and walked the camera to the van.

I had his age at late thirties to early forties. He was average height and build. He had brown hair cut short, ears that would lift him off the ground if they caught enough wind, and his eyes were hidden behind Oakleys. He was wearing a wrinkled short-sleeved, collared knit shirt and khakis that were bagged out and creased at the crotch. I was guessing he had no wife, and his mother was either dead or lived out of state.

"What happens to the camera now?" I asked him.

"We'll take it to the shop and have a look at it."

I felt a flash of heat pass through my entire body and my heart jumped in my chest. Major adrenaline rush. It was the voice. I looked down at his shoes. Jackpot.

I was afraid to talk. I didn't trust my voice. I smiled and nodded. "Okay, then," I managed to say.

I backed away and walked stiff-legged across the street. I slipped into Morelli's house and closed and locked the door. I tried to call Morelli on my cell, but my hand was shaking so bad I couldn't get the numbers right. I held my breath and tried again.

"Morelli here," he said.

"It's the crime lab tech," I told him. "He's across the street. He just took the camera down, and I recognized his voice and the shoes. He's the fourth partner."

"Are you sure?"

"Absolutely." Mostly.

"I'm on my way. Where are you?"

"In your house."

"Stay there. Lock the doors. You know where I keep my extra gun?"

"Yes."

"Get it."

"What's going on?" Mooner wanted to know.

"I think the crime lab tech might be Dom's fourth partner. Stay in the house. Morelli is on his way home."

I ran upstairs, got Morelli's gun, and returned to the living room. Mooner was standing guard at a window with his potato bazooka. Gary was behind him with a basket of potatoes.

"We're ready to defend the house," Mooner said.

"Okay," I said, "but don't fire anything off unless I tell you to."

Mooner and Gary saluted.

I shoved Morelli's gun into the waistband of my jeans at the small of my back, and I stood beside Mooner and looked out the window. The gun was cold and hard and uncomfortable. I popped the snap on my jeans, but it didn't help a lot. I removed the gun and shoved it under a couch cushion for safekeeping. It was a semiautomatic Glock, and I didn't actually know how to use it, anyway.

The crime lab tech stowed the ladder and was about to drive off when Dom rolled to a stop in front of Morelli's house. Dom got out and nodded at the tech. The tech got out of his van and crossed to Dom.

Crap!

I didn't know what to do. I had no idea what was being said. I didn't want to rush out and blunder into a perfectly benign conversation, but I also didn't want Dom to disappear, forever.

"Should we shoot them?" Mooner asked.

"No!"

The tech was talking, and Dom was nodding in agreement. Dom gave a quick glance to Morelli's house, took his phone out of his pocket, and punched a number in. Seconds later, my phone rang.

"I need the keys," Dom said.

"That's not a good idea."

"It *is* a good idea."

"At least try to stall him so I can set something up."

"For crissake," Dom said. "Just bring me the keys. He gets the van with the money and I get Loretta."

"Okay, I'll send the keys out, but I'm staying here."

"Whatever," Dom said.

If I was the partner, I'd want a hostage to ensure my escape. And I'd make a better hostage than Loretta, since the lack of toes had to slow her down. I supposed he could take Dom, but I wasn't sure anyone would care.

I retrieved the keys from my purse, opened the front door, and pitched the keys into the street. Dom scuttled over and scooped them up, and both men got into the tech's van and drove off.

I saw the van turn right at the corner, and I sprinted to my car. Mooner and Gary ran with me and jumped into the backseat. Mooner still had his bazooka and Gary had his basket of potatoes. I got to the corner and looked right. They were two blocks in front of me.

"Keep your eyes on the van," I told Mooner and Gary. "I don't want to lose them, but I can't get too close."

The van turned left, into the Burg. This was the logical place for Dom to hide the money. Dom had friends there, and there were lots of unused garages. I looked in my rearview mirror. Brenda's film crew was a car length away. Could it get any worse?

I followed the tech van as it wove through the Burg. It turned into an alley, and I hesitated. I would be clearly visible if I followed. I took a chance and drove down a street running parallel. I waited at the cross street, but the van didn't emerge. Five minutes passed, and still no van. I parked in front of a small corner deli, and we all got out. Brenda and the film crew did the same. Mooner had his potato gun and Gary had his basket of potatoes, and Stephanie had nothing, since the Glock was still under the couch cushion.

I told everyone to stay where they were, out of sight, and not to go into the alley. There were garages on both sides. Hard to tell from where I stood, but I was guessing twelve to sixteen garages in all. The older garages, originally built with the row houses, were singles. The newer garages were two-car. I walked the alley, looking for open garage doors, listening at closed doors. Halfway down the alley, I heard an engine catch. A door to a two-car garage rolled up and a maroon Econoline with Pennsylvania plates jumped out of the garage and turned in my direction. The tech was driving. No sign of Dom. The Econoline roared at me, and I dove between garages to avoid getting hit. He missed me by inches and continued to race down the alley.

"It's him!" I yelled. "It's the fourth partner!"

"No problemo," Mooner said. "Raw russet," he told Gary.

And *phoonf!* Direct hit to the windshield. The van swerved, took out a parked car, ran into the back of the deli, and exploded. Nine million dollars in hundreds shot into the air and floated down, plus the contents of the deli's frozen-food locker.

"Sweet," Mooner said.

"Are you filming?" Brenda yelled to her camera-man. "It's raining money and popsicles!"

And in that instant, Brenda got hit with a family-size frozen pizza. Pepperoni, black olives. It whacked her in the face and knocked her to her knees.

"Ulk," she said. Her eyes rolled into the back of her head, and she went facedown.

The cameraman grabbed her feet, and the sound-man grabbed her under the armpits, and they carried her back to the news truck.

The maroon Econoline was a fireball. Sirens were screaming in the distance. People were running from neighboring houses, scarfing up the money and frozen fish sticks and disappearing back into their homes. Mooner was running everywhere, stuffing hundred-dollar bills into his pants and his shirt.

I looked down the alley, and saw Dom jogging my way.

"Are you okay?" I asked him.

"I'm better than okay. I'm fucking fabulous. The so-novabitch blew himself up."

"You were in the garage a long time."

"The battery was dead," Dom said. "We had to give it a jump start."

"I thought the key disabled the bomb. Why did it explode?"

Dom was grinning. "I don't know. I'm guessing it just went off when the van rammed into the deli. The asshole should have moved the boxes of money to a different car before he took off, but he was in a rush to get away. Tell you the truth, I was practically crap-ping in my pants, giving the van a jump. Allen was the one who rigged the bomb, and between you and me, Allen wasn't the sharpest tack on the board."

"Did you find out about Loretta?"

"She's in the basement of the lab guy's house. He lives two blocks from Morelli. He said she's okay."

I jogged back to the deli with Dom and stuffed him into my car. Brenda was on her feet, with a big Band-Aid across her nose and tissues stuffed up her nostrils, and she was interviewing Mooner. Gary was rocked back on his heels, smiling. His prophecy had come true. The only thing left was the business about Brenda sitting on a toilet on Route 1, and I was hoping I wouldn't be around for that one.

I was moving the car so the fire trucks could get better access and saw Morelli fly in with his roof light flashing. I pulled alongside him.

"We're all okay," I said. "The fourth partner was in the van with the money. It looks like a lot of the money survived. I don't think the lab tech made it."

"What about Loretta?"

"The lab tech told Dom she's locked away in his basement."

"I've got his address," Morelli said. "Spanner fed me the information on my way over. The tech's name is Steve Fowler, and besides being a crime scene tech, he also did some moonlighting as security at the bank ten years ago."

I followed Morelli and we wound through the Burg and took a left into Morelli's neighborhood. He parked in front of a row house that looked like all the other row houses on the street. Two stories. Small front yard. Neat but unexceptional. No indication that a killer lived inside.

We all piled out of our cars and went to the door. We all looked a little grim. We weren't sure what we'd find. Amputation isn't pretty. And for that matter, we weren't convinced Loretta was still alive.

Morelli tried the door. Locked, of course. He moved to a window. Also locked. He put his elbow to it, and it shattered. He cleared some glass away, opened the window, and went in. He opened the door for us and told everyone to stay in the foyer. He drew his gun and moved to the cellar door.

Dom and I were silent, gnawing on our lower lips, barely breathing. A couple minutes passed, and there were footsteps on the cellar stairs, and next thing, Loretta was standing there in front of us. She was pale and shaking and her hair was snarled. She was crying and laughing. Borderline hysteria.

We all stared at her feet and hands. No big bandages. No sign of amputation.

"You have all your toes," I said to her.

She looked down at herself. "Yeah," she said. "What do you mean?"

"He said he chopped off two toes. I saw them."

"Not mine," Loretta said.

I looked at Morelli, and Morelli shrugged. He hadn't a clue who belonged to the toes.

It was six o'clock, and we were all in front of the television eating meatball subs, tuned in to the news. Mooner, Gary, Zook, Loretta, Dom, Morelli, Bob, and me. Lula had declined in favor of a night with her big Honey Pot. The party was thrown by Mooner with money he'd collected when the Econoline exploded. Mooner'd given twenty thousand to Loretta and Zook, ten thousand to the animal shelter so they could offer free cat-spaying, and he'd bought a very used mellow yellow Corvette with the remaining money. True, the money was slightly illegal, but hell, this was Mooner we were talking about. Almost *everything* he did was slightly illegal.

Brenda's theme song came up, and we all sat forward. Brenda popped onto the screen wearing a low scoop-neck sweater and a tiny skirt. She had two black eyes and a Band-Aid on her nose.

"Here I am with an exclusive on the nine-million-dollar-mystery conclusion," Brenda said. "You'll have to excuse my appearance, as I was in a freak pizza accident."

There was film of the maroon Econoline going out of control, crashing into the deli, and exploding. And then Brenda was on film with the tissues up her nose. "And here we have an interview with the man who took down the vicious criminal responsible for murder, mayhem, and kidnapping."

The camera panned to Mooner, and everyone in Morelli's living room yelled and whistled.

"Tell us exactly how you did it," Brenda said, pointing the mic at Mooner.

"It was with my potato rocket," Mooner said, looking into the camera. "And my munitions man, Gary, deserves some credit for giving me exactly the right potato."

The camera returned to Brenda. "There you have it," she said. "Another exclusive from Brenda. And, sadly for you, but happily for me, this is my last piece of news on this station. I'm going national with my own reality show. And I'm cohosting the show with my very own stalker and psychic, Gary."

There was more whistling and cheering on our part, and Gary took a bow.

Dom stood and raised a bottle of beer. "Now that all this is over and Loretta's safe, I want to say, let bygones be bygones, and I still think Morelli's a piece of shit for getting Loretta pregnant and walking away, but I'm not gonna kill him like I planned."

Loretta looked up at Dom. "What the heck are you talking about? Morelli isn't Mario's father. Morelli was a jerk. I wouldn't have anything to do with him."

"Then who's the father?" Dom wanted to know.

"It was Lenny Garvis. I got pregnant the night before he died. I didn't want to make a big deal about it. Mario always knew, but I didn't tell anyone else."

Lenny Garvis! He was in Morelli's class. Two years ahead of me and mentally a few years behind. I remembered his death. The idiot choked on a peanut butter and banana sandwich. I mean, how could you possibly choke on a peanut butter sandwich?

Dom wasn't convinced. "I saw you in the garage with Morelli."

"That wasn't me," Loretta said. "That was Jenny Ragucci. She was *such* a slut."

Morelli smiled. "It could have been Jenny Ragucci. That makes much more sense. I had good luck with sluts."

I looked over at him.

"All in the past," Morelli said. "I'm a cupcake man now."

"Whoa, dude," Mooner said. "That's so, like, *cosmic*."

FINGER
LICKIN'
FIFTEEN

This book is dedicated to Lauren Tsai

Thanks to Ann and Chris Duffy
for suggesting the title for this book.

ONE

When I was a kid, I was afraid of spiders and vegetables. As an adult, I've eliminated vegetables from my fright-o-meter, but I've added a whole bunch of other stuff. Homicidal maniacs, serial rapists, cellulite, Joe Morelli's Grandma Bella, rabid bats, and any form of organized exercise.

My name is Stephanie Plum, and I work as a bond enforcement officer for Vincent Plum Bail Bonds. It's not a great job, but it allows me to avoid organized exercise, and I hardly ever encounter rabid bats. The remaining fright-o-meter items lurk in the dark shadows of my daily life. Fortunately, there are also good things in those shadows. Joe Morelli without his Grandma Bella, fellow bounty hunter Ranger without his clothes, my crazy family, my hamster, Rex . . . and Lula. Lula actually fits somewhere between the rabid bats and the good stuff. She's a former 'ho, now working as the office file clerk and apprentice bounty hunter. Lula's got a plus-size personality and body, and a petite-size wardrobe. She's got brown skin, blond hair, and last week she had tiny rhinestones pasted onto her eyelids.

It was Monday morning. Connie, the office manager, and I were in the bonds office enjoying our morning coffee, and Lula slid her red Firebird to a stop at the curb. We watched Lula through the big plate-glass window in the front of the small office, and we did a joint grimace. Lula was in a state. She lurched out of the Firebird, beeped it locked, and burst into the office, her eyes wild, rolling around in their sockets, her hands waving in the air.

"I saw it all," she said. "It was terrible. It was horrible. I couldn't believe it was happening. And right in front of me." She looked around. "What do we got? Do we got doughnuts? 'Cause I need a doughnut. I need a whole bag. And maybe I need one of them breakfast sandwiches with the egg and cheese and bacon and grease. I got a big grease craving."

I knew it would be a huge mistake to ask Lula what she'd seen, but I couldn't stop myself.

"What was terrible and horrible?" I asked.

Connie leaned forward, elbows on her desk, already knowing the telling of the story would be a car crash. Connie is a couple years older than me, and while my heritage is half Hungarian and half Italian, Connie is Italian through and through. Her hair is jet black, her lipstick is fire-engine red, her body is *va-va-voom*.

Lula paced in front of Connie's desk. "First off, I hardly had time for anything this morning. I had a big date last night, and by the time I booted his butt out of my bed, I already missed a lot of my beauty sleep. Anyways, I got up late, and then I couldn't decide what to wear. One day it's hot out and next thing it's cold. And then I had to decide if I needed to wear shoes that kicked ass or were good for ass kicking, on account of there's a difference, you know."

"Jeez Louise," Connie said. "Could you get to it?"

"The point bein' I was late," Lula said. "I was tryin' to put makeup on and drive, and I missed a turn, and before I knew it I was someplace I didn't want to be. So I pulled over to look around and figure things out, and when I did that my makeup case rolled off the seat next to me, and everything went all over the floor. So I was bent over to get my makeup, and I guess it looked like there was no one in the car, because when I came back up there were two big hairy morons standing right in front of my Firebird, and they were removing a head from some guy's body."

"Excuse me?"

"This one moron had a giant meat cleaver. And the other moron had a hold of this man in a suit. And *whack*! No head. The head popped off its neck and bounced down the street."

"And then what happened?" Connie said.

"Then they saw me," Lula said. "They looked real surprised. And I know *I* looked real surprised. And then I laid down about two feet of rubber and took off."

"Do you know who they were?"

"No."

"Did you know the guy in the suit?"

"No, but it was a real nice suit. And he had a nice striped tie, too."

"Did you go to the police?" Connie asked.

"No. I came straight here. It's not like the police were gonna put Humpty Dumpty back together again," Lula said. "Didn't seem like there was a big rush, and I needed a doughnut. Holy cow. Holy shit. I really need a doughnut."

"You need to call the police," Connie told Lula.

"I hate the police. They give me the willies. Except for Stephanie's Morelli. He's a hottie."

Joe Morelli is a Trenton plainclothes cop, and Lula is right about Morelli being a hottie, but Lula is wrong about Morelli belonging to me. Morelli and I have had an off-and-on relationship for as long as I can remember, and we are currently off. Two weeks ago, we had a disagreement over peanut butter that turned into a disagreement over everything under the sun, and we haven't seen each other since.

Connie dialed into the police band, and we listened for a couple minutes to see if we could pick up anything to do with decapitation.

"Where did this happen?" Connie asked.

"The three hundred block of Ramsey Street. It was right in front of the Sunshine Hotel."

The Sunshine Hotel is a roach farm that rents rooms by the hour. No one coming or going from the Sunshine Hotel would ever report anything to anyone.

"I seen lots of stuff," Lula said, "but this was disgustin'. Blood shot out like one of them oil gushers. And when the head hit the ground, I swear the eyes were lookin' at me. I guess I need to tell the police, but I only want Morelli." Lula fixed on me. "You gotta call Morelli."

"No way. I'm not talking to him. *You* can call him."

"I don't know him like you know him."

"I don't know him that way anymore. I'm done with him. He's a jerk."

"All men are jerks," Lula said. "That don't mean they aren't good for some things. And Morelli's a *hot* jerk. He could be a movie star or a underwear model if he wasn't a cop. He got all that wavy black hair and dreamy brown bedroom eyes. He's kind of puny compared to some men I know, but he's hot all the same."

Morelli was actually six foot tall and solid muscle, but Lula used to be engaged to a guy who was a cross between an Army tank and Sasquatch, so I suppose by comparison Morelli might measure up short.

"I'll call Morelli," Connie said. "He's a cop, for crying out loud. You don't need a complicated relationship to call a cop."

I was halfway to the door. "I'm leaving. Things to do. And I don't want to see Morelli."

"Oh no," Lula said. "You get your boney ass back here. We're in this together. Through thick and through thin."

"Since when?"

"Since now. And before that, too. Remember when I rescued you from that big snake in the mobile home? And what about when we were lost in the Pine Barrens?"

"You ran screaming like a little girl when you *thought* you saw the snake. And Ranger found us in the Pine Barrens."

"Yeah, but if he hadn't found us, I would have got us out."

"You were up to your armpits in a cranberry bog."

"I don't never want to see another cranberry, neither," Lula said.

Twenty minutes later, Morelli sauntered in to the bonds office. He was dressed in jeans and running shoes, a blue button-down shirt that was open at the neck, and a navy blazer. He looked entirely edible and a little wary.

"What's up?" Morelli asked, eyes on me.

Okay, so I was no longer interested in Morelli. At least I was pretty sure I wasn't interested. Still, I was wishing I'd spent more time on my hair and makeup this morning, so he'd feel really rotten about what he was missing. I have naturally curly shoulder-length brown hair that was currently pulled back into a ponytail. I have blue eyes that look a lot better when they have a swipe of liner and mascara, an okay mouth that so far hasn't needed artificial plumping, and a little nose that I consider my best feature. Morelli always thought my best feature was located considerably lower on my body.

"It was horrible! It was terrible!" Lula said. "I almost fainted."

Morelli shifted his attention to Lula. He didn't say anything, but he looked over at her and raised his eyebrows a little.

"I never saw nothin' like it," Lula told him. "One minute, I was having a day like any other, and then *whack* and this guy didn't have no head. And blood came out of him like he was a fountain. And when his head hit the ground, his eyes were lookin' at me. And I think the head might have smiled at me, too, but I'm not sure of that."

Morelli was back on his heels, thumbs hooked into his jeans pockets. "Is this for real?"

"Hell yeah," Lula said. "Who makes up shit like that? Don't I look traumatized? I'm practically turned white. I think my hand might even be shaking. Look at my hand. Is it shaking?"

Morelli's eyes cut back to me. "Were you with her?"

"Nope."

"Did anyone call 911?"

"Nope."

Lula was hands on hips, starting to look pissed. "We called *you*," she said to Morelli.

Morelli did a fast office scan. "You don't have the head here, do you?"

"So far as I know, the head and everything else is still in front of the Sunshine Hotel," Lula told him. "And I'm not sure I like your attitude. I'm not sure you're takin' this seriously."

Morelli stared down at his shoe. Hard to tell if he was trying hard not to laugh or if he was getting a migraine. After a five-count, he took out his cell phone, called dispatch, and sent a uniform to the Sunshine Hotel.

"Okay, ladies," Morelli said when he got off the phone. "Let's take a field trip."

I made a big show of looking at my watch. "Gee, I've got to run. Things to do."

"No way," Lula said. "I need someone with me in case I get faint or something."

"You'll have *him*," I said.

"He's a fine man, but he's the cop representative here, and I need someone from my posse, you see what I'm saying. I need a BFF."

"It's not gonna be me," Connie said. "Vinnie is picking up a skip in Atlanta, and I have to run the office."

Morelli looked at me and gave his head a small shake, like he didn't believe any of this. Like I was a huge, unfathomable pain in the ass, and in fact maybe that was how he felt about women in general right now.

I understood Morelli's point of view because it was precisely my current feeling about men.

"Terrific," I said on a sigh. "Let's get on with it."

Lula and I followed Morelli in my ten-year-old Ford Escort that used to be blue. We didn't take the Escort because we liked riding in it. We took it because Lula thought she might be too overwrought to drive her Firebird, and she suspected she would need a bacon cheeseburger after visiting the scene of the crime and Morelli might not be inclined to find a drive-through for her.

There were already two cruisers angled into the curb in front of the Sunshine Hotel when Lula and I arrived. I parked, and Lula and I got out and stood next to Morelli and a couple uniforms. We all looked down at a red splotch that sprayed out over about a four-foot diameter. A couple smaller splotches trailed off the big splotch, and I assumed that was where the head had hit the pavement. I felt a wave of nausea slide through my stomach, and I started to sweat.

"This here's the spot," Lula said. "You can see it's just like I told you. There was a big gusher of blood when they whacked the head off. It was like Old Faithful going off, only it was blood. And then the head rolled down the sidewalk. It was like the head was a bowlin' ball with eyes. And the eyes were like big googly eyes kinda popping out of the head and lookin' at me. And I think I might have heard the head laughin', or maybe it was the guys who did the whackin' who were laughin'."

The uniforms all did a grimace, Morelli was impassive, and I threw up. Everyone jumped away from me, I gagged one last time and did some deep breathing.

"Sorry," I said.

"No problem," Morelli told me. "I feel like throwing up a lot on this job."

One of the uniforms brought me some paper towels and a bottle of water, and Lula stood a good distance away.

"You got lots of room for lunch now that you're empty," she yelled to me. "I could get a early start with one of them extra-crispy bird burgers they're servin' at Cluck-in-a-Bucket. Have you heard about them? They got some new secret sauce."

I wasn't interested in secret sauce. I wanted to go home and go to bed and not get up until it was a new day. I was done with this one.

"We got a couple footprints heading south," a uniform said. "One of these guys had real big feet. Looks like a size fourteen. And there's some skid marks where they dragged the body to the curb. Imagine they dumped it into a car and took off."

"You need to come downtown and give me some information," Morelli said to Lula.

"No way. Nuh-ah. I got a allergic reaction to police stations. I get irritable bowel and hives and the heebie-jeebies."

"You witnessed a murder."

"Yeah, but there's extenuating circumstances here. I got a medical condition. I got a extreme sensitivity to cops."

Morelli looked like he wanted to pull his gun out of its holster and shoot himself.

"I'll get you some cheeseburgers and a side of onion rings," he said to Lula.

Lula stood hands on hips. "You think I could be bought for some lame-ass burgers? What kinda woman you think I am?"

"I'll throw in a bucket of chicken and an ice cream cake from Carvel," Morelli said. "That's my final offer."

"Deal," Lula told him. "We goin' in your car? On account of I'm not riding in a cop car, and I hate to say this, but Stephanie don't smell too good."

Twenty minutes later, I parked in the lot to my apartment building. My building straddles the line between Trenton proper and Trenton improper. It's a three-story utilitarian brick box filled with tenants who are struggling to make ends meet. Frequently, I have a gap between my ends, resulting in a lot of dinners mooched from my parents, who live ten minutes away in a blue-collar chunk of Trenton called The Burg.

My apartment is on the second floor and my windows look out at the parking lot. My only roommate is a hamster named Rex. I manage to keep a good supply of hamster food in my fridge and in my cupboards. People food is spotty. I own a fry pan and a pot. Perfectly adequate since I mostly eat peanut butter sandwiches. Peanut butter and banana, peanut butter and jelly, peanut butter and potato chips, peanut butter and olives, and peanut butter and marshmallow goo. So sue me, I like peanut butter. The rest of the apartment consists of dining alcove, living room with television, one bedroom, and bath.

I hustled from my car to my apartment, stripped, and jumped into the shower. I was approaching boiled lobster skin tone when I finally emerged and wrapped myself in a towel. I stepped out of the bathroom and spotted Ranger lounging in the club chair across from my bed. I gave a startled yelp and jumped back into the bathroom.

"Babe," Ranger said.

I stuck my head out and looked at him. "What are you doing here?"

"I need to talk to you."

"You could have called. Or how about ringing my doorbell?"

Ranger looked like he was thinking about smiling. His attention focused on the top of my towel and slowly moved to the bottom hem that hung a half-inch below my doodah. His brown eyes dilated black, and I took a stronger grip on my towel.

Ranger was the second biggest complication in my life, and now that Morelli was out of the picture, I supposed Ranger was elevated to numero uno. He's close to six foot, one way or the other, is Latino, with medium brown skin and dark brown hair cut short. His teeth are white and even, and he has a killer smile that is seen only on special occasions. He dresses in black, and today he was wearing a black T-shirt and black cargo pants. His given name is Carlos Manoso. His street name, Ranger, is a holdover from time spent in Special Forces. These days, he does the occasional high-risk bond enforcement job, and is the managing partner of a security firm located in a stealth building in center city. I've seen him naked, and you can take it to the bank when I tell you he's all hard muscle and perfect in every possible way. And I mean *every* possible way.

Ranger and I have three things in common. We're the same age. We're both single. And we both were previously married for about ten seconds. That's where the common ground ends. I'm an open book with a lot of blank pages. His book is filled with life experience but written in disappearing ink. I have three locks on my front door, plus a sliding bolt, and I was sure they were all in place. Somehow, this never stops Ranger. He's a man of mysterious talents.

Ranger crooked his finger at me. "Come here."

"No way."

"Afraid?"

"Cautious."

"That's no fun," Ranger said.

"I didn't know you were interested in fun."

There was a very slight curve to the corners of his mouth. "I have my moments."

I had a big, cuddly pink robe in my closet, but I had to cross in front of Ranger to get to it. I wasn't worried Ranger would jump me. My fear was that if I got too close, I'd get sucked into his force field, and I'd jump *him*. And jumping Ranger was a dangerous deal. He'd made it clear that his emotional involvement would always have limitations. Plus, there was Morelli. Morelli was currently out of the picture, but he'd been out before, and he'd always slid back in. Getting naked with Ranger would make a reconciliation with Morelli much more difficult. Of course, that wasn't currently an issue, because I wasn't in a mood to reconcile anything.

"What did you want to talk to me about?" I asked him.

"Three of my clients have been robbed in the last

two months. All three had state-of-the-art security systems. And in all three cases the systems were shut down for exactly fifteen minutes and then reactivated. My clients weren't home at the time. There was no sign of physical tampering."

"I see them using gizmos in the movies that can figure out codes."

"This isn't a movie. This is real life."

"Someone hacked into your system?"

"No."

"That leaves an unpleasant possibility," I said to Ranger.

"In theory, there are only a few people in my organization who have access to the codes, and I can't imagine any of those men being involved in this. For that matter, *everyone* I employ is rigorously screened. Plus, the entire building, with the exception of private living spaces, is monitored twenty-four hours."

"Have you changed the codes?"

"I changed them after each break-in."

"Wow."

"Yeah," Ranger said. "Someone on the inside is beating my system."

"Why are you telling this to me?"

"I need you to come in and snoop around without raising suspicion. I can't trust anyone already inside."

"Even Tank?"

"Even Tank."

Tank is exactly what his name would imply. He's big and solid inside and out. He's second in command at Rangeman, and he's the guy who watches Ranger's back.

"You've worked for me before doing computer searches, and that's where I'd like to put you again. Ramon has been doing the searches, but he'd like to get out of the cubby and back on the street. You'd be working on the fifth floor in the control room, but you'd have total access within the building. Every man in my organization knows you and understands that you're my personal property, so they're not going to talk freely when you're around, but they're also not going to think I hired you to snoop. They'll assume I gave you the job to have you close to me."

"Personal property?"

"Babe, you're the only one who would question it."

I narrowed my eyes at him. "I am *not* personal property. A car is personal property. A shirt is personal property. A human being is not personal property."

"In my building, we share cars and shirts. We don't share women. In my building, you're my personal property. Deal with it."

At a later time, when I was alone and had given it some thought, I'd probably find the flaw in that reasoning, but oddly enough it made sense at the moment.

"What about my cases at the bonds office?" I asked him.

"I'll help you."

This was a really good deal, because I was a crappy bounty hunter and Ranger was the best. Not to mention I'd be drawing salary from Rangeman. All I had to do was keep my hands off Ranger and everything would be peachy.

"Okay," I said. "When do you want me to start?"

"Now. Do you have uniforms left from the last time you worked for me?"

"I have a couple T-shirts, and I have some black jeans."

"Good enough. I'll have Ella order some more."

Ella and her husband, Louis, serve as live-in property managers for Rangeman. They keep the building clean and running efficiently, and they keep the men fed and clothed. They're both in their early fifties, and

Ella is dark-haired, and dark-eyed, and pretty in a no-nonsense kind of way.

"I assume you still have your key fob?" Ranger asked.

"Yep."

The key fob got me into the high-security Rangeman building, and it also got me into Ranger's private seventh-floor apartment. In the past, I'd used the apartment when I felt I was in danger. It wasn't a move I made lightly, because I had to weigh the danger at hand against the danger of living with Ranger.

Ranger's cell phone buzzed, and he looked at the screen. "I have to go," he said. "Tank and Ramon are expecting you. Ramon will bring you up to speed and then you should be able to take over. You know the drill." His eyes moved from my face to the towel and then back to my face. "Tempting," he said. And he left.

TWO

I dried my hair and put on makeup that stopped just short of slut. I dressed in black jeans and one of the black V-neck stretchy girl-type T-shirts I had left from my last stint at Rangeman. I topped the T-shirt with a black Rangeman hooded sweatshirt, grabbed my bag, and headed out.

I stopped at the bonds office on my way to Rangeman. Connie was alone when I walked in.

"Oh crap," Connie said, eyeballing my outfit. "You aren't quitting again, are you?"

"No. The Rangeman job is temporary."

"What about the stack of skips I gave you last week?"

"Ranger is going to help me."

"My lucky day," Connie said.

"Have you heard anything from Lula?"

"She called to say she was on her way back to the office, and she had a bucket of chicken."

That was worth the wait. I could get lunch at Rangeman, but it would be tuna salad on multigrain bread, and it would be made with fat-free mayo. And for dessert, I could score an apple. Ranger encouraged healthy eating. Truth is, Ranger was a tyrant. If you worked at Rangeman, you had to be physically strong, mentally tough, loyal without question, and survive random drug tests. I was exempt from all those things, and that was a good deal, because the only one I could fly through was the drug test.

I saw Morelli's green SUV pull to the curb and make a Lula drop. Lula slammed the passenger-side door closed and waved Morelli off as best she could considering her arms were filled with fast-food buckets and bags and drink holders. She used her ass to push open the door to the bonds office and crossed to Connie's desk to dump her food.

"I got that done and over," Lula said. "And it wasn't so bad as I expected, on account of while I was there the head came in, so that speeded up a lot of stuff."

Connie leaned forward a little. "The head came in?"

"Yeah. One of the camera dudes at the television station went outside to smoke, and when he opened the back door, he saw a head sitting by the Dumpster. And here's the best part. This guy recognized the head right off. Turns out the head belongs to Stanley Chipotle."

"The celebrity chef?"

"Yep. He's on The Food Channel all the time. I don't know why I didn't recognize him. Guess I'm used to seeing him in his chef's clothes. You know how he wears that puffy chef hat, and lately, he's always got on the red apron advertising his barbecue sauce. Anyway, they brought the head in, and I identified it, and then Morelli said I could go home." Lula opened the bucket of chicken and dug in. "Help yourself," she said. "There's plenty."

Connie poked around in the bucket, looking for a recognizable chicken part. "What was Chipotle doing in Trenton? Did anyone know?"

"The camera dude said Chipotle was supposed to be in a big-deal national barbecue cook-off that's gonna be held at Gooser Park. He was gonna be talking about it on the station's cooking show this afternoon, but since only his head showed up, they got someone from Dawn Diner to make rice pudding instead."

"Chipotle's famous for his barbecue sauce," Connie said.

I polished off a mystery chicken part and selected another. I was out of the loop. I never watched The Food Channel, and I didn't do a lot of cooking. Mostly, I mooched food from my parents.

"What are you doing dressed up like Rangegirl?" Lula asked me.

"I'm temporarily filling in on a desk job." I glanced at my watch. "I need to run. Ramon is waiting for me."

Rangeman is housed in a small office building on a side street in center city Trenton. The inside has been renovated into a high-tech, self-contained, secure corporate Batcave that operates 24/7. Ranger's private apartment occupies the top floor. Ella and Louis live on the sixth floor. The control room, dining area, and assorted offices are located on the fifth floor. And the remaining space is given over to efficiency apartments made available to some of the Rangeman employees, a gym, a gun range, meeting rooms, and more offices. The exterior façade of the building is nondescript, with only a small brass nameplate beside the front door to tell the world this is Rangeman.

I used my key fob to access the underground garage. I parked and fobbed my way into the elevator and up to the fifth floor. There were three uniformed men in the control room, watching monitors, and four men were in the kitchen area. All eyebrows raised when I stepped out of the elevator. I smiled and gave everyone a small wave and went directly to Ramon's cubicle.

"Hallelujah," Ramon said when he saw me. "I'm

going back out into the land of the living. I hate this cubicle. The sun doesn't shine in here. There isn't even a window. After a half hour at this desk, I've got a cramp in my ass."

Ramon had dark hair, dark eyes, and dark skin, and eyelashes I'd kill for. He was a couple inches taller than me, and looked to be around my age. He had pierced ears but no earrings. Rangeman employees weren't allowed jewelry other than a watch when they were on the job.

"How did you get behind the computer in the first place? I thought you were a car guy."

"I got a speeding ticket, and Ranger stuck me here. This is like the dunce desk. I was lucky I didn't get fired."

Great. I was working the dunce desk.

"What did you do to deserve this?" Ramon asked me.

"I needed extra money, and this is what Ranger had available."

"Gotta pay the bills," Ramon said. "Let me show you what I've got on my desktop."

An hour later, I was on my own. A variety of searches passed through this position. There were background searches on employees and prospective clients, searches for outsourced services, plus security searches requested by clients.

Some of it was interesting, but after an hour of staring at the screen, it all grew monotonous. By five o'clock, I had a cramp in my ass. I put my computer to sleep and walked the short distance down the hall to Ranger's office.

"Knock, knock," I said.

Ranger looked up at me. "Babe."

"I have a cramp in my ass."

"I could kiss it and make it better."

"I was thinking more along the line of a new chair," I told him.

"Tell Louis. He'll get you whatever you want. Do you have plans for tonight?"

"No."

"Hang out for another hour. I want to talk to you, but I need to go through this paperwork first."

A little after six, Ranger ambled into my cubicle and collected me.

"Ella has dinner ready upstairs," he said. "We can eat and talk."

There was a time, not too long ago, when Ranger's address was a vacant lot. It turns out besides being a very tough guy, he's also a very smart businessman, and he now lives in an extremely upscale one-bedroom inner sanctum of civilized calm. The apartment was tastefully decorated by a professional, and is now maintained by Ella. The furniture is comfortable contemporary. Leather, chrome, dark woods, with earth-tone accents. It's clearly masculine but not overpowering. The apartment feels surprisingly warm in spite of the fact that there are no personal touches. No family photographs. No favorite books stacked at bedside. No clutter. I've spent a reasonable amount of time in Ranger's apartment, and I've always thought it was a place where he slept but didn't live. I've never been able to find the place he would call *home*. Maybe it doesn't exist. Maybe he carries it inside him. Or maybe it's a place he hasn't yet discovered.

We were silent in the elevator and small foyer that preceded Ranger's apartment. He fobbed his door open, and I stepped into the hall, with its subdued lighting and plush carpet. Ranger dropped his keys onto a small silver tray on the sideboard and followed me to the kitchen. His appliances were top-of-the-line stainless. His countertops were granite. Ella kept everything immaculate. I lifted the lid to the blue Le Creuset casserole dish on the stovetop. Chicken, rice, spicy sausage, and vegetables.

"This smells wonderful," I said to Ranger. "You're lucky to have Ella."

"If I can't stop these break-ins, I'm not going to have Ella or anyone else."

"What about security cameras? Weren't any of the thefts caught on tape?"

"All the burglaries were residential with no cameras in place." Ranger poured out two glasses of wine and handed one to me. "Without going into detail, I can tell you there are a lot of safeguards in the system to prevent this from happening."

"But it happened anyway."

"Three times."

"Is there anyone you especially want me to watch?"

"Martin Beam is the newest man in the building. He's been with me for seven months. Chester Rodriguez and Victor Zullick were on deck for all three break-ins. There are four men who rotate shifts monitoring the code computer. Beyond that, I have nothing."

"You've done recent background checks?"

"So far as I can tell, none of my men are in trouble, financial or otherwise."

I ladled the stew onto plates, Ranger cut into a loaf of bread set out on a breadboard, and we took our wine and plates of food to the table, where Ella had laid out placemats and silverware.

"Do you think this is someone needing money?" I asked Ranger. "Or do you think it's someone trying to ruin you?"

"Hard to tell, but if I had to choose, I'd go with trying to ruin me."

"That's ugly."

Ranger selected a slice of bread. "The men I hire

aren't stupid. They have to know stealing the codes will end badly, and the items and cash taken can't compensate them for the risk. They'd be better off stealing from an ATM."

"Was there a pattern to the break-ins?"

Ranger refilled my wineglass. "Only that they all happened at night."

I've never known Ranger to have more than one glass of wine or beer. And usually, he didn't finish his first glass. Ranger never placed himself in a position of weakness. He sat with his back to the wall, and he was always sober. I, on the other hand, from time to time slipped into dangerous waters and counted on Ranger to scoop me out.

"So," I said to him. "If I drink this second glass of wine, will you drive me home?"

"Babe, you have no alcohol tolerance. If you drink a second glass of wine, you won't *want* to go home."

I blew out a sigh and pushed the glass away. He was right. "I have five open cases that need immediate attention," I told him. "You said you would help me."

"Do you have the files with you?"

I went to the kitchen and retrieved my bag from the counter, handed the five files over to Ranger, and returned to my place at the table.

Ranger paged through the files while he ate.

"You have two armed robberies, one exhibitionist, a mid-level drug dealer, and an arsonist," he said. "The dealer is a no-brainer. Kenny Hatcher. Better known as Marbles. I know where he works. He deals from the six hundred block of Stark Street."

"I've been checking. He isn't there."

"He's there. You just aren't seeing him."

I stared down at my dinner plate and wineglass. Empty. Damn. "Someone drank my wine," I said to Ranger.

"That would be you."

I looked around. "Do we have dessert?"

"No."

Big surprise. Ranger *never* had dessert.

"Why can't I see my drug dealer?" I asked him.

Ranger leaned back in his chair and watched me. The lion assessing his prey. "He's using a runner," Ranger said. "If you want to find Hatcher, you have to follow the runner."

"How do I recognize the runner?"

"You pay attention."

"Okay, I'll give it another shot," I said, pushing away from the table, taking the files from Ranger. "I'm going to Stark Street."

I started to leave, and Ranger snagged me by the back of my shirt and dragged me up against him.

"Let me get this straight," he said. "You're going to Stark Street *now*?"

"Yeah."

"Alone?"

"Yeah."

"I don't think so."

"Why not?"

Ranger smiled down at me. I was amusing him.

"I can think of at least a half-dozen reasons," he said. "Not the least of which is you'll be the only one on Stark Street not carrying a gun. It'll be like open season on Plum pudding."

"I can take care of myself," I told him.

"Maybe, but I can take care of you better."

No argument there.

THREE

A half hour later, Ranger and I were parked on the six hundred block of Stark Street. Stark Street starts down by the river, cuts through the center of the city, and runs straight to hell. Storefronts are grimy, decorated with gang graffiti and the accumulated grit of day-to-day life in the breakdown lane. Hookers stake out corners, knots of kids going nowhere strut the street, men chain-smoke in doorways, and pushers work the sidewalks.

Ranger was behind the wheel of a shiny black Cadillac Escalade with tinted windows and fancy chrome wheel covers. No one could see us sitting in the SUV, and we were left unmolested as a sign of respect by the general population of Stark Street, who assumed the car belonged to contract killers, badass hip-hop gangsters, or high-level drug dealers.

The sun had set, but there was ambient light from streetlights and headlights and doors opening into bars. Enough light to determine that Marbles wasn't on the street.

"I don't see anyone who looks like a runner," I said to Ranger.

"The kid in the oversize sweatshirt, white T-shirt, and homeboy jeans."

"How do you know?"

"He's making deals."

"And?"

"And this block belongs to Marbles. The kid would be dead if he wasn't working for Marbles. Marbles isn't a charitable kind of guy."

"Maybe Marbles sold his real estate and left town."

"Not his style. He's in one of these buildings, conducting business. Besides owning drugs on the six hundred block, he also manages a couple hookers. Marbles read the memo on diversification. I ran into him two years ago, and he was operating an all-night dog-grooming and cockfighting operation. The cockfighting didn't involve poultry."

It took me a couple beats to figure that out. And even then, how the heck did a guy go about it? Was it like thumb wrestling? I was debating asking about the rules and regulations of cockfighting, but just then the kid in the sweatshirt ambled into a building halfway down the block.

"He's going back to the mother ship," Ranger said.

Mostly, Stark Street is filled with narrow redbrick town houses, two to four stories tall. Small businesses in varying degrees of failure occupy ground floors, and the upper floors are given over to cramped apartments and rented rooms. At odd intervals on the street, you might find a garage or a warehouse or a funeral home. The kid went into a four-story brick town house. All the windows had been painted black.

Ranger and I left the Escalade, crossed the street, and followed the kid into the building. The foyer was dimly lit by a bare bulb in an overhead fixture, the walls were entirely covered with graffiti. A door labeled HEAD MOTHERFUCKER opened off the foyer.

Ranger and I exchanged glances and went directly to the Head Motherfucker door. Ranger pushed the door open, and we looked inside at what at one time had probably been an efficiency apartment but was now a rat's nest office. The desk was piled high with papers, empty fast-food boxes, a laptop computer, a multiline phone, and two half-filled cups of coffee. There was a chair behind the desk and a two-seater leather couch against a wall. Nobody home.

We left the office, closing the door behind us. We returned to the foyer and took the stairs to the second floor, where a dull-eyed wannabe junior gangsta sat on a plastic lawn chair. He was hooked up to an MP3 player, and he had a small wooden table beside him. There was a cigar box and a roll of tickets on the table.

"Yuh?" he said. "You want a ticket for the night or just for a run-through?"

"Run-through," Ranger said.

"Twenty bucks each. Forty each, if you want a jumpsuit."

"Just the run-through ticket," Ranger said.

"You know the rules? You collect a ticket from the dude without no mess, and you get a kewpie doll. You're gonna be on the third floor."

Ranger and I climbed the stairs to the third floor and stood in the hallway.

"Do you have any idea what he was talking about?" I asked Ranger.

"No. Knowing Marbles, it could be most anything."

There were two doors that opened off the hallway. The doors were labeled PUSSY and MOTHERFUCKERS.

"I'm taking the Motherfucker door," I said to Ranger.

"No way. That's my door."

"Well, I'm sure as hell not taking the Pussy door."

"It's just a door, Babe."

"Great. Then *you* take it."

Ranger moved to the Pussy door and shoved it open. He walked through the front room and looked into two other rooms. "It's an apartment. Looks like it was decorated by someone on 'shrooms. No one home."

I opened the Motherfucker door and stepped inside. The door closed behind me, neon red, green, blue, and white strobe lights activated and flickered across the front room, and hip-hop boomed from overhead speakers. I opened a door. Closet. I opened another door and a crazy-eyed, woolly-haired, scrawny guy in too-big pants and too-big shoes shouldered a gun at me from across the room.

"Gonna put a cap up your pussy ass," he said.

And *POW*.

I felt the bullet hit my shoulder, knock me back an inch or two, and something splattered out across my chest.

"What the?" I said.

"Run, Pussy!"

"What?"

"Run!"

And *POW*. I got shot again. *POW*. *POW*.

An arm wrapped around my waist, and I was lifted off my feet and whisked out of the room and back into the hall. Ranger kicked the door closed and set me down.

"What? Why?" I asked.

"Paintball. Are you okay?"

"No! It hurt. It's like getting hit with a rock. Why on earth do people do that? You'd have to be crazy."

"It's a game," Ranger said. "Usually. This version is more like shooting sitting ducks."

I checked myself out. I was completely splattered with blue, pink, and yellow paint. It was in my hair and on my shoes and everywhere in between. There was no paint on Ranger.

"You don't have a drop of paint on you," I said. "Why is that?"

Ranger smiled, liking that he hadn't gotten hit. "I guess they were hunting pussy."

"But I walked into the Motherfucker room."

"Yeah, but babe, you're clearly pussy."

"That is so sexist and *annoying*. These are my favorite sneakers, and now they're ruined. I'll never get this paint out."

"I'm sure it's water-based. Throw them in the washer."

"I don't have a washer."

Ranger took my hand and tugged me toward the stairs. "Then throw them in your mother's washer."

"You wouldn't be this cheery if *you* were covered in paint."

He pushed my back to the wall and leaned in to me. "Would you like me to take your mind off your sneakers?"

I bit into my lower lip.

"Well?" he asked, kissing me just below my ear, making the little man in the boat pay attention.

"I'm th-th-thinking."

Actually, I was thinking he'd have half my paint on him when he pried himself loose. And along with that I was thinking he felt great plastered against me. He was big and warm and strong.

A door banged open on the first floor and conversation carried up to us. Ranger listened for a moment and eased away. I followed him down the stairs and into the first-floor hall, where the kid in the white T-shirt and homeboy jeans stood talking to a stocky older man with wiry gray hair. Both guys looked up when we stepped into the hall. The kid froze in his tracks. The older guy spun around, ran to the office, and locked himself inside.

Ranger dismissed the kid and knocked on the locked office door. He waited a couple beats and knocked again. When there was no response to his second knock, he put his foot to the door and kicked it open.

"Jeez Louise," I said to Ranger, knowing he could have finessed the lock and opened the door.

Ranger smiled. "Making a statement."

The guy inside the office was behind his desk, waving his arms, his eyes rolling around in their sockets, popped out like marbles.

"This must be Marbles," I said to Ranger.

"Only one of them is real," Ranger said.

"You broke my door," Marbles said. "You're gonna pay. You think doors grow on trees?"

"Bond enforcement," Ranger said.

"That's bullshit. You owe me for a door. And she owes me for playing. Does she have a ticket? Where's her fuckin' ticket?"

Ranger never shows much emotion. I saw him walk into a room once, knowing he was going to get shot and maybe die, and he was perfectly composed. Only because I've spent a decent amount of time with him did I know the limit to his patience. So I took a step back and gave him some room, because I knew he was done talking.

"And another thing . . ." Marbles said, finger pointed at Ranger, eyes all googly-woogly.

Marbles never finished the sentence, because in a matter of moments, he was on the ground and cuffed. Ranger dragged Marbles to his feet and set him in his chair. Marbles opened his mouth to speak, Ranger looked at him, and Marbles clamped his mouth shut.

"You have a choice," Ranger said to me. "We can take him to the station and get him booked in, or I can have one of my men do it, and I can take you home so we can get you out of your clothes."

"*We* can get me out of my clothes? Are you planning on making it a group activity?"

"Figure of speech, Babe. I don't need help getting you undressed." He answered his cell phone, listened for a moment, and disconnected. "Change in plans," he said, yanking Marbles out of his chair. "There's been another break-in. We'll take Marbles with us and pass him off on site."

FOUR

The house was a big white colonial with black shutters and a massive mahogany front door. The grounds were professionally landscaped. A dusty and battered police cruiser and two gleaming black Rangeman SUVs were parked in the circular drive. Ranger parked behind one of the Rangeman SUVs, we got out, and Tank and Hal came forward to meet us.

I gave Hal my paperwork for Marbles, Hal got behind the wheel, backed the Escalade out of the drive and disappeared down the street.

"Same MO," Tank told Ranger. "The clients attended a political fund-raiser, came home, and found money and jewelry missing." He handed Ranger a list. "We interrogated the system and found it had been briefly disarmed and then reset."

"Anything missing besides the money and jewelry?"

"Some electronics. They're going through the house now, trying to make sure the list is complete."

"I want Stephanie to walk through the house and look at it from a woman's point of view. Make sure she has total access. Assure the owners her paint isn't wet."

Tank looked at my paint-splattered hair and clothes. He paused for a beat, but he didn't smile or frown or grimace. "Yessir," he said to Ranger.

I wandered around, checking out the kitchen with its professional-level appliances, marble countertops and splash plates, warming ovens and wine cooler. I thought it would be nice to have a kitchen like this, although most of it would go unused. All I actually needed was a butter knife, a loaf of white bread, and a jar of peanut butter. And can you fill a wine cooler with Bud Light?

The upstairs master bath had a crystal chandelier and a bidet. I knew the *purpose* for the bidet, because I had seen *Crocodile Dundee* about a hundred times, but I wasn't sure how one actually *used* a bidet. I mean, does it shoot water up your cooter or do you splash it around? And I thought I might have issues with the crystal chandelier. I wasn't sure I could do number two in a room with a crystal chandelier.

I'd looked at the list, so I knew what had been taken and what had been left. There was a safe in the master bedroom, but it hadn't been touched. Madame's jewelry had been easy access in a jewelry case on display in her walk-in closet. A couple thousand in twenties had been left on the dresser. All this stuff was gone. Plus two laptop computers from the home office, and a Patek Philippe man's watch.

I wandered around in the house for a half hour while the police did their thing, and Ranger did his thing, and the burgled house owners, a conservatively dressed middle-aged couple, quietly sat in the living room, looking shell-shocked.

Ranger caught up with me in the front foyer. "Any ideas?" he asked me.

"The thieves only hit two rooms. The master bedroom and the home office. There was a woman's rose gold and diamond Cartier watch on the kitchen counter. And there were four icons that looked priceless in a display case in the living room. All untouched. Is this always the pattern?"

"Yes. They disable the alarm for precisely fifteen minutes, and they move directly to the master bedroom and office."

"Why fifteen minutes?"

Ranger did palms-up. "I don't know."

"No prints left on doorknobs?"

"None."

"And they only hit residential accounts?"

"So far."

"This house has two security keypads. Can you tell which was used?"

"They always enter and exit through the garage."

"The garage in this house opens into a short hall that leads to the kitchen. That means they walked through the kitchen twice and didn't take the watch."

"Correct," Ranger said.

"Do you have anyone working for you who's OCD or superstitious?"

"Almost everyone. I'm going to have Tank take you back to Rangeman so you can get your car. I need to stay here for a while and then I have paperwork to complete."

"So I'm off the hook with the undressing thing?"

"Rain check," Ranger said.

I drove home and did my own undressing, lathering, and shampooing. When I flopped into bed, my hair was still multicolored.

I stopped at the bonds office on my way to Rangeman. It was a little before nine in the morning, and the air was warm, and the sky was almost blue. It was Indian summer in Jersey.

Connie and Lula looked over when I walked through the door.

"What the heck happened to you?" Lula wanted to know. "You got tutti-frutti hair. Is this some new fashion statement?"

"No, this is the result of a paintball encounter on Stark Street. The good news is I apprehended Kenny Hatcher."

"Your mother's going to have a cow when she sees your hair," Connie said. "You try water? You try paint thinner?"

"I've tried everything."

"I like it," Lula said. "You should add some more pink. Pink's a good color on you. And by the way, have you been listening to the radio? There's a big reward being offered to anyone who brings in the guy who whacked Stanley Chipotle."

"How big?"

"A million dollars. It's from the barbecue sauce company he did all those advertisements for. Fire in the Hole Red Hot Barbecue Sauce. He was supposed to represent them in this cook-off coming up. And I'm gonna get that reward. I know what those guys look like. All I have to do is find them. So I thought I'd cut you and Connie in on it, and between us we could track them down and we'd each get a third of a million dollars."

"I'm so there," Connie said. "I could pay my mortgage off with that money."

"What would you do with the money?" Lula asked me.

I didn't know what I'd do. My mind was blank. The amount was incomprehensible to me. I could put a crystal chandelier in my crapper for that kind of money. I could buy a case of motor oil and feed it to my $700 car. I could download all the *3rd Rock from the Sun* episodes from iTunes. I could get the works on my pizza. I could buy new sneakers. I *really* needed new sneakers. I could probably buy a house, for crying out loud. Except I didn't actually *want* a house. I had a hard enough time keeping people out of my apartment. If I had a house, the weirdos would be coming in every door and window and down the chimney like Santa. Plus, I'd have to cut grass and paint the porch and caulk the tub.

"I think this is about barbecue sauce," Lula said. "Everyone knows it's dog-eat-dog out there in barbecue land. You wait and see, someone didn't want Stanley Chipotle in that barbecue contest. I looked into it, and he always wins those contests. He was the one who come up with Fire in the Hole Red Hot Barbecue Sauce. He invented that recipe, and when he's in a contest, he has a secret ingredient he puts in. I'm tellin' you, Stanley Chipotle's killer is a sauce freak. So I figure we just gotta bust into the barbecue circuit and we'll find the killer."

"Bust into the circuit?"

"All I gotta do is enter the contest as one of them chefs. I bet I could even win."

"You can't cook."

"That's true so far, but that could change. I'm real good at eatin'. I got a highly developed palate. Especially for barbecue. I just gotta take some of my eatin' talent and make it into cookin' talent. Anyways, I only gotta come up with sauce. How hard could it be? I mean, you start out with ketchup and keep adding pepper until you feel it burnin' a hole in your stomach."

"I don't think it's that easy," Connie said. "I watch these contests on The Food Channel, and you have to use the sauce on ribs and chicken and stuff. Can you cook ribs or chicken?"

"Not yet," Lula said. "But I know I could be real good at it. Look at me. Don't I look like a woman who could cook the shit out of chicken? I'm like a combination of Paula Deen and Mario Whatshisname. I'm just around the corner from bein' the Mrs. Butterworth of barbecue sauce."

"The cook-off is in a week," Connie said. "Is there still time for you to enter? Do you have to qualify or something?"

"I don't have to do nothin' but sign up," Lula said. "I already looked into it, and the idiot who's runnin' the cook-off used to be a customer of mine back when I was a 'ho. He was what you call a drive-by. He'd pick me up on my corner, and two blocks later, we'd concluded our business."

"That's more information than I need," Connie said.

"Well, I'm just sayin' so you get the picture."

"I have to run," I told them. "I'm late for work."

"After we win the contest and capture the killer, none of us is gonna have to work," Lula said. "We're all gonna be ladies of leisure."

It was noon, and Ranger's men were moving around, breaking for lunch, so I left my cubicle and went to the kitchen area to mingle. Ella kept the large glass-fronted refrigerator filled with sandwiches, fruit, raw veggies, yogurt, low-fat milk, snack-size cheeses, a variety of fruit juices, plus individual cups of chicken salad and vegetable soup. Early in the morning, Ella supplemented this with a caldron of oatmeal and a chafing dish of scrambled eggs. The dinner offering was always some sort of Crock-Pot stew, plus a bread-basket.

Ranger almost always ate breakfast and dinner in his apartment. And lunch was usually a sandwich and piece of fruit from the common kitchen, taken back to his office. There were three small round tables set to one side of the kitchen. Each table held four chairs. Two men I didn't know were eating at one of the tables.

Hal and Ramon were at another. The third table was empty. I selected a sandwich and joined Hal and Ramon. I've known Hal for a while now. Hal isn't the sharpest tack on the corkboard, but he tries hard. His nickname is Halosaurus, because there's a stegosaurus resemblance.

"You're my new favorite person," Ramon said. "You got me out of that cubicle. I was dying in that cubicle."

"It's not my favorite job, either," I said, "but I needed the money."

I unwrapped my sandwich and examined it. Multigrain bread, pretty ruffled green lettuce, thin-sliced chicken, a slice of tomato, slices of hard-cooked egg, and salad dressing that was for sure low fat. It looked good, but it would look even better with bacon.

"No bacon," I said, more to myself than to Hal and Ramon.

Hal grinned. "Ranger thinks bacon is the work of the devil."

"Sometimes I walk past Ella's apartment, and I smell bacon frying," Ramon said. "I think she makes it for Louis." He looked over at me. "Have you ever seen Ranger eat bacon?"

"No," I said. "Not that I can remember."

"I think sometimes he cheats and goes to eat with Louis," Ramon said.

"No way," Hal said. "Ranger's pure."

Both men looked at me.

"Forget it," I said. "I'm not commenting on that one."

Hal flushed red, and Ramon gave a bark of laughter.

I finished my sandwich and pushed back from the table. "I'm going for a walk around the building. Is there anyplace off-limits for us worker people?"

"Only the seventh floor. No one would mind if you

went into the men's locker room, but there could be a lot of wood if you stayed too long. And then Ranger would probably fire us all," Ramon said.

"I don't want to get anyone fired."

"That's good," Hal said, "because everyone here wants to keep their job."

"Not everyone," Ramon said.

I cut my eyes to him.

"You were on the job last night," he said to me. "I'm sure you know the problem. *Everyone* in the building knows the problem."

"Then why isn't the problem solved?" I asked him.

Ramon did palms-up. "Good question. If I knew, I would tell immediately. And so would Hal. And before this happened, I would say every man in the building would tell and would lay down their life for Ranger."

"Maybe it's not in the building," I said to Ramon.

"I would like to believe that."

I glanced at Hal. "What do you think?"

Hal shook his head. "I don't know what to think. It used to be we were a team here, and now we're all pulled up inside ourselves. It's creepy working with people who are looking at you funny."

I stood and gathered my trash off the table. "I'm sure Ranger has it under control. He doesn't seem overly worried."

"I saw Ranger jump off a bridge into the Delaware River in January once. He was going after a skip, and he didn't seem overly worried," Ramon said. "He handed me his gun, and he did about a sixty-foot free fall into black water."

"Did he get the skip?" I asked him.

"Yeah. He dragged the guy out and cuffed him."

"So he was right not to be worried."

"Anyone else would have fuckin' died. Excuse the language."

I wandered out of the kitchen, walked past my cubicle and down the hall to Ranger's office.

"Knock, knock," I said at his open door.

He looked up from his computer. "Babe."

"Do you have a minute?"

"I've got as much time as you need."

I knew he wasn't just talking about conversation, and there was a quality to his voice that gave me a rush. And then, for some inexplicable reason, I thought about Morelli. Morelli didn't flirt like Ranger. Morelli would say *sure* and then he'd look down my shirt to try to see some boob. It was actually very playful, and it felt affectionate when Morelli did it.

Ranger relaxed back in his chair. "I'm pretty sure I lost you for a couple beats."

"My mind wandered."

"As long as it always comes back."

I repeated my conversation with Hal and Ramon.

"This business runs on trust," Ranger said. "Ninety-five percent of the time, the work is mundane. When it rolls over into the other five percent, you need total confidence that the man watching your back is on the job. Knowing there's an unidentified weak link in the organization puts stress on everyone."

I left Ranger and walked through the building. I couldn't listen at doors or rifle through files, because I was always on camera. I peeked into the conference rooms and strolled halls. I stuck my head into the gym but stayed away from the locker room. The garage, the practice range, some high-security holding rooms were below ground, and I didn't go there. The men I encountered gave me a courteous nod and returned to work. No invitations to stay and chat.

I returned to Ranger. "You have a well-oiled machine," I told him. "Everything looks neat and clean and secure."

He almost raised an eyebrow. "That's it?"

"Yep."

"How much am I paying you?"

"Not enough."

"If you want more money, you're going to have to perform more services," he said.

"Are you flirting with me again?"

"No. I'm trying to bribe you."

"I'll think about it."

"Would you like to think about it over dinner?"

"No can do," I said. "I promised Lula I'd test-drive some barbecue sauce with her."

FIVE

I dropped into the office a little after five. Connie was shuffling papers around and Lula was nowhere to be seen.

"Where's Lula? I thought we were supposed to eat barbecue tonight?"

"Turns out, Lula only has a hot plate in her apartment, and she couldn't get the ribs to fit on it, so she had to find someplace else to cook."

"She could have used my kitchen."

"Yeah, she considered that, but we didn't have a key. And we thought you might not have a lot of equipment."

"I have a pot and a fry pan. Is she at your house?"

"Are you insane? No way would I let her into my kitchen. I won't even let her work the office coffee-maker."

"So where is she?"

"She's at your parents' house. She's been there all afternoon, cooking with your grandmother."

Oh boy. My father is Italian descent and my mother is Hungarian. From the day I was born to this moment, I can't remember ever seeing anything remotely resembling barbecue sauce in my parents' house. My parents don't even have a grill. My mom *fries* hot dogs and what would pass for a hamburger.

"I guess I'll head over there and see how it's going," I said to Connie. "Do you want to come with me?"

"Not even a little."

My parents and my Grandma Mazur live in a narrow two-story house that shares a common wall with another narrow two-story house. The three-hundred-year-old woman living in the attached house painted her half lime green because the paint was on sale. My parents' half is painted mustard yellow and brown. It's been that way for as long as I can remember. Neither house is going to make *Architectural Digest*, but they feel right for the neighborhood and they look like home.

I parked at the curb, behind Lula's Firebird, and I let myself into the house. Ordinarily, my grandmother or mother would be waiting for me at the door, driven there by some mystical maternal instinct that alerts them to my approach. Today they were occupied in the kitchen.

My father was hunkered down in his favorite chair in front of the television. He's retired from the post office and now drives a cab part-time. He picks up a few people early morning to take to the train station, but mostly the cab is parked in our driveway or at the lodge, where my father plays cards and shoots the baloney with other guys his age looking to get out of the house. I shouted *hello,* and he grunted a response.

I shoved through the swinging door that separated kitchen from dining room and sucked in some air. There were racks of ribs laid out on baking sheets on the counter, pots and bowls of red stuff, brown stuff, maroon stuff on the small kitchen table, shakers of cayenne, chili pepper, black pepper, plus bottles of various kinds of hot sauce, and a couple cookbooks turned to the barbecue section, also on the table. The cookbooks, Lula, and Grandma were dotted with multicolored sauce. My mother stood glassy-eyed in a corner, staring out at the car crash in her kitchen.

"Hey, girlfriend," Lula said. "Hope you're hungry, on account of we got whup-ass shit here."

Grandma and Lula looked like Jack Sprat and his wife. Lula was all swollen up and voluptuous, busting out of her clothes, and Grandma was more of a deflated balloon. Gravity hadn't been kind to Grandma, but what Grandma lacked in collagen she made up for with attitude and bright pink lipstick. She'd come to live with my parents when my Grandfather Mazur went in search of life everlasting at the all-you-can-eat heavenly breakfast buffet.

"This here's a humdinger dinner we got planned," Grandma said. "I never barbecued before, but I think we got the hang of it."

"Your granny's gonna be my assistant at the cook-off," Lula said to me. "And you could be my second assistant. Everybody's got to have two assistants."

"We're gonna get chef hats and coats so we look professional," Grandma said. "We're even gonna get our names stitched on. And I'm thinking of making this a new career. After I get the hat and the coat, I might go get a chef job in a restaurant."

"Not me," Lula said. "I'm not working in no restaurant. After I win the contest, I'm gonna get a television show."

"Maybe I could help you with that on my day off," Grandma said. "I always wanted to be on television."

I took a closer look at the ribs. "How did you cook these?"

"We baked them," Lula said. "We were supposed to grill them, but we haven't got no grill, so we just baked the crap out of them in the oven. I don't think it matters, anyways, after we get the sauce on them. That's what we're fixin' to do now."

"We got a bunch of different sauces we're trying out," Grandma said. "We bought them in the store and then we doctored them up."

"I don't think that's allowed," I said. "This is supposed to be your own sauce recipe."

Lula dumped some hot sauce and chili pepper into the bowl of red sauce. "Once it gets out of its bottle, it's my sauce. And besides, I just added my secret ingredients."

"What if they want to see your recipe?"

"Nuh-ah. No one gets to see Lula's recipe," Lula said, wagging her finger at me. "Everybody'll be stealing it. I give out my recipe, and next thing it's in the store with someone else's name on it. No sir, I'm no dummy. I'm gonna take the winning recipe to my deathbed."

"Should I start putting the sauce on these suckers?" Grandma asked Lula.

"Yeah. Make sure everybody gets all the different sauces. Since I'm the chef, I got the most refined taste buds, but we want to see what other people think, too."

Grandma slathered sauce on the ribs, and Lula eyeballed them.

"I might want to add some finishing touches," Lula said, pulling jars off my mother's spice rack, shaking out pumpkin pie spices. "These here ribs are gonna be my holiday ribs."

"I would never have thought of that," Grandma said.

"That's why I'm the chef and you're the helper," Lula said. "I got a creative flare."

"What are we eating besides ribs?" I asked.

Lula looked over at me. "Say what?"

"You can't just serve ribs to my father. He'll want vegetables and gravy and potatoes and dessert."

"Hunh," Lula said. "This is a special tasting night and all he's gettin' is ribs."

My mother made the sign of the cross.

"Gee," I said. "Look at the time. I'm going to have to run. I have work to do. Rex is waiting for me. I think I'm getting a cold."

My mother reached out and grabbed me by my T-shirt. "I was in labor twenty-six hours with you," she said. "You owe me. The least you could do is see this through to the end."

"Okay," Lula said. "Now we put these ribs back into the oven until they look like they been charcoaled."

Twenty minutes later, my father took his seat at the head of the table and stared down at his plate of ribs. "What the Sam Hill is this?" he said.

"Gourmet barbecue ribs," Grandma told him. "We made them special. They're gonna have us rolling in money."

"Why are they black? And where's the rest of the food?"

"They're black because they're supposed to look grilled. And this is all the food. This is a tasting menu."

My father mumbled something that sounded a lot like *taste, my ass*. He pushed his ribs around with his fork and squinted down at them. "I don't see any meat. All I see is bone."

"The meat's all in tasty morsels," Lula said. "These are more pickin'-up ribs instead of knife-and-fork ribs. And they're all different. We gotta figure out which we like best."

My mother nibbled on one of her ribs. "This tastes a little like Thanksgiving," she said.

My father had a rib in his hand. "I've got one of them, too," he said. "It tastes like Thanksgiving after the oven caught on fire and burned up all the meat."

What I had on my plate was charred beyond rec-ognition. I loved Grandma and Lula a lot, but not enough to eat the ribs. "You might have cooked these a smidgeon too long," I said.

"You could be right," Lula said. "I expected them to be juicier. I think the problem is I bought grillin' ribs, and we had to make them into oven ribs." She turned to Grandma. "What's your opinion of the ribs? Did you try them all? Is there some you like better than others?"

"Hard to tell," Grandma said, "being that my tongue is on fire."

"Yeah," Lula said. "I made one of them real spicy 'cause that's the way I like my ribs and my men. Nice and hot."

My father was gnawing on a rib, trying to get something off it. He was making grinding, sucking sounds and really concentrating.

"You keep sucking like that, and you're gonna give yourself a hernia," Grandma said.

"It'd be less painful than eating these burned black, tastes like monkey shit, dry as an old maid's fart bones."

"Excuse me," Lula said. "Are you trash-talkin' my ribs? 'Cause I'm not gonna put up with slander on my ribs."

My father had a grip on his knife, and I thought the only thing stopping him from plunging it into someone's chest was he couldn't decide between Grandma and Lula.

"Are you really going to enter the competition?" I asked Lula.

"I already did. I filled out my form and gave it over to the organizer. He wanted me to do a favor for him, and I said *nuh-ah*. I said I don't do that no more. Not that I don't still have my skills, but I moved on with my life, you see what I'm sayin'."

"Did he take your form anyway?"

"Yeah. I got pictures of him from when he was a customer."

"You'd blackmail him?"

"I like to think of it as reminders of happy times," Lula said. "No need to negatize it. What happens is, he looks at the picture of himself and thinks bein' with me was better than a fork in the eye. And then he thinks it's special if that shit stay between him and me and for instance don't be seen on YouTube. And then he takes my contest application and gives it the stamp of approval."

"You got a way with people," Grandma said.

"It's a gift," Lula said.

"I'm making myself a peanut butter and olive sandwich," I said. "Anyone else want one?"

"I got to go to the lodge," my father said, pushing away from the table.

I figured he might get there eventually, but he'd stop at Cluck-in-a-Bucket on the way.

"I don't need a sandwich," Lula said. "But I'll help clean the kitchen."

Lula, Grandma, my mother, and I all trooped into the kitchen and set to work.

"I don't see any more barbecue sauce anywhere," Grandma finally said. "The floor's clean, the counters are clean, the stove's clean, and the dishes and pots are clean. Only thing dirty is me, and I'm too pooped to get clean."

"I hear you," Lula said. "I'm goin' home, and I'm goin' to bed."

I drove back to my apartment, changed into comfy worn-out flannel pajamas, and was about to settle in to watch television and *bang, bang, bang.* Someone was hammering on my door. I looked through the security peephole at Lula.

"I been shot at," she said when I let her in. "I'm lucky I'm not dead. I parked in front of my house, and I got out of my car, and just as I got to my front porch, these two guys jumped out of the bushes at me. It was the guys who whacked Stanley Chipotle, and the one had a meat cleaver, and the other tried to grab me."

"Are you serious?"

"Fuckin' A. Don't I look serious? I'm friggin' shakin'. Look at my hand. Don't it look shaky?"

We looked at her hand, but it wasn't shaking.

"Well, it used to be shakin'," she said. "Anyways, I hit the one asshole in the face with my pocketbook, and I kicked the other one in the nuts, and I turned and ran back to my car and took off. And one of them shot at me while I was driving away. He put bullet holes in my Firebird. I mean, I can stand for a lot of shit, but I don't tolerate bullet holes in my Firebird. What kind of a moron would do that, anyway? It's a Firebird, for crissake!"

"But you're okay?"

"Hell yeah, I'm okay. Don't I look okay? I'm just freakin' is all. I need a doughnut or something." She went to my kitchen and started going through cabinets. "You don't got nothin' in here. Where's your Pop-Tarts? Where's your Hostess Twinkies and shit? Where's your Tastykakes? I need sugar and lard and some fried crap."

"Did you call the police?"

"Yeah. I called them from my car. I told them I was coming here."

I got out my only fry pan, put a big glob of butter in it, slathered a lot of Marshmallow Fluff between two slices of worthless white bread, and fried it up for Lula.

"Oh yeah," Lula said when she bit into the bread and Fluff. "This is what I'm talkin' about. I feel better already. Another four or five of these, and I'm gonna be real calm."

There was a polite knock at the door, and I opened it to two uniforms. Carl Costanza and Big Dog. I made First Communion with Carl, and Big Dog had been his partner long enough that I felt like I made communion with him, too.

"What's up?" Carl said.

"I been shot at," Lula said. "That's what's up. And before that I almost got my head chopped off. It was terrifyin'."

Carl looked at me. "This isn't like the time she fell in the grave and thought the devil was after her, is it?"

"Your ass," Lula said to Carl.

"Just asking," Carl said.

"I got bullet damage to my Firebird," Lula told him. "It wasn't done by no devil, either. It was done by a certified killer."

Morelli appeared behind Carl. Morelli looked like he'd fallen asleep watching the ballgame, was jolted awake by dispatch, and reluctantly dragged his ass out to investigate. His black hair was overdue for a cut and curling along his neck in waves. His five o'clock shadow was way beyond shadow. He was wearing running shoes, jeans, and a faded navy blue sweatshirt with the sleeves pushed up to his elbows.

"I'll take it," he said to Carl and Big Dog.

"What are you doing here?" I asked him.

"I'm assigned to the Chipotle murder. Dispatch got a report of attempted murder by the same perps."

"That's right," Lula said. "I almost got my head chopped off. It was the same two idiots. And the one had a meat cleaver. Just like he used on Stanley Chipotle. Biggest meat cleaver I've ever seen. And this one with the meat cleaver was giggling. Not normal giggling, either. It was eerie. It was like horror movie giggling."

"Why didn't they chop your head off?" Morelli wanted to know.

"I kicked the one in the nuts and smashed my pocketbook in the other one's face."

"I guess that would slow them down," Morelli said. "Dispatch said this happened in front of your house?"

"Yeah. They were waiting for me. See, here's what happened. Stephanie and her granny and me were makin' ribs, only the ribs had to go in the oven, so they didn't cook right. Personally, I been thinking about it and I bet that oven was faulty."

Morelli blew out a sigh and went to my refrigerator. "There's no beer in here," he said.

"I need to go to the store."

Morelli closed the door and went back to Lula. "And?"

"And we had three special sauces, but it was hard to tell what was what since the ribs were all the same color when they come out of the oven."

"Has this got anything to do with Chipotle's murderers?"

"I'm gettin' to it," Lula said.

Morelli looked at his watch. "Could you get to it faster?"

"Boy, you're Mr. Cranky Pants tonight. What, do you got a date or something?"

I felt a small twinge of pain in the vicinity of my heart, and I narrowed my eyes at Morelli.

Morelli was hands on hips. "I haven't got a date. I just want to go home and see the end of the game."

"I guess there isn't much more to tell," Lula said. "They were waiting for me. They come at me with the mother of all cleavers. I kicked the guy in his nuts and got back in my car. And they shot at me when I drove away. And now my Firebird's full of bullet holes."

"I checked it on my way in," Morelli said. "I counted two in the right rear quarter panel and one in the back bumper. I don't suppose you noticed what kind of car these guys were driving?"

"I wasn't paying attention to that."

"Any distinguishing features? Anything you can add to your description of them?"

"One of them's got a broken nose and the other's walkin' funny."

"Did they say anything to you?"

"Nope. The one just was giggling."

"I'll send a uniform to check on your house, but it's unlikely your assailants are still there," Morelli told Lula.

"Okay, but I'm not going back there. I'm still freaked out. I'm staying here."

"Good luck with that one," Morelli said.

I cut my eyes to him. "What's that supposed to mean?"

He blew out another sigh. "Forget it."

I felt my eyes get squinchy and my lips compress. *"What?"*

"You're not exactly the easiest person to live with these days."

"Excuse me? I happen to be very easy to live with. You're the one who has issues."

"I don't want to get into this now," Morelli said. "Call me when you calm down."

"I'm *calm*!" I yelled at him.

He gave his head a shake and moved to the door. He turned, looked at me, and shook his head again. He murmured something I couldn't catch, and he left.

"He's hot," Lula said, "but he's a pig. All men are pigs."

"Do you really believe that?"

"No, but it's a point of view to keep in mind. You don't want to go around thinkin' shit is your fault. Next thing you know, they got you makin' pot roast and you're cutting up your MasterCard."

"I don't know how to make pot roast."

"Good for you," Lula said. "I don't suppose you got anything that would fit me. Like a big T-shirt. I'm all covered in barbecue sauce, and I'm beat."

I gave Lula an extra quilt and pillow and a worn-out T-shirt that belonged to Morelli. I said good night and I closed the door to my bedroom. I didn't especially want to see Lula in Morelli's T-shirt. Lula was a lot shorter than Morelli and a lot wider. Lula wearing Morelli's T-shirt wasn't going to be a pretty sight.

I woke up in a panic a little after midnight, thinking someone was sawing through my bedroom door. A couple seconds later, my head cleared, and I realized it was Lula snoring in my living room. I put my pillow over my head, but I could still hear Lula. Three hours later, I was thrashing around, plotting out ways to kill her. I got out of bed, marched into the living room, and yelled in her face.

"Wake up!"

Nothing.

"Wake up! Wake up! *WAKE UP!*"

Lula opened her eyes. "Huh?"

"You're snoring."

"You woke me up to tell me that?"

"Yes! My first choice was to suffocate you, but I don't have the energy to drag your lifeless body out to the Dumpster."

"Well, I happen to know I don't snore. You must have dreamed it."

"I didn't dream it. You snore loud enough to wake

the dead. Roll over or something. I have to go to work in the morning. I need my sleep."

Brrrrrp. Lula let one go.

"Holy Toledo!" I said, backing away, fanning the air. "That's disgusting."

"I don't think it's so bad," Lula said. "It smells a little like ribs."

I drove to Rangeman in pouring rain. The temperature had dropped overnight, and the heater was broken on my car, so I was freezing my butt off. I parked in the underground garage, took the elevator to the fifth floor, and shuffled past the control desk to my cubicle. I turned my computer on, and next thing I knew, Ranger was standing over me.

"Rough night?" he asked.

"How did you know?"

"You were asleep at your desk. I was afraid you were going to fall out of your chair and get a concussion."

I told him about Lula and the meat cleaver giggler, and the shooting, and the sleeping and snoring.

"Go to my apartment and take a nap," Ranger said. "I'll be out all morning on a job site. I'll catch up with you when I come back."

Ranger left and I finished a computer search I was doing on a job applicant. I took the elevator to the seventh floor and let myself into Ranger's apartment. It very faintly smelled like citrus, and everything was in perfect order. No thanks to Ranger. This was Ella's handiwork.

First thing in the morning Ella went through, polishing and straightening. Ranger's bed was made with fresh linens. His bathroom was gleaming clean, his towels neatly folded.

I kicked my shoes off, wriggled out of my jeans, slid under the covers, and thought this might be as close as I'd ever come to paradise. Ranger's three hundred thread count sheets were smooth and cool and heavenly soft. His pillows were just right. His mattress was just right. His feather quilt was just right. If Ranger were the marrying type, I'd marry him in a heartbeat just for his bed. There were other good reasons to hook up with Ranger, but the bed would be the clincher. Unfortunately, there were also some major reasons *not* to hook up with Ranger.

SIX

I opened my eyes and looked at my watch. It was almost one o'clock. I rolled out of bed, pulled my jeans on, and was tying my shoes when I heard the front door to Ranger's apartment open. Keys clinked onto the silver tray on the hall sideboard. A beat later, there was a heavy clunk, and I suspected this was his gun getting dropped onto the kitchen counter. Moments later, Ranger strode into the bedroom.

He was wearing a black ball cap, black windbreaker, black cargo pants, and black boots. He was soaking wet, and he didn't look happy.

"Still raining out?" I asked him.

It was a rhetorical question since I could hear the rain pounding on the bedroom window.

He bent to unlace his boots. "Everything I had to do this morning was outdoors. I'm soaking wet, and I'm late for a meeting." He kicked his boots off and moved to the bathroom. "Get me some dry clothes."

"What kind of clothes?"

"Any kind of clothes."

Ranger has a walk-in dressing room I would kill for. Shirts, slacks, blazers, T-shirts, sweatshirts, cargo pants, socks, underwear, gym clothes, shoes are all perfectly hung on hangers, stacked on shelves, or neatly placed in a drawer. Again, this is done by Ella.

It was easy for me to pick clothes for Ranger because everything he owns is black. The only question is dressy or casual. I went with casual and gathered together the same outfit he was wearing when he walked in.

There was a time a while ago when I searched for underwear in Ranger's dressing room and found just one pair of silky black boxers. Today, he had a drawer full of underwear. Boxers, bikini briefs, and boxer briefs. I closed my eyes and grabbed and came up with boxer briefs.

I brought the clothes to the open bathroom door in time to see Ranger strip off the last of his wet clothes.

"Sorry," I said. "I didn't mean to barge in on you."

"Babe, you've seen it all before."

"Yeah, but not lately."

"So far as I know, nothing has changed." He pulled the briefs on and arranged himself. "If I had more time, I'd let you figure that out for yourself." He removed his watch and tossed it to me. "Set this out to dry and get me a new one. Top drawer in the chest in my dressing room."

I brought him the exact duplicate of the watch he'd discarded, plus I handed him socks and shoes.

"On my desk in the den I have a list of items taken from all the break-ins. I'd like you to take a look at it. Plus, I have a map with the houses marked. I haven't been able to find anything significant, but maybe something will jump out at you." He finished lacing his shoes and stood. "I also have a list of every man in the building, his position, and his background. I'd like you to read through it."

I followed him to the door and watched him take his keys from the sideboard and pocket them. He pushed me to the wall, leaned in to me, and kissed me. "Later," he said, his lips brushing against mine. And he left.

It was a really great kiss, and if he'd said *now,* I might have been in trouble, but after a couple beats, when my heart had stopped jumping around in my chest and I wasn't pressed up against Ranger, I decided *later* was a scary idea.

I took the break-in and employee information down to the fifth floor, grabbed a sandwich from the kitchen, and went to my cubby. After a couple minutes, I realized my cubby didn't give me the privacy I needed, so I commandeered Ranger's office. The items taken were similar in all the houses. Jewelry, cash, iPods, laptop computers, handheld electronic games. The map showed the houses in three different neighborhoods. I saw nothing to tie them together. I was about a third of the way through the men's employment files when Ranger came in.

"I expected you'd stay in my apartment," Ranger said.

"I was worried about the *later* thing."

"And you think moving from my apartment to my office will save you?"

"I'm doing good so far."

Ranger slouched into a chair on the opposite side of the desk. "Is this move into my office permanent?"

"Is that a possibility?"

"No."

I looked around. "It's a really nice office. It has a window."

The corners of Ranger's mouth curved into the beginnings of a smile. "Would you like to negotiate for this office?"

"No, but I'd like to stay here until I finish reading. I have no privacy in my cubicle."

"Deal," Ranger said. "When you're done reading, I'd like you to find a way to talk to the four men who have access to the computer that holds the codes. Roger King, Martin Romeo, Chester Deuce, and Sybo Diaz. I don't want you to interrogate them. I just want you to make a fast character assessment. Chester Deuce is on the desk until six o'clock. Sybo Diaz will take the next six-hour shift. Romeo goes on at midnight. You should be able to catch him in the kitchen early afternoon. He occupies one of the Rangeman apartments and prefers Ella's cooking to his own."

"Okeydokey," I said. "I'm on it."

It was almost four when I finished reading. Ranger's men were a motley group, chosen for specific skills and strength of character over other more mundane attributes such as lack of a criminal record. From what I could tell, Ranger employed safecrackers, pickpockets, computer hackers, linebackers, and a bunch of vets who'd served overseas. He also had on his payroll a second-story burglar who the papers compared to Spider-Man, and a guy whose murder conviction was overturned on a technicality. I wouldn't want to be caught in a blind alley with any of these guys, but Ranger found something in each of them that inspired his trust. At least until a couple weeks ago.

I pulled two men out of the group for a closer look. One of them was Sybo Diaz, the evening monitor for the code computer. He was with Special Forces in Afghanistan and took a job as a rent-a-cop in a mall when he got out. His wife divorced him two months later. His wife's maiden name was Marion Manoso. She was Ranger's cousin. I didn't know the details of the divorce, but I thought there was the potential for some bad feelings. The other file I pulled was Vince Gomez. Vince wasn't one of the men with code computer access, but he caught my attention. He was a slim little guy with the flexibility of a Romanian acrobat. The inside joke was that he could crawl through a keyhole. He did system installation and troubleshooting for Ranger. I flagged him because he lived beyond his means. I'd seen him around, and I knew he drove an expensive car, and when he wasn't working he wore expensive jewelry and designer clothes. And he liked the ladies, a lot.

I left the paperwork in Ranger's office and returned to my desk. I worked at my computer for a half hour and wandered out to the kitchen. No one there, so I stopped in at the monitoring station and smiled at Chester Deuce.

"I've always wondered what you guys did out here," I said to him.

"There are always three of us on duty," he said. "Someone monitors the cars and responds to the men off-site. Someone watches the in-house video and is responsible for maintaining building integrity. And I watch the remote locations and respond to emergency calls and alarms."

"So if an alarm went off, what would you do?"

"I'd call the client and ask if they were okay, and then I'd ask for their password."

"How do you know if they give you the right password?"

"I have the information in an off-line computer."

I looked at the computer sitting to his right. "I guess it has to be off-line for security purposes."

He shrugged. "More that there's no reason for it to be on-line."

I returned to my desk and packed up. I had seven messages on my phone. All were from Lula, starting at three this afternoon. All the messages were pretty much the same.

"You gotta be on time for supper at your mama's

house tonight," Lula said. "Your granny and me got a big surprise."

Thoughts of the big surprise had me rolling my eyes and grimacing.

Ranger appeared in my doorway. "Babe, you look like you want to jump off a bridge."

"I'm expected for dinner at my parents' house again. Grandma and Lula are taking another crack at barbecue."

"Has Lula had any more contact with the Chipotle hitmen?"

"I don't think so. She didn't mention anything in her messages."

"Keep your eyes open when you're with her."

My father was slouched in his chair in front of the television when I walked in.

"Hey," I said. "How's it going?"

He cut his eyes to me, murmured something that sounded like *just shoot me now*, and refocused on the screen.

My mother was alone in the kitchen, alternately pacing and chopping. Everywhere I looked there were pots of chopped-up green beans, carrots, celery, potatoes, turnips, yellow squash, and tomatoes. Usually when my mother was stressed, she ironed. Today she seemed to be chopping.

"Run out of ironing?" I asked her.

"I ironed everything yesterday. I have nothing left."

"Where's Lula and Grandma?"

"They're out back."

"What are they doing?"

"I don't know," my mother said. "I'm afraid to look."

I pushed through the back door and almost stepped on a tray of chicken parts.

"Hey, girlfriend," Lula said. "Look at us. Are we chefs, or what?"

Grandma and Lula were dressed in white chef's jackets. Grandma was wearing a black cap that made her look like a little old Chinese man, and Lula was wearing a puffy white chef's hat like the Pillsbury Doughboy. They were standing in front of a propane grill.

"Where'd you get the grill?" I asked.

"I borrowed it from Bobby Booker. He brought it over in his truck on the promise he was gonna get some of our award-winning barbecue chicken some-day. Now that we got this here grill, my barbecue is gonna turn out perfect. Only thing is, I can't get it to work. He said there was lots of propane in the tank. And my understanding is, all I have to do is turn the knob."

"I got some matches," Grandma said. "Maybe it's got one of them pilot lights that went out."

Lula took the matches, bent over the grill, and *Phunnf!* Flames shot four feet into the air and set her chef's hat on fire.

"That did it," Lula said, stepping back, hat blazing. "It's cookin' now."

Grandma and I had a split second of paralysis, mouths open, eyes bugged out, staring at the flaming hat.

"What?" Lula said.

"Your hat's on fire," Grandma told her. "You look like one of them cookout marshmallows."

Lula rolled her eyes upward and shrieked. "Yow! My hat's on fire! My hat's on fire!"

I tried to knock the hat off her head, but Lula was running around in a panic.

"Hold still!" I yelled. "Get the hat off your head!"

"Somebody do something!" she shouted, wild-eyed, arms waving. "Call the fire department!"

"Take the damn hat off," I said to her, lunging for her and missing.

"I'm on fire! I'm on fire!" Lula yelled, running into the grill, knocking it over. Her hat fell off her head onto the ground and ribbons of fire raced in all directions across my parents' yard.

Growing grass was never a priority for my father. His contention was if you grew the grass, you had to cut the grass. And what was the point to that? The result was that most of our backyard was dirt, with the occasional sad sprinkling of crab grass. In seconds, the fire burned up the crabgrass and played itself out, with the exception of a half-dead maple tree at the back of the yard. The tree went up like Vesuvius.

I could hear fire trucks whining in the distance. A car pulled into the driveway, a car door opened and closed, and Morelli strolled into the yard. Lula's hat was a lump of black ash on the ground. The tree was a torch in the dusky sky.

"I saw the fire on my way home from work," Morelli said. "I stopped by to help, but it looks like you have everything under control."

"Yep," I said. "We're just waiting for the tree to burn itself out."

He looked at the grill and the chicken. "Barbecuing tonight?"

A pack of dogs rounded the corner of the house, ran yapping up to the chicken, and carried it off.

"Not anymore," I said. "Want to go for pizza?"

"Sure," he said.

We each took our own cars, sneaking out between the fire trucks that were angling into the curb. I followed Morelli to Pino's, parked next to his SUV in Pino's lot, and we pushed through the restaurant's scarred oak front door into the heat and noise of

dinner hour. At this time of day, the majority of tables were filled with families. At ten in the evening,
Pino's would be crammed with nurses and cops un-
winding off the second shift. We were able to snag
a small table in the corner. We didn't have to read
the menu. We knew it by heart. Pino's menu never
changes.

Morelli ordered beer and a meatball sub. I got the
same.

"Looks like you're working for Rangeman,"
Morelli said, taking in my black T-shirt and sweatshirt
with the Rangeman logo on the left front. "What's
that about?"

"It's temporary. He needed someone to fill in on the
search desk, and I needed the money."

Back when we were a couple, Morelli hated when
I associated with Ranger. He thought Ranger was a
dangerous guy from multiple points of view, and of
course Morelli was right. From the set of his jaw,
I suspected he still hated that I was associating with
Ranger.

"What have you got on your desk these days?" I
asked him, thinking it best to get off the Ranger topic.

"A couple gang slayings and the Chipotle thing."

"Are you making any progress with Chipotle?"

We paused while the waitress set two glasses of
beer on the table.

Morelli sipped his beer. "Originally, I thought
it felt like a couple professionals had come in from
out of town, but that didn't make sense after they
went for Lula. These guys are afraid Lula will finger
them."

"She gave you a description. Have you had any luck
with that?"

"Lula's description fit half the men in this country.

Average height, one shorter than the other, brown hair, average build, late forties to early fifties, she wasn't close enough to see eye color. No distinguishing features, and she said they dressed like white men. What the hell is that supposed to mean?"

"So you have nothing?"

"Worse than that, we have more than we can manage. The million-dollar reward brought out every crackpot in the state. We had to pull Margie Slater off traffic duty and sit her in a room with a phone so she could field the calls coming in. They were clogging the system."

"Lula's convinced Chipotle was killed over barbecue sauce, and she figures the killers will be at the cook-off. She's entered the contest so she'll have the inside track at identifying them."

"That'll make sense if she lives that long."

"Do you have someone watching her house?"

"That kind of surveillance only happens in the movies. We're so underbudgeted we're one step away from holding bake sales to pay for toilet paper."

"Have you considered the barbecue sauce connection?"

"I've considered a lot of connections. Chipotle had so much bad juju going it's a wonder he wasn't killed sooner. He has three ex-wives who hated him. Everyone on his television show hated him. His sister hated him. He was suing his manager. And the tenants in his New York co-op signed a petition to get him evicted."

"Who would have thought? He was all smiley on the jar of barbecue sauce."

"It's not that easy to slice off someone's head," Morelli said.

"The way Lula tells it, there wasn't any struggle."

"Yeah. That bothers me. Would you stand there and let someone decapitate you? And what about the guy who did it? Why would he choose decapitation? There are so many easier, cleaner ways to kill someone. And this was done in broad daylight in front of the Sunshine Hotel. It was almost like it wasn't planned."

"A spontaneous decapitation?"

Morelli grinned. "Yeah."

"And he just happened to be carrying a meat cleaver around with him?"

"Maybe he was a butcher."

"So all we have to do is look for an impulsive butcher."

Morelli signaled for another beer. "I'm having fun."

"Me, too."

"Do you want to go home and go to bed?"

"Jeez," I said. "Is that all you ever think about?"

"No, but I think about it a lot. Especially when I'm with you."

"I thought we were supposed to be mad at each other."

Morelli shrugged. "I don't feel mad anymore. I can't even remember what we were fighting about."

"Peanut butter."

"It was about more than peanut butter."

"So you *do* remember?"

"You called me an insensitive clod," Morelli said.

"And?"

"I'm not a clod."

"But you admit to being insensitive?"

"I'm a guy. I'm supposed to be insensitive. It's my birthright."

I was pretty sure he was kidding. But then, maybe not. "Okay," I said. "I'll take half of it back. You're not a clod."

The waitress brought our food and Morelli took out

his credit card. "We'll take the check now, and we'd like a to-go box."

"Since when?" I said.

"I thought we decided to go home."

"I can't go home. I have to go back to work."

"Doing what?"

"Doing what I do. I'm working at Rangeman."

"At night?"

"It's complicated," I said.

"I bet."

I felt my eyebrows squinch together. "What's that supposed to mean?"

"It means I don't trust him. He's a total loose can-non. And he looks at you like you're lunch."

"It's a job. I need the money."

"You could move in with me," Morelli said. "You wouldn't have to pay rent."

"Living with you doesn't work. Last time we tried to cohabitate, you threw my peanut butter away."

"It was disgusting. It had grape jelly and potato chips in it. And something green."

"Olives. It was just a little cross-contamination. Sometimes I'm in a hurry and stuff gets mixed into the peanut butter. Anyway, when did you get so fussy?"

"I'm not fussy," Morelli said. "I just try to avoid food poisoning."

"I have never poisoned you with my food."

"Only because you don't cook."

I blew out a sigh because he was right, and this was going to lead to another contentious topic. Cooking. I'm not sure why I don't cook. In my mind, I cooked a lot. I made whole mental turkey dinners, baked pies, roasted tenderloins, and whipped up rice pudding. I even owned a mental waffle maker. So to some extent, I understood Lula's delusional belief that she could barbecue. The difference between Lula and me being that I knew fact from fiction. I knew I was no kind of cook.

The waitress came back with a couple plastic take-out boxes and the check.

"Well?" Morelli asked me.

"Well what?"

"Are we eating here or are we taking these subs back to my house?"

"I'd rather eat here. I have to go back to work tonight, and this is closer to Rangeman."

"So you're choosing Ranger over me?"

"Rangeman. Not *Ranger*. I have a project I can only do in the evening. You should understand that. You choose your job over me all the time."

"I'm a cop."

"And?"

"And that's different," Morelli said. "*I'm* serving the public, investigating murders, and *you're* working for . . . Batman."

"Gotham City would have been a mess without Batman."

"Batman was a nutcase. He was a vigilante."

"Well, Ranger isn't a nutcase. He's a legitimate businessman."

"He's a loose cannon hiding behind a veneer of legitimacy."

We'd had this conversation about a hundred times before, and it never had a happy ending. Problem was, there was an element of truth to what Morelli said. Ranger played by his own rules.

"I don't want to get into a shouting match," I said to Morelli. "I'm going to pack up this sandwich and go back to work. We can try this again when I'm done working for Ranger."

* * *

The rhythm of Rangeman was always the same. As a security facility, it worked around the clock. The fifth-floor control room, the dining area, and most of the satellite offices were interior to the building and without windows. If you worked in these areas, it was difficult to tell if it was night or day.

The evening shift was in place when I came on the floor. Sybo Diaz was kicked back in his chair, watching several monitors. The code computer was to his right; the screen was blank. I'd never spoken to Diaz, but I'd seen him around. He wasn't the friendliest guy in the building. Mostly, he stayed to himself, eating alone, not making eye contact that would encourage conversation. According to his work profile, he was five foot nine inches tall and thirty-six years old. His complexion was dark. His face was scarred from acne he probably had as a teenager. He was built chunky, but he didn't look like he had an ounce of fat. He walked like his shorts were starched.

"Hey," I said to him, passing the desk on my way to my cubicle. "How's it going?"

This got me a polite nod. No smile.

I plunked myself into my chair and turned my computer on. I could see Diaz from where I sat. I watched him for twenty minutes, and he never moved or blinked or looked my way. I wanted to talk to him, but I didn't know how to go about it. The man was a robot. For lack of something better to do, I ran one of my assigned security checks. I printed the report and attempted to staple the pages, but the stapler was jammed. I pressed the button that was supposed to release the staples, I poked at it with my nail file, I banged it against the top of my desk. *Bang, bang, bang.* Nothing. I looked up and found Diaz staring at me.

"Stapler's jammed," I said to him.

His attention turned back to his monitors. No change in facial expression. Also no change in my stapler condition, so I hit it against my desktop some more. *Bang, bang, bang, bang, bang!* Diaz swiveled his head in my direction, and I think he might have sighed a little.

I left my station and took my stapler over to Diaz. "I can't get it to work," I told him, handing him the stapler.

Diaz examined the stapler. By now the stapler had a bunch of dents, and the part that holds the staples was all bashed in. Diaz pushed the button that was supposed to release the staples, but of course nothing happened.

"It's dead," Diaz said. "You need a new stapler."

"How do I get a new stapler?"

"Storeroom on the second floor."

"Will it be open at this time of the night?" I asked him.

"It's always open."

This was like talking to a rock. "I don't suppose I could borrow your stapler?"

Diaz so looked like he wanted me to go away that I almost felt sorry for him.

"I don't have a stapler," he said.

"Would you like me to get one for you from the storeroom?"

"No. I don't need one. I haven't got anything to staple."

"Yeah, but what if suddenly you had to staple something and you didn't have a stapler? Then it would be a stapling emergency."

"Somebody put you up to this, right? Martin? Ramon?"

"No! Cross my heart and hope to die. I came in to catch up on my work, and I had this stapler issue."

Diaz looked at me. Not saying anything.

"Jeez," I said. And I went back to my cubicle.

I fiddled around for ten or fifteen minutes, drawing doodles in the margins of the report I'd just done, and Ranger called.

"This guy isn't human," I said to Ranger. "Does he ever talk to anyone?"

"No more than necessary to be a team member."

"I get the feeling he's been the brunt of some practical jokes."

"I'm not supposed to know, but I think there's a lottery going to see who's the first to get him to crack a smile."

"Why did your cousin divorce him?"

"She found someone she liked better."

"Gee, hard to believe there's someone better than Mr. Charming here."

"He's a good man," Ranger said. "He's steady."

"He's emotionally closed."

"There are worse things," Ranger said. And he disconnected.

Truth is, Ranger was every bit as silent and unemotional as Diaz. Always in control. Always on guard. What made the difference was an animal intelligence and sexuality that made Ranger mysterious and compelling, while Diaz was simply annoying.

I ambled down to the second floor and prowled through the storeroom in search of a stapler. I finally found them and selected a small handheld. I took it back to the fifth floor and showed it to Diaz on the way to my desk.

"Got my stapler," I said. "Thanks."

Diaz nodded and resumed staring at his collection of monitors. I walked around his desk and looked over his shoulder. He was watching multiple locations in the building. No activity at any of them.

"I thought for sure one of these would be tuned to the Cartoon Network," I said.

No response.

"What's this computer?" I asked, referring to the code computer. "Why isn't there anything on the screen?"

"I don't need it right now."

"What happens if you have to go to the bathroom?"

"One of the other men will cover. There's always an extra man in the control room."

I stood there for a while, watching Diaz ignore me.

"This is a little boring," I finally said to him.

"I like it," Diaz said. "It's quiet. It lets me think."

"What do you think about?"

"Nothing."

I found that easy to believe. I returned to my cubicle and my cell phone buzzed.

"Hey, girlfriend," Lula said. "Your granny needed a ride to a viewing at the funeral parlor tonight, so after the fire department hosed the tree down, I took her over here to pay respects to some old coot. Anyways, we were just about to leave and who do you think walked in? Junior Turley, your exhibitionist FTA. I didn't recognize him at first. It was your granny who spotted him. And she said she almost missed him, bein' he had all his clothes on. She said usually he's in her backyard waving his winkie at her when she's at the kitchen window. And she said she wouldn't mind seeing his winkie up close to make a positive identification, but I thought we should wait until you got here."

"Good call. I'm about fifteen minutes away."

I grabbed my purse and took the stairs, deciding they were faster than the elevator. I wanted to capture Turley, but even more I didn't want Grandma trying to make a citizen's arrest based on identification of Turley's winkie. I rolled out of the garage and called Ranger.

"Lula has one of my skips cornered," I told him. "I'll see you tomorrow."

"Babe," Ranger said. And he disconnected.

SEVEN

The funeral parlor is part renovated Victorian and part brick bunker. I found on-street parking and jogged to the front porch. Hours were almost over, but there were still a lot of mourners milling around. A group of men stood to one side on the wraparound porch. They were smoking and laughing, smelling faintly of whiskey. The funeral parlor had several viewing rooms. Two were presently occupied. Knowing Grandma, she probably visited both. Viewings were at the core of Grandma's social scene. On a slow week, Grandma would go to the viewing of a perfect stranger if nothing better popped up.

I found Grandma and Lula at the back of Slumber Room #3.

"He's up there at the casket," Lula said. "He looks like he knows the stiff's ol' lady."

"They're relations," Grandma said. "Nothin' anyone would want to admit to. That whole family is odd. I went to school with Mary Jane Dugan, the wife of the deceased. She was Mary Jane Turley then. Up until fourth grade, she quacked like a duck. Never said a blessed word in school. Just quacked. And then one day she fell off the top of the sliding board in the park and hit her head and she started talking. Never quacked again. Not to this day. Junior's father, Harry, was Mary Jane's brother. He electrocuted himself trying to pry a broken plug out of a wall socket with a screwdriver. I remember when it happened. He blew out one of them transformer things, and four houses on that block didn't have electric for two days. I didn't see Harry after the accident, but Lorraine Shatz said she heard they had to put him in the meat locker to get him to stop smokin'."

"Stay here," I said to Lula. "I'm going to make my way up to the casket. You grab Junior if he bolts and tries to leave by this door."

"Don't you worry," Lula said. "Nobody's gonna get past me. I'm on the job. He come this way, and I'll shoot him."

"No! No shooting. Just grab him and sit on him."

"I guess I could do that, but shooting seems like the right thing to do."

"Shooting is the *wrong* thing to do. He's an exhibitionist, not a murderer. He's probably not even armed."

Grandma helped herself to a cookie set out on a tray by the door. "You wouldn't be saying that if you saw him naked."

I eased my way along the wall, inching past knots of people who were more interested in socializing than in grieving. Not that this was a bad thing. Death in the Burg was like pot roast at six o'clock. An unavoidable and perfectly normal part of the fabric of life. You got born, you ate pot roast, and you died.

I came up behind Turley and snapped a cuff on his right wrist. "Bond enforcement," I whispered in his ear. "Come with me, and we don't have to make a big scene. We'll just quietly walk to the door."

Turley looked at me, and looked at the cuff on his wrist. "What?"

"You missed your court date. You need to re-schedule."

"I'm not going to court. I didn't do anything wrong."

"You flashed Mrs. Zajak."

"It's my thing. Everybody knows I'm the flasher. I've been flashing for years."

"No kidding. This is the third time I've captured you for failing to appear. You should get a new hobby."

"It's not a hobby," Turley said. "It's a calling."

"Okay, it's a calling. You still have to reschedule your court date."

"You always say that, and then when I get to the courthouse with you, I get locked up in jail. You're a big fibber. Does your mother know you tell fibs?"

"Does your mother know you flash old ladies?"

Turley's attention switched to the door where Lula and Grandma were standing. "What are the police do-ing here?" he asked.

I turned to look, and he jumped away.

"Hah! Fooled you," he said. And he scuttled around to the other side of the casket.

I lunged and missed, bumping into Mary Jane Du-gan. "Sorry about your loss," I said, shoving her aside.

"What's going on?" she wanted to know. "Stepha-nie Plum, is that you?"

Turley took off for the double doors at the front of the room, and I ran after him. He knocked some lady on her ass, and I tripped over her.

"Sorry," I said, scrambling to my feet in time to see Grandma do a flying tackle at Turley.

Turley wriggled away from Grandma and escaped into the ladies' room. Two women ran shrieking out, and Grandma, Lula, and I barged in.

Turley was trapped against the wall between the tampon dispenser and the sanitary hand dryer.

"You'll never take me alive," he said.

"Do you have a gun?" I asked him.

"No."

"Are you booby-trapped?"

"No."

"Then how are you going to die?"

"I don't know," Turley said. "I just always wanted to say that."

"Could we hurry this up?" Lula said. "I'm missing my Wednesday night television shows."

"I'll make a deal," Turley said. "I'll go with you if I can flash everyone on my way out of the ladies' room."

"No way," I told him.

"Eeuw," Lula said. "Ick."

Grandma slid her dentures around a little, thinking. "I wouldn't mind seeing that," she said.

Turley unzipped his pants and reached inside.

"Hold it right there," Lula said. "I got a stun gun here, and you pull anything out of your pants, I'll zap you."

Next thing there was a *zzzzt* from the stun gun and Junior Turley was on the floor with his tool hanging out.

"Whoa, Nellie," Lula said, staring down at Junior.

"Yep," Grandma said. "He's got a big one. All them Turleys is hung like horses. Not that I know firsthand, except for Junior. And maybe Junior's Uncle Runt. I saw him take a leak outside the Polish National Hall one time, and it was like he had hold of a fire hose. I tell you, for a little guy, he had a real good-size wanger."

"We need to get that thing back in his pants before we drag him out of here," I said.

"I'll do it," Grandma said.

"I think you done enough," Lula said. "You're the one encouraged him to take it out in the first place."

They looked over at me.

"No, no, no," I said. "Not me. No way, Jose. I'm not touching it."

"Maybe we could drag him out facedown," Lula said. "Then no one would see. All's we have to do is flip him over."

That seemed like an okay plan, so we rolled him over, and I finished cuffing him. Then Lula took a foot, and I took a foot, Grandma got the door, and we hauled him out of the ladies' room.

All conversation stopped when we dragged Junior through the lobby. It was like everyone inhaled at precisely the same time and the air all got sucked out of the room. Halfway across the oriental carpet, Junior's eyes popped open, his body went rigid, and he let out a shriek.

"Yow!" Junior yelled, flopping around like a fish out of water, wrangling himself over onto his back. He had a *huge* erection and a bad case of rug burn.

"I gotta tell you, I'm impressed," Lula said, checking out Junior's stiffy. "And I don't impress easy."

"It's a pip," Grandma said.

It was a pip and a half. I was going to have nightmares.

By now, the funeral director was hovering over Junior, hands clasped to his chest, face red enough to be in stroke range. "Do something," he pleaded. "Call the police. Call the paramedics. Get him out of here!"

"No problemo," I said. "Sorry about the disturbance."

Lula and I pulled Junior to his feet and muscled him to the door. We got him outside, onto the porch, and he kicked Lula.

"Hey," Lula said, bending over. "That hurts."

He gave Lula a shove, she grabbed me by my sweatshirt, and Lula and I went head-over-teakettle down the wide front stairs.

"Adios," Junior yelled. And he ran away into the night.

I was flat on my back on the sidewalk. My jeans had a tear in the knee, my arm was scraped and bleeding, and I was worried my ass was broken. I went to hands and knees and slowly dragged myself up to a semivertical position.

Lula crawled to her feet after me. "I'm surprised he could run with that monster boner," she said. "I swear, if it was two inches longer, it'd be draggin' on the ground."

I dropped Grandma off at my parents' house, drove to my building, parked, and limped to my apartment. I flipped the light on, locked the door behind me, and said hello to Rex. Rex was working up a sweat running on his wheel, beady black eyes blazing bright. I dropped a couple raisins into his cage and my phone rang.

"Myra Baronowski's daughter has a good job in the bank," my mother said. "And Margaret Beedle's daughter is an accountant. She works in an office like a normal human being. Why do I have a daughter who drags aroused men through funeral parlors? I had fourteen phone calls before your grandmother even got home."

The Burg has a news pipeline that makes CNN look like chump change.

"I think it must have happened when he got rug burn," I told my mother. "He didn't have an erection when I cuffed him in the ladies' room."

"I'm going to have to move to Arizona. I read about this place, Lake Havasu. No one would know me there."

I disconnected, and Morelli called me.

"Are you okay?" he asked. "I heard you dragged a naked guy through the funeral parlor, and then shots were fired, and you fell down the stairs."

"Who told you that?"

"My mother. Loretta Manetti called her."

"He wasn't naked, and no shots were fired. He kicked Lula, and Lula took me down the stairs with her."

"Just checking," Morelli said. And he hung up.

I dropped my clothes on the bathroom floor and washed the blood away in the shower. I pulled on my old flannel pajamas and went to bed. Tomorrow would be a better day, I thought. I'd get a good night's sleep in my nice soft jammies and wake up to sunshine.

My phone rang at 5:20 A.M. I reached for it in the dark and brought it to my ear.

"Who died?" I asked.

"No one died," Ranger said. "I'm coming into your apartment, and I didn't want you to freak."

I heard my front door open and close, and moments later, Ranger was in my bedroom. He flipped the light on and looked down at me.

"I'd like to crawl in next to you, but there was another break-in tonight. This time it was a commercial account. I want you to take a look at it with me."

"Now? Can't it wait?"

Ranger grabbed jeans from my closet and tossed them at me. The jeans were followed by a sweatshirt and socks. "I want to go through the building before people arrive for work."

"It's the middle of the night!"

"Not nearly," Ranger said. He looked at his watch. "You have thirty seconds to get dressed, or you're going in your pajamas."

"Honestly," I said, rolling out of bed, scooping my clothes up into my arms. "You are such a *jerk*."

"*Twenty* seconds."

I stomped off into the bathroom and slammed the door closed. I got dressed and was about to brush my hair when the door opened and Ranger pulled me out of the bathroom.

"Time's up," Ranger said.

"I didn't even have time to fix my hair!"

Ranger was dressed in a black Rangeman T-shirt, cargo pants, windbreaker, and ball cap. He took the ball cap off his head and put it on mine.

"Problem solved," he said, taking my hand, towing me out of my apartment.

The building that had gotten hit was just four blocks from my apartment. Police cars and Rangeman cars were angled into the curb, lights flashing, and lights were on inside the building. Ranger ushered me into the lobby and one of his men brought me a cup of coffee.

"This building is owned by a local insurance company," Ranger said. As you can see, the first floor is mostly lobby, with a front desk and satellite glass-fronted offices. Executive offices, a boardroom, a small employee kitchenette, and a storeroom are on the second floor. It's not a high-security account. They have an alarm system. No cameras. For the most part, there's nothing of value in this building. The computers are antiquated. There are no cash transactions. The only thing of value was a small collection of Fabergé eggs in the company president's office. And that's what was taken."

"Was the routine the same?"

"The thief entered through a back door that had a numerical code lock. He deactivated the alarm, went directly to the second-floor office, took the eggs, reset the alarm, and left. The alarm was off for fifteen minutes."

"He had to be moving to get all that done in fifteen minutes."

"I had one of my men run through it. It's possible."

"Was the president's office locked?"

"The office door was locked, but it wasn't a complicated lock, and the thief was able to open it. He didn't bother to close the door or relock it when he left."

"How much were the eggs worth?"

"There were three eggs. One was especially valuable. Collectively, he probably lost a quarter of a million."

"Is this guy going to have a hard time fencing the eggs?"

"I imagine they'll go out of country."

I looked around. There was one uniform left in the building and one plainclothes guy from Trenton P.D. I didn't know either of them. Ranger had four men on site. Two were at the front door, and two were at the elevator.

"How was this discovered?" I asked Ranger. "Is there a night watchman or something?"

"The company president likes to get an early start. He's here at five every morning."

Morelli was awake at five. Ranger was awake at five. And now here was another moron at work at five. As far as I was concerned, five was the middle of the night.

"What am I supposed to do?" I asked Ranger.

"Look around."

I went to the back door and looked outside. From what I could see, there was an alley, a small blacktop parking lot with six designated spaces. No light.

There should be a light. I stepped outside and looked up at the building. The light had been smashed. There were some glass shards on the ground under the light.

I went back inside and looked for the alarm pad. On the wall to my right. Exactly where I would have put it. I walked to the stairs, imagining the thief doing this in the dark. Probably had a penlight and knew exactly where he was going. And he was in a hurry, so he would take the stairs rather than the elevator.

I prowled through the second floor, peeking into offices, the kitchen, the storeroom. It all looked pretty normal. The president's office was nice but not extravagant. Corner office with windows. Executive desk and fancy leather chair. Couple smaller chairs in front of the desk. Built-in bookcase behind the desk with an empty shelf. I guessed that was where the eggs used to be.

I sat in the fancy leather chair and swiveled a little, checking out the pictures on the desk. Balding, overweight guy with a cheesy mustache, posing with a preppy dark-haired woman and two little boys. The corporate family photo display placed next to the corporate pen-and-pencil set that some decorator probably requisitioned and the guy never used. Matching leather blotter. And alongside the desk was the matching corporate wastebasket. A single Snickers wrapper was in the wastebasket.

I called Ranger on my cell phone. "Where are you?" I asked.

"Downstairs with Gene Boran, the president of the company."

"How did the thief know about the eggs?"

"The Trenton paper ran a feature on them two weeks ago."

"Perfect."

"Anything else?" Ranger asked.

"It looks like the cleaning crew came through here last night."

"They left at eleven-thirty."

"There's a Snickers wrapper in the wastebasket."

There was some discussion at the other end, and Ranger came back on. "Gene said he saw it on the floor, so he put it in the wastebasket."

"It could be a clue," I said to Ranger.

Ranger disconnected.

I ambled downstairs and slouched into a man-size chair in the lobby. The police had cleared out, and there were only two Rangeman employees left. Ranger spoke to the company president for another five minutes, they shook hands, and Ranger crossed the room to where I was sitting.

"I'm leaving Sal and Raphael here until the building opens for business," Ranger said. "We can go back to Rangeman."

"It isn't even seven A.M.! Normal people are still asleep."

"Is this going somewhere?" Ranger asked.

"Yes. It's going to . . . *take Stephanie home so she can go back to bed.*"

"Babe, I'd be happy to take you back to bed."

Unh. Mental head slap.

It was almost noon when I left my apartment for the second time that morning. I'd run out of Rangeman clothes, so I was dressed in jeans and a stretchy red V-neck T-shirt. My hair was freshly washed and fluffed. My eyes were enhanced with liner and mascara. My lips were comfy in Burt's Bees lip balm.

I stopped at the bonds office on my way to Rangeman.

"Just in time for lunch," Lula said when I walked in

the door. "Me and Connie are feeling like we should try the chicken at the new barbecue place by the hospital."

"That's sacrilege. You always get your chicken at Cluck-in-a-Bucket."

"Yeah, but we gotta do barbecue research. I don't have my just-right gourmet barbecue sauce yet. I might have had it on the chicken last night, but the dogs run off with it. Anyways, I thought it wouldn't hurt to shop around. And I hear the guy who owns the barbecue place is gonna be in the contest."

"Sorry, no can do. I'm late for work."

"Just tell Ranger you needed barbecue," Lula said. "Everybody understands when the barbecue urge comes over you. And besides, there's no place to park by that barbecue place. I need a ride up there. It'll take you a minute, and it's the least you can do since I rescued you from that embarrassing experience last night."

"You didn't rescue me! You pulled me down the stairs and let Junior escape."

"Yeah, but people was watching me go ass-over-elbows down the stairs, and they hardly noticed you at all."

That could be true. "Okay, I'll give you a ride, but then I have to go to work."

Lula hiked her purse onto her shoulder. "We got it all planned out what me and Connie want to eat. All's I gotta do is run in and out."

Lula and I stepped out of the office onto the sidewalk and stood for a moment squinting into the sun.

"This here's a beautiful day," Lula said. "I got a real good feeling about today."

A black Mercedes with tinted windows pulled out of a parking space half a block away and cruised up to the bonds office. It slowed, the side window slid down, a gun barrel appeared, there was maniacal giggling, and four rounds were fired off.

I heard a bullet whistle past my ear, the plate-glass window behind me cracked, and Lula and I hit the ground. Connie kicked the bonds office door open and aimed a Glock at the Mercedes, but the car was already too far away.

"That asshole took out my computer," Connie said.

Lula hauled herself up off the sidewalk and pulled her lime green spandex miniskirt down over her butt. "Someone call the police. Call the National Guard. Those guys are out to get me. That was one of those Chipotle killers behind that gun. I saw his idiot face. And I heard that crazy-ass giggling. Did someone get that license plate?"

Vinnie appeared in the doorway and cautiously peeked outside. "What's going on?"

Vinnie was my rodent cousin. Good bail bondsman. Scary human being. Slicked-back hair, face like a ferret, dressed like Tony Soprano, had a body like Pee-wee Herman.

"Someone's trying to kill Lula," Connie said.

Vinnie put his hand to his heart. "That's a relief. I thought they were after me."

"It's no relief to me," Lula said. "I'm a nervous wreck. And stress like this is bad for your immune system. I read about it. I could get shingles or something."

People from nearby businesses migrated onto the sidewalk, looked around, and realized it was just the bonds office getting shot at. Their faces registered that this was no big whoopity-do, and they drifted back into their buildings.

Lights flashed in the distance on Hamilton, and a fire truck and an EMS truck rumbled to a stop in front of the office.

"Hey!" I yelled to the fire truck. "You're blocking me in. I have to go to work. We don't need you."

"Of course we need them," Lula said. "Do you see that big beautiful man drivin' that fire truck? I think I saw him on one of them Fire Truck Hunks calendars." Lula stood on tiptoes in her spike heels and waved to him. "Yoohoo, sweetie! Here I am. I been shot at," she called. "I might be faint. I might need some of that mouth-to-mouth."

Ten minutes later, I was still waiting for the fire truck to take off, and Morelli strolled over.

"Now what?" he said.

"A guy in a black Mercedes shot at Lula. She said it was one of the Chipotle killers."

Morelli cut his eyes to Lula. "Guess they didn't tag her."

"No, but they got Connie's computer."

"Anyone see the license plate?"

"Nope."

"I like this red shirt you're wearing," Morelli said, tracing along the neckline with his fingertip. "Did you get fired from your new job already?"

"No. I ran out of black clothes."

"What happens if you don't dress in black? Do you have to go to detention? Do you get fined?"

I did an eye roll.

"I'm serious," Morelli said, laugh lines crinkling the corners of his eyes. "Are all the towels in the building black? Is there black toilet paper?"

I did a five-count of deep breathing as an alternative to kicking him in the knee.

"If you could get that fire truck to move, I could go to work," I finally said.

Morelli was still smiling. "You would owe me."

"What did you have in mind?"

"A night of wild gorilla sex."

"Good grief."

"How bad do you want to go to work?" he asked.

"Wild gorilla sex isn't going to happen. I'm not interested. I'm done with men."

"Too bad," he said. "I learned some new moves."

"We are no longer a couple," I told him. "And you better not have learned those moves from Joyce Barnhardt."

Morelli and I went to school with Joyce Barnhardt, and she'd always had a thing for Morelli. For as long as I can remember, Joyce Barnhardt has been like a needle in my eye. I severely disliked Joyce Barnhardt.

It was close to two o'clock when I walked through the fifth-floor control room and settled myself in my cubicle.

My intercom buzzed and Ranger came on. "My office," he said.

I walked the short distance to his office and looked in at him. "What?"

"Come in and close the door."

I closed the door and sat in a chair opposite him. He was at his desk, and I was struck by the same thought I had every time I came into his office. Ranger always looked at ease, but he never actually looked like he belonged behind a desk. He looked like he should be scaling a wall, or jumping out of a helicopter, or kicking the crap out of some bad guy.

"Do you like doing this?" I asked him. "Do you like running this security firm?"

"I don't love it," he said. "But I don't hate it, either. It's a phase in my life. It's not so different from being a company commander in the military. Better work conditions. Less sand."

I wondered if my job was also just a phase in my life. Truth is, I felt a little stalled.

"Do you have any new thoughts on my problem?" he asked.

"Nothing big. Sybo Diaz gets the prize for most suspicious guy so far, but he doesn't fit into the puzzle right. He's like trying to ram a square peg into a round hole. Diaz was on duty when two of the break-ins occurred, so he'd have to be working with someone else. Problem is, I don't see Diaz having a partner in this kind of operation. He's totally closed. He'd have to do it all himself.

"The computer with the security codes is actually available to a lot of people. Four men have primary responsibility, but a bunch of other guys fill in for them when they take a break. And all the other men who are watching other monitors have the ability to see the screen on the code computer. You already knew this.

"The thing is, the longer I'm here, the less likely I'm inclined to believe this is an inside job. Everyone is watching everyone now. And the code computer is under constant scrutiny. And yet there was a new break-in. I think you have to look at outside possibilities. Maybe a rival security firm. Or a techno freak you fired or didn't hire. Or maybe someone not associated with you at all who's doing it for the rush."

"This isn't a large firm," Ranger said. "We offer quality personal service to a select group of clients. If I remove all clients with video surveillance, I cut the list in half. If I only look at residential accounts, the list gets much smaller. I was able to increase the number of cars I have patrolling video-free, residential accounts during hours when the break-ins occurred. If I have to enlarge that list to include commercial accounts spread over a two-shift period, I'm short manpower."

"Maybe you can get more accounts to use video."

"That's like announcing my system is corrupted.

I'm trying to keep this quiet." He handed me a list of names. "These are non-video clients, both residential and commercial. The clients that have been hit by this guy are printed in red. I'd like you to ride around and see if anything jumps out at you."

EIGHT

I took the list back to my apartment, made myself a peanut butter sandwich, and marked Ranger's at-risk accounts on a map of Trenton. Commercial accounts in green Magic Marker. Residential accounts in pink Magic Marker. Accounts already hit in red.

Grandma called on my cell phone. "Guess who's standing in the backyard waving his winkie at me?"

"I'll be right there."

I called Ranger and told him I needed help with an FTA who was currently in my mom's backyard. I shoved the map and the client list into my purse and ran out of my apartment, down the stairs, and across the lot to my car. If I had luck with traffic, I could make my parents' house in five minutes. It would take Ranger ten to twenty minutes.

I called my grandmother when I was two minutes away. "Is he still there?"

"He's making his way through backyards. I can see him from the upstairs window. I think he's going to Betty Garvey's house. She gives him cookies."

I went straight to Betty Garvey. I parked at the curb in front of her house and walked around back. I didn't see Junior Turley, but Betty was at her kitchen door.

"Have you seen Junior?" I asked her.

"Yes. He just left. I gave him an oatmeal raisin cookie, and he thanked me and went on with his walk. He's such a nice, polite man."

"Which way did he go?"

"He was walking toward Broome Street."

I jogged through the next two yards, crossed the street, and saw Junior at the end of the block. He was eating his cookie with one hand and shaking his wanger at Mrs. Barbera with the other. He looked my way and shrieked and took off running.

I chased Junior for half a block and lost him when he cut through Andy Kowalski's driveway. I stopped a moment to catch my breath and answer my phone.

"Babe," Ranger said.

"I lost him at the corner of Green and Broome. I think he's doubling back toward my parents' house. You can't miss him. He's eating a cookie, and he's got his barn door open."

I looked between houses and saw Ranger's black Porsche Turbo glide down the street. I stood perfectly still and listened for footsteps. A dog barked on the next block, and I ran in that direction. I crossed the street, hopped a fence, bushwhacked through a jungle of out-of-control forsythia, and spotted Junior Turley displaying his wares to old Mrs. Gritch.

I bolted out of the bushes and tackled Turley. We both went down to the ground, where we wrestled around, Turley trying to get away and me holding on.

"Stop that this instant," Mrs. Gritch said. "You're going to roll over my mums." And she turned the hose on us.

A black boot came into my line of vision, the water stopped, and Ranger lifted Turley off me and held him out at arm's length, Turley's feet not touching the ground, his pride and joy hanging limp against his drenched pants like a giant slug.

"I'm guessing this is the flasher," Ranger said.

I got to my feet and pushed my wet hair back from my face. "Yep. Junior Turley. And he owes me cuffs."

"I left them with your granny," Junior said.

I was soaked to the skin and getting cold. "I need to get out of these wet clothes," I said to Ranger.

"Go home and change. I'll have one of my men drop Mr. Turley at the police station."

"Thanks. I'll start riding around, checking things out for you, as soon as I get dry clothes."

I took a shower, put on clean jeans and my last clean sweater, and carted my overflowing laundry basket out to my car. The plan was to ride around and do a fast look at the Rangeman accounts that were between my house and my parents' house. This included Hamilton Avenue. Then I would mooch dinner from my mom and do my laundry at her house. There were machines in the basement laundry room of my apartment building, but I was pretty sure the place was inhabited by trolls, and I'd eat dirt before I'd go down there.

I drove by two houses and three businesses. The third business was the insurance company that had already been robbed. I didn't see anything suspicious at any of the locations. No one skulking in the shadows, casing the joint. No one throwing Snickers wrappers on the ground. The two houses were large, set in the middle of large landscaped lots. Easy to burgle if you didn't have to worry about the alarm system. The two remaining businesses were on Hamilton and would be more difficult to break into. They were both in high-visibility areas with poor back access. In both cases, the rear entrance opened to a chain-link-fenced lot that was gated at night.

I motored over to my parents' house and was

surprised not to find Lula's car parked at the curb. I thought for sure this would be another barbecue night.

My mom and dad and Grandma Mazur were already seated when I walked in. I told them not to get up, but my mother and grandmother jumped to their feet and set a place for me. My father kept eating.

"Leave the laundry," my mother said. "I'll do the laundry later."

I sat at the table and filled my plate with pot roast, potatoes, gravy, and green beans.

"Where's Lula?" I asked Grandma Mazur. "I'm surprised you aren't barbecuing again tonight."

"She had a date with some hot fireman," Grandma said. "She said she was gonna give him brown sugar, and I said that was okay so long as she had some left for the barbecue sauce."

The phone rang and my mother and grandmother looked at each other and sat firm.

"Aren't you going to answer the phone?" I asked.

"It's been ringing off the hook," Grandma said. "I don't want to talk to any more grumpy women. Who'd think this would make such a stink? I help my granddaughter do her job, and next thing, we're all in the doghouse."

"It's about Junior Turley," my mother said to me. "Some of the women in the neighborhood are upset because you put him in jail."

"He exposed himself," I said. "Men aren't supposed to go around exposing themselves at unsuspecting women."

"Well, technically none of us was unsuspecting," Grandma said. "We wait for him to show up. I guess it's one of them generation things. You get to an age and you look forward to seeing a winkie at four in the afternoon when you're peeling potatoes for supper.

The thing about Junior and his winkie is, you don't have to do anything about it. You just take a look and he moves on."

I poured more gravy over my potatoes. "Mrs. Zajak filed a complaint against him."

"She was in a snit because he skipped her that day," Grandma said. "It was starting to rain and he cut his circuit short. Everybody's mad at her, too."

"He won't be in jail forever," I said. "I'm sure Vinnie will bail him out again in the morning."

"Yeah, but I think his winkie-waggin' days are over," Grandma said.

It was dark when I left my parents' house. Clouds had rolled in and a light drizzle was falling. I did a sweep past the accounts I'd checked out earlier, and I went on to Broad Street and the area around the arena. Traffic was relatively heavy, and I was only able to catch glimpses of Ranger's buildings. The drizzle turned to rain, and I decided to quit for the night and start over in the morning.

An hour later, I was changed into my pajamas, watching television, and Lula showed up.

"I swear I don't know what things are coming to," Lula said, bustling through my front door and heading straight for the refrigerator. "What have you got in here? Did you eat at your mama's house tonight? Do you got leftovers? I need something to calm my stomach. This keeps up, and I'm gonna get a ulcer or diarrhea or something." She by-passed the pot roast and mashed potatoes and went straight for the pineapple upside-down cake. "You don't mind if I eat this, do you?"

"Knock yourself out."

Lula found a fork and dug into the cake. "First off, I got myself a date with that hot-lookin' fireman. You remember the one. The big brute with muscles bulgin' out everywhere. So he came over, and we did some talkin'. And then one thing led to another, and he said would I mind if he go into my bedroom. And I told him he was sittin' on my bedroom on account of I had to turn the bedroom into a closet. I mean, where's a girl supposed to put her shoes and her dress-up clothes? Anyways, I supposed he had things to do with himself, so I pulled out my sleep sofa, and I wasn't paying much attention to him, and next thing he's all dressed up in one of my cocktail dresses from the Dolly Parton collection."

"Get out."

"Swear to God. And he didn't look good in it, either. It was all wrong for him. He sees me lookin' at him and he says, *I hope you don't mind I'm wearing your dress.* And I say, hell yeah, I mind. You don't fit in that dress. You're bustin' out of it. You're gonna ruin it, and it's one of my favorites."

"And then what?"

"Then he gets all huffy, saying he thought he looked pretty darn good in the dress, and I shouldn't be talkin' about bustin' out of stuff. So I ask him exactly what that's supposed to mean, and he says, *figure it out, fatso.*"

I sucked in some air on that one. Calling Lula fatso was like asking to die.

"It got ugly after that," Lula said. "I don't want to go into the depressin' details, but he got his ass out of my apartment, and he wasn't wearin' my dress when he exited, either." She looked down at the empty cake plate. "What happened to the cake?"

"You ate it."

"Hunh," Lula said. "I didn't notice."

"Easy come, easy go," I said.

"That's so true. It's true about cake and men."

"Doesn't sound traumatic enough to give you an ulcer," I said.

"That wasn't the traumatic part. The traumatic part came after I booted him out. I was putting my gown away, and I heard someone knockin' at my door. I figured it was the moron fireman coming back to get his clothes. . . ."

"He left without his clothes?"

"He was in a hurry after I got my gun. The thing is, I already threw his clothes out my window. You know I live on the second floor of the house, so the clothes kind of floated down and landed in some bushes, and maybe he didn't notice. So I'm thinkin' it's just this loser again, and I open the door, and it's the Chipotle killers, and the one's got the big-ass meat cleaver and the other's got a gun."

"Omigosh."

"Yeah, that's what I said. I jumped back real quick and slammed the door shut, and *bang, bang, bang*, there was three bullets shot through my door. Can you imagine the nerve of them defacing my door? And it's not even like I own the door. This here's a rental property. And I don't see where I should be held responsible to pay for that door."

"What happened next?"

"I got *my* gun and *I* shot a whole bunch more holes in the door while they were trying to kick it in."

"Did you hit anyone?"

"I don't know. I emptied about half a clip in the door, and when I stopped shooting, there weren't any sounds coming from the other side. So I waited a minute, and then I peeked out, and I didn't see no decapitators. And there wasn't any blood all splattered around, either, although hard to believe I missed them, on account of they had their foot to the door when I started shooting."

It was easy for me to believe. Lula was the worst shot ever. Lula couldn't hit the side of a barn if she was three feet away from it.

"So that's why I'm here," Lula said, retrieving a big black garbage bag she'd left in the outside hall. "I brought some clothes and stuff with me because I figure I could stay with you while my door is getting fixed. It looks like Swiss cheese, and the lock's broke from those assholes kickin' at it." Lula closed my door behind her and took a look at it. "You got a real good door here. It's one of them metal fire doors. I only had a wimp-ass wood one."

I was speechless. Lula's a good friend, but having her as a roommate would be like getting locked in a closet with a rhinoceros in full attention deficit disorder mode.

"You don't have Morelli coming over or nothin', do you?" she asked. "I don't want to interfere. And I'll be gone as soon as they get my new door put up. Don't seem to me there's much to it. You get a new door and you put it up on those hinges, right?"

I nodded. "Yuh," I said.

"Are you okay?" Lula asked. "You look all glassy-eyed. Good thing I'm here. You might be coming down with something." She settled into my couch and focused on the TV screen. "This is one of my favorite shows. I watch this every Thursday."

I joined her on the couch and tried to relax. It'll be fine, I told myself. It's just for tonight. Tomorrow she'll get the door fixed, and I'll have my apartment back. And Lula's a good person. This is the least I could do.

Three minutes after sitting down, Lula's head dropped forward, and she was asleep, softly snoring. The snoring got louder and louder, until finally it was drowning out the sound from the television and I was sitting on my hands to keep from choking her.

"Hey!" I yelled in her ear.

"What?"

"You're snoring."

"No way. I was watching television. Look at me. Do I look like I'm asleep?"

"I'm going to bed," I said.

"You sure you don't want to see the end of this? This is a real good show."

"I'll catch it on reruns."

I closed the door to my bedroom, crawled into bed, and shut my light off. I took a couple deep breaths and willed myself to go to sleep. Relax, I told myself. Calm down. Life is good. Think of a gentle breeze. Think of the moon in a dark sky. Hear the ocean. My eyes snapped open. I wasn't hearing the ocean. I was hearing Lula snoring. I put my pillow over my head and went back to talking myself into sleep. Hear the ocean. Hear the wind in the trees. *Shit!* It wasn't working. All I could hear was Lula.

Okay, I had a choice. I could kick her out of my apartment. I could hit her in the head with a hammer until she was dead. Or I could leave.

I parked in the Rangeman garage and fobbed myself into the elevator and up to the seventh floor. I knew all eyes were on me in the control room. I waved at the Minicam hidden in the far corner of the elevator and tried to look nonchalant. I was wearing sneakers, flannel pajamas, and a sweatshirt. I'd called Ranger on the way across town and told him I needed a room. He said he was out on surveillance, and the only room available was his bedroom . . . so that was where I was headed.

I walked through his apartment in the dark and debated sleeping on the couch, but in the end Ranger's bed was too alluring. He was working a double shift, doing drive-bys on accounts he felt were at highest risk for break-in. That meant he wouldn't be back until six A.M. All I had to do was set the alarm so I'd be out of his bed before he rolled in.

The next morning, I was still in my pajamas and was standing in Ranger's kitchen when he got home. I wasn't entirely with the program, needing at least another two hours of sleep and a lot of hot coffee. Ranger had been up for more than twenty-four hours and looked annoyingly alert.

He wrapped an arm around me and kissed me just above my ear. "There's something wrong with this picture," Ranger said. "You're in my bed a lot, but never with me."

"It was nice of you to let me stay here. Lula has taken over my apartment."

"Nice has nothing to do with it," Ranger said.

"How was your night?"

"Long. And uneventful. I need to get some sleep. Are you coming back to bed with me?"

"No. I'm up for the day. Gotta get to work and solve all your problems."

"If you call Ella, she'll bring breakfast. Or you can get dressed and have breakfast on the fifth floor."

"I haven't got any clothes."

"Ella has clothes for you."

He took a bottle of water from the refrigerator, kissed me on the forehead, and left the kitchen. I called Ella, told her I was in Ranger's apartment, and ten minutes later, Ella was at the door with a breakfast tray and a shopping bag filled with Rangeman gear.

Ella wore Rangeman black just like everyone else

in the building. Today she was in a girl-style V-neck T-shirt and black jeans.

I took the bag and tray from her at the door and thanked her.

"Let me know if the clothes don't fit," she said. "I saw you in the building yesterday, and I took a guess at the size. I didn't think you'd changed from the last time you worked here."

"I didn't see you," I said. "I never see you! Food just mysteriously appears and disappears in the fifth-floor kitchen."

"I try to stay invisible and not disrupt the men's routine."

Ella left, and I ate a bagel with cream cheese, drank a couple cups of coffee, and picked at some fresh fruit. My eyes were pretty much open, but I wasn't sure my heart was beating fast enough to propel me through the day. I collapsed on Ranger's couch and woke up a little before eight A.M. I picked some clothes out of the shopping bag, tiptoed past Ranger, and quietly closed the bathroom door.

I took a shower, brushed my teeth, dressed in my new clothes, and emerged from the bathroom feeling like a functioning human being. I was awake. I was clean. The caffeine had kicked in and my heart was racing. Okay, maybe it wasn't the caffeine. Maybe it was the sight of Ranger with a day-old beard, sleeping in the bed I'd recently vacated.

I left the apartment and took the elevator to the fifth floor. Roger King was monitoring the station that included the code computer. I paused in front of him to watch him work. He was on the phone with an account that had accidentally tripped their alarm. He was polite and professional. The conversation was short. The account gave King their password, King verified the password and ended the call.

"That's the first time I've seen someone verify a password," I said to King.

King was a nice-looking guy with a voice like velvet. I knew from his human resources file that he was twenty-seven years old and had a degree in criminal justice from a community college. He'd worked as a cop in a small town in Pennsylvania but quit to take the job with Rangeman.

"If you work this shift, you get a lot of bogus alarms," King said. "People get up in the morning and forget the alarm is on. By the time Chet takes over, this desk is like a graveyard."

When Chet showed up for his shift, I ventured out of my cubicle again and attempted small talk. Chet was polite but not stimulating, and I was feeling like I was contributing to the graveyard syndrome, so I moseyed on back to work, starting a computer search on a deadbeat client.

Louis had made good on the new chair, and my ass no longer cramped after a half hour. I was wearing black slacks that had some stretch, and a short-sleeved V-neck knit shirt with *Rangeman* stitched on it and my name stitched below the *Rangeman*. Ella had also given me cargo pants and matching button-down-collared shirts with roll-up sleeves, a couple stretchy little skirts, black running shoes, black socks, a black zippered sweatshirt, and a black windbreaker. I was on my own for underwear.

A little before noon, I sensed a shift in the climate and looked up to find Ranger on deck. He spoke briefly to each of the men at the monitoring stations, grabbed a sandwich from the kitchen, and stopped at my cubicle on his way to his office. He was freshly showered and shaved and perfectly pressed in black dress slacks and shirt.

"I have a client meeting in the boardroom in fifteen minutes," he said. "After that, I need to catch up on paperwork, and then I'll take another surveillance shift at six. How far did you get on the accounts list yesterday?"

"Not that far. I was getting ready to pack up here and spend the afternoon riding around."

"Do you need a company car?"

"No. I'm okay in the Escort."

I stuffed myself into my new Rangeman sweatshirt, hiked my purse onto my shoulder, and went to the kitchen to load up on free food. Ella had set out vegetable soup and crackers, assorted sandwiches, a salad bar, and a large display of fresh fruit. I looked it all over and blew out a sigh.

Ramon was behind me, and he burst out laughing. "Let me guess what that sigh was about. You want a hot dog, fries, and a brownie with ice cream."

"I'd kill for a meatball sub and a hunk of birthday cake, but this is better for me," I said, selecting a barbecue chicken sandwich.

"Yeah, I keep telling myself that. If I get shot dead on the job, there won't be an ounce of fat on me."

"Do you worry about that?"

"Getting shot dead? No. I don't do a lot of worrying, but the reality is most of this job is routine, with the occasional potential for really bad shit."

I dropped the sandwich into my purse, along with an apple and an organic granola bar. "Gotta go," I said. "Things to do."

"Knock yourself out."

I took the elevator to the garage, wrenched open the rusted door on my p.o.s. Escort, and motored out to the street. Probably it was stupid to refuse Ranger's offer of a company car, but it seemed like the right thing to do at the time. I had lousy car karma, and I always felt crappy when I used Ranger's Porsche and it got stolen or crushed by a garbage truck.

I had my map on the seat beside me, and I drove from one account to the next according to neighborhood. By four o'clock, I'd gone through all the accounts and had checked off a handful that I thought had the potential for a future break-in. I'd gone full circle around the city and ended on lower Hamilton, a half mile from the bonds office.

Lula hadn't called about the door, but I felt confident the door had been replaced and everything was cool. I drove up Hamilton to talk to Connie and Lula and found Connie was manning the office all by herself.

"Where is everyone?" I asked Connie.

"Vinnie is writing bond for someone, and Lula is at your apartment. She said she lives there now."

"I let her stay last night because her door was broken."

"I guess her door is still broken," Connie said.

"That's ridiculous. How long does it take to replace a door? You go to Home Depot, buy a door, and hang it on those doohickey hinge things."

"Something about it being a crime scene. The door can't be replaced until the lab checks it out."

"Who said that?"

"Morelli. He stopped by the office to talk to her after she reported the shooting."

Unh! Mental head slap.

I dialed Morelli and did some anti-hyperventilation exercises while I waited for him to pick up.

"What?" Morelli said.

"Did you tell Lula she couldn't replace her door?"

"Yeah."

"That's stupid. She has to replace her door. How can she live in her apartment without a door?"

"It's a crime scene that's part of an ongoing murder investigation, and we couldn't schedule evidence collection today. I'll have a guy out there tomorrow, and then she can replace her door."

"You don't understand. She's camped out in my apartment."

"And?"

"I can't live with her! She rumbles around. She takes up space. *Lots of space!* And she snores!!"

"Listen," Morelli said. "I have my own problems."

"Such as?"

"You don't want to know."

A woman's voice called out in the background. "Get off the phone. I need help with my zipper."

My heart felt like it had stopped dead in my chest. "Is that who I think it is?" I asked Morelli.

"Yeah, and I can't get rid of her. Thank God her zipper's stuck. I'm moving in with my brother."

For a moment, my entire field of vision went red. Undoubtedly due to a sudden, violent rise in blood pressure once my heart started beating again. It was Joyce Barnhardt. I hated Joyce Barnhardt. She was a sneaky, mean little kid when we were in school together. She spread rumors, stole boyfriends, alienated girlfriends, cheated on tests, and looked under stall doors in the girls' bathroom. And now that she was all grown up, she wasn't much different. She stole husbands, boyfriends, and jobs, cheating in any way possible. Her very presence in Morelli's house sent me into the irrationally enraged nutso zone.

I sucked in some air and pretended I was calm. "You're a big strong guy," I said, my voice mostly steady, well below the screaming level. "You could get rid of her if you wanted."

"It's not that easy. She walked right into my house. I'm going to have to start locking my doors. And she came in with a tray of lasagna. I'm afraid to touch it. She's probably got it laced with roofies."

Okay, get a grip here. She walked into Morelli's house. She wasn't invited. It could be worse, right?

"Why is she suddenly bringing you food?" I asked him.

"She's been up my ass ever since you broke up with me."

"Hey, stud," Joyce yelled to Morelli. "Get over here."

"Shit," Morelli said. "Maybe I should just shoot her and get it done with."

I had a bunch of bitchy comments rolling through my head, but I clamped my mouth shut to keep the comments from spewing out into the phone. I mean, honestly, how hard is it to shove a woman out your back door? What am I supposed to be thinking here?

"I have to go," Morelli said. "I don't like the way she's looking at my olive oil."

I made a sticking-my-finger-down-my-throat gagging motion and hung up.

"What was that about?" Connie wanted to know.

"Barnhardt is trying to feed her lasagna to Morelli."

"She's fungus," Connie said.

"I'm not too happy with Morelli, either."

"He's a man," Connie said. As if that explained it all.

"I suppose I should go home and see what Lula is doing."

"I know what she's doing," Connie said. "She's brewing barbecue sauce with your grandmother."

"In my apartment?"

"That was the plan."

Eek! Okay, so I know my apartment isn't going to get a full-page spread in *Home Beautiful,* but it's all I've got. Bad enough I have Lula in it. Lula and Grandma together are total facaca.

"Gotta go," I said to Connie. "See you tomorrow."

Vinnie stuck his head out of his office. "Where are you going? Why are you dressed up in Rangeman stuff? Christ, you're not moonlighting, are you? You aren't any good when you're working for me full-time. Now I'm sharing you with Ranger?"

"I brought two skips in this week."

"Big deal. What about all the others still in the wind? This isn't a goddamn charity. I'm not buying these idiots out of jail for my health. And it's not like you're the only bounty hunter out there," Vinnie said. "You could be replaced."

"Lucille's been talking redecorating again," Connie said to me. "Vinnie needs money."

Lucille was Vinnie's wife. She tortured Vinnie by constantly redecorating their house and by spending his money faster than he could make it. We figured this was retribution for Vinnie boinking anything that moved. The good part of the deal was that all Vinnie could do was pedal twice as fast, since Lucille's father, Harry the Hammer, financed the bonds office. If Vinnie left Lucille, not only would he be unemployed, there was a good chance he'd be dining with Stanley Chipotle.

"She's killing me," Vinnie said. "I haven't got money to buy a hot dog for lunch. My bookie took me off his iPhone."

Actually, it wasn't a good thing when Vinnie got this broke, because instead of buying favors from professionals on Stark Street, we suspected Vinnie was forced to chase down ducks at the park.

NINE

I left the bonds office, drove a couple blocks on Hamilton, and took a right into Morelli's neighborhood. Best not to examine my motives too closely. I was telling myself morbid curiosity was the driving force, but my heart was beating pretty hard for something that benign. I left-turned onto Morelli's street, cruised half a block, and stopped in front of his house. His SUV was gone, and there was no sign of Joyce's car. No lights on in the house. No sign of activity. I turned at the next corner and headed for the Burg. I drove past Morelli's brother's house. No SUV there, either.

Okay, get a grip, I told myself. No reason to get crazy. Morelli is a free man. He can do whatever the heck he wants. If he wants to act like a jerk and get friendly with Barnhardt, it's his problem. Anyway, I have to expect that he'll be seeing other women. That's what happens when people break up . . . they spend time with other people, right? Just because I don't want to spend time with other people doesn't mean Morelli has to feel that way. I'm one of those people who needs space between relationships. I don't just jump into stuff. And I don't do one-night stands. Usually. There was that time with Ranger, but you couldn't really categorize it as a one-night stand. It was more like a onetime-only ticket to *WOW*.

I turned out of the Burg onto Hamilton, and five minutes later, I pulled into my parking lot. I parked next to Lula's Firebird and looked up at my windows. No smoke. No sign of fire. No one running screaming out of the building. That was good. Maybe I wasn't too late. Maybe they hadn't started cooking yet. Maybe they'd discovered I only had one pot and decided to watch television.

I jogged across the lot, up the stairs, and down the hall to my apartment, reminding myself to stay calm. Lula and Grandma were in my kitchen and my counters were filled with bottles of barbecue sauce, dry rub, vinegar, cooking sherry, a half-empty bottle of rum, lemons, onions, oranges, a keg of ketchup, and a ten-pound can of tomato sauce. Grandma and Lula were in their chef's clothes, except Lula was missing her hat. My sink was filled with dirty measuring cups, assorted utensils, bowls, and measuring spoons. There was a large pot hissing on the stove.

"What the heck is that?" I asked Lula.

"I got my pressure cooker goin' here," Lula said. "I saw it advertised on QVC. It cuts cookin' time in half. Maybe more. And it preserves all the goodness of the food. It was real expensive on television, but I got this one off of Lenny Skulnik. It's good quality, too, because it was made in China."

Lenny Skulnik sold knockoff handbags and kitchen appliances out of the trunk of his car. I went to school with Lenny. He was totally without scruples, and one of the more successful graduates.

"Are you sure it's supposed to make those noises?" I asked Lula. "And what about all that steam?"

"It's supposed to steam," Lula said. "It's why you

call it a pressure cooker. And if you look close, you could see the pressure indicator is all red. That's the sign of good pressure cookin'. You wouldn't want no green shit on a pressure-cookin' indicator."

"Are you sure? Did you read the instructions?"

"This one didn't come with no instructions. This was the economy model."

I kept Rex's cage on the kitchen counter. It was lost behind the bottles and cans, but I could see Rex running on his wheel for all he was worth, every now and then sneaking a peek at the pot on the stove.

The pot had gone beyond hissing and was now whistling a high keening wail. *We-e-e-e-e-e-e.* Red sauce was sputtering out of the steam hole and the pot was vibrating.

"Don't worry," Lula said. "It's just workin' itself up to maximum pressurizin'."

"It's a modern miracle," Grandma said.

I had a bad feeling in the pit of my stomach. I always worried when the little bulb at the top of anything went red. And I recognized the sound the pot was making. I felt like that sometimes, and it never ended well.

"Maybe you should turn the heat down a little," I said to Lula.

"I guess I could do that," Lula said. "It must almost be done. We've been cooking it for over an hour."

Lula reached for the knob on the stove and at that exact moment there was a *popping* sound and the two latches flew off the lid.

"Holy cats," Lula said.

"She's gonna blow!" Grandma yelled. "Run for your life!"

Rex darted into his soup can. Lula and Grandma and I turned tail and bolted. And the lid exploded off the pot. *BANG!* The lid hit the ceiling like it had been launched from a rocket, and barbecue sauce was thrown onto every exposed surface. There was a hole in the ceiling where the lid had impacted, and sauce dripped from the ceiling and slimed down cabinets.

"Guess we aren't having barbecue for dinner tonight," Grandma said, creeping back to the stove to look in the pot.

Lula swiped at some of the sauce on the counter and tasted it. "Not exactly right yet, anyways."

A splotch of sauce dripped off the ceiling onto Grandma's head, and she retreated out of the kitchen.

"I feel like getting some of that Cluck-in-a-Bucket chicken," Grandma said. "I wouldn't mind the Clucky Dinner Tray with the extra-crispy chicken and mashed potatoes."

"That's a good idea," Lula said. "I could use some chicken, and I got a coupon for the Clucky Dinner Tray."

"What about my kitchen?" I asked Lula.

"What about it?"

"It's a mess!"

Lula glanced at the kitchen. "Yeah, it don't look too good. You're gonna have to use one of them degreasers on it."

"I'm not cleaning this kitchen."

"Well, somebody gotta do it," Lula said.

I narrowed my eyes at her. "That would be you."

"Hunh," Lula said. "In my opinion, that pot manufacturer should be responsible for the cleanup. I got a faulty pot."

"The manufacturer in China?" I asked her.

"Yeah. That's the one. I'm gonna tell Lenny Skulnik he needs to get in touch with them."

"And you think they're going to send someone from China to clean my kitchen?"

"I see your point," Lula said. "I guess I could do

some cleaning, but I'd need a stepladder. Or else I'd need a big strong fireman to help me out."

"I thought you pulled a gun on him."

"Yeah, but he might be persuaded to overlook that if I let him wear my dress again."

Twenty minutes later, Lula rolled her Firebird into the Cluck-in-a-Bucket parking lot. Cluck-in-a-Bucket is a fast-food hot spot in Trenton. The food is surprisingly good, if you like nice greasy chicken, heavily salted gelatinous potatoes, and gravy so thick you could walk across a vat of it. Lula, Grandma, and I gave it five stars. And the very best part of Cluck-in-a-Bucket is the giant red, yellow, and white chicken impaled on a thirty-foot candy-striped pole that rotates high above the red-roofed building 24/7. Paris has the Eiffel Tower, New York has the Empire State Building, and Trenton has the revolving chicken.

On weekends and during the dinner rush, there was always some poor sap dressed up in a Mister Clucky chicken suit. He clucked at kids, and he danced around and annoyed the heck out of everyone. The guy who owned Cluck-in-a-Bucket thought the dancing chicken was great, but the truth was everyone would have been happy to pay more for the chicken if Mister Clucky never clucked again.

Lula was one of three people out of ten thousand who liked Mr. Clucky.

"Lookit here," Lula said. "It's the dancin' chicken. I love that chicken. I like his red hat and his big chicken feet. I bet there's a real cute guy inside that chicken suit. You'd have to be cute to get a job as Mister Clucky."

I was betting there was a scrawny kid with a bad complexion inside the suit.

Lula got out of the car and went up to Mister Clucky. "You're a big Mister Clucky," Lula said. "You must be

new. I got a bet with my friend that you're a real cutie-
pie. How'd you like to give us a look?"

"How'd you like my beak up your ass?"

"Excuse me?"

"You heard me. Fuck off, fatso."

"Fatso? Did I hear you call me fatso? Because I better be mistaken."

"Fatso. Fatso. Fatty fatty fatso."

Lula took a closer look at Mister Clucky. "Hold on
here. I recognize your voice."

"No you don't," Mister Clucky said.

"Larry? Is that you?"

"Maybe."

Lula turned to Grandma and me. "This is Larry, the
fireman I was telling you about."

"The one who wears dresses?" Grandma asked.

"Yep. That's the one," Lula said.

"Lots of men wear dresses," Mister Clucky said.
"It's not against the law."

"That's real true," Lula said. "And I've been reviewing our unfortunate date, and I decided you didn't look
all that bad in that turquoise cocktail dress. Now that
I'm thinking about it, that gown might have brought
out the color of your eyes."

"Do you really think so?"

"Yeah. That gown was made for you," Lula said. "In
fact, if you want to let bygones be bygones, I might let
you try it on again."

"I saw you had a beaded sweater that looked like it
might match," Mister Clucky said.

"Yeah, you can wear the sweater, too."

He adjusted his clucky head and hiked up his pri-
vates. "I have to work until nine."

"That's fine," Lula said. "Only thing is, I'm staying
someplace else. I'll get my food and come back with
my new address."

We put our orders in and moved to the pickup station.

"He seemed like a real nice chicken," Grandma said.

"Yeah," Lula said. "I guess he's not so bad. And he's a real good dancer in his chicken suit. And on top of that, I bet he could get me a discount on chicken. He just took me by surprise the other night, causing me to overreact about the dress."

We all had the Clucky Dinner Tray, plus Lula supplemented hers with a side of biscuits and a bucket of barbecue chicken, which she said was research. She wrote my address on a napkin and handed it to Mister Clucky when we left.

"It must be fun to be Mister Clucky," Lula said to him.

"Yeah, the suit is pretty cool, and I get to dance around. Mostly, I do it for spending money, though. I do okay as a fireman, but nice handbags don't come cheap."

We all piled into the Firebird, and Lula drove a couple blocks to the supermarket.

"I'll be right back," Lula said. "I just gotta get some cleaning products."

"I'll go with you," Grandma said. "We could take another look at the barbecue aids."

I stayed in the car and called Ranger. "Just checking in," I said. "Anything interesting going on?"

"Nada. And you?"

"Lula and Grandma exploded a pot of barbecue sauce in my kitchen, Lula has a date later tonight with Mister Clucky, and it looks like I'll be spending the night in your apartment again."

"Something to look forward to," Ranger said. "Do you have any thoughts on my accounts?"

"Yes. I picked out several that I think have break-in potential." I gave him the addresses and told him Vinnie was having a cow over my open files. "I'm going to need some time off tomorrow to look for one of these guys," I said.

"Done," Ranger said. And he disconnected.

Lula swung her ass out of the supermarket and Grandma trotted behind her. They hustled across the lot to the car, Lula rammed herself behind the wheel, and in moments we were back on the road.

"Next stop is my house," Lula said. "I gotta get clothes for Larry."

Grandma leaned forward from the backseat. "What if the killers are waiting for you?"

"That would be good luck," Lula said. "We could take them down and get the reward. I'd shoot the heck out of them, and then we'd drag their carcasses to the police station."

"We'd kick their asses," Grandma said.

"Damn skippy," Lula said.

Lula eased the Firebird to the curb in front of her house, and we all piled out. Lula lived in an emerging neighborhood of hardworking people. Homes were small, yards were postage stamp size, and aspirations were modest. Lula rented half of the second floor of a two-story Victorian house that had been painted lavender with pink gingerbread trim. It was possibly the most inappropriate house in the entire universe for Lula. It was too small, too dainty, and too lavender. Every time I saw her walk through the front door, I had the feeling she was going through a portal into another dimension . . . like Harry Potter at the train station.

We got to the top of the stairs and gaped at Lula's bullet-hole-riddled door. Yellow-and-black crime scene tape had been plastered over the door, but it hadn't been applied in such a way that it prevented the door from being used.

"Cheap-ass plywood hollow-core door," Lula said. "Bird shot would go through this crap-ass door."

Grandma and I followed Lula into the one-room apartment and waited by the door while she went to her giant closet.

"This won't take long," Lula said. "I got everything organized in here by collection, so depending who I want to be, it's easy to find."

Lula opened her closet door and two men jumped out at her.

One had a gun and the other had a cleaver, and they were both wearing gorilla masks.

"It's the killers! *It's the killers!*" Lula shrieked.

"Grab her," the cleaver guy said. "Hold her still so I can chop off her head." And then he giggled and all the hair stood up on my arms.

His partner was trying to sight his gun on Lula. "For crying out loud, get out of the way and let me shoot her. Big deal, you're a butcher. Get over it."

The guy with the cleaver swung out at Lula, giggling the whole time. Lula ducked, and the cleaver got stuck in the wall.

Lula scrambled hands and knees under a table, around an overstuffed chair, out her door, and thundered down the stairs.

The killers ran after Lula, not even noticing Grandma and me standing with our eyes bugged out and our mouths open.

"Don't that beat all," Grandma said.

She hauled her .45 long-barrel out of her big black patent-leather purse, stepped into the hall, planted her feet, and squeezed off a couple shots at the two guys running down the stairs.

The gorilla guys disappeared out the front door, into the night. There was the sound of car doors opening and slamming shut. An engine caught, and I heard the car drive away. A moment later, Lula appeared at the front door. She had a bunch of leaves stuck in her hair and a big dirt smudge on her wraparound blouse.

"What happened?" she said. "I don't hardly remember anything except I fell in a big bush."

"It was the killers," Grandma said. "We kicked their asses."

"Oh yeah. Now it's all coming back to me." Lula climbed the stairs and sleepwalked through her door. "It's a nightmare," she said. "It's a friggin' nightmare."

Grandma rooted through Lula's cabinets in the little kitchenette area of the room and came up with a bottle of Jack Daniel's. She took a pull from the bottle and handed it over to Lula. "This'll fix you up," Grandma said. "Take a snort of this."

Lula chugged some Jack Daniel's and looked a little better. "This is bullshit," she said. "This gotta end."

TEN

I took Grandma home, and then I drove to my apartment building and walked Lula into the apartment.

"Smells like barbecue in here," Lula said.

It *looked* like barbecue.

"Are you going to be okay?" I asked Lula.

"Yeah, I'm fine. I'm gonna hang my Dolly Parton dress and sweater up and get to work. I want to be working when Larry gets here."

"You should call Morelli."

"I guess, but I don't see where it does any good."

"He's working on finding these guys, and it gives him a more complete picture." And most important, it probably annoys the hell out of him and interrupts whatever he's doing.

"What's with you two?" Lula said. "Are you really calling it quits?"

"Hard to say. Every time we see each other we get into an argument. We don't agree on anything."

"Sounds to me like you're talkin' about the wrong things. Why don't you talk about other things? Like you could make a list of things you won't fight over and then you only talk about those things."

"I think he might be seeing Joyce Barnhardt."

"What?" Lula's eyes almost popped out of her head.

"I hate Joyce Barnhardt. She's Devil Woman. And she's a skank. Men have relations with her and their dicks fall off. If I was you, and I found out Morelli was foolin' around with Joyce Barnhardt, I'd drop-kick his ass clear across the state."

I wrapped my arms around the hamster cage. "I'm taking Rex to Rangeman while you clean the kitchen."

"That's a good idea," Lula said. "We don't want to traumatize him with cleaning fumes. And he might not want to see a giant hairy man in a turquoise cocktail dress. I'm not sure I even want to see it."

I set Rex's cage on the counter in Ranger's kitchen and scrubbed the barbecue sauce off the glass sides.

"This is temporary," I said to Rex. "Don't get attached to Ranger. I know he's strong and sexy. And I know he smells nice, and he has good food, and his apartment is always the right temperature. Problem is, he's got secrets. And he's not in the market for a wife. Okay, so the wife thing might not be a deal breaker since I'm having commitment issues anyway, but the secrets he carries are troublesome."

I gave Rex fresh water and a chunk of bread, and I poured myself a glass of red wine. I took the wine into Ranger's small den, got comfy on the couch, and clicked the television on. I watched an hour-long show on Spain on the Travel Channel, and after that I couldn't find anything of interest. I dropped one of Ranger's T-shirts over my head by way of pajamas, crawled between his orgasmic sheets, and couldn't decide if I wanted him to come home early or stay away until morning.

I came awake with a start, not knowing where I was for a moment, and then remembering. Ranger's bed. I looked at the clock. 6:20 A.M. The light was on in the bathroom. Ranger emerged, still dressed in Rangeman tactical gear. He came to his side of the bed and kicked his shoes off.

"Either get out of the bed or else take your clothes off," he said. "I'm not in a mood to compromise."

"You've been working for eighteen hours. You're supposed to be tired."

"I'm not *that* tired." He removed his watch and set it on the bedside chest. "I saw Rex in the kitchen. Is this going to be an extended stay?"

"Would that be a problem?"

"We'd have to negotiate terms."

"Rent?"

"Sex and closet space," Ranger said.

I heaved myself out of bed. "If you sleep on my side, it's already warm."

I took a shower, dried my hair, and tiptoed past Ranger. He looked dangerous even in sleep, with a beard that was eight hours past five o'clock shadow and a shock of silky brown hair falling across his forehead. I dressed in Rangeman black, grabbed a sweatshirt, and went to the kitchen to say hello to Rex.

"Remember what I said about Ranger," I told Rex, but I'm not sure Rex cared. Rex was asleep in his soup can.

I pocketed my Rangeman key fob, hung my bag on my shoulder, and took the stairs to the fifth floor. Hal and Ramon were sitting at a table in the kitchen. Ramon looked fresh as a daisy. Hal looked like he'd just come off a shift. I got coffee and a bagel and joined them.

"What's going on?" I asked them.

"Same ol', same ol'," Ramon said.

Hal didn't say anything. Hal looked like he was asleep, with a spoon in his hand.

"Earth to Hal," I said.

Ramon cut his eyes to Hal. "Hal's working a double shift in the car."

"It's killing me," Hal said. "I don't know if it's morning or night anymore."

"Big guys like Hal need sleep," Ramon said. "Wiry little guys like me can do with less. And people who aren't exactly human, like Ranger, hardly need sleep at all."

"When we find out who's doing these break-ins, I'm going to personally beat the crap out of him," Hal said. "Then I'm going to sleep for a week."

I ate my bagel, and when Hal and Ramon left for parts unknown, I took a second cup of coffee to my desk. Aside from a couple men looking a little bedraggled from double shifts, everything was business as usual. I ran employee background checks for a start-up company in Whitehorse for almost three hours. My ass didn't cramp in my new chair, but my mind went numb from the tedium of staring at the screen. At ten o'clock, I stopped working for Rangeman and pulled Vinnie's remaining three current files from my bag.

Ernie Dell was wanted for setting fire to several abandoned buildings at the bombed-out end of Stark Street. This strip of Stark was so bleak and devoid of anything resembling civilized society that only a whacked-out crazy person like Ernie Dell would set foot there. Ernie was my age, and for as long as I've known him, which is pretty much my whole life, Ernie has been handicapped with a shape like a butternut squash. Narrow, gourd-like head, narrow shoulders, huge butt.

The second guy on my list was Myron Kaplan. Myron was seventy-eight years old, and for reasons not given in my file, Myron had robbed his dentist at gunpoint. At first glance, this would seem like an easy apprehension, but my experience with old people is that they don't go gently into the night.

That left Cameron Manfred. If I asked Ranger to help me with an apprehension, this is the one I'd choose. Manfred didn't look like a nice guy. He was twenty-six years old, and this was his third arrest for armed robbery. He'd been charged with rape two years ago, but the charge didn't stick. He'd also been accused of assault with a deadly weapon. The victim, who was a rival gang member, lost his hearing and right eye and had almost every bone in his body broken but refused to testify, and the charges were dropped for insufficient evidence. Manfred lived in the projects and worked for a trucking company. His booking photo showed two teardrops tattooed onto his face. Gang members were known to tattoo a teardrop below their eye when they killed someone.

I left a text message for Ranger that I'd be away from Rangeman. I stuffed myself into my sweatshirt, swiped a couple granola bars from the kitchen, and took the elevator to the garage. Traffic was light at mid-morning. Gray sky. The temperature was in the fifties. It felt cold for September.

I parked in front of the bonds office behind a truck that was repairing the front window. Connie was inside, and Lula was nowhere to be seen.

"She called a couple minutes ago," Connie said. "She said she was having a wardrobe issue, but she'd solved it, and she was coming in to work."

The door banged open, and Lula waddled in dressed in a flak vest and riot helmet. "Is it all safe in here?" she asked. "You checked the back room and all, right? I'm not taking no chances until those Chipotle killers are caught."

"Did you drive here dressed like that?" I asked her.

"Yeah. And it wasn't easy. I'm sweating like a pig

in this. And this helmet is gonna ruin my hairdo, but it's better than having my head ventilated with bullet holes."

"Did you talk to Morelli this morning?"

"I did. Jeez Louise, he was in a mood. That man needs to get some. He was cranky."

I tried not to look too happy about that. "Have they made any progress finding the killers?"

"He said they had an out-of-town lead."

"Are you going to take that helmet off, or are you wearing it all day?" Connie asked.

"I guess I could take it off in here."

"I'm looking for Ernie Dell today," I said to Lula. "Do you want to ride shotgun?"

"Is he the firebug?"

"Yep."

"I'm in."

"I don't mind if you wear the flak vest," I told her, "but I'm not riding around with you in the helmet. You look like Darth Vader."

"Okay, but I'm gonna hold you responsible if I get killed."

Ernie lived alone in a large house on State Street. No one knew how he got the house, since no one could ever remember Ernie having a job. Ernie alternately claimed to be a movie producer, a stockbroker, a racecar driver, and an alien. I thought alien was a good possibility.

I idled in front of his house, and Lula and I craned our necks and gaped up at it. It was on about a half acre, on a hill high above the street. Shingles had blown off the roof and lay sprinkled across the yard. Window frames were down to bare wood and were splintered and split. The clapboard siding was charcoal gray. I wasn't sure if it was water stain, battleship paint, or mold.

"Holy crap," Lula said. "Are you shitting me? Someone lives in that? It's falling apart. And there must be a hundred steps to get up the hill. I'll get shin splints climbing those steps."

"There's an alley behind the house. And there's a back driveway and a two-car garage."

I drove around the block, took the alley, and parked in Ernie's driveway.

"What's the deal with this guy?" Lula asked. "Has he always set fires?"

I thought back to Ernie as a kid. "I can't remember him setting fires, but he did a lot of weird things. One time, he entered a talent show and tried to burp "The Star-Spangled Banner," but he was hauled off the stage halfway through. And then he went through a period where he was sure he could make it rain, and he'd start chanting strange things in the middle of arithmetic. *Oowah doowah moo moo hooha*."

"Did it rain?"

"Sometimes."

"What else did he do? I'm starting to like this guy."

"He took a goat to the prom. Dressed it up in a pink ballerina outfit. And he went through a fireworks stage. You'd wake up at two in the morning and fireworks would be going off in your front yard."

We got out of the Escort, and I transferred cuffs from my purse to my back pocket for easier access.

"We don't want to spook him if he's home," I said to Lula. "We're just going to walk to the back door and be calm and friendly. Let me do the talking."

"Why do you get to do the talking?"

"I'm the apprehension agent."

"What am I then?"

"You're my assistant."

"Maybe I don't want to be the assistant. Maybe I want to be the apprehension agent."

"You have to talk to Vinnie about that. Your name has to be on the documentation."

"We could write me in. I got a pen."

"Good grief."

"How about if I just say *hello*."

"Fine. Terrific. Say *hello*."

I knocked on the back door, and Ernie answered in his underwear.

"Hello," Lula said.

Ernie looked like he'd just rolled out of bed. His thinning sandy blond hair was every which way on his head. "What's up?" he asked.

"You missed your court date," I said. "You need to go downtown with me and reschedule."

"Sure," he said. "Wait in the front room while I get dressed."

We followed him through the kitchen that was circa 1942, down a hall with peeling, faded wallpaper, and into the living room. The living room floor was bare, scarred wood. The furniture was minimal. A lumpy secondhand couch. Two folding chairs with the funeral home's name engraved on the back. A rickety end table had been placed between the two folding chairs. No lamps. No television.

"I'll be right back," Ernie said, heading for the stairs. "Make yourself comfortable."

Lula looked around. "How are we supposed to get comfortable?"

"You could sit down," I told her.

Lula sat on one of the folding chairs, and it collapsed under her weight.

"Fuck," she said, spread-eagle on the floor with the chair smashed under her. "I bet I broke a bone."

"Which bone did you break?"

"I don't know. Pick one. They all feel broke."

Lula struggled to her feet and felt around, testing out

her bones. Ernie was still upstairs, getting dressed, but I didn't hear him walking overhead.

I went to the bottom of the stairs and called. "Ernie?"

Nothing. I climbed the stairs and called his name again. Silence. Four rooms, plus a bathroom, led off the center hall. One room was empty. One room was filled with bizarre junk. Store mannequins with broken arms, gallon cans of cooking oil, stacks of bundled newspapers, boxes of firecrackers and rockets, gallon cans of red paint, a wooden crate of rusted nails, a birdcage, a bike that looked like it had been run over by a truck, and God only knows what else. The third room housed a sixty-inch plasma television, an elaborate computer station, and a movie house popcorn machine. A new leather La-Z-Boy recliner sat in the middle of the room and faced the television. The fourth room was his bedroom. A sleeping bag and pillow had been thrown onto the floor of the fourth room. Clothes were scattered around in no special order. Some looked clean and some looked like they'd been worn a lot.

The window was open in the bedroom, and two large hooks wrapped over the windowsill. I crossed the room to the window and looked down. Rope ladder. The sort you might stash in a room as a fire precaution.

I ran downstairs and headed for the kitchen. "He's gone."

Lula and I reached the back door just as an engine caught in the garage, and a baby diarrhea green VW bug chugged out to the alley. We ran for the Escort, jumped in, and took off. I could see the bug two blocks away. Ernie turned right and I floored it, bouncing along the pot-holed service road. I turned right and caught a flash of green a block away. I was gaining on him.

"Do you smell something?" Lula asked.

"Like what?"

"I don't know, but it's not good."

I was concentrating on driving and not on smelling. Ernie was going in circles. He was driving a four-block grid.

"It's like a cat was burning," Lula said. "I never actually smelled a cat burning, but if I did, it would smell like this. And do you think it's getting smokey in here?"

"Smokey?"

"Yow!" Lula said. "Your backseat is on fire. I mean, it's a inferno. Let me out of this car. Pull over. I wasn't meant to be extra crispy."

I screeched to a stop, and Lula and I scrambled out of the car. The fire raced along the upholstery and shot out the windows. Flames licked from the under-carriage and *Vrooosh!* The car was a fireball. I looked up the street and saw the pea green VW lurking at the corner. The car idled for a few moments and sedately drove away.

"How long do you think it's gonna take the fire trucks to get here?" Lula wanted to know.

"Not long. I hear sirens."

"This is gonna be embarrassing. This is the second thing we burned up this week."

I dialed Ranger. "Did I wake you?" I asked.

"No. I'm up and functioning. I just got a report that the GPS unit we attached to your car stopped working."

"You know how when you toast a marshmallow it catches fire and gets all black and melted?"

"Yeah."

"That would be my car."

"Are you okay?"

"Yes, but I'm stranded," I told him.

"I'll send Tank."

* * *

I watched the fire truck disappear down the street, followed by the last remaining cop car. What was left of my Escort was on a flatbed.

"Where do you want me to take this?" the flatbed guy asked me.

"Dump it in the river."

"You got it," he said. And he climbed into the cab and rumbled away.

"Guess you gotta be careful when you're going after someone who likes fire," Lula said.

I had a shiny new black Porsche Cayenne waiting for me. Tank had dropped it off, made sure I didn't need help, and returned to Rangeman. The car was one of several in Ranger's personal fleet. It was immaculate inside, with no trace of Ranger other than a secret drawer under the driver's seat. The drawer held a loaded gun. All cars in Ranger's personal fleet had guns hidden under the seat.

I remoted the car open, and Lula and I got in.

"Now what?" Lula said.

"Lunch."

"I like that idea. And I think we should take something to Larry on account of he's still working on your kitchen."

"It sounds like things went okay last night."

"One thing you learn when you're a 'ho is there's all kinds in this world. Bein' a 'ho is a broadening experience. It's not just all hand jobs, you know. It's listenin' to people sometimes and tryin' to figure out how to make them happy. That's why I was a good 'ho. I didn't charge by the hour."

"And Larry fits in there somewhere."

"Yeah. He's a real interesting person. He was a professional wrestler. His professional name was Lady Death, but he was one of them niche market wrestlers, and his feelings got hurt when the fans didn't like him in his pink outfits. So he quit, and he got a job as a fireman. Turns out he's a hottie, too. He likes wearing ladies' clothes, but he isn't gay."

We decided Larry was probably tired of chicken, so we got ham and cheese and hot pepper subs and brought them back to my apartment.

"Boy, that's great of you to bring me lunch," Larry said. "I'm starving."

He was still wearing the Dolly Parton number. It had a fitted bodice with spaghetti straps and a swirly chiffon skirt, and there was a lot of chest hair and back hair sticking out of the top of the dress. There was also a lot of armpit hair, leg hair, and knuckle hair. He'd accessorized the dress with heels and rubber gloves.

"I know this looks funny," he said, "but I like to feel pretty when I clean."

"Go for it," I told him. And I meant it. I didn't care what he was wearing as long as I was getting barbecue sauce removed from my walls.

My cell phone buzzed, and I recognized Morelli's number.

"I'm trying to find Lula," he said. "I called the office, and they said she was with you."

"Why didn't you just call her cell?"

"She's not answering her cell."

"Do you want to talk to her?"

"I need to show her a photograph. Where are you?"

"We're in my apartment."

"Stay there. I'm a couple minutes away."

"That was Morelli," I said to Lula. "He's coming here with a photograph he wants you to look at. He said you're not answering your cell phone."

"It's out of juice. I forgot to plug it in."

Five minutes later, I opened my door to Morelli. He looked at me in my Rangeman clothes, and the line of his mouth tightened. "Why don't I just lie down in the parking lot and let you run over me a couple times. It would be less painful."

"Been there, done that," I said.

The bright red splotches in my kitchen caught his attention. "Remodeling?" he asked.

"Pressure cooker full of barbecue sauce."

That got a smile. "Where's Lula?"

"Eating lunch in the dining room."

The smile widened when Morelli walked into the dining room and eyeballed Lula in her flak vest and Larry in his cocktail dress.

"This here's Larry," Lula said to Morelli. "He's Mister Clucky."

"I'm a fireman full-time," Larry said. "Being Mister Clucky is my part-time job."

Morelli extended his hand. "Joe Morelli. Isn't it early in the day for a cocktail dress?"

"I guess," Larry said, "but I stayed over, and this was all I had to wear."

Morelli cut his eyes to me. "He stayed over?"

"It's complicated."

"I bet."

"Are those pictures you're holding for me?" Lula asked. "You need to be figuring this out, because I'm gettin' tired of this *kill Lula* bullshit."

Morelli gave her the photos, and Lula flipped through them.

"This one," Lula said. "This guy with the bad haircut and a nose like Captain Hook. He's one of the killers. He's the one with the meat cleaver."

"That's Marco the Maniac," Morelli said.

"Oh shit," Lula said. "I got a killer named Maniac. Where's my helmet? I need my helmet. I think I left it at the office."

"His profile finally popped out of the system," Morelli said. "He's from Chicago. Works as a butcher, but he makes spare change by chopping off fingers and toes of people who annoy the Chicago Mob. Mostly gets off on insufficient evidence, but did some time a couple years ago. I don't know how he's connected to Chipotle. I'm assuming it was a contract hit, but we don't really know."

"You're gonna arrest him, right?" Lula said.

"As soon as we find him."

"Well, what are you doing standing here!" Lula said. "You gotta mobilize or something. Put out one of them APB things. I need all my fingers and toes. I got some Via Spiga sandals that aren't gonna look right if I only got nine toes. And what about the guy with the gun? Why don't you got a picture of him?"

"We're working on it," Morelli said.

"Working on it, my ass," Lula said. "I'm gettin' the runs. I need a doughnut."

Morelli grabbed my wrist and tugged me to the door. "I need to talk to you alone," he said, moving me into the hall and down toward the elevator.

"I don't want to argue about Rangeman," I told him.

"I don't care about Rangeman," Morelli said, his voice cracking with laughter. "I want to know about the guy in the dress. What the heck is that about?"

"Lula exploded the barbecue sauce in my kitchen and didn't want to clean it up, so she told this cross-dresser he could wear her dress if he scrubbed the sauce off the walls and ceiling."

"And he spent the night?"

"Lula's guest."

"The crime lab got to her apartment first thing this morning. She can change out that door anytime she wants."

"I'm not sure she'll go back there. She's really freaked."

"From what I can tell, Marco is an animal with a very small brain. He's dangerous and disgusting but not smart. At the risk of sounding insensitive, Lula is a large target, and anyone else would have killed her by now."

"So you think she shouldn't be worried?"

"I think she should be terrified. If this goes on long enough, Marco is going to get lucky, and Lula is going to lose a lot more than a toe." He punched the elevator button. "Is that Ranger's Cayenne in your parking lot?"

A small sigh escaped before I could squelch it. "I tried to capture Ernie Dell, but he torched my car and got away. Ranger gave me a loaner."

The elevator doors opened, and Morelli stepped inside.

"How close are you to catching Marco?" I asked him.

"Not close enough."

I returned to the apartment and finished my lunch.

"We should have got dessert," Lula said. "I don't know what we were thinking about, not getting dessert."

"You have to stop obsessing about food," I told her. "You're going to weigh four hundred pounds."

"Are you sayin' I'm fat? Because I think I'm just a big and beautiful woman."

"You're still beautiful," I said. "But I think the *big* is getting a little *bigger.*"

"That's a valid point," Lula said. She locked on to Larry. "Do you think I'm fat?"

Larry was deer in headlights. He'd already traveled this road. "Well, you're not *too* fat," he said.

"Not too fat for what?" Lula wanted to know.

"For me. For this dress. I'm sure you look much better in this dress than I do."

"Damn right," Lula said. "Take that dress off and I'll show you. This dress fits me perfect."

Larry stood and reached for the zipper, and I clapped my hands over my eyes.

"It's okay," Larry said to me. "I'm wearing boxers. I didn't have any nice lingerie with me."

"It doesn't matter," I said. "I don't want to see Lula, either. Tell me when it's over."

"Well, what the heck is wrong with this dress?" Lula said a couple minutes later. "I can't get this thing together."

I opened my eyes, and Lula had the dress on, but it wasn't zipped. There was fat bulging out everywhere, and Larry had his knee against Lula's back and was two-handing the zipper, trying to pull it up.

"Suck it in," Larry said. "I have this problem sometimes, too."

"I'm all sucked," Lula said. "I can't suck no more."

Veins were standing out in Larry's temples and bulging in his neck. "I'm getting it," he said. "I can press two hundred pounds, and there's no reason why I can't get this zipper closed."

The heck there wasn't. The dress wasn't made out of spandex. And even spandex had limits.

"I've almost got it," Larry said, sweat dripping off his flushed face, running in rivers down his chest. "I've got an inch to go. One lousy, motherfucking, cocksucking inch."

Lula was standing tall, not moving a muscle.

"Yeah, baby!" Larry said. "I got it! Woohoo! *Yeah!*" He stepped back and pumped his fist and did a white boy shuffle in his boxers.

Lula still wasn't moving. Her eyes were all wide and bulging, and she was looking not so brown as usual.

"Can't breathe," Lula whispered. "Feel faint."

And then *POW,* the zipper let loose, and Lula flopped onto the floor, gasping for air.

Larry and I peered down at her.

"Maybe I could use to lose a pound or two," Lula said.

We got Lula out of the dress and back into her marigold yellow stretch slacks, matching scoop-neck sweater, and black flak vest. And neither of us mentioned that she looked like a giant bumblebee.

"Are you okay?" Larry asked her.

"Pretty much, but I need a doughnut."

"No doughnuts!" Larry and I said in unison.

"Oh yeah," Lula said. "I forgot."

"I have to get back to work," I said to Lula. "Are you coming with me?"

"I guess," Lula said. "But we gotta stop at your mama's house. Your granny was supposed to cook up a recipe I gave her."

ELEVEN

My mother and Grandma Mazur were in the kitchen. My mother was at the stove, stirring red sauce, and Grandma was at the sink, drying pots stacked in the Rubbermaid dish drainer.

"I made up the recipe just like you said," Grandma told Lula. "And then I put the sauce on some pulled pork. It's in the casserole dish in the refrigerator."

"How does it taste?" Lula asked. "What do you think of it?"

"It tastes okay, but I got the trots as soon as I ate it. I've been in the bathroom ever since. I got hemorrhoids on hemorrhoids."

"Get it out of the refrigerator before your father gets hold of it," my mother said to me. "Bad enough I've got your grandmother running upstairs every ten minutes. I don't want to have to listen to the two of them fighting over who gets in first."

I took the casserole dish out of the refrigerator and lifted the lid. It looked good, and it smelled great.

"Do you want to try some?" I asked Lula.

"Ordinarily," Lula said. "But I'm on a diet. Maybe you should taste it."

"Not in a hundred years," I told her.

"It could just be a fluke that your granny got the trots," Lula said. "It could be one of them anemones."

"I think you mean anomaly."

"Yeah, that's it."

"We're having ham tonight," my mother said to me. "And pineapple upside-down cake. You should bring Joseph to dinner."

"I'm not seeing him anymore."

"Since when?"

"Since weeks ago."

"Do you have a new boyfriend?"

"No. I'm done with men. I have a hamster. That's all I need."

"That's a shame," my mother said. "It's a big ham."

"I'll come to dinner," I said. "I love ham."

"No Joseph?"

"No Joseph. I'll take his share home and eat it for lunch tomorrow."

"I know what we can do with this casserole," Lula said. "We can take it to the office and feed it to Vinnie. He don't care what he puts in his mouth."

I thought that sounded like a decent idea, so I carted the pulled pork out to Ranger's Porsche and carefully set it on the floor in the back. Lula and I buckled ourselves in, and I headed for Hamilton Avenue.

"Holy cats," Lula said, half a block away from the office. "You see that car parked on the other side of the street? It's the bushy-headed killer. It's Marco the Maniac. He's sitting there waiting to kill me."

"Don't panic," I said. "Get his license plate. I'm dialing Morelli."

"It's them or me," she said, launching herself over the consul onto the backseat, powering the side window down. "This is war."

"Stay calm! Are you getting the license number?"

"Calm, my ass." And she stuck her Glock out the

window and squeezed off about fifteen shots at the two guys in the car. "Eat lead," she yelled, "you sons of bitches!"

Bullets ricocheted off metal wheel covers and bit into fiberglass, but clearly none hit their intended mark because the car took off and was doing about eighty miles an hour before it even got to the corner. I hung a U-turn in front of the bonds office, sending oncoming cars scrambling onto curbs, screeching to a stop.

Lula had discarded the flak vest, rammed herself through the side window, and was half in and half out, still shooting at the car in front of us.

"Stop shooting," I yelled at her. "You're going to kill someone."

The car turned left onto Olden, and I was prevented from following by heavy traffic.

"Get back into the car," I said to Lula. "I've lost them."

"I can't get back," Lula said. "I'm stuck."

I looked over my shoulder at Lula. All I could see was bright yellow ass. The rest of her was out the window.

"Stop fooling around," I told her.

"I'm not fooling. I'm stuck!"

Cars were passing and honking.

"Your ass," Lula said to the cars.

I checked her out in my side mirror and saw that not only was she stuck, but her boobs had fallen out of the scoop-neck sweater and were blowing in the wind. I turned onto a side street and pulled to the curb to take a look. By the time I got out of the car, I was laughing so hard tears were rolling down my cheeks and I could hardly see.

"I don't see where this is so funny," Lula said. "Get me out of the window. I'm about freezing my nipples off. It's not like it's summer or somethin'."

Short of lubing Lula up with goose grease, I didn't know where to begin.

"Do you think it's better if I pull or push?" I asked her.

"I think you should pull. I don't think I'm gonna get my titties and my belly back through the window. I think my ass is smaller. And I don't want no wise-crackin' comment on that, neither."

I latched on to her wrists, planted my feet, and pulled, but she didn't budge.

"I'm losing circulation in my legs," Lula said. "You don't get me out of here soon, I'm gonna need amputation."

I went around to the other side, got into the back-seat, and almost fainted at the sight of the big yellow butt in front of me. I broke into a nervous giggle and instantly squashed it. Get it together, I told myself. This is serious stuff. She could lose the use of her legs.

I put my hands on her ass and shoved. Nothing. No progress. I put my shoulder to her and leaned into it. Ditto. Still stuck. I got out of the Porsche and went around to take another look from the front.

"Maybe I should call roadside assistance," I said to Lula. "Or the fire department."

"I don't feel so good," Lula said. And she farted.

"Jeez Louise," I said. "Could you control yourself? This is Ranger's Porsche."

"I can't help it. I'm just a big gasbag. I still got left-over barbecue gas." She squeezed her eyes shut tight and did a full minute-long fart. "Excuse me," she said.

I was horrified and impressed all at the same time. It was a record-breaking fart. On my best day, I couldn't come near to farting like that.

"I feel a lot better," Lula said. "Look at me. I got room in the window opening." She wriggled a little and eased herself back into the SUV. "I'm not so fat after all," she said. "I was just all swelled up."

My cell phone buzzed, and I saw from the screen that it was Morelli.

"Did I miss a call from you?" he asked.

"Yeah. Marco and his partner were parked in front of the bonds office. They were in a black Lincoln Town Car. I didn't get their license. I followed them to Olden and then lost them."

"I'll put it on the air."

"Thanks."

Ten minutes later, Lula and I trudged into the office with the casserole and came face-to-face with Joyce Barnhardt.

Joyce had been a pudge when she was a kid, but over the years the fat had shifted to all the right places. Plus, she'd had some sucked out and added some here and there. Truth is, most of the original equipment had been altered one way or another, but even I had to admit the end result was annoyingly spectacular. She had a lot of flame-red hair that she did up in waves and curls. Hard to tell which of it was hers and which was bought. Not that it mattered when she swung her ass down the street in spike-heeled boots, skintight low-rider jeans, and a black satin bustier. She wore more eye makeup than Tammy Faye and had lips that were inflated to bursting.

"Hello, Joyce," I said. "Long time no see."

"I guess you could say that to Morelli, too," Joyce said.

Lula cut her eyes to me. "You want me to shoot her? 'Cause I'd really like to do that. I still got a few bullets left in my gun."

"Thanks, but not today," I said to Lula. "Some other time."

"Just let me know when."

"So what are you doing here in the slums?" I asked her.

"Ask Connie."

"Vinnie hired her again," Connie said. "He decided you weren't bringing the skips in fast enough, so he brought Joyce in to take up the slack."

"I don't take up slack," Joyce said. "I take the cream off the top."

From time to time, Joyce had worked for Vinnie, mostly because she was good with a whip and once in a while Vinnie felt like a very bad boy.

"What's in the casserole?" Joyce asked.

I opened the lid. "It's barbecue. Grandma Mazur made it for me for dinner. She knows how I love this recipe."

Joyce spit on the pulled pork. "Just like old times," she said. "Remember when I used to spit on your lunch in school?"

"How about now?" Lula asked. "Can I shoot her now?"

"No!"

Joyce took the casserole dish from me. "Yum," she said. "Dinner." And then she sashayed out of the bonds office, got into her black Mercedes, and roared off down the street with the barbecue.

"I got a dilemma here now," Lula said. "I don't know whether I want her to like my barbecue sauce or get the squirts from it."

Vinnie stuck his head out of his office. "Where is she? Did she leave? Christ, she scares the crap out of me. Still, there's no getting around it. She's a man-eater. She'll clean up the list."

Connie and Lula and I did a collective eye roll because Joyce had tried her hand at bounty hunting before and the only man she ate was Vinnie.

"Am I fired?" I asked Vinnie.

"No. You're the B team."

"You can't have an A team and a B team going after the same skips. It doesn't work."

"Make it work," Vinnie said.

"We should have saved the barbecue for Vinnie," I said to Lula.

"Wasn't me that gave Barnhardt the barbecue," Lula said. "I wanted to shoot her."

I hiked my bag onto my shoulder. "I'm out of here. I'm going to see if Myron Kaplan is home."

"I'm with you," Lula said. "I'm not staying here with this Barnhardt-hiring idiot."

"What about the filing?" Vinnie yelled at Lula. "There's stacks of files everywhere."

"File my ass," Lula said.

According to the information Connie had given me, Myron Kaplan was seventy-eight years old, lived alone, was a retired pharmacist, and two months ago, he robbed his dentist at gunpoint. Myron's booking photo was mostly nose. Several other photos taken when bail was written showed Myron to be slightly stooped, with sparse, wild gray hair.

"There it is," Lula said, checking house numbers while I crept down Carmichael Street. "That's his house with the red door."

Carmichael was a quiet little side street in the center of the city. Residents could walk to shops, restaurants, coffeehouses, corner groceries, and in Myron's case . . . his dentist. The street was entirely residential, with narrow brick-faced two-story row houses.

I parked at the curb, and Lula and I walked to the small front stoop. I rang the bell, and we both stepped aside in case Myron decided to shoot through his door. He was old, but he was known to be armed, and we'd been shot at a lot lately.

The door opened, and Myron looked at me and then focused on Lula in the yellow stretch suit and black flak vest.

"What the heck?" Myron asked.

"Don't mess with me," Lula said. "I'm off doughnuts, and I feel mean as a snake."

"You look like a big bumblebee," Myron said. "I thought I slept through October, and it was Halloween."

I introduced myself and explained to Myron he'd missed his court date.

"I'm not going to court," Myron said. "I already told that to the lady who called on the phone. I got better things to do."

"Like what?" Lula wanted to know.

"Like watch television."

Myron had a cigarette hanging out of his mouth. He was gumming it around, sucking in smoke and blowing it out, all at the same time.

"That's disgustin'," Lula said. "You shouldn't be smoking. Didn't your doctor tell you not to smoke?"

"My doctor's dead," Myron said. "Everybody I know is dead."

"I'm not," Lula said.

Myron considered that. "You're right. You want to do knicky-knacky with me? It's been a while, but I think I can still do it."

"You better be talkin' about some kind of card game," Lula told him.

"We need to go now," I said. "I'm kind of on a schedule."

"Listen, missy," Myron said. "I'm not going. What part of *not going* don't you understand?"

I hated capturing old people. If they didn't cooperate, there was no good way to bring them in. No matter how professional and respectful I tried to act, I always looked like a jerk when I dragged their carcass out the door.

"It's the law," I said. "You're accused of a crime, and you have to go before a judge."

"I didn't commit a crime," Myron said. "I just got a refund. This quack dentist made me false teeth. They didn't fit. I wanted my money back."

"Yes, but you got it back at gunpoint."

"That's because I couldn't get an appointment to see him until January. Couldn't get past his snippy receptionist. When I went in with the gun, I got to see him right away. It's not like I have forever to wait for money. I'm old."

"What about the teeth?" Lula asked him. "Where's the teeth?"

"I left them with the dentist. I got my money back, and he got his teeth back."

"Sounds fair to me," Lula said.

"The court decides what's fair," I said. "You have to go to court."

Myron crossed his arms over his chest and narrowed his eyes. "Make me."

"This is gonna get ugly," Lula said. "We should have left this for Barnhardt."

"I'll make a deal," I said to Myron. "If you come with me, I'll get you a date with my grandmother. She's real cute."

"Does she put out for knicky-knacky?"

"No!"

"Criminy," Lula said to Myron. "What's with you and the knicky-knacky? Do it by yourself and get it over with just like the rest of us."

"He's not real big," I said to Lula. "Probably about a hundred and sixty pounds. If we hog-tie him, we should be able to cart him out to the car."

"Yeah, and he don't have no teeth, so we don't have to worry about him biting us."

"You can't do that to me," Myron said. "I'm old. I'll have a heart attack. I'll pee my pants."

Lula was hands on hips. "I hate when they pee their pants. It's a humiliating experience. And it ruins the upholstery."

I cut my eyes to Myron. "Well? How do you want us to do this?"

"I gotta go to the bathroom before you hog-tie me," Myron said. "Or else I'll pee for sure."

"You've got three minutes," I said to him.

"I can't go in three minutes. I'm old. I've got a prostate the size of a basketball."

"Just *go*!"

Myron trotted off to the bathroom, and Lula and I waited in the front room. Five minutes passed. Ten minutes. I went to the bathroom door and knocked. No answer.

"Myron?"

Nothing. I tried the door. Locked. I called again and rapped louder. *Shit!*

"I need something to pop the lock," I said to Lula. "Do you have a safety pin? Chicken skewer? Knitting needle?"

"I got a bobby pin."

Lula bent the pin open, shoved it in the little hole in the knob, and the door unlocked and we peeked in. No Myron in the bathroom. Open window.

"He gets around, for bein' he's so old," Lula said, looking out the window.

This was the second time today I'd lost a skip through a window. I couldn't even categorize myself as incompetent. I had to go with pathetically stupid.

"Now what are we gonna do?" Lula asked.

Ordinarily, I'd walk the neighborhood and try to

ferret out my skip. Problem was, I had Lula in her yellow spandex, and we were way too visible. You could probably see Lula from the space shuttle.

"I'm going to drop you at the office, and I'm going back to work for Ranger," I said. "Morelli told me the crime lab was done with your apartment. Is your landlord replacing your door?"

"I don't know. I gotta call and find out."

I drove past the bonds office twice before pulling to the curb to let Lula out.

"I don't see anything suspicious," I said to her. "I think you're safe."

"This has been another disturbin' day, what with those two assholes lookin' to kill me, and findin' out that I'm fat. I might go back on that bacon diet."

"The bacon diet is unhealthy. And you had packs of dogs chasing you down the street when you were on the bacon diet. All you need to do is control your portions. Stay away from the doughnuts and only eat one piece of chicken or one pork chop or one hamburger at a meal."

"That's ridiculous," Lula said. "Nobody eats just one pork chop. I'd get weak and die."

"Lots of people only eat one pork chop."

"Who?"

"Me."

"Hunh," Lula said. "That's un-American. How am I supposed to stimulate the economy when I'm only eating one plain-ass pork chop? Probably I can't even have gravy on that pork chop."

I made sure Lula got into the office without getting shot or decapitated, and then I pulled my map out of my handbag and started another run through Ranger's accounts.

Morelli called a little after four. "We found the Town

Car," he said. "It was parked on a side street near the Bank Center. Easy to spot, since it had a bunch of bullet holes in it. No blood inside. I don't know how she always manages to miss her target. It's uncanny."

"Owner?"

"It was stolen from a car service last night. The lab guys are doing their thing, but that car has been handled by half of New Jersey."

"Thanks. I'll pass this on to Lula."

"Is she with you?"

"No. I dropped her at the bonds office. I'm riding a circuit for Ranger right now."

"Word around town is that he's losing accounts. Having a Rangeman security system has turned into a liability."

"He's working on it."

I was halfway through my account route, and I realized it was almost six o'clock. I took Olden to Hamilton, turned into the Burg, and slid to a stop in front of my parents' house precisely on time.

I could smell the ham the minute I stepped into the foyer. It was an intoxicating aroma of warm, salty goodness and special occasions. My father was already at the table, waiting to stab into the first piece of ham. My grandmother was also seated. And a strange man sat beside Grandma.

"This is Madelyn Mooney's boy, Milton," my mother said to me, setting the green bean casserole on the table. "He just moved back to Trenton."

"Yep," Grandma said. "We thought we'd fix you up with some hotties since it's kaput with Morelli."

"I'm not interested in getting fixed up," I said.

"You're not getting any younger," Grandma said. "You wait too long, and all the good ones get taken."

I looked over at Milton. He was a sandbag. Overweight, slumped in his chair, pasty white skin, bad complexion, balding orange hair. I was guessing mid-thirties. Not to be judgmental, but he wasn't at the top of the list when God was handing stuff out.

"Milton used to work in the auto industry," Grandma said. "He had a real good job on the line at the factory."

"Yeah," Milton said. "It was sweet until I got fired. And then the bank foreclosed on my house, and my wife left me and took the dog. And now I'm hounded by collection agencies."

"That's awful," I said. "So what are you doing?"

"Nothing."

"He's living with his mother," Grandma said. "Until he gets on his feet."

"I guess it's hard to get a job these days."

"I'm not actually looking for a job," Milton said. "The doctor who treated me after I had the nervous breakdown and set fire to my house said I should take it easy for a while."

"You set fire to your house?"

"Technically, it wasn't my house anymore. It was the bank's house, and between you and me, I think they were happy I burned it down. They were real nice to me while I was in the mental hospital." He speared a piece of ham, studied it, and turned his attention back to me. "My outpatient advisor tells me I need to get out of my mother's house, so that's why I'm considering marrying you. I was told you have your own apartment."

My father picked his head up and paused with his fork halfway to his mouth. "Good God," he said.

"I bet a big, strapping young guy like you has a lot of special talents," Grandma said to Milton.

"I can make French toast," Milton said. "And I can whistle."

"Isn't that something," Grandma said. "Whistling's a lost art. You don't find many whistlers anymore."

Milton whistled "Camptown Races" and "Danny Boy."

"That's pretty good," Grandma said. "I wish I could whistle like that."

My father shot my mother a look like he was in intense pain.

"Pass the potatoes to your father," my mother said to me. "And give him more ham."

I tried to sneak an inconspicuous peek at my watch.

"Don't even think about it," my mother said. "You leave now, and you don't get dessert . . . ever."

TWELVE

Milton left at eight o'clock so he could get home in time to take his meds. I helped my mom with the dishes, had an extra piece of cake, and said good night at nine, pulling away from my parents' house reconsidering my feelings toward Morelli. After two hours of Milton, I was thinking Morelli might be worth a second look.

I drove two blocks down, hooked a left, and turned into his neighborhood. This was blue-collar Trenton at its best. Houses were small, cars were large, green referred to dollars in the bank. At eight o'clock, kids were doing homework and parents were in front of the television. At ten o'clock, the houses were dark. This neighborhood got up early five mornings out of seven and went to work.

Morelli lived in a row house he inherited from his Aunt Rose. He was gradually making it his own, but Rose's curtains still hung in most of the windows. Hard to explain, but I liked the combination of Morelli and his aunt. There was something about the mix of generations and genders that felt right for the house. And I thought it said something good about Morelli that he didn't have to entirely erase the house's history.

I cruised down Morelli's street and had a moment of breathless panic at finding Barnhardt's Mercedes parked in front of Morelli's green SUV. The moment passed, and I continued on to the corner. I made a U-turn and parked on the opposite side three houses down, taking some time to collect myself. In the past, this sort of dilemma would have sent me straight to the nearest 7-Eleven, where I'd clean them out of Reese's Peanut Butter Cups and Snickers bars. Since I'd just had three pieces of my mother's cake, a bag of candy wasn't where I wanted to go.

I did some deep breathing and told myself slashing tires never really solved anything. And besides, here I was sitting in Ranger's car, sleeping in his bed, wearing his stupid uniform, and I was all bent out of shape because Barnhardt was in Morelli's house. I rolled my eyes and thunked my forehead against the steering wheel. Jeez Louise, I was a mess.

Morelli's front door opened, and Barnhardt made a theatrical exit, blowing kisses and smiling. She got into her Mercedes and drove off, rolling past me, never noticing that I was watching.

There were two other vehicles parked by Morelli's house. A red F150 truck and a clunker Subaru. Now that my breathing was returning to normal and my brain was more or less functioning, I realized I recognized the car and truck. The truck belonged to Morelli's brother, Anthony. And the Subaru belonged to Morelli's cousin Mooch.

I got out of the Cayenne, crossed the street, crept up to Morelli's house, and carefully inserted myself into the azalea bushes planted under his front window. I stood on tiptoe and saw that Morelli, Morelli's dog, Bob, and Mooch, and Anthony were on the couch, watching the game on television. The coffee table in front of them was littered with empty beer cans, opened bags of chips, a cardboard pizza box from Pino's, some plates with forks, and the casserole dish Joyce had taken from me. The casserole dish was empty. Holy crap. Joyce had fed the toxic barbecue to Morelli.

I extricated myself from the bushes and danced around, pumping my fist and thinking, *YEAH! Woohoo! Whoopie!* After about thirty seconds of this, I realized I looked stupid, and it would be beyond embarrassing for Morelli to come out and find me on his lawn. And beyond that, I probably shouldn't have been so happy about three men and a dog getting diarrhea, but the truth is, the only one I felt bad about was Bob. Bob was a big, shaggy-haired, entirely lovable beast. And he didn't deserve diarrhea. I stopped dancing and skulked back to the Cayenne.

I put the Cayenne in gear and drove to my apartment building. I pulled into the lot and found Lula's Firebird parked next to Mr. Macko's Cadillac, and light shining from my apartment windows. I'd been hoping to find my apartment dark and deserted. I loved Ranger's apartment, but it wasn't home. Looking up at my windows, I wasn't sure *that* was home, either. I'm in limbo, I thought. My whole friggin' life is in limbo.

I thought I should go in to see the kitchen progress and verify that Lula was staying the night. Unfortunately, that might involve more of Larry in the blue cocktail dress. Or even worse, Larry in his shorts. I felt like I'd had enough weird for one day, so I maneuvered the Cayenne out of the lot and headed for Rangeman.

I was sound asleep when the bedside phone rang.

"He just hit two accounts," Ranger said. "They phoned in minutes apart. Both of the houses were on your high-risk list. Tank is waiting for you in the garage. I want you to take a look at these houses from the inside."

I looked at the clock. It wasn't quite midnight. I took a moment to come awake, and ten minutes later, the phone woke me up a second time.

"Tank has a key," Ranger said. "And he'll come in and get you if you're not in the garage in five minutes."

I managed to get myself out of bed and vertical, but I wasn't firing on all cylinders. I was wearing Ranger's T-shirt as a nightshirt, and I left the shirt on, tugged on cargo pants, socks, sneakers, and a sweatshirt and grumbled my way to the elevator and down to the garage.

"Whoa!" Tank said when he saw me.

I narrowed my eyes. "What?"

"Nothin'," Tank said. "Guess you were asleep. You just took me by surprise, with the hair and all."

I rolled my eyes up to the top of my head, but I couldn't see my hair.

"I'm feeling grouchy," I said to Tank.

"Do you want to see a picture of my cat?" Tank asked. "That always makes me happy."

I climbed into Tank's Rangeman SUV, buckled my seat belt, and looked at the picture of his cat.

"Cute," I said.

"Do you feel happy?"

"No." Crawling back into bed would make me feel happy.

Both houses were north of town in a high-rent neighborhood by the river. The first house Tank took me to looked like Mount Vernon if Mount Vernon was built in 2008. It was Faux Vernon. Tank drove into a circular driveway and parked behind Ranger's Porsche. A police car and another Rangeman SUV were in front of Ranger. The front door was open and every light was on in the house. We walked in and met Ranger in the foyer.

"Why was this house on your *at risk* list?" he asked me.

"It had some things in common with the houses that were already hit. All houses are single family on large lots. All houses have attached garages that open off a side drive court. All houses have trees and bushes that throw shadows and partially screen the house. None of the houses are on streets with on-street parking."

"Our guy likes to have cover," Ranger said.

"Exactly."

"Look through the house and see if you come up with anything. I'm sending Tank with you so you're not mistaken for a vagrant and arrested."

I flipped Ranger the bird.

Ranger smiled at me. "Cute."

"That's what I said about Tank's cat."

"He made you look at his cat picture?"

"I thought it would make her happy," Tank said.

Ranger's smile widened. "Did it make you happy?" he asked me.

"A little."

I suspected I was to Ranger what Tank's cat was to Tank.

"Take good care of her," Ranger said to Tank.

Ranger left for the second break-in, and Tank and I set off on our exploration. The exploration didn't take long. I was getting to know what to expect. Start with the door leading from the garage and take the shortest route to the master bedroom. Check out the home office, the den, the kids' rooms. Proceed to the front door or possibly back door. Locate the keypads.

I felt like the keypads held the answer to the mystery. There were three keypads in this house. One in the master bedroom, one on a wall by the front door, and one by the door to the garage. None of the keypads were visible from a window.

Tank and I had gone through the house and returned to the door leading to the garage. We were standing in a small hallway behind the kitchen. The laundry room and a half bath opened off the hallway.

"I think this guy is getting the code from the keypad," I said to Tank.

"I've been thinking that, too. It's like when people watch you at the ATM and they get your bank code. It's like someone's looking through walls."

We left Faux Vernon and went to house number two. The second house was only three blocks away in the same neighborhood. It was a huge redbrick box with white columns and a porte cochere.

Ranger met us at the door. "The drill is the same. Cash and jewelry taken from the upstairs master."

"Are the police making any progress on these robberies?"

"Not that I can tell. Not a lot of talent assigned to this desk."

"It's odd that these two houses were hit together."

"Both clients were at the same dinner party," Ranger said. "Somehow, our bandit knew the houses would be empty. Originally, I thought he randomly hit houses that were dark. Now I think he plans ahead. We need to go over the original report taken after each break-in to see if there's a common service provider. Someone who might have talked to the homeowner. And we probably want to go back and reinterview all of the clients who were robbed."

"That still doesn't tell us how he got the codes."

"Trust me, if I catch this guy, he'll tell me how he got the codes."

The first thing I noticed when I woke up was that I wasn't alone. Ranger was in bed with me. And he was asleep. I reviewed the night, and I couldn't remember anything amazing happening. Tank had driven me back to Rangeman around two in the morning. Ranger hadn't come back with us. It was now nine o'clock. I checked around and determined I was wearing all the clothes I was supposed to be wearing. Panties and T-shirt. I slipped out of bed, and Ranger woke up.

"When did you get home?" I asked him.

"A little after five."

"I'm surprised I'm not naked."

"You weren't in the mood," Ranger said. "You told me you'd shoot me with my own gun if I touched you."

"What did you do?"

"I got up and locked my gun in the safe. You were asleep when I came back to bed."

"I was tired."

"Are you tired now?"

"No, but I'm going to work. I have three skips to catch. I need to check in on Lula. And I want to go over the reports from your break-ins."

"The reports are on my desk," Ranger said.

A half hour later, I rolled out of the garage in Ranger's Cayenne and dialed Lula.

"What's going on today?" I asked her. "And where are you?"

"I'm getting ready to leave your apartment. Your kitchen is all clean, and they're putting my new door up this morning. I'm having brunch with Mister Clucky, and then I'm going to your mama's house to cook with your granny. You could have brunch at Cluck-in-a-Bucket with me if you want."

"Cluck-in-a-Bucket has brunch?"

"Only on Sunday. You get orange juice and biscuits and a bucket of nuggets."

"How is that different from every other day?"

"It's the orange juice. Usually, you get a soda."

"Okay," I said. "I'll meet you at Cluck-in-a-Bucket."

I'd grabbed a to-go cup of coffee from the fifth-floor kitchen before I left Rangeman, but I hadn't bothered with breakfast, so biscuits and orange juice sounded good.

I drove through the center of the city and reached Cluck-in-a-Bucket just as Lula was pulling into the lot. Mister Clucky was dancing around in front of the building, and the hideous impaled chicken was spinning overhead.

"Yoohoo, Mister Clucky, honey," Lula called, getting out of her Firebird and waving.

"Boy, you must really like him," I said.

"He's an excellent scrubber, and besides, it's not everybody gets to know Mister Clucky personally. He's one of them minor celebrities."

Mister Clucky was surrounded by kids, so we bypassed him and put our order in.

"I'm going to try my luck with Ernie Dell again," I said to Lula. "Are you in?"

"As long as it don't take too long. Larry gave me his barbecue recipe, and Granny and me are trying it out this afternoon."

I got an orange juice and two biscuits. Lula got an orange juice, a bucket of biscuits, and a bucket of nuggets.

"Crikey," I said, looking at her tray. "I thought you were cutting back on the food."

"You said only have one pork chop and one burger and one steak. So I only got *one* bucket of biscuits and *one* bucket of nuggets. You got a problem with that?"

"You could feed a family of six on that food."

"Not in my neighborhood. I live in a three-pork-chop neighborhood."

Mister Clucky came inside dancing and singing his Mister Clucky song, going table by table.

"I know him personally," Lula said to the woman at the table next to her.

Lula was still wearing the flak vest. She ate half the bucket of nuggets, and she released the Velcro straps to give herself more room.

"Is that a bulletproof vest?" the woman next to Lula asked.

"Yep," Lula said. "And it's hard to make a fashion statement in this on account of it don't come in a lot of colors. I gotta wear it because there's a couple guys tryin' to kill me."

The woman gave a gasp and hustled her two kids out the door.

"Hunh," Lula said. "She just up and left. She didn't even finish her Clucky Burger."

"Next time, say you're wearing a back brace."

We finished eating, Lula said good-bye to Mister Clucky, and we saddled up. We left Lula's Firebird in the lot, and I drove.

"I love this car," Lula said. "My personality don't fit a SUV, but this car is still excellent. It got buttons all over the place. What's this button do?"

"I don't know."

Lula pushed the button and my GPS screen went blank. "Oops," Lula said.

The car phone rang, and I opened the connection.

"This is Hal in the control room," a voice said on the hands-free phone. "Are you all right?"

"Yes."

"You just dropped off my screen. Did you disable your GPS?"

"It was an accident. How do I fix it?"

"Push the button again."

"Where's that voice comin' from?" Lula wanted to know. "It sounds like the voice of God, floatin' around in space."

I disconnected Hal, reconnected the GPS, and turned off Hamilton.

"This time we'll cover all exits," I said. "You take the front door, and I'll take the back door."

"Sounds like a plan. Who's going in first?"

"I'll go in first. You don't go in at all unless I yell for you. You keep your eyes open in case he goes out a front window."

I drove a couple blocks into Ernie's neighborhood, found the alley that ran past the back of his house, and crept along until I reached his driveway. I pulled in and angle-parked behind the garage, blocking his exit.

"I'll give you time to walk around the house, and then I'm going in," I said to Lula. "Just stay put until you hear from me."

Lula checked the Velcro on her vest to make sure everything was secure. "Gotcha."

We left the Cayenne and went our separate ways. I counted off two minutes and knocked on the back door. No answer. I knocked again and tried the door. Unlocked. I stepped into the kitchen and listened. No sound. "Bond enforcement!" I yelled. "Ernie, are you in here?" Nothing. I walked through the house, stood at the bottom of the stairs and called out again. I climbed the stairs and went room by room. No Ernie. I returned to the first floor and opened the door to Lula.

"He's not here," I said. "I'll try again later."

We walked through the house and let ourselves out.

"There's something wrong here," Lula said, standing on the back stoop. "I get the feeling something's not right. What is it?"

A wave of nausea swirled through my stomach. "It's Ranger's Cayenne," I said. "It's gone."

"Yep," Lula said. "That's it, all right. There's a big empty space where the car used to be."

I dialed Rangeman and got Hal. "Is Ranger on the floor yet?"

"No," Hal said. "I haven't seen him. Would you like me to transfer you?"

"No. I don't want to bother him. Is the GPS still working on the Cayenne?"

"Yes."

"Maybe you could send someone after it, since it's been sort of . . . stolen."

There was a beat of silence. "Stolen?" Hal said. "Someone stole Ranger's Cayenne?"

I blew out a sigh. "Yes."

"Uh-oh," Lula said, staring off into the distance. "I don't like the looks of this."

I followed her line of sight and felt my heart skip a couple beats. Black smoke billowed skyward about a quarter mile away.

"Has the car stopped?" I asked Hal.

"Yes."

"No rush," I told him. "It's going to be there for a while."

"Now what?" Lula asked when I got off the phone.

I wanted to get on a plane and leave the country. Get a job in St. Bart's and never come back.

"Hal's sending a car to pick us up," I said.

Ten minutes later, a black SUV rolled into the driveway. Ramon was at the wheel.

"I need to get my car at Cluck-in-a-Bucket," Lula told him. "I gotta go cook up barbecue."

Ramon glanced over at me. "Ranger would like me to take you back to Rangeman."

"Sure," I said. "Drop Lula at the Bucket and take me to the Batcave."

Ranger was in the shower when I got to the apartment. I flopped onto the couch, pulled a pillow over my head, and hoped when he came out he wouldn't notice me lying there.

Pretend you're in a good place, I told myself. You're on a beach. Hear the waves swooshing in and out. Hear the seagulls.

The pillow got lifted off my face and Ranger looked down at me. "You can run, but you can't hide," he said.

"Just shoot me and get it over with."

"Talk to me."

"Ernie Dell."

Ranger yanked me to my feet, pulled me into the hall and out the door. "He needs to find another hobby."

Ranger is a master of control. He can lower his heart rate at will and walk past a bakery and never be tempted. On the surface, Ranger would appear to have no emotion. It's anyone's guess what rages below the surface. What I do know about Ranger is that he's most dangerous when he's dead calm. And right now he was pretty calm, except for having his hand clamped around my wrist.

Neither of us said a word in the elevator. Ranger guided the Turbo out of the garage, and I gave him directions to Ernie's house. He looked relaxed at the wheel. No angry little lines in his forehead. No tense muscles working in his jaw. He also wasn't talking. He was in his zone.

We drove down the alley behind Ernie's house and parked in his driveway, Ranger still not saying anything, looking at the wreck of a haunted mansion in front of him. We got out of the Porsche and walked to the building's back door. Ranger listened for a moment and knocked. No answer. Ranger knocked again.

There was a sound overhead like a window being raised. I looked up to see and *Splooosh*. I was doused head to foot with red paint.

Ranger was standing inches from me, and he didn't have a drop on him. He was in black Rangeman tactical gear of T-shirt, cargo pants, and windbreaker, and he was pristine. He looked at me and did a small *I can't believe these things always happen to you* gesture with his hands.

"If you so much as crack a smile, that's the end of our friendship," I said to him.

The corners of his mouth twitched a little, and I knew he was smiling inside.

"Babe," he said.

"I'm a mess."

"Yes, but we're going to have fun washing this paint off you when we get back to my apartment." He unholstered his gun and handed it to me. "Stay here and don't move from this spot. If you see Ernie Dell, shoot him."

"What if he isn't armed?"

"He'll be armed by the time the police get here."

Ranger disappeared inside the house, leaving the kitchen door open. A minute later, I heard something crash overhead. The crash was accompanied by a loud grunt, as if the air had been knocked out of someone. I'd seen Ranger in action on other manhunts, and I suspected this was Ernie Dell getting thrown against a wall. There was a moment of silence and then more thumping and crashing. I looked inside, past the kitchen, and saw Ernie sprawled on the floor at the foot of the stairs. Ranger hauled him to his feet and wrangled him to the back door.

"What was all that crashing?" I asked Ranger.

"He slipped on the stairs."

Ernie's hands were cuffed behind his back, and he wasn't looking happy. I was relieved to have captured Ernie, but it was annoying that it was so easy for Ranger to execute a takedown and next to impossible for me.

"You have other talents," Ranger said, reading my thoughts.

"Such as?"

He tucked my hair behind my ear so it wouldn't drip paint on my face. "You're smart. You're intuitive. You're resilient." He thought about it for a beat. "You're stubborn."

"Stubborn is a good thing?"

"Not necessarily. I ran out of good things."

A Rangeman SUV glided into the driveway and parked. Tank and Ramon got out and went pale when they saw me.

"It's paint," Ranger said to them. "Mr. Dell was feeling playful."

Tank clapped a hand to his heart.

"Sweet Mother of God," Ramon said.

Ranger handed Ernie over to Tank. "I'll get the paperwork for you, and you can turn him in for Stephanie. And I need a thermal blanket from the emergency kit for her."

Five minutes later, Ernie was shackled to the floor in the backseat of the Rangeman SUV and trundled off to the police station. This left me with two open files, and as far as I was concerned, Joyce was welcome to both of them. I kicked my shoes off at carside, wrapped myself in the aluminum blanket from the emergency kit, and eased myself into the Turbo, next to Ranger.

"I'm trying not to drip," I said to him.

"I saw the can in the upstairs bedroom. It's water-based. It should wash off."

"Why don't you have any paint on you? It's always me. Why isn't it ever you?"

"I don't know," Ranger said. "But I like it this way."

Ranger backed out of the driveway and drove toward Olden. I was soaked through with paint and wrapped in an aluminum foil blanket like a baked potato. I'd left my shoes in the driveway, and my feet were getting cold.

"Take me to my apartment," I said to Ranger.

"Isn't Lula there?"

"No. She's cleared out."

THIRTEEN

I let myself into my apartment and went to my kitchen first thing. It was sparkling clean, with only a few pale pink stains in the ceiling paint and a small chunk of the ceiling chipped away from the lid impact. The living room and dining room were nice and neat. No sign of Lula. Yay. Yippee.

The bedroom wasn't nearly so happy. Lula's clothes were still there. Okay, don't panic, I told myself. Maybe she was in a hurry to go to brunch and just hasn't come back to collect her clothes. I was holding a big plastic garbage bag that I'd taken from the kitchen. I stripped down and put everything, including the disposable aluminum blanket, into the garbage bag. There was a limit to how much paint you could wash out of a shirt, and my clothes were way beyond the limit.

I stepped into the shower and, after a lot of scrubbing and shampooing, finally emerged red-free. I fluffed my hair out with the dryer, swiped some mascara on my lashes, and dressed in a ratty T-shirt, washed-out jeans, and a denim jacket. Not a high-fashion day, since my laundry basket with all my clean clothes was still at my mother's house.

I'd promised to test-drive more barbecue sauce to-

night at my parents' house. I called Lula for a ride and
went down to the parking lot to wait for her.

Mostly seniors on fixed incomes lived in my building. There were a couple Hispanics and a young single
mom with two kids, but everyone else had a subscrip-
tion to *AARP The Magazine*. It was almost five, and
half of my building was out taking advantage of the
early bird specials at the diner, and the other half was
in front of the television, eating a defrosted entrée.

Lula barreled into the lot and came to a sharp stop
in front of me. "Hop in," she said. "I gotta get back to
help your granny. We're in the middle of saucin' up
some chicken."

"Is this Mister Clucky's recipe?"

"Yeah, and I think it's a good one. His secret ingredient is blackberry jelly. Leave it to a cross-dresser to
come up with something real creative like that."

Lula was wearing a stretchy orange sweater with a
low V-neck and short sleeves, and a matching orange-
and-black tiger-striped skirt. No flak vest.

"What happened to the flak vest?" I asked her.

"I was always sweating under it and it gave me a
rash. I just gotta be on a more vigilant outlook for those
idiot killers. If I get rid of the rash in time, I might wear
the vest to the cook-off. Although I hate for it to interfere with my chef outfit."

"Do you still think Chipotle's killers will be at the
cook-off?"

"They'll be there," Lula said. "And we'll catch them
and be rich. I got a bracelet all picked out at the jewelry store. And I'm going on a cruise down to the
Panama Canal. I always wanted to see the Panama
Canal."

I agreed with Lula. I thought there was a good
chance the killers would be at the cook-off. They

were sticking around, and the cook-off seemed to be the logical reason. Although for me, it wouldn't have been reason enough. If I whacked someone's head off and was worried about being recognized, I'd get out of town. These guys didn't seem to be all that smart. They were focused on getting rid of the witness, and in the bargain they were getting more witnesses.

Lula parked at the curb in front of my parents' house and looked around before getting out of the car.

"I guess the coast is clear," she said. "I don't see no killers anywhere."

Everything was business as usual in my parents' house. My dad was in his chair in front of the television. My mom and Grandma Mazur were in the kitchen.

"I got all the chicken soaking in the sauce," Grandma said. "I got batter for biscuits, and we made some coleslaw."

"I got Larry comin' over as soon as he's off his shift," Lula said. "He's gonna show us how to do the grillin'. He should be here any minute."

The doorbell chimed, and Grandma went to open the door.

"Well, lookit you," I heard Grandma say. "You must be Larry. Come on in. We're all in the kitchen waiting for you. And this here's my son-in-law, Frank."

"For the love of everything holy," my father said. "What the hell are you supposed to be?"

"This is from my Julia Child collection," Larry said. "I know she didn't barbecue, but I just love the simplicity of her clothes and the complexity of her dishes."

I stuck my head out the kitchen door and looked beyond the dining room into the living room. Larry was wearing a curly brown wig, a lavender-and-pink flower-print blouse, navy skirt, and navy pumps with very low heels. There actually was a frightening resemblance to Julia Child.

My father muttered something that might have sounded like *flaming fruitcake* and went back to reading his paper.

Larry followed Grandma into the kitchen, and Grandma introduced him to my mother.

"Very nice to meet you," my mother said. And then she made the sign of the cross and reached for the liquor bottle in the cupboard next to the stove.

"We had a mishap with the grill a couple days ago," Lula said to Larry. "But we got it put together again and we're pretty sure it'll work. It's out back."

"And here's the chicken," Grandma said. "We got it sitting in the sauce just like you told us."

"Lookin' good, ladies," Larry said. "Let's barbecue."

Lula grabbed the tray with the chicken. My mother had her hand wrapped around a highball glass. And my grandmother had a broom.

"What's the broom for?" Larry wanted to know.

"Dogs," Grandma said.

We went outside, Larry approached the grill, and the rest of us hung back. Not that we didn't trust Larry's manly ability to ignite a grill; more that we suspected this was the grill from hell.

After a couple minutes of fiddling around, Larry got the grill up and running. He adjusted the flame just so, and he arranged the chicken.

"Good thing you got the night off from being Mister Clucky," Grandma said.

"I never get the Sunday night shift," Larry said. "Sunday night is dead. All the action takes place for the brunch and the early-dinner crowd. They always give those times to me because I'm the best Mister Clucky."

"You're a pretty good Julia Child, too," Grandma said. "I bet you're fun on Halloween."

At six o'clock, my father took his seat at the table and we all hustled into the dining room with the food. We took our seats and I realized there was an extra plate set.

"You didn't do what I think you did," I said to my mother.

"He seemed like a nice young man," my mother said. "I met him in the supermarket. He helped me pick out a grapefruit. And it turned out he's related to Biddy Gurkin."

The doorbell rang and Grandma jumped out of her chair. "I'll get it. I like when we have a new man at the dinner table."

"You have to stop doing this," I said to my mother. "I don't want a new man."

"I'll be dead someday," my mother said. "And then what? You'll wish you had someone."

"I have a hamster."

"This here is Peter Pecker," Grandma said, leading a tall, bald, red-faced guy into the room.

Lula spewed water out of her nose, and my father choked on a piece of bread.

"Sorry," Lula said. "I never met anyone named Peter Pecker before."

"And he looks just like one, too," Grandma said. "Did anyone else notice that? Isn't that something?"

My mother drained her highball glass and looked to the kitchen.

"Sit here and have a piece of chicken," Grandma said to Peter Pecker. "We made it special."

Pecker sat down and looked across the table at Julia Child. "I thought you died."

"It's not really Julia Child," Grandma said. "It's

Larry all dressed up. Earlier today, he was Mister Clucky."

"That's weird," Peter said.

"Not as weird as being named Peter Pecker," Larry said.

"I can't help it if that's what I'm named, asshole."

"Who are you calling an asshole?"

"You, Mister Fruity Tutti."

"You must have heard wrong," Grandma said. "He's not Mister Fruity Tutti. He's Mister Clucky."

"Biscuits," my father said. "Where the hell are the biscuits?"

My mother and grandmother and I snapped to attention and passed the biscuits to my father.

"What do you do at the supermarket?" Grandma asked Pecker.

"I'm assistant manager for produce. I'm the vegetable specialist."

"That sounds like a real good job," Grandma said.

"I know all the vegetables," Pecker said. "And I know all about fruits, too." He looked across the table to Larry. "Nothing personal."

"What's that supposed to mean?" Larry asked. "Are you calling me a fruit?"

"If the high heel fits."

"You're a jerk."

"Hey, pal, I'm not the one wearing ladies' panties."

"This is the United States of America," Larry said. "I can wear whatever kind of pants I want."

"You should stop pickin' on him," Lula said to Peter Pecker. "You don't watch your step, and I'll put my foot up your runty butt."

"Oh, I'm so scared," Pecker said. "Now the fat chick's going to protect the pussy-boy."

Lula was on her feet. "Did someone call me a fat chick? I better not have heard that."

"Fat, fat, fat," Pecker said.

"Pecker head, pecker head, pecker head," Larry said.

"Nobody calls me pecker head and lives," Pecker said. And he launched himself across the table and tackled Julia Child.

The two men went to the floor, punching and grunting, rolling around locked together.

"Look at that," Grandma said, leaning across the table. "He *is* wearing ladies' panties."

My father kept his head down, shoveling in buttered biscuits and barbecued chicken, and my mother went to the kitchen to refill her glass.

Lula hauled her Glock out of her purse and fired off a round at the ceiling. A small chunk of plaster fell down onto the table, and Larry and Pecker stopped gouging each other's eyes out long enough to look around.

"We got chicken on the table," Lula said, pointing the gun at the two men. "And I want some respect for it. What the hell are you thinking, rolling around on the floor like that at dinner hour? You need to get your asses into your chairs and show some manners. It's like you two were born in a barn. Not to mention I got a contest coming up, and I need to know if this is gonna give you all diarrhea on account of everything I've cooked so far has gone through people like goose grease."

Larry righted his chair and sat down, and Pecker went to his side of the table. Pecker's nose was bleeding a little, and Larry had a bruise developing on his cheekbone.

"I hope this chicken's okay," Grandma said, spooning coleslaw onto her plate. "I'm hungry."

Everyone looked to my father. He'd been shoveling food into his face nonstop, including the chicken.

"What do you think of the chicken?" my mother asked him.

"Passable," my father said. "It would be better if it was roasted."

Pecker tested out a leg. "This is pretty good," he said, reaching for another piece.

"It's Larry's recipe," Grandma said.

Pecker looked over at Larry. "No kidding? How do you get that sweet but spicy taste?"

"Blackberry jelly," Larry said. "You add a dab to the hot sauce."

"I would never have thought of that," Pecker said.

I ate a biscuit and nibbled at the chicken. Pecker was right. The chicken was good. *Really good.* I didn't have any delusions about winning the contest, but at least we might not poison anyone.

My father reached for the butter and noticed the chunk of plaster in the middle of the table. "Where'd that come from?" he asked.

No one said anything.

My father looked up to the ceiling and spotted the hole. "I knew when we hired your cousin to do the plastering it wasn't going to hold," my father said to my mother.

"He plastered that ceiling thirty years ago," my mother said.

"Well, some of it fell down. Call him after dinner and tell him he better fix it."

"I heard some interesting news today," Grandma said. "Arline Sweeney called and said they were going to hold the Chipotle funeral here in Trenton."

"Why would they do that?" Lula asked.

"I guess he had three ex-wives who didn't want him in their plot. And his sister didn't want him in her plot. So the barbecue company decided to take charge and bury him here since that's where his head is. And he's gonna be at the funeral home on Hamilton. Right here in the Burg."

"That's weird," Lula said. "Are they going to have a viewing?"

"Arline didn't know anything about that, but I guess they'd have a viewing. There's always a viewing."

"Yeah, but they only got a head," Lula said. "How do they have a viewing with just a head? And what about the casket? Would they put just the head in a whole big casket?"

"Seems like a waste," Grandma said. "You could just put the head in a hatbox."

An hour later, Grandma waved good-bye to Larry and Pecker and closed the front door. "That went well," she said. "We need to have company to dinner more often."

I was holding my laundry basket of clean clothes and the keys to my Uncle Sandor's baby blue and white '53 Buick. He'd bequeathed it to Grandma Mazur when he went into the nursing home, but Grandma Mazur didn't drive it. Grandma didn't have a license. So I got to borrow the gas-guzzling behemoth when I had a transportation emergency. The car was a lot like my apartment bathroom, not nearly what I would choose but utterly indestructible.

"What's the deal with your apartment?" I asked Lula. "Is your door fixed?"

"Yeah, and I'm moving back in. I just have to stop at your place to get my clothes. I'll be over in a little while. I gotta get some groceries first."

I carted my laundry out to the Buick and slumped a little when confronted with the reality of my life. I would have preferred a new Porsche Turbo, but my car budget was old borrowed Buick. And the truth is, I was lucky to have anything at all. I put the basket in the trunk, slid onto the couch-like bench seat, gripped the wheel, and turned the key in the ignition. The engine rumbled in front of me. Testosterone shot out the exhaust pipe. Big, wide-eyed headlights blinked on.

I slowly backed out of the garage and chugged down the street. Without thinking too much about it, I turned down Adams Street and after a couple blocks found myself in Morelli's neighborhood. On nights like this, after suffering through dinner with a guy dressed up like Julia Child and a guy who looked like an ad for erectile dysfunction remedies, I found myself missing Morelli. He wasn't perfect, but at least he didn't look like a penis.

FOURTEEN

I thought I would quietly cruise by Morelli's house unnoticed, but it turned out Morelli was standing in his small front yard and spotted me half a block away. Hard to miss me in the Buick. I pulled to the curb and he walked over to me.

"What's going on?" I asked. As if I didn't know. Bob was hunched on the lawn, head down, tail up.

"Bob's got problems," Morelli said.

"Must have eaten something that disagreed with him."

"Yeah, I've got the same problem," Morelli said. "Mooch and Anthony came over to watch the game and I think we got some bad food."

"Bummer."

"I thought you were driving Ranger's Cayenne."

"It sort of burned up."

"Sort of?"

"Totally."

Morelli gave a bark of laughter. "That's the first thing I've had to smile about all day. No one was hurt?"

"No. Ernie Dell stole it and torched it."

"I bet that went over big with Ranger."

"He went after Ernie and rooted him out like a rat in his nest."

"I don't always like Ranger, but I have to admit he gets the job done."

Bob had taken to dragging his butt on the ground, going in circles around the yard.

"Maybe he needs to go to the vet," I said to Morelli.

"This is nothing," Morelli said. "Remember when he ate your red thong? And the time he ate my sock?"

"That was my favorite thong."

"Mine, too," Morelli said. His face broke out in a cold sweat, and he bent at the waist. "Oh man, my intestines are in a knot. I have to go inside and lie down in the bathroom."

"Do you need help? Do you want me to get you Pepto-Bismol or something?"

"No, but thanks for the offer." Morelli waved me away, collected Bob, and they shuffled into the house.

Okay, that was sad. I thought it might be satisfying, but it wasn't at all. I drove on autopilot to my apartment building, surprised when I realized I was parked in the lot. I hauled my laundry basket to the second floor, let myself in, and listened to the silence of my empty apartment. The silence felt lonely. Rex was still with Ranger. I wasn't greeted by rustling pine bedding or the squeak of Rex's wheel. I carted the basket into my bedroom, set it on the floor, and my cell phone rang.

"Bitch," Joyce Barnhardt said when I answered.

"Do you have a problem?"

"You poisoned me."

"I don't know what you're talking about."

"Don't play dumb. You knew exactly what you were doing when you forced that pork on me."

"Gee, I'd really like to talk to you, Joyce, but I have to go do something."

"I'll get you for this . . . as soon as I can leave the bathroom."

I hung up with Joyce, and I heard the front door open.

"I hope you don't mind I let myself in," Lula called from the foyer. "I still got the key you gave me."

"No problem," I said, and I came out to meet her.

There was a *BANG* from the parking lot, followed by the sound of glass breaking.

"That sounded like a window next door," Lula said.

We stuck our heads out the dining room window and looked down at the lot. Two guys were standing there, and one had some sort of shotgun. They were wearing masks like Zorro, but they were still recognizable because one of them was giggling. They were the Chipotle killers.

"Imbecile," the one guy yelled at the other guy. "You can't even shoot a stupid firebomb into the right window. You're a total screwup. You never do anything right."

"You said she lived in the apartment on the end."

"I said *next* to the end."

"Looks to me like there's smoke comin' from your neighbor's apartment," Lula said.

The fire alarm went off next door, and I could hear doors opening and closing in the hall and people shouting. I turned my attention back to the lot and saw the smaller of the two men shoulder the gun.

"Uh-oh," Lula said. "Duck!"

We went flat to the floor, and *BANG!* A small black ball sailed past us, crashed against the far wall, and burst into flames. The flames raced across the carpet and the curtains caught.

"Fire!" Lula yelled. "Fire! Fire! We're gonna die. We're gonna burn up like we was in hell."

I ran to the kitchen, got the fire extinguisher from under the sink, and ran back to the dining room with it. By now, the fire had spread to the living room, and the couch was on fire. I shot some foam at the couch and the living room curtains, and then I turned tail and ran for the door. I grabbed my purse on the way out, relieved that Rex was at Rangeman.

Lula was already in the hall, along with Dillon Ruddick, the building super. Dillon had a fire hose working on my neighbor's apartment. Mr. Macko was helping him. Lula and I stumbled down the smoke-filled hall to the stairs.

"I don't know if we should go out," Lula said when we got to the ground floor. "What if they're still there?"

Good point. I opened the door and peeked out into the small lobby. A bunch of tenants were milling around. Red and blue lights from cop cars and fire trucks flashed from the parking lot. A bunch of firemen in boots and gear entered the building and clomped past us, taking the stairs to the second floor. I looked out again and saw that the police were clearing the lobby.

"They're going to make us leave the building," I said to Lula.

"No way," Lula said. "I'm here to stay. There's crazy-ass Marco the Maniac out there."

"I'm sure he's gone by now. The parking lot is crawling with cops."

"Some of those cops aren't real smart."

"Even the dimmest bulb would be suspicious of two guys wearing Zorro masks."

"How'd they find me here anyway?" Lula wanted to know.

"They've probably been following your Firebird."

"Well, I'm not drivin' it no more. I'm leaving it here, and I'm calling a cab. And I'm not going home, neither. I'd be sitting there waiting for them to set me on fire."

"Where are you going?"

"I don't know. I haven't figured that out."

We left the stairwell and inserted ourselves into the middle of a clump of displaced tenants. Lula called for a cab, and I called Morelli.

"Are you out of the bathroom yet?" I asked him.

"Yeah, but it's probably temporary."

"How's Bob doing?"

"He's looking better."

"Our two hit men, dumb and dumber, just fire-bombed my apartment. I think they must have been following Lula and figured out that she was living here."

"Was anyone hurt?"

"I don't think so. The firemen are here. And a bunch of cops. Everyone's out of the building, and I don't see the EMTs treating anyone. Marco and his partner are so inept, they shot the first firebomb into my neighbor's window by mistake."

"Were they captured?"

"No. Lula and I heard the shot and went to the window. We saw them in the lot, and they saw us in the window, and next thing, there was a firebomb in my dining room."

"How bad is the fire?"

"I think it was confined to the two apartments. I don't see any more flames coming out the windows, so I'm thinking it's under control. I won't know how much damage was done for a while."

"I'd offer to come rescue you, but I'm not sure I can drag myself to the car."

"Thanks for the thought, but I'm okay. I'll fill you in on the details tomorrow."

I disconnected and Ranger called.

"Babe," Ranger said.

"You heard?"

"The control room picked the call up on the police scanner."

"It was my apartment, but I'm not hurt. I think most of the fire is out, but the firemen are still working in the building."

"Hal is sitting just outside your lot in case you need help."

"Thanks."

The parking lot was clogged with emergency vehicles and fire trucks fighting for space around the parked cars. Fire hoses snaked over the pavement and it was difficult to see past the glare of spotlights and strobe lights.

"The cab's gonna pick me up on the road," Lula said. "It'll never get into the lot."

I walked through the tangle of trucks and gawkers with Lula, keeping alert for the Chipotle killers. Hard to believe they'd still be around, but they were so stupid it was hard to predict what they'd do. We reached the street running parallel to the lot. The Rangeman SUV was parked about twenty feet away. I waved to Hal and he waved back at me. After a couple minutes, the cab arrived.

"I'm gonna have this guy take me to Dunkin' Donuts," Lula said. "I need a bag of doughnuts."

"No! You're supposed to be off doughnuts."

"Oh yeah. I forgot. I'll have him take me to the supermarket, and I'll get a bag of carrots."

"Really?"

"No, not really. You think I'm gonna feel better eatin' a carrot? Get a grip. There's two idiots out there trying to kill me, and you think I'm gonna waste my last breath on a vegetable?"

Lula climbed into the cab, and I returned to the parking lot. Water dripped down the side of the building and pooled on the blacktop. Some of the tenants were being allowed to return to their apartments. Dillon Ruddick was talking to a couple cops and the fire chief. I walked over to join them.

"I knew it would only be a matter of time before we met again," the chief said to me, referring to the fact that this wasn't the first time my apartment had been firebombed. Or maybe he was talking about the two cars that just got toasted.

"Not my fault," I said, thinking that covered all the possibilities.

"What can you tell me about this?" he said to me.

Morelli was the principal on the Chipotle case, and I didn't know how much he wanted divulged, so I didn't say much. I described the firebomb and left it at that.

I looked up at my smoke-stained window. "How bad is it?"

"Some damage in the dining room and living room. Mostly rugs and curtains. The couch is gone. Some water damage and smoke damage. You should be able to get in tomorrow to look around, but you're not going to want to live in it until a cleaning crew goes through."

"What about the bathroom?"

"It didn't reach the bathroom."

I'd been hoping the bathroom was destroyed. I really needed a bathroom remodel.

It was another hour before the fire trucks rumbled out of my lot and I was able to move the Buick. Hal was still at curbside. I rolled my window down and told him he could go back to Rangeman.

"I'm going to spend the night at my parents' house," I said.

"Do you want me to follow?"

"No. I'll be fine on my own."

I drove down Hamilton, cut into the Burg, and

parked in front of my parents' house. The house was dark. No lights shining anywhere. Everyone had turned in for the night.

There are three small bedrooms and one bath on the second floor. My parents share a room, Grandma has a room, and the third room was mine when I lived at home. It hasn't changed much over the years. A new bedspread and new curtains that look exactly like the old ones. I quietly crept up the stairs, carefully opened the door to my room, and had a couple beats of utter confusion. Someone was in my bed. Someone huge. Someone snoring! It was like Goldilocks, but reversed. The mountain of quilt-covered flesh turned and faced me. It was Lula!

I was dumbstruck.

When she said she'd find a place to stay, it never occurred to me it would be with my parents, in *my bed*. I was torn between hauling her out of my room and silently skulking away into the night. I debated it for a moment, took a step back, and closed the door. Let's face facts, there was no way I could haul Lula anywhere. I tiptoed out of the house, got into the Buick, and drove to Rangeman.

Ranger was in his apartment when I walked in. He was in the kitchen, standing at the counter and eating a sandwich.

"Sorry," I said. "I didn't mean to barge in on you. I didn't realize you were here."

"I wouldn't have given you a key if I felt I needed privacy," Ranger said. "You can come and go as you please."

"Any more sandwiches?"

"In the refrigerator."

I took a sandwich, unwrapped it, and bit into it. "It's been a long night."

"I can see that," Ranger said. "You look like you've been dragged through a swamp fire."

My sneakers were soaked, my jeans had wicked water up to my knees, and I was head-to-toe soot.

"The Chipotle killers firebombed my apartment. I saw them in the parking lot. I think they were after Lula."

"Is Morelli making any progress?"

"He's got a name for one of them." I went to the fridge and found a beer. "I thought you'd be on patrol."

"My route took me through town, so I decided to take a break and get something to eat." Ranger finished his sandwich and washed it down with a bottle of water. "I'm going back out."

I walked him to the door and watched him take a key from the silver server on the breakfront. Ranger always kept three cars for his personal use. The Porsche Turbo, a Mercedes sedan, and a Porsche Cayenne. He used to have a truck that he loved, but it went to truck heaven and was never replaced. The key he chose tonight was for a Cayenne.

"Replaced already?" I asked him.

"It would have been here sooner, but they had to install the lockbox under the seat."

"I guess you're all about instant gratification."

Ranger grabbed me and kissed me. "If I was all about instant gratification, you'd be naked and in bed."

And he left.

FIFTEEN

I opened my eyes and looked at the bedside clock. Almost six in the morning. I heard keys clink onto the silver server in the hall, and I knew Ranger was home. I vacated the bed and sleepwalked into the dressing room. Not a lot of variety to my clothing choices. Black everything. Life was simple at Rangeman, and this was a good thing at this hour because I wasn't capable of complicated thoughts, such as red shirt or blue shirt.

I grabbed some clothes and hustled into the bathroom. When I came out, Ranger was eating breakfast at the small dining room table.

"It looks like Ella's been here," I said to him.

"She brought you coffee and an omelet."

There was also a breadbasket, plus a fresh fruit platter with raspberries, blackberries, and kiwi. Ranger had a bagel with cream cheese and smoked salmon.

"How was your night?" I asked him.

"Uneventful. And yours?"

"Uneventful once I got here," I said.

Ranger pushed back from the table and stood.

"What are your plans for today?"

"I want to take another stab at capturing Myron Kaplan. I'm hoping to get into my apartment to at least look around. And we have to sign in for the barbecue cook-off this afternoon. Tomorrow is the big day."

"I hate to point out the obvious, but so far as I know, you can't cook."

"It's about barbecue sauce," I said. "You take some ketchup and add pepper, and you've got sauce."

Ranger grinned down at me. "And this is why I love you." He kissed me on the top of my head. "I need to get some sleep. Take whatever car you want."

I finished my omelet, had a second cup of coffee, and headed out, grabbing the keys to the new Cayenne. It would be fun to drive the Turbo, but it wasn't practical for hauling felons back to jail. I stepped into the elevator, pushed the button for garage level, and waved at the little camera in the corner up by the ceiling, knowing someone was manning a monitor, looking at me. And that's when it hit me. The camera.

I got to the garage and hit the button to go back to the seventh floor. I let myself into Ranger's apartment and yelled out to him. "I've got it!"

"I'm in the bedroom," Ranger said.

"Are you naked?"

"Do you want me to be?"

"No." That was a total lie, but I was too chicken to say yes. Even if a woman was sworn off men for life, she'd still want to see Ranger naked. And I was only sworn off men for the time being.

He walked out to see me. "What do you have?"

"Suppose our man gets into the house under some pretext. Like maybe he's checking phone lines or cable lines. And then he plants a small camera in such a way that it gets a video of the owner punching in the code. And then a couple days later, he comes back and gets the camera. Or maybe the camera sends the video out to an exterior location and then he gets the camera when he commits the robbery. Could he do that?"

"I suppose it could be done, but there've been a lot of break-ins, and no one has noticed a camera."

"Yeah, but these cameras are small. And maybe they get placed alongside other devices like smoke detectors or motion sensors."

"I like it," Ranger said. "Run with it."

"Would you mind if I went to some of your accounts and did a fast check of the areas where touch pads have been installed?"

"Make sure you show them your Rangeman ID and tell them you're a tech."

I rolled out of the garage and realized it was barely seven o'clock. What on earth is a person supposed to do at this hour? I could go to breakfast at the diner, but I'd just eaten. My parents would be getting up around now, and it might be fun to see everyone fighting over the bathroom. But then, maybe not. I drove past the office. No lights on. Connie never came in this early. I cruised past Morelli's house. No one on the front lawn. His SUV parked at curbside. A single light on upstairs. Morelli was most likely moving a little slow this morning. I avoided my apartment building. It was too soon to get in, and I knew the sight of the fire-blackened windows would make me feel sad.

That left me with Myron Kaplan. I returned to the center of the city and parked across the street from Kaplan's house. It was Monday morning and some houses showed signs of life, but not Kaplan's. If I was a television bounty hunter, I'd kick the door down and go in guns drawn to catch Kaplan by surprise. I elected not to do this because it seemed like a mean thing to do to a guy who just wanted to return his teeth,

I wasn't any good at kicking doors down, and I didn't have a gun. My gun was home in my cookie jar, and it wasn't loaded, anyway.

So I hung out in Ranger's brand-new Cayenne, watching Kaplan's house, telling myself I was doing surveillance. Truth is, I was snoozing. I had the seat reclined and was feeling very comfy inside the big car with the dark tinted windows.

I woke up a little after nine and saw movement behind Kaplan's front window. I got out of the car and rang Kaplan's bell.

"Oh jeez," Kaplan said when he saw me. "You again."

"I'll make a deal," I said. "I'll take you to breakfast if you go to the police station with me when you're done."

"I don't want to go to breakfast. I haven't got any teeth. I have to gum everything to death. And if I swallow big chunks of stuff, I get indigestion. Can't eat bacon at all."

"You got your money back. Why don't you go to another dentist and get new teeth?"

"I called some other dentists and couldn't get an appointment. I think they're all in cahoots. I'm on a blacklist."

"Dentists don't have blacklists."

"How do you know? Are you *sure* they don't have blacklists?"

"Pretty sure."

"Pretty sure doesn't cut it, chickie."

"Okay, we'll go to plan B. Let's pay a visit to your old dentist."

"The quack?"

"Yeah. Let's talk to him about your teeth."

"Do you have a gun?"

"No."

"Then it's a waste of time," Myron said. "You'll never get in."

"Trust me, I'll get in."

William Duffy, DDS, had an office suite on the fifth floor of the Kreger Building. The waiting room was standard fare. Durable carpet, leatherette chairs, a couple end tables holding artfully arranged stacks of dog-eared magazines. A receptionist desk presided over one wall and guarded the door that led to Duffy.

"That's her," Myron said. "Miss Snippity."

Miss Snippity was in her forties and looked pleasant enough. Short brown hair, minimal makeup, blue dental office smock with the name *Tammy* embroidered on it.

"Don't come any closer," Tammy said. "I'm calling Security."

"That's not necessary," I told her. "We aren't armed." I glanced over at Myron. "We aren't, right?"

"My daughter took my gun away," Myron said.

"We'd like to talk to Dr. Duffy," I said to Tammy.

"Do you have an appointment?"

"No."

"Dr. Duffy only sees by appointment."

"Yes," I said, "but you just opened for the day and there's no one in the waiting room."

"I'm sorry. You'll have to make an appointment."

"Fine," I said. "I'd like an appointment for *now*. Do you have that available?"

"Dr. Duffy doesn't see patients until 10 A.M."

"Okay. Give me an appointment at 10 A.M."

"That's not available," she said, thumbing through her appointment book. "The next available appointment would be three weeks from now."

"Here's the deal," I said to her. "Poor Mr. Kaplan

has no teeth. He's getting indigestion, and he can't eat bacon. Can you imagine a life without bacon, Tammy?"

"I thought Mr. Kaplan was Jewish."

"There's all kinds of Jewish," Mr. Kaplan said. "You sound like my daughter. Maybe you want to tell me to get a colonoscopy, too."

"Oh my goodness, you haven't had a colonoscopy?"

"No one's sticking a camera up my rump," Mr. Kaplan said. "I never like the way I look in pictures."

"About Mr. Kaplan's teeth," I said to Tammy.

"I have *no* appointments," Tammy said. "If I break the rule for Mr. Kaplan, I have to break the rule for everyone."

Tammy was starting to annoy me.

"Just this once," I said. "No one will know. I know Dr. Duffy is in. I can hear him talking on the phone. We want five minutes of his time. We just want to talk to him. Five minutes."

"No."

"I told you," Mr. Kaplan said to me. "She's snippity."

I put palms down on Tammy's desk and I leaned in real close to her. Nose to nose. "If you don't let me in, I'm going to picket this building and let everyone know about the shoddy work Dr. Duffy is doing. And then I'm going to run a personal computer check on you and get the names of all your high school classmates and tell them you have relations with ponies and large dogs."

"You don't scare me," Tammy said.

So that was when I went to plan C and broke into my imitation of Julie Andrews, singing, "The hills are alive, with the sound of music. . . ."

Dr. Duffy almost immediately stuck his head out the door. "What the heck?"

"We'd like to talk to you for a moment," I said.

"Mr. Kaplan is very sorry he held you up, and he'd like to discuss his teeth."

"I'm not sorry," Mr. Kaplan said. "This office gives me a pain in my behind."

"You aren't armed, are you?" Dr. Duffy asked.

"No."

"Come back to my office. I have a few minutes until my first appointment."

Myron stuck his tongue out at Tammy, and we followed Dr. Duffy down a short corridor, past dental torture rooms.

"What would you like to discuss?" Dr. Duffy said, settling himself behind his desk.

"Do you still have Myron's teeth?"

"The police have them. They're evidence."

"Can they be fixed so they fit him and they're comfortable?"

"They seemed to fit him when he left my office."

"They were fine, and then a week later, they were terrible," Myron said.

"You should have made an appointment to get them rechecked," Dr. Duffy said.

"I couldn't get an appointment," Myron said. "Your snippity secretary wouldn't give me one."

"It would be really great if you could drop the charges against Mr. Kaplan and fix his teeth," I said to Duffy. "He's not a bad guy. He just wants teeth. And for the record, your secretary *is* snippity."

"I know she's snippity," Duffy said. "She's my wife's first cousin, and I can't get rid of her. I'll see what I can do about getting the charges dropped, and I'll call you as soon as the police release your teeth."

"That would be real nice of you," Myron said. "I'm getting tired of oatmeal."

Ten minutes later, we were in front of the courthouse.

"I have to check you in," I said to Myron, "but Connie is on her way to bail you out again. And hopefully, you'll be cleared of charges soon."

"That's okay," Myron said. "I didn't have anything to do today, anyway."

I had my map and a summary of Ranger's accounts in front of me. My plan was to take a look at those accounts I'd tagged as high risk and those accounts that had already been hit. The first two houses were high risk. Each of the houses had a touch pad by the front door and a touch pad by the garage entrance. I couldn't find any evidence of filming devices in the touch-pad areas. The next stop was the only commercial account on my list. It was the insurance company that had been burgled four days ago.

I went directly to the rear-entrance touch pad and looked to find possible lines of sight. Rangeman had installed a motion sensor over the door. This was the spot I'd choose if I wanted to snoop on the touch pad. I'd set the camera above the motion sensor, and it would look like it belonged there. There was no camera there now, but it looked to me like some of the paint above the motion sensor had flaked off.

I asked building maintenance to get me a stepladder. I climbed up, took a closer look, and I was pretty sure something had been taped there. When the tape was removed, the paint had peeled away with it. I took a picture with my cell phone and thanked the maintenance guy for the ladder.

"No problem," he said. "The guy last week needed a ladder, too."

"What guy?"

"The Rangeman guy. What is it that you people keep checking?"

"Do you remember exactly when he was here?"

"Yeah, he was here twice. Monday morning and Wednesday morning."

"Can you describe him?"

"Sure. He was young. Maybe eighteen or nineteen. Slim. About my height. I'm five ten. Brown hair, brown eyes. Sort of dark skin. Nice-looking kid. Is something wrong?"

"No, but I'll check with the office to make sure we're not both doing the same route. Did you get his name?"

"No. He didn't tell me his name. At least, I can't remember."

I had to work hard not to run out of the building. I was so excited, I could barely concentrate on driving. I screeched to a stop in the Rangeman garage and danced in the elevator all the way to the seventh floor. I ran through Ranger's apartment, rushed into his bedroom, and jumped on the bed.

"I've got it! I know how the robberies were done and I know what the guy looks like!"

I was straddling Ranger, who fortunately was under a quilt, because from what I could see, he looked deliciously naked.

Ranger put his hands on my waist. "You've got my attention."

"I noticed the paint was flaked away near a motion sensor that was opposite the touch pad at the insurance company. So I asked for a ladder, and sure enough, you could see where something had been taped to the wall."

"Keep talking."

"Are you sure you're listening? Your hand just moved to my breast."

"You're so soft," Ranger said, his thumb brushing across my nipple.

I got a rush, followed by a lot of desire spread all

over the place. "Oh," I heard myself murmur. "That feels good." *No!* Wait a minute. Get a grip. "Jeez," I said. And I scrambled off the bed.

"I almost had you," Ranger said.

"I'm not ready for you. I'm currently off men."

"Taking a hiatus."

"Something like that."

"Tell me more about my break-in expert."

"The maintenance man said a Rangeman employee had been in twice to check on the same motion sensor. I figure, once to install the camera and once to remove it. He said the tech was eighteen or nineteen years old. Around five ten. Brown hair, brown eyes, sort of dark skin. Nice-looking."

"I don't have anyone that young," Ranger said, "but I have several men who would fit the rest of the description and might look younger than they actually are."

"So we're back to someone in-house. That's ugly."

Ranger slipped out of bed. "I'm going to take a shower, and then I'll follow up on this."

I stared at him. He was naked, all right.

"You're staring," he said, smiling.

"I like to look."

"Nice to know," Ranger said, "but we should be able to do better than that for you."

I rummaged through Ranger's refrigerator while he took a shower. Fresh fruit, low-fat cottage cheese, orange juice, nonfat milk, white wine. No leftover pizza. No birthday cake. Ranger was hot, but he didn't know much about food.

I went down to the fifth floor, got an assortment of sandwiches and sides, and brought it all back to Ranger's apartment.

Ranger strolled in and took a turkey club. "Did you get the name of the maintenance guy?"

"Mike. He'll be there until three o'clock today."

"Do you want to ride with me?"

"I can't. I need to check on my fire damage and see if Lula needs help with the cook-off."

"How are you doing with FTAs?"

"I have one open. I saved the worst for last. Cameron Manfred. Armed robbery. Connie has him living in the projects. Works for Barbara Trucking."

"I can go out with you tonight," Ranger said.

I pulled the Cayenne into the parking lot to my building and looked up at my windows. One window was broken. Looked like it was boarded over from the inside. All were ringed with black soot. Grimy water stains streaked down the yellow brick exterior. Water still pooled in the parking lot. What looked like the remains of my couch sat black and sodden alongside the Dumpster. Sometimes it was good not to have a lot of expensive stuff. Less to feel bad about when it got firebombed.

I took the stairs and stepped into the second-floor hall. Dillon had a couple giant fans working at drying the carpet. The door to my apartment was open, and Dillon was inside.

Dillon was around my age, and he'd been the building super for as long as I could remember. He lived in the bowels of the building in a free but tomb-like efficiency. He was a nice guy who'd do anything for a six-pack of beer, and he was always mellow, in part from the small cannabis farm in his bathroom. He was a little sloppy in a hip super-casual kind of way, and he tended to show some butt-crack when he came up to fix your plumbing, but you didn't actually mind because his butt-crack was kind of cute.

"I hope it's okay I'm in your apartment," Dillon

said. "I wanted to get some of the waterlogged stuff out, and I have an insurance agent due any minute."

"Fine by me," I said. "I appreciate the help with the furniture."

"It was a lot worse last time you were firebombed," Dillon said. "Most of the damage this time is from water and smoke. It didn't touch your bedroom at all. And it didn't get to your bathroom."

I blew out a sigh.

"Yeah," he said. "I'm sorry it didn't get to your bathroom. I thought about spreading some gasoline around and lighting a match in there, but I was afraid I'd blow myself up. On the bright side, I'm sure this isn't the last time you'll ever get firebombed, so maybe you'll have better luck next time."

"There's a cheery thought."

"Yeah, I'm a glass is half full kind of guy."

"Speaking of glasses. I could use a beer."

"I put some in your fridge. I figured you'd need a cold one."

I cracked open a beer and slogged through my apartment. The curtains were history. The couch I already knew about. The rugs were sort of melted and waterlogged. No biggie on the rugs. They weren't wonderful to begin with, and the building would replace them. My dining room table and chairs were grimy but probably would clean up okay. Everything in my bedroom smelled like smoke. Dillon had another fan working in there.

"How long before I can move in?" I asked him.

"I've got professional cleaners coming in later today. The carpet's been ordered. I'll bring a couple of my buddies in, and we'll do the painting. If all the moons line up right, I'd say a week."

Oh boy. Another week with Ranger. And once he solved his break-in problem, he'd stop working nights, and he'd go to bed early . . . with me. My first thought was *YUM!* My second thought was *Help!*

I stuffed Lula's clothes into a plastic garbage bag, carted it out to the Cayenne, and drove it to the office. Connie was out when I arrived, and Lula was at Connie's desk, answering phones.

"Vincent Plum Bail Bonds," she said. "What do you want?" There was a pause, and Lula said, "Un-hunh, un-hunh, un-hunh." Another pause. "What did you say your name was? Did I hear Louanne Harmon? Because I'm not bailin' out no Louanne Harmon. I suppose there's some good Louanne Harmons out there, but the one I know is a skank 'ho. The Louanne Harmon I know told my customers I was overchargin' for my services when I was workin' my corner. Is this that same Louanne Harmon?" Another pause. "Well, you can kiss my ass," Lula said. And she hung up.

Vinnie stuck his head out of his office. "What was that?"

"Wrong number," Lula said. "They wanted the DMV."

"Where's Connie?" I asked.

"She went to write bond for your Mr. Kaplan, and she didn't come back yet."

"Any word from Joyce?"

"Connie called and told her there was only one open file, and she told Connie you had breast implants and one of them diseases that you get from the toilet seat. I forget what it was."

Terrific. "It looks like you're doing okay."

"Yeah, I'm not dead. Nobody's even shot at me today. I think this is my lucky day. I bet we're gonna win that cook-off tomorrow and catch the Chipotle killers and be on easy street. I even stopped by the travel agency and got a brochure for my Panama Canal cruise. It's one of them boats that had a virus epidemic and everyone got sick and now their rates are real low. I have a chance to get a good deal. Not that I need it anymore."

"So you're still planning on entering the cook-off."

"Damn skippy, I'm gonna enter. We gotta go to the Gooser Park and sign in this afternoon. And I gotta get my car, too. I was hoping you could give me a ride to your parking lot as soon as Connie gets back."

An hour later, I was back in my parking lot with Lula.

"There's my baby," Lula said. "Good thing I parked way at the end of the lot where nobody else parks. It didn't hardly get any soot on it. And it was out of the water spray. I'm gonna take it to get detailed this afternoon, so it looks fine when I win the contest and capture the bad guys. I'll probably be on television."

I pulled up next to the Firebird, Lula got out, unlocked her car, and slid behind the wheel. I waited for the engine to catch, and then I put the Cayenne in gear and drove out of the lot. I realized Lula was still sitting there, so I returned to the lot, parked next to her, and got out.

"Something wrong?"

"It's making a funny sound. You hear it?"

"Are any of the warning lights on?"

"No. I'm gonna take a look under the hood."

"Do you know anything about cars?"

"Sure I know about cars. I know there's an engine up there. And lots of other shit, too."

Lula popped the hood, and we took a look.

"What are we supposed to be looking for?" I asked her.

"I don't know. Something unusual. Like I once had a neighbor who found a cat in his car. At least, he thought it used to be a cat. It was something with fur.

It might have been a raccoon or a big rat or a small beaver. It was hard to tell."

"What's that package wrapped in cellophane with the wires?" I asked her.

"I don't know," Lula said, leaning closer. "I think that might be the problem, though, on account of it's ticking."

"Ticking?"

"Oh shit!" Lula said.

We jumped back and ran for all we were worth and hid behind the Dumpster. Nothing happened.

Lula stuck her head out. "Maybe that was the carburetor, and it was supposed to tick," she said. "Do carburetors tick?"

BABOOOM! Lula's car jumped five feet in the air. The doors and hood flew off into space, and the car burst into flames. There was a second explosion, the Firebird rolled over onto Ranger's Cayenne, and the Cayenne caught. In a matter of minutes, there was nothing left of either car but smoking, twisted, charred metal.

Lula's mouth opened, but no words came out. Her eyes got huge, rolled back into her head, and she keeled over in a dead faint. By the time the fire trucks arrived, the fire had played itself out. Lula was sitting propped against the Dumpster, still not making sense.

"It . . . and . . . my . . . how?" she asked.

I was numb. These idiots were still trying to kill Lula, and I'd just destroyed another Cayenne. I'd been involved in so many fires in the past week, I'd lost count. I had no place to live. I had no idea what I wanted to do about my personal relationships. And I still couldn't get all the red paint out of my hair. I was a disaster magnet.

I suddenly felt warm, and all the little hairs stood up on my arms. I turned and bumped into Ranger.

"This has to be a record," he said. "I've had that car for twenty-four hours."

"I'm sorry," I said. And I burst into tears.

Ranger wrapped his arms around me and cuddled me into him. "Babe. It's just a car."

"It's not just the car. It's me," I wailed. "I'm a mess."

"You're not a mess," Ranger said. "You're just having one of those emotional girl moments."

"Unh," I said. And I punched him in the chest.

"Feel better?"

"Yeah, sort of."

He stepped back and looked at Lula. "What's wrong with her?"

"She's in a state. Her Firebird got blown up."

"She spends all this time with you, and she's not used to cars getting blown up?"

"They aren't usually hers."

"Does she need help?"

"I think she'll come around," I said. "She's breathing now. And her eyes have mostly gone back into their sockets."

I looked past Ranger and saw Morelli come on the scene. He picked me out of the crowd of bystanders and jogged over.

"Are you okay?" he asked me. "What's with Lula?"

"One of those cars used to be her Firebird."

"And the other used to be my Cayenne," Ranger said.

Morelli looked down at Lula. "Does she need a medic?"

"Someone's gonna pay," Lula said. And she farted.

Morelli and Ranger smiled wide, and we all took a step back.

"That should help," I said.

"Yep," Morelli said, still grinning. "Always makes me feel better."

"I have to get back to the office," Ranger said. "Ramon is in a car on the street if you need anything."

Morelli watched him walk away. "It's like he's SpiderMan with Spidey sense. Something happens, and he suddenly appears. And then when the disaster is contained, he vanishes."

"His control room listens to the scanners."

"That was my second guess," Morelli said.

"It was some sort of bomb," I said to Morelli. "It was next to the engine, and it ticked. We were lucky we weren't killed."

"It ticked? Bombs don't tick anymore. Where did they get their material, WWI surplus?"

"Maybe it was something rubbing against a moving part. I don't know anything about this stuff. It was making a noise that sounded like ticking. Anyway, these guys aren't smart."

"I noticed. It makes it all the more annoying that we can't catch them."

"How's Bob?" I asked.

"Bob is fine. His intestines are squeaky clean."

"How are you?"

"I'm clean, too."

And then I couldn't help myself. The bitch part of me sneaked out. "How's Joyce?"

"Joyce is Joyce," Morelli said.

Lula hauled herself to her feet. "I'm in a bad mood," she said. "I'm in a mood to get me some Marco the Maniac. I've had it with this shit. It's one thing to kill me, but blowin' up my Firebird is goin' too far." She looked at her watch. "We gotta get to the park. We gotta sign in."

"We haven't got a car. The Buick is parked at Rangeman."

"I'll call Connie. She can take us."

SIXTEEN

Connie drove a silver Camry with rosary beads hanging from her rearview mirror and a Smith & Wesson stuck under the driver's seat. No matter what went down, Connie was covered.

I was in the backseat with Grandma, and Lula was next to Connie. We were in the parking lot adjacent to the field where the cook-off was to be held, and we were watching competitors pull in, dragging everything from mobile professional kitchens to U-hauls carrying grills and worktables.

"I didn't expect this," Grandma said. "I figured we come with a jar of sauce, and they'd have some chicken for us."

"We got a grill," Lula said, getting out of the Camry. "We just didn't bring it yet."

"Did you get a set of rules when you registered?" Connie asked Lula.

"No. I did the express register, bein' that the organizer was under some duress. And on top of that, I didn't have to pay no registration fee, so he might have been trying to save on paper."

A registration table had been set up at the edge of the lot. Competitors were signing in, taking a set of instructions, and leaving with a tray.

"What's with the tray?" Lula asked the guy in line in front of us.

"It's the official competition tray. You put the food that's going to be judged on the tray."

"Imagine that," Grandma said. "Isn't that something?"

We got our tray and our rules, and we stepped aside to read through the instructions.

"It says here that we can't use a gas grill," Connie said. "We need to cook on wood or charcoal. And we have to pick a category. Ribs, chicken, or brisket."

"I'm thinking ribs," Lula said. "Seems to me it's harder to poison someone with ribs. I guess there's always that trichinosis thing, but you don't know about that for years. And I'm gonna have to get a different grill."

"All these people got tents and tables and signs with their name on it," Grandma said. "We need some of that stuff. We need a name."

"How about Vincent Plum Bail Bondettes," Connie said.

"I'm not being nothin' associating me with Vincent Plum," Lula said. "Bad enough I gotta work for the little pervert."

"I want a sexy name," Grandma said. "Like Hot Vagina."

"Flamin' Assholes would be better," Lula said. "That's what happens when you eat our sauce. Can you say Flamin' Assholes on television?"

"This is big," I said, looking out over the field. "There are flags with numbers on them all over the place. Every team is assigned a number."

"We're number twenty-seven," Lula said. "That don't sound like a good number to me."

"What's wrong with it?"

"It's not memorable," Lula said. "I want to be number nine."

My eye was starting to twitch, and I had a dull throb at the base of my skull. "Probably, they gave us Chipotle's number," I said.

"Do you think?"

"Absolutely. He got decapitated, and you registered late, so you got his number."

I hoped she bought this baloney, because I didn't want to hang out while Lula pulled a gun on the registration lady.

"That makes sense," Lula said. "I guess it's okay then. Let's find our spot."

We walked down rows of flags and finally found twenty-seven. It was a little patch of grass between the red-and-white-striped canopy of Bert's BBQ and the brown canopy of The Bull Stops Here. Our neighbors had set up shop and taken off. From what I could see, that was the routine. Stake out your territory, get your canopy and table ready to go. Hang your sign. Leave for the day.

"The instructions say we can get back in here at eight o'clock tomorrow morning," Connie said. "We can start cooking anytime we want after that. The judging is at six in the evening."

"We got a lot of stuff to get together," Lula said. "To start, we gotta find one of them canopies and a grill."

"Not everybody has a canopy," Grandma said.

"Yeah, but the canopy is classy, and it keeps the sun off the top of your head, so you don't get a sunburn," Lula said.

We all looked at the top of Lula's head. Not much chance of sunburn there. Not a lot of sunlight reached Lula's scalp.

"I've got a couple hours free this afternoon," I said to Lula. "We can go around and try to collect some of

the essentials. We just have to stop by Rangeman, so I
can get the Buick."

"I'll go with you," Grandma said.

The first thing we gotta do is get us a truck," Lula said.
"This Buick isn't gonna hold a grill and all. I bet we
could borrow a truck from Pookey Brown. He owns
that junkyard and used-car lot at the end of Stark
Street. He used to be a steady customer of mine when
I was a 'ho."

"Boy," Grandma said. "You had lots of customers.
You know people everywhere."

"I had a real good corner. And I never had a business manager, so I was able to keep my prices down."

I didn't want to drive the length of Stark, so I cut
across on Olden and only had to go two blocks down
to the junkyard. The name on the street sign read C.J.
SCRAP METAL, but Pookey Brown ran it, and scrap
metal was too lofty a description for Pookey's business.
Pookey was a junk collector. He ran a private dump.
Pookey had almost two acres of broken, rusted,
unwanted crapola. Even Pookey himself looked like
he was expired. He was thin as a reed, frizzy haired,
gaunt featured, and his skin tone was gray. I had no
clue to his age. He could be forty. He could be a hundred and ten. And I couldn't imagine what Pookey
would do with a 'ho.

"There's my girl," Pookey said when he saw Lula.
"I never get to see you anymore."

"I keep busy working at the bond office," Lula told
him. "I need a favor. I need to borrow a truck until tomorrow night."

"Sure," Pookey said. "Just take yourself over to the
truck section and pick one out."

If you had a junker car or truck, and somehow you
could manage to get it to C.J. Scrap, you could park

it there and walk away. Some of them even had license plates attached. And every now and then, one got parked with a body in the trunk. There were thirteen cars and three pickup trucks in Pookey's "used car" lot today.

"Any of these trucks run?" Lula asked.

"The red one got a couple miles left," Pookey said. "I could put a plate on for you. You need anything else?"

"Yeah," Lula said. "I need a grill. Not one of them gas grills, either."

"I got a good selection of grills," Pookey said. "Do you need to cook in it?"

"I'm entered in the barbecue contest at the park tomorrow," Lula said.

"So then you need a *barbecuing* grill. That narrows the field. How about eating? Are you gonna personally eat any of the barbecue?"

"I don't think so. I think the judges are eating the barbecue."

"That gives us more selection," Pookey said.

By the time Lula was done shopping at C.J. Scrap, she had a grill and a card table loaded into her truck. The plate on the truck was éxpired, but you could hardly tell for the mud and rust. I followed her down Stark and parked behind her when she stopped at Maynard's Funeral Home.

"I gotta make a pickup here, too. You stay and guard the truck," Lula said, sticking her head in the Buick's window. "Bad as it is, if I leave it alone for ten minutes in this part of town, it'll be missing wheels when I get back." She looked at Grandma, sitting next to me. "Do you have your gun?"

"You betcha," Grandma said. "I got it right here in my purse. Just like always."

"Shoot whoever comes near," Lula said to Grandma. "I won't be long."

I looked over at Grandma. "If you shoot *anyone,* I'm telling my mother on you."

"How about those three guys coming down the street? Can I shoot them?"

"No! They're just walking down the street."

"I don't like the looks of them," Grandma said. "They look shifty."

"Everyone looks like that on Stark Street."

The three guys were in their early- to mid-twenties, doing the ghetto strut in their ridiculous oversize pants. They were wearing a lot of gold chains, and one of them had a bottle in a brown paper bag. Always a sign of a classy dude.

I rolled my window up and locked my door, and Grandma did the same.

They got even with the Buick and looked in at me.

"Nice wheels," one of them said. "Maybe you should get out and let me drive."

"Ignore them," I said to Grandma. "They'll go away."

The guy with the bottle took a pull on it and tried the door handle. Locked.

"Are you sure you don't want me to shoot him?" Grandma asked.

"No. No shooting."

They tried to rock the car, but the Buick was a tank. It would take more than three scrawny homies to rock the Buick. One of them dropped his pants and pressed his bare ass against the driver's side window.

"You're gonna have to Windex that window when we get home," Grandma said.

I was looking at the funeral home, sending mental telepathy to Lula to get herself out to her truck, so we could leave, and I heard the back door to the Buick get wrenched open. I hadn't thought to lock the back door.

One of the men climbed onto the backseat, and another reached around and unlocked the driver's door. I reached for the ignition key, but my door was already open, and I was getting pulled out of the car. I hooked my arm through the steering wheel and kicked one of the guys in the face. The guy in the back was grabbing at me, and the third guy had hold of my foot.

"We're gonna have fun with you and the old lady," the guy in the backseat said. "We're gonna do you like you've never been done before."

"Shoot!" I said to Grandma.

"But you said . . ."

"Just fucking *shoot* someone!"

Grandma carried a gun like Dirty Harry's. I caught sight of the massive barrel in my peripheral vision and *BANG.*

The guy holding my foot jumped back and grabbed the side of his head, blood spurting through his fingers. "Son of a bitch!" he yelled. "Son of a fuckin' bitch! She shot off my ear."

I knew what he was saying because it was easy to read his lips, but I wasn't hearing anything but a high-pitched ringing in my head.

The guy in the backseat scrambled out of the Buick and helped drag the guy with one ear down the street.

"Do you think he'll be all right?" Grandma asked.

"Don't know. Don't care."

The door to the funeral home opened, and Lula and a mountain of a guy came out carrying a bundle of what looked like aluminum poles partially wrapped in faded green canvas. They threw the bundle into the back of the truck, and the guy returned to the funeral home. Lula said something to Grandma and me, but I couldn't hear.

"What?" I said.

"HOME!" Grandma yelled.

I followed Lula to my parents' house and dropped Grandma off. I think Grandma said they were going to put the truck in the garage, so no one would steal the grill. Personally, I didn't think she had to worry about anyone wanting the grill.

I drove through town to Rangeman and went straight to Ranger's apartment. I kicked my shoes off and flopped onto his bed. When I woke up, I was covered with a light blanket, and I could see Ranger at his desk in the den. The ringing wasn't nearly so loud in my head. It was down to mosquito level.

I rolled out of bed and went into the den.

"Tough day?" Ranger asked.

"You don't even want to know. How was your day?"

"Interesting. I showed your maintenance man Mike file pictures of all Rangeman employees remotely fitting his description, and he couldn't identify any of them. Our bad guy wears a Rangeman uniform but doesn't work here."

"Could he be a former employee?"

"There were only two possibilities, and I got a negative on them."

"Now what?"

"I have someone checking all the accounts for evidence of touch-pad surveillance. He's also cataloging Rangeman visits on those accounts."

"It wouldn't be difficult to duplicate a Rangeman uniform. Black cargo pants and a black T-shirt with *Rangeman* embroidered on it."

"My men all know to show their ID when entering a house, but the accounts are lax at asking. Most people see the uniform and are satisfied."

I was suddenly starving, and there was a wonderful smell drifting in from the kitchen. "What's that smell?"

Ella brought dinner up a half hour ago, but I didn't want to wake you. I think we've got some kind of stew."

We went to the kitchen and dished out the stew.

"I've got a fix on Cameron Manfred," Ranger said. "During the day, he works for a trucking company that's a front for a hijacking operation. It would be awkward to make an apprehension there. Lots of paranoid people with guns. Manfred leaves the trucking company at five, goes to a neighborhood strip bar with his fellow workers until around seven, and then heads for his girl's apartment. He gives his address as the projects, but he's never there. It's actually his mother's address. We're going to have to hit him at the girl's place tonight. If there isn't enough cover to tag him on the street, we'll have to let him settle and then go in after him. I have to take a shift at eleven, but we should have this wrapped up by then."

We were in a Rangeman-issue black Explorer. Ranger was behind the wheel, and we were parked across from a slum apartment building one block over from Stark Street, where Cameron Manfred was holed up with his girlfriend. It was a little after nine at night, and the street was dark. Businesses were closed, steel grates rolled down over entrances and plate-glass windows. There was a streetlight overhead, but the bulb had been shot out.

We'd been sitting at the curb for ten minutes, not saying anything, Ranger in hunt mode. He was watching the building and the street, taking the pulse of the area, his own heart rate probably somewhere around reptilian.

He punched a number into his phone. A man answered, and Ranger disconnected. "He's there," Ranger said. "Let's go."

We crossed the street, entered the building, and silently climbed to the third floor. The air was stale. The walls were covered with graffiti. The light was dim.

A small rat scuttled across Ranger's foot and disappeared into the shadows. I shuddered and grabbed the back of his shirt.

"Babe," Ranger said, his voice barely audible.

There were two apartments on the third floor. Maureen Gonzales, Manfred's girlfriend, lived in 3A. I stood flat to the wall on one side of her door. Ranger stood on the other side and knocked. His other hand was on his holstered gun.

A pretty Hispanic woman opened the door and smiled at Ranger. She was wearing a man's shirt, unbuttoned, and nothing else. "Yes?" she said.

Ranger smiled back at the woman and looked beyond her, into the room. "I'd like to speak to Cameron."

"Cameron isn't here."

"You don't mind if I look around?"

She held the shirt wide open. "Look all you want."

"Nice," Ranger said, "but I'm looking for Cameron."

"I told you he's not here."

"Bond enforcement," Ranger said. "Step aside."

"Do you have a search warrant?"

There was the sound of a window getting shoved up in the back room. Ranger pushed past Gonzales and ran for the window. I turned and raced down the stairs and out the front door. I saw Manfred burst out of the alley between the buildings and cross the street. I took off after him, having no idea what I'd do if I caught him. My self-defense skills relied heavily on eye-gouging and testicle rearrangement. Beyond that, I was at a loss.

I chased Manfred to Stark and saw him turn the corner. I turned a couple beats behind him, and the sidewalk was empty in front of me. No Manfred.

The only possibility was the building on the corner. There was a pizza place on the ground floor and what looked like two floors of apartments above it. The pizza place was closed for the night. The door leading to the apartments was open, the hallway was dark. No light in the stairwell. I stood in the entry and listened for movement.

Ranger came in behind me. "Is he up there?"

"I don't know. I lost him when he turned the corner. I wasn't that far away. I don't think he had time to go farther than this building. Where were you? I thought you'd be on top of him."

"The fire escape rusted out underneath me at the second floor. It took me a minute to regroup." He looked up the stairs. "Do you want to come with me, or do you want to keep watch here?"

"I'll stay here."

Ranger was immediately swallowed up by the dark. He had a flashlight, but he didn't use it. He moved almost without sound, creeping up the stairs, pausing at the second-floor landing to listen before moving on.

I hid in the shadows, not wanting to be seen from the street. God knows who was walking the street. Probably, I should carry a gun, but guns scared the heck out of me. I had pepper spray in my purse. And a large can of hair spray, which in my experience is almost as effective as the pepper spray.

I was concentrating on listening for Ranger and keeping watch on the street, and was completely taken by surprise when a door to the rear of the ground-floor hallway opened and Manfred stepped out. He froze when he saw me, obviously just as shocked to find me standing there as I was to see him. He whirled around and retreated through the door. I yelled for Ranger and ran after Manfred.

The door opened to a flight of stairs that led to the cellar. I got to the bottom of the stairs and realized this was a storeroom for the pizza place. Stainless-steel rolling shelves marched in rows across the room. Bags of flour, cans of tomato sauce, and gallon cans of olive oil were stacked on the shelves. A dim bulb burned overhead. I didn't see Manfred. Fine by me. Probably the only reason I wasn't already dead was that he'd left his girl's house in such a rush, he'd gone out unarmed.

I cautiously approached one of the shelves, and Manfred stepped out and grabbed me.

"Give me your gun," he said.

My heart skipped a beat and went into terror tempo. *Bang, bang, bang, bang*, knocking against my rib cage.

"I don't have a gun," I said.

And then, without any help from my brain, my knee suddenly connected with Manfred's gonads.

Manfred doubled over, and I hit him on the head with a bag of flour. He staggered forward a little, but he didn't go down, so I hit him again. The bag broke, and flour went everywhere. I was momentarily blinded, but I reached back to the shelf, grabbed a gallon can of oil, and swung blind. I connected with something that got a grunt out of Manfred.

"Fuckin' bitch," Manfred said.

I hauled back to swing again, and Ranger lifted the can from my hand.

"I'm on it," Ranger said, cuffing Manfred.

"Jail's better than another three minutes with her," Manfred said. "She's a fuckin' animal. I'm lucky if I can ever use my nuts again. Keep her away from me."

"I didn't see you come down the stairs," I said to Ranger. "It was a whiteout."

"Any special reason you grabbed the flour?"

"I wasn't thinking."

Manfred and I were head-to-toe flour. The flour sifted off us when we moved and floated in the air like pixie dust. Ranger hadn't so much as a smudge. By the time we got to the Rangeman SUV, some of the flour had been left behind as ghostly white footprints, but a lot of it remained.

"I honestly don't know how you manage to do this," Ranger said. "Paint, barbecue sauce, flour. It boggles the mind."

"This was all your fault," I said.

Ranger glanced over at me and his eyebrows raised a fraction of an inch.

"You could have taken him down in the apartment if you hadn't spent so much time staring at his naked girlfriend."

Ranger grinned. "She wasn't naked. She was wearing a shirt."

"You deserved to fall off that fire escape."

"That's harsh," Ranger said.

"Did you hurt yourself?" I asked him.

"Do you care?"

"No," I said.

"Liar," Ranger said. He ruffled my hair and flour sprang out in all directions.

Manfred said something to Ranger in Spanish. Ranger answered him as he assisted him into the backseat of the Explorer.

"What did he say?" I asked Ranger.

"He said if I let him go, I could have his girl."

"And your answer?"

"I declined."

"You'll probably regret that as the night goes on," I said to him.

"No doubt," Ranger said.

Ranger and I had Manfred in front of the docket lieutenant. It was a little after ten, and things were heating up. Drunk drivers, abusive drunk husbands, and a couple drug busts were making their way through the system. I was waiting for my body receipt when Morelli walked in. He nodded to Ranger and grinned at me in my whiteness.

"I was at my desk, and Mickey told me I had to come out to take a look," Morelli said.

"It's flour," I told him.

"I can see that. If we add some milk and eggs, we can turn you into a cake."

"What are you doing here? I thought you were off nights."

"I came in to cover a shooting. Fred was supposed to be on, but he got overexcited at his kid's ball game and pulled a groin muscle. I was just finishing up some paperwork."

Mickey Bolan joined us. Bolan worked Crimes Against Persons with Morelli. He was ten years older than Morelli and counting down to his pension.

"I wasn't exaggerating, right?" Bolan said to Morelli. "They're both covered with flour."

"I'd tell you about it," I said to Bolan, "but it's not as good as it looks."

"That's okay," Bolan said. "I got something better, anyway. The rest of Stanley Chipotle just turned up at the funeral home on Hamilton."

We all stood there for a couple beats, trying to process what we'd just heard.

"He turned up?" Morelli finally said.

"Yeah," Bolan said. "Someone apparently dumped him on the doorstep. So I guess someone should talk to the funeral guy."

"I guess that someone would be me," Morelli said. He looked at his watch. "What the hell, the game's over now, anyway."

"I need to get back to Rangeman," Ranger said to me. "If you have an interest in Chipotle, I can send someone with a car for you."

"Thanks. I don't usually get excited about seeing

headless dead men, but I wouldn't mind knowing more."

"I can give her a ride," Morelli said. "I don't imagine this will take long."

SEVENTEEN

Eddie Gazarra was standing in the funeral home parking lot, waiting for Morelli. Eddie is married to my cousin Shirley-the-Whiner. Eddie is a patrolman by choice. He could have moved up, but he likes being on the street. He says it's the uniform. No choices to make in the morning. I think it's the free doughnuts at Tasty Pastry.

"I was the first on the scene," Gazarra said when we got out of Morelli's SUV. "The drop was made right after viewing hours. Morton shut the lights off, and ten minutes later, someone rang the doorbell. When Morton came to the door, he found Chipotle stretched out and frozen solid."

Eli Morton is the current owner of the funeral home. For years, Constantine Stiva owned the place. The business has changed hands a couple times since Stiva left, but everyone still thinks of this as Stiva's Funeral Home.

"Where is he now?" Morelli asked.

"On the porch. We didn't move him."

"Are you sure it's Chipotle?"

"He didn't have a head," Gazarra said. "We sort of put two and two together."

"No ID?"

"None we could find. Hard to get into his pockets, what with him being a big Popsicle."

We'd been walking while we were talking, and we'd gotten to the stairs that led to the funeral home's wide front porch. I recognized Eli Morton at the top of the stairs. He was talking to a couple uniformed cops and an older man in slacks and a dress shirt. A couple guys from the EMT truck were up there, too. The body wasn't visible.

"Maybe I'll wait here," I said.

"It's not so bad," Gazarra told me. "He's frozen stiff as a board. All the blood's frozen, too. And the head was cut off nice and clean."

I sat down on the bottom step. "I'll *definitely* wait here."

"I'll get back to you," Morelli said, walking the rest of the way with Gazarra.

The medical examiner's truck rolled past and pulled into the lot. It was followed by a TV news truck with a dish. I saw Morelli glance over at the news truck and move a couple of the uniformed guys from the porch to the lot to contain the media.

I sat on the step for about a half hour, watching people come and go. Finally, Morelli came back and sat alongside me.

"How's it going?" I asked him.

"The forensic photographer just finished, and the ME is doing his thing, and then we're moving the body inside to a meat locker. He's starting to defrost."

"Is he staying here for the funeral?"

"Eventually. The body will have to go to the morgue for an autopsy first, and then it'll get released for burial. Right now, I need someone to identify the body."

"Do you think it might not be Chipotle?"

"This is a high-profile case, and there was no identification on the body."

"Aren't there tests for that sort of thing?"

"Yeah, and they'll do them when they do the autopsy. I just need someone to eyeball this guy for a preliminary ID."

"His sister?"

"We haven't been able to reach her."

"One of his ex-wives? His agent?"

"They're all over the place. Aspen, New York, L.A., Sante Fe."

"So who are you going to get?"

"Lula."

"You're kidding."

"She saw him get murdered," Morelli said. "I'm hoping she remembers his clothes and enough of his build to give me an ID. I've got two television trucks and a bunch of reporters sitting in the lot. If I don't give them something, they'll make something up, so I'm going to have to talk to them. Before I do that, my chief wants an ID."

"Have you called Lula?"

"Yeah. She's on her way over."

There was activity at the top of the porch, and Morelli stood.

"Looks like they're getting ready to move the body," he said. "I'm keeping it on ice here for Lula. I thought it was easier than trying to get her to go to the morgue. I'd appreciate it if you could wait here for her and bring her in when she arrives."

"Sure."

Twenty minutes later, I saw my father's cab drive into the lot. The cab parked, and Lula got out and waved to the knot of newsmen standing by one of the trucks.

"Yoohoo, I'm Lula," she said to them. "I got called in to identify the body."

I jumped up and sprinted to the lot, intercepting the horde that rushed at her.

"Lula will talk to you later," I told them, herding Lula out of the lot. "She has to talk to the police first."

"Do I look okay?" Lula asked me. "I didn't have a lot of time to fix my hair. And I didn't have my full wardrobe at my disposal."

"You look fine," I said. "The silver sequined top and matching skirt is just right for an evening decapitation identification."

"You don't think it's too dressy?"

On everyone but Lula and Tina Turner, yes. On Lula and Tina Turner, no. It was perfect.

"I thought there might be television here," Lula said. "You know how television always likes a little bling."

"Does my father know you have his cab?"

"Everyone was asleep, and I didn't want to bother no one, so I helped myself to the cab. I would have rather taken your mother's car, but I couldn't find the key."

We went up the stairs and into the foyer. No problem for me now. I was real brave once the body was removed.

Morelli ambled over. "Thanks for coming out to do this," he said to Lula.

"Anything to help the police," Lula said. "Are the television cameras in here? Is that a tabloid photographer over there?"

"No television cameras," Morelli said. "And the photographer is the department's forensics guy."

"Hunh," Lula said. "Let's get this over with then. It's not like I was sitting around thinking I'd like to go look at a dead guy with no head. I got sensibilities, you know. The thing is, I hate dead guys."

"It's just a fast look," Morelli said. "And then you can go home."

"After I talk to the television people."

"Yeah," Morelli said. "Whatever. Follow me. We have the body in one of the freezers downstairs."

"Say what? I'm not going downstairs to no freezer compartments. That's too creepy. How many bodies does this guy have in his freezer?"

"I don't know," Morelli said. "I didn't ask, and I didn't look. Would you rather see this body in the morgue?"

"Hell no. Only way you're getting me in a morgue is toes up."

"Can we get on with it?" Morelli said. "I've had a long day and my intestines are a mess."

"I hear you," Lula said. "I got issues, too. I think there must be something going around."

"I'll wait here," I said. "No reason for me to tag along."

"The hell," Lula said. "I'm needing moral support. I wasn't even gonna come until Morelli told me you'd do this with me."

I cut a look at Morelli. "You said that?"

"More or less."

"You're scum."

"I know," Morelli said. "Can we *please* go downstairs now?"

The funeral home had originally been a large Victorian house. It had been renovated, and rooms and garages had been added, but it still had the bones of the original structure. We followed Eli Morton down a hallway off the lobby. To our right was the kitchen. To our left was the door to the basement.

A couple years ago, the basement had been destroyed in a fire. It had all been rebuilt and was now nicely finished off and divided into rooms that opened off a center hall. Morton led us to the room farthest from the stairs.

"I have three cold-storage drawers and three freezer drawers in here," Morton said. "I almost never use the freezer drawers. They were put in by the previous owner."

The floor was white tile, and the walls were painted white. The fronts to the freezer drawers were stainless steel. Gazarra pulled a freezer drawer out, and it was filled with tubs of ice cream.

"Costco had a sale," Morton said. "Your guy is in drawer number three."

He rolled number three out, Lula gaped at the body without the head, and Lula fainted. *Crash*. Onto the white tile floor. I didn't faint because I didn't look. I walked in staring at my feet, and I never raised my eyes.

"Crap," Morelli said. "Get her out of here. Someone take her feet. I've got the top half."

Gazarra and Morelli lugged Lula into the hall and stepped back. Lula's eyes snapped open, and we all stared down at her.

"You fainted," I told her.

"Did not."

"You're on the floor."

"Well, anybody would have fainted. That was disgusting. People aren't supposed to be going around without their head," Lula said. "It's not right."

"Was that Chipotle?" Morelli asked.

"Might have been," Lula said. "Hard to tell with the frost on him, but it looked like the same clothes. I don't know where they been keeping him, but he got freezer burn."

Morelli and Gazarra helped Lula to her feet.

"Are you going to be okay?" Morelli asked her.

"I could use a drink," Lula said. "A big one."

"I have some whiskey," Morton said, leading the way up the stairs and into the kitchen.

Morton poured out a tumbler of whiskey for Lula and took a shot for himself. The rest of us settled for a rain check.

"Does that count as an ID?" I asked Morelli.

"Good enough for me."

"Where do you suppose Marco the Maniac has been keeping the body? It was frozen straight out. That means it was kept in a commercial freezer."

"There are commercial freezers all over the place."

"Still, it's not like Marco and his partner are just hanging out around the house here. They know someone well enough to let them store a dead guy in the freezer."

"There are probably dead guys in half the commercial freezers in Trenton," Morelli said.

Lula chugged the whiskey. "This is good stuff," she said. "I'm feeling much better. Maybe I need just a teensy bit more."

Morelli got the bottle off the counter and poured out more for Lula. He draped an arm across my shoulders and brought me into the hallway.

"She's going to be in no shape to talk to the reporters," he said. "You're going to have to drive her directly home."

"Gotcha."

He leaned in to me. "I could have whispered that in your ear in the kitchen, but I thought this was more romantic."

"You think this is romantic?"

"No, but it's all I've got," Morelli said. "This is the highlight of my week."

"I thought you were dating Joyce."

"If I was dating Joyce, I'd have fang marks in my neck and I'd be down a couple quarts of blood."

"Not to change the subject, but why would Marco take a chance by coming out and dropping the body off on the porch? Why not throw it in the river, or bury it, or make it into hamburger? He's a butcher, right?"

"Good question. Of course, he's known as Marco the Maniac, so this might not have been a rational act." Morelli kissed me just above the collar of my T-shirt. "Do you think we can overlook the fact that we're in a funeral home for a moment?"

"No. For one thing, Gazarra is trying to get your attention."

Gazarra was waving from the front door. "Can the ME take over?" Gazarra hollered.

"Yes," Morelli said. "I'm done with Chipotle for now."

"I'm going to get the cab," I told Morelli. "I'll bring it around to the front door, and you can hustle Lula into it."

I got the key from Lula's purse and jogged to the lot. My father's cab was white with CAB printed in red all over it. CAB was an acronym for a small company named Capitol Area Buslettes.

I got into the cab, cranked it over, and drove out of the lot. I stopped in front of the funeral home, and an elderly man got in the backseat.

"Excuse me," I said. "I'm off duty."

"Two Hundred Eldridge Road," he said. "It's one of the new high-rises down by the river."

"This is a private cab. You have to get out."

"But I called for a cab. And now here you are."

"You didn't call for *my* cab."

Morelli and Gazarra had their arms locked across Lula's back. They whisked her down the stairs and across the sidewalk without her feet touching once. They came up to the cab parked at the curb and looked inside.

"What's going on?" Morelli wanted to know.

"He thinks I'm driving a cab."

"Cupcake," Morelli said, "you *are* driving a cab."

"Yes, but . . . oh hell, just dump Lula in with him."

Morelli stuffed Lula into the backseat with the man, leaned through the driver's side window and kissed me, and waved me away.

"Who's this?" Lula asked.

"I'm Wesley," the man said. "You can call me Wesley."

"How come I'm in a cab with you?"

"I don't know," Wesley said. "This is a very strange cab company."

"Hunh," Lula said.

She slumped in her seat, put her head on Wesley's shoulder, and fell asleep. Fifteen minutes later, I dropped Wesley at 200 Eldridge Road.

"How much do I owe you?" he asked.

"I don't know," I said. "It's free."

"Thanks," he said, giving me a dollar. "Here's a tip."

I turned around and drove Lula to my parents' house. I made sure she got in the house and up the stairs, and then I drove to Rangeman. I parked the cab next to the Buick and took the elevator to the seventh floor. I looked in at Rex and said hello. Someone had given him fresh water and filled his food dish with nuts and vegetables and what looked like a tiny piece of pizza. I went to the bedroom, dropped my clothes on the floor, and crawled into bed.

I was just coming awake when a warm body slipped into bed next to me.

"What time is it?" I asked him.

"A little after seven A.M."

He threw an arm and a leg over me and nuzzled my neck.

"I have just enough energy left to make both of us happy," he said.

He kissed my shoulder and the pulse point in my neck. He got to my mouth and my cell phone rang.

"Ignore it," he said.

It kept ringing.

"I can't ignore it," I told him. "I can't concentrate."

"Babe, I'm going to be so good to you, you won't need to concentrate."

I snatched at the phone. "What?"

It was my father. "You've got the cab, and I'm supposed to pick up Melvin Miklowski at seven-thirty."

"Use Mom's car."

"I can't use her car. I have to have the cab. And anyway, she's at Mass."

"Have the company send another cab."

"There are no other cabs. Everyone has morning pickups. That's what we do. We take people to the train station. For three years, I've taken Melvin Miklowski to the train station precisely at seven-thirty, every Tuesday. He has a Tuesday meeting in New York, and he catches the train at eight A.M. He counts on me. He's a regular."

"I'm all the way across town at Rangeman."

"Then you can pick him up. He's downtown at 365 Front Street."

"Okay. Fine."

I hung up and blew out a sigh.

"That doesn't sound good," Ranger said.

"It was my dad."

"Heart attack?"

"Cab pickup."

EIGHTEEN

I got to 365 Front Street with five minutes to spare. At 7:30, Melvin exited his house and quickly walked to the cab.

"I'm Frank's daughter," I told him. "My father couldn't make it."

"Do you drive a cab for a living, too?"

"No. I'm a bounty hunter."

"Like on television."

"Yeah." It wasn't at all like on television, but it was easier to go with it. Besides, people were always disappointed when I told them what I did every day.

"Are you packin'?" Melvin asked.

"No. Are you?"

"It would be cool if you were packin'. It would make a better story."

"You could pretend," I said. "Who would know?"

"Do you at least own a gun?"

"Yeah. I have a Smith & Wesson."

"Have you ever shot anyone?"

"No." That was a fib, too, but shooting someone isn't something you brag about.

"What do I owe you?" Melvin said when I dropped him at the train station.

"I don't know," I told him. "I don't know how to

work the meter. You can settle with my father next week."

I'd rushed out of Rangeman without breakfast, and now I had some choices. I could return to Rangeman, I could go to Cluck-in-a-Bucket, or I could get my mom to make pancakes. My mom won by a mile.

I drove to Hamilton and cut into the Burg. I reached my parents' house and had lots of parking choices. The Buick wasn't there. Lula's Firebird wasn't there. And I was in the cab.

Lula was at my mother's small kitchen table when I walked in. She was drinking coffee, and she looked like she was at death's door.

"That was an upsetting experience last night," she said. "Police identifications give me a headache."

"Maybe you should take more pills," Grandma said. "You gotta cook barbecue today."

"I'll be okay," Lula said. "I'm feeling better now that I've got coffee."

"Have you had breakfast?" my mom asked me.

"No."

"What would you like?"

"Pancakes!"

My mom has a special pancake bowl. It has a handle on one side and a pour spout on the other. And it makes the world's best pancakes. I helped myself to a mug of coffee and sat across from Lula while my mom whipped up the batter.

"We've got lots of things to do this morning," Lula said. "Grandma and me are taking the truck to the park to get our mobile kitchen going. Connie said she'd get the ribs. And I thought you could go to the grocery store and get all the odds and ends."

"Sure."

"I even got a special surprise coming. I had this brainstorm yesterday on making sure we got on television. Larry's delivering it to the park later this morning."

My mother brought butter and pancake syrup to the table and set out knives and forks for everyone.

"Where's Dad?" I asked my mother. "I thought he'd be waiting for me to bring his cab back."

"He took my car to get serviced. He went early, since he didn't have to pick Mr. Miklowski up."

Terrific. That meant I was stuck with the cab until I got back to Rangeman and swapped it for the Buick. And truth is, I couldn't say which of them I hated more.

My first stop was the supermarket. Not bad this early in the morning because it takes the seniors time to get up and running. By ten, they'd start to roll in, clogging up the lot with their handicap-tagged cars. Being a senior citizen in Jersey is a lot like belonging to the Mob. A certain attitude is expected. If you don't respect a Mob member in Jersey, you could get shot. If you don't respect a senior, they'll ram a shopping cart into your car, rear-end you at a light, and deliberately block you from going down the nonprescription meds aisle by idling in the middle of it in their motorized basketed bumper cars while they pretend to read the label on the Advil box.

I worked my way through the list Lula had given me. A giant-size ketchup, Tabasco sauce, molasses, cider vinegar, orange juice, a bunch of spices, some hot sauce, M&Ms, aluminum foil, a couple disposable baking pans, Pepto-Bismol, nonstick spray oil.

"Looks to me like you're making barbecue," the lady at the checkout said to me.

"Yep."

"Did you hear about that barbecue cook? The one who got his head cut off? It's on the news that they found his body. It's all everyone's talking about. I heard the *Today* show is sending Al Roker and a film crew to the cook-off in the park today."

I loaded everything into the trunk and drove to Tasty Pastry to get doughnuts for Larry. I parked at the curb, ran inside, and got a dozen doughnuts. When I came out, there was a woman sitting in the backseat of the cab.

"I'm off duty," I told her.

"I'm only going a couple blocks."

"I'm late, and I still have to go to the hardware store. You have to get out."

"What kind of a cab is this that doesn't want to make money?"

"It's an off-duty cab!"

The woman got out and slammed the door. "I'm going to report you to the cab authority," she said. "And I know who you are, too. And I'm telling your mother."

The hardware store was on Broad. I took a shortcut through the Burg, hit Broad, went one block, and parked in the small lot attached to the hardware store. I ran inside and gathered together a bag of charcoal, fire starter, and one of those mechanical match things.

"Is this to barbecue?" the checkout kid asked.

"Yeah."

"You should get a couple bundles of the special wood we've got. You put it in the grill, and it makes everything taste great."

"Sure," I said. "Give me a couple bundles."

He swiped my credit card, and I started to sweat. Barbecuing was expensive. Thank goodness I had the extra job with Rangeman.

I threw everything into the trunk alongside the groceries and peeled out of the lot. I stopped for a light, and an old guy got into the backseat.

"Out!" I said. "I'm off duty."

"What?"

"Off duty."

"I'm going to the senior center on Market."

"Not in this cab you're not."

"What?"

"I'm off duty!" I yelled at him.

"I don't hear so good," he said.

"Read my lips. *Get out.*"

"I got rights," he said.

The light turned, and the woman behind me gave me the finger. I stepped on the gas, raced the half mile to the senior center, and came to a screeching stop at the wheelchair ramp. I jumped out of the cab and yanked the old guy out of the backseat. I got back behind the wheel, made sure all the doors were locked, and took off. I looked in the rearview mirror and saw the old guy was standing there, waving money at me. I hooked a U-turn, drove up to him, snatched the money out of his hand, and kept going. Three dollars. Good deal. I'd put it toward my credit card.

I had everything on the list, so I pointed the cab toward Gooser Park. The sun was struggling to shine through scattered clouds, and the air was crisp. Perfect weather for a barbecue.

I turned into the park and cruised the lot, looking for a space close to the cook-off area. If the event had been held on a weekend, the lot would have been packed to overflowing by now. As it was, it was only half full. I'd been told they scheduled the event for a Tuesday to obtain better television coverage. Fine by me. I was happy not to have to battle a couple thousand people for a parking place and private time in a portable potty.

I did the best I could with the parking, loaded myself up with the groceries, and set off for our assigned space. All over the field, teams were working at marinating meat and chopping vegetables. The air smelled

smoky from applewood and hickory fires, and the barbecue kitchens were colorful with striped awnings
and checkered tablecloths. Except for our kitchen. Our
kitchen looked like the Beverly Hillbillies were getting
ready to barbecue possum.

The green awning over our area advertised Maynard's Funeral Home. The grill was rusted. The table
was rickety. A handwritten sign with our team name
was taped to the table. FLAMIN'. The rest of the name
had been ripped off. I assume this was done by a horrified cook-off organizer. Grandma and Lula were at
the ready, spatula and tongs in hand, all dressed in
their white chef's jackets and puffy white chef's hats.

I dumped my stuff on the rickety table. "I'll be right
back," I said. "I have to go back for the charcoal. I
couldn't carry it all at once. Where's Connie?"

"She should be here any minute," Lula said. "She
got a late start on account of she had to write bail for
some drunken loser who pissed on the mayor's limo."

I walked back to the cab, got the rest of the stuff
out of the trunk, and my cell phone rang.

"We got lucky," Ranger said. "We found a camera
watching a touch pad in one of the houses you tar-
geted. I had Hector install a video system of the area,
and we can monitor it from Rangeman."

"It's going to be interesting to see who's doing this.
There's a good chance it's someone you know."

"I just want the break-ins stopped. It's bad for business, and I'm tired of riding surveillance every night.
I assume you're at the park?"

"Yes. I'll be here all afternoon. The cook-off ends
at six tonight with the judging."

"You're driving a vehicle that isn't monitored. We
don't have a blip for you on the screen."

"I'm still in my father's cab."

"Be careful." And he was gone.

I lugged the charcoal and wood and fire starter stuff across the field to Lula and Grandma. Lula filled the bottom of the grill with charcoal and piled the wood on top. She poured accelerant on and used the gizmo to light it. *WHOOOSH!* The accelerant caught, flames shot up, and the canopy caught fire. One of the guys in the kitchen next to us rushed over with a fire extinguisher and put the canopy fire out.

"Thanks," Grandma said to him. "That was quick thinking. Last time that happened, it burned up Lula's chef hat and cremated our maple tree."

"You might want to move the canopy so it's not over the grill," the guy said. "Just a suggestion."

Connie hurried to the table and set two bags on it. "I saw the flames from the parking lot," she said. "What happened?"

"The usual," Grandma said. "No biggie."

Connie, Lula, Grandma, and I each took a pole and moved the canopy back a few feet. There was a large black-rimmed, smoking hole in the top and a smaller one in the front flap where the funeral home name was written. It now said MAYNARD FUN HOME. I thought it was an improvement. God works in mysterious ways.

We all set to work mixing the sauce and getting the ribs into the marinade.

"I was talking to some people in the parking lot," Connie said. "One of them was on the barbecue committee, and they said Al Roker and his crew were going to be walking around all afternoon. They were waiting for the van to show up."

"Al Roker is a big star," Grandma said. "He might be about the most famous person we've had in Trenton."

"There was that singer last year," Lula said.

"Whatshername. She was pretty famous. And Cher came through once. I didn't see her, but I heard she rode a elephant."

"We're not as fancy as some of these people," Grandma said. "I don't know if Al Roker is gonna want to film us."

"I got it covered," Lula said. "You'll see soon as Larry gets here, we'll have it locked in."

Connie looked up at the sign. "It just says Flamin'."

"One of the committee people got a stick up her butt about cussing," Grandma said. "We tried to explain Assholes wasn't being used as a cuss, that it was the part of the body effected by our sauce, but she wasn't having any of it."

"Bein' that we burned a hole in our roof, it turns out Flamin' isn't such a bad name for us, anyway," Lula said.

Weekday or not, there were a lot of people at the cook-off. Swarms of them were milling around in front of the kitchens and strolling the grounds. I could see Larry's head bobbing above the crowd as they all made their way along the path. He reached us and handed a big box to Lula.

"I can't stay," he said. "I have to work today."

"Thanks," Lula said. "This is gonna make celebrities out of us. This could get me my big break."

"I couldn't get exactly what you wanted," Larry said. "So I got you the next best thing."

Larry left, and Lula tore the box open. "I got the idea from Mister Clucky," she said. "Cluck-in-a-Bucket got Mister Clucky the dancin' chicken, and we're going to have the dancing barbecue sparerib."

No one said anything for a full thirty seconds. I mean, what was there to say? A dancing sparerib. As if the funeral home canopy and the massacred sign wasn't enough humiliation for one day.

Grandma was the first to find her voice. "Who's gonna be the sparerib?" she asked.

"I don't know," Lula said. "I didn't decide. Probably everyone wants to be. I guess I could do eenie meenie minie mo."

"There's no way in hell you're getting me in a spare-rib suit," Connie said.

"Let's see what we got," Lula said, pulling the suit out of the box. "What the heck? This isn't no sparerib. This isn't even a pork chop."

"It looks like a hot dog," Grandma said. "I guess it was all Larry could get on short notice."

"This don't work," Lula said. "How can someone be the Flamin' dancing hot dog when we're cooking ribs?"

"It could be a pork hot dog," Grandma said.

"That's true," Lula said. "A pork hot dog's pretty close to a rib. It's sort of like a ground-up rib."

She held the suit up. It looked to be about six feet from top to bottom. The hot dog was in a padded bun and was enhanced with a stripe of yellow mustard.

"It's a real colorful costume," Grandma said. "I wouldn't mind wearing it, but then no one would know who I was when I was on television."

That sounded like a good deal to me. "I'll wear it," I said.

There were holes in the bottom where my legs could stick out, armholes in the sides of the bun, and part of the hot dog was made of mesh, so I could sort of see. I got the thing on, and Grandma zipped me up.

"This is disappointing," Lula said. "It's not as good as Mister Clucky."

"She's got a saggy bun," Grandma said.

Connie squished my bun. "It's foam. It needs re-shaping."

Everyone worked on the bun while I stood there.

"It's hot in this thing," I said. "And I can't see through the hot dog skin. Everything's brown. And there's only a little window to look through."

"I can't hardly hear what you're saying through all that padding," Grandma said. "But don't worry, we got you looking pretty good."

"Yeah," Lula said. "Dance around. Let's see what you got."

"What kind of dance?" I asked her.

"I don't know. Any kind of dance."

I jumped around a little and fell over.

"This is top-heavy," I said.

"It don't look top-heavy," Lula said. "It's all one size top to bottom. Imagine if we got a pork chop instead of a hot dog."

I was on my back, and all I saw was brown sky. I rolled side to side, trying to flip over. No luck. I was stuck in the stupid bun. I flopped around, flailing my arms and kicking my feet. I got some decent momentum going rocking back and forth in my bun, but in the end, it didn't get me anywhere.

Lula looked down at me. "Stop clownin' around. You're scarin' the kids. You're even creepin' out the big people. It's like someone threw away a giant twitching hot dog."

"I can't get up!"

"What?"

"*I can't fucking get up*. What part of that don't you understand?"

"Well, you should have said so instead of just layin' there thrashin' around."

Connie and Lula grabbed my arms and hauled me to my feet.

"This might not be a good idea," I told them. "This suit is unwieldy."

"You just gotta get used to it," Lula said. "I bet Al

Roker will be here any minute. Anybody seen Al Roker?"

Some people stopped to look at me.

"What is it?" a man asked.

"It's a dancing hot dog," Lula said.

"It's not dancing," the man said.

There was a kid with the man. "I want to see the hot dog dance," the kid said.

I did a couple moves and fell over. "Shit!"

The kid looked up at the man. "The hot dog said *shit*."

Everyone hurried away.

"Dancing hot dogs don't say *shit*," Lula said to me, pulling me upright.

"What do they friggin' say?"

"They say *oops*."

"I'll try to remember."

"And that's a cranky tone I'm hearing," Lula said. "Hot dogs are happy food. If you was a brussels sprout, you could be cranky. Or maybe a lima bean."

"I don't feel happy. I'm sweating like a pig in this thing."

"Hey," Lula said. "You were the one who wanted to be the hot dog. Nobody *made* you be the hot dog. And you better learn how to dance before Al gets here, or you're going to miss your chance at having a national television debut."

My stomach got queasy, and I felt my skin crawl at the back of my neck. "What's out there that I can't see?" I asked. "Spiders? Snakes?"

"It's Joyce Barnhardt," Grandma said.

I turned around, and sure enough, it was Barnhardt. Her red hair was piled high on her head, her mouth was high-gloss vermilion. Her breasts were barely contained in a red leather bustier that matched skintight red leather pants and spike-heeled red leather boots.

"Who's the hot dog?" Joyce wanted to know.

"It's Stephanie," Grandma said.

"Figures. I suppose you wanted her to be the hot dog so it would have a nice straight line. Nothing worse than a hot dog with boobs, right?"

I gave Joyce the finger. "Boobs this, Joyce."

"What are you doing here?" Grandma asked Joyce. "Are you in the barbecue competition?"

"I put a couple things together," Joyce said, and she turned to face Lula. "I listen to the police bands. I know all about the Chipotle killers stalking you. And I figure those guys are here looking to put a bullet in you. Or maybe carve you up for barbecuing."

"So you're here to protect me?" Lula said.

"No, Dumbo. I'm here to capture the idiots and get the reward."

Joyce sashayed away, and we all made the sign of the cross.

"I always smell sulfur burning when she's around," Connie said.

"I want to do some walking and look at the other kitchens," Grandma said. "We got an hour before we have to start cooking the ribs."

"That's a good idea," Lula said. "We should be looking for the killers, anyway. I'm all ready for a take-down. I got my gun and my stun gun and some pepper spray. And I got body armor on under this white jacket."

NINETEEN

Connie, Lula, Grandma, and I eased into the crowd that was slowly making its way past the cook-off teams.

"Look at this group," Grandma said. "They've got one of them drums for cookin' a pig."

I couldn't see the drum. The drum was lost behind my hot dog skin. I turned to look and bumped into a kid.

"The hot dog stepped on me," the kid said.

"Sorry," I said. "Excuse me." I stepped to the side and knocked a woman over.

Connie picked the woman up. "It's her first time as a hot dog," Connie told the woman. "Cut her some slack."

Lula had me by my bun, steering me forward. "Watch out for the hot dog," she was telling people. "Make way for the hot dog."

"I think I'm getting the hang of this," I said to Lula. "I'm okay as long as I only go forward."

Lula's grip tightened on my arm. "It's him."

"Who?"

"The Chipotle killer. Marco the Maniac."

"Where?"

"Up there in front of us. The guy who's all dressed up in a cheap suit."

I squinted through the hot dog skin. I couldn't see a guy in a suit. "Does he have a cleaver?"

"No. He's got an ice-cream cone."

Lula hauled her gun out of her purse. "Hey! Marco the Maniac!" she yelled at him. "Hold it right there. I'm making a citizen's arrest."

Marco looked around, spotted Lula, and froze.

"Guess it's not so funny when he don't have his cleaver," Lula said.

A family walked between us and Marco, and Marco threw his ice-cream cone down and took off.

"He's running away," Lula said. "After him!"

After him? Was she kidding?

Lula had one side of my costume, Connie had the other, and I could feel Grandma pushing from behind. "Wait," I said. "I can't run. I can't . . ." *CRASH.* I knocked over a prep table. "Sorry!"

Lula kept dragging me. "He's going for the parking lot," Lula said.

"I see him," Connie said. "He's getting into that silver BMW. Who's got a car here?"

"What about *your* car?" Grandma asked.

"It's way on the other side of the lot."

I wriggled my arm out of the armhole and pulled the keys to the cab out of my pants pocket. "I've got the keys to the cab."

Connie got behind the wheel, Lula sat next to her, and Grandma got into the backseat. I tried to sit next to Grandma, but I couldn't get all of me in. Everyone jumped out and ran around to my side and pushed and shoved.

"She's too fat," Grandma said. "She don't fit in the door."

"Bend the bun," Connie said. "There's too much bun."

"Stand back," Lula said. And she put her butt to me and rammed me in.

Everyone rushed back into the car, Connie rocketed out of the parking place and whipped around the lot. "I see him," she said. "He turned left out of the park."

"If you get close enough to him, I can shoot out his tires," Lula said.

"Yeah, me, too," Grandma said. "You take the right-side tires," she said to Lula, "and I'll take the left-side tires."

We were on a two-lane road that ran for almost a mile before hooking up with a four-lane highway.

"I can't catch him in this cab," Connie said after a half mile. "I've got it floored, and we're losing him." Her eyes flicked to her side mirror. "Crap," she said. "It's a cop."

Lula and Grandma stuffed their guns back into their purses, and Connie popped the button on her shirt so she showed more cleavage. She pulled over, and the cop stopped behind her, lights flashing. We'd crossed the line, and we were in Hamilton Township. I didn't know any of the Hamilton Township police.

"Do you know why I pulled you over?" the cop asked Connie.

Connie leaned back to give him a good look at the girls. "Because you couldn't catch the guy in front of me?"

"We were trying to run down a killer," Grandma said. "And the hot dog is a personal friend of Joe Morelli."

"Morelli is the reason my bowling team lost the trophy," the cop said. "I hate Morelli."

Morelli was waiting for us when we rolled into the cook-off lot. Lula had called him and told him about Marco the Maniac, and now Morelli was leaning against his SUV, watching Connie park the cab. Lula and Connie and Grandma got out, but I was stuck.

"What are you, some superhero?" Lula asked Morelli. "How'd you get here so fast?"

"I was already here. We have some men on-site." Morelli looked into the cab. "There's a hot dog in the backseat."

"It's Stephanie," Grandma said. "She's stuck. Her bun's too big."

"Gotta cut back on the dessert," Morelli said.

"Very funny," I said to him. "Just get me out of here."

Morelli pulled me out of the cab and gave me the once-over. "What are you doing in a hot dog suit?"

"It was supposed to be a sparerib, but the costume shop was all out, so the best we could get was a hot dog."

"Yeah, that makes sense," Morelli said. "What have you got in your hand?"

"We got stopped by Officer Hardass. Connie got a speeding ticket, and I got a ticket for not wearing a seat belt. I was in the backseat. Do you have to wear a seat belt in the backseat?"

Morelli took the ticket from me and put it in his pocket. "Not if you're a hot dog."

"I hope we didn't miss Al Roker," Grandma said.

Morelli looked over at her. "Al Roker?"

"He's bringing a whole crew with him, and he's going to film the cook-off, and we're going to be on television," Grandma said.

"It's not Al Roker," Morelli said. "It's Al Rochere. He's got a cooking show on some cable channel."

"How do you know that?" Lula said. "They could both be coming."

"I have a list of media and celebrities present," Morelli said. "There's extra security for this event because of the Chipotle murder."

"Look at the time," Grandma said. "We gotta get the ribs going."

Connie, Lula, and Grandma set off power-walking across the field. I tried to follow, but I walked into a trash can and fell over.

"Oops," I said.

Morelli looked down at me. "Are you okay?"

"I can't see in this stupid suit."

Morelli picked me up. "Would you like me to get you out of this thing?"

"Yes!"

He worked at the zipper in the back and finally peeled me out of the hot dog suit. "You're soaking wet," he said.

"It was hot in the suit."

Morelli wrapped an arm around me and shuffled me off to a booth selling cook-off gear. He bought me a T-shirt, a hat, and a sweatshirt, stuffed the hot dog suit into a bag, and sent me to the ladies' room to change.

"This feels much better," I said to him when I came out. "Thanks."

"You look better, too."

"Out of Rangeman black?"

"Yeah." Morelli wrapped his arms around me. "I miss you. Bob misses you. My grandmother misses you."

"Your grandmother hates me."

"True. She misses hating you." Morelli straightened the hat on my head. "Maybe I could learn to like peanut butter."

"You don't have to like peanut butter. Just stop yelling at me."

"That's the way my family communicates."

"Find another way to communicate. And why are we arguing all the time? We argue over everything."

"I think it's because we aren't having enough sex."

"And that's another thing. Why are you so obsessed with sex?"

"Because I don't get any?"

I tried not to laugh, but I couldn't help myself. "I guess that could do it."

I saw flames shoot into the sky and then black smoke.

"It looks like Lula fired up the grill," I said to Morelli. "I should get back to them."

We made our way through the crowd, back to the Flamin' kitchen. The guy from the kitchen next to us was standing with the fire extinguisher in his hand, shaking his head.

"Unbelievable," he said. "You moved the canopy back, and then you set your ribs on fire and torched your hat."

Lula still had the hat on her head, but the top was all black and smoking, and foam dripped off the hat onto Lula's white chef coat.

"Looks to me like the ribs are done," Grandma said, peering over the grill at the charred bones. "You think they need more sauce?"

"I think they need a decent burial," Connie said.

The rusted bottom of the grill gave way, and everything fell out onto the ground.

"Don't that beat all," Grandma said.

Morelli's cell phone buzzed. He walked away to talk, and when he returned he was smiling.

"They caught Marco," he said. "He was trying to get to the airport in Philly. He's being brought back to Trenton."

"Do we get the reward?" Lula wanted to know. "We gave information that got him captured."

"I don't know," Morelli said. "That's up to the company offering the reward."

"The barbecue sauce company," Lula said. "The one with the picture of Chipotle on the jar. Fire in the Hole sauce."

"Yep."

"What about the other moron?" Lula said. "What about the guy who was always shooting at me?"

"Marco fingered him the minute he was caught. Zito Dudley. Marco said as far as he knew, Dudley was still on the cook-off grounds."

"We gotta find Dudley before anyone else," Lula said. "Or we might have to split the reward, bein' that there were two killers and only one million dollars. We should spread out, and if you see him, shoot him."

"I wouldn't mind shooting him, but I don't know what he looks like," Grandma said.

"He looks sort of like the Maniac," Lula said. "Only shorter."

"Dudley sounds familiar," Connie said. "I just saw that name somewhere. Zito Dudley. Zito Dudley."

The fire-extinguisher guy was basting the ribs on his grill. He looked over when Connie said Zito Dudley.

"Zito Dudley is presenting the check to the winner of the cook-off," he said. "He's associated with Chipotle's barbecue sauce."

Lula's eyes went wide. "Get out. That wiener is part of Chipotle's company?"

"It's not actually Chipotle's company," the guy said. "Chipotle got money for putting his name on the jar. The company is owned by someone else." He reached behind him to his prep table, grabbed the cook-off program, and handed it to Lula. "His picture is in here. It's on the last page. He's standing with the cook-off committee."

We all looked at the picture of Dudley.

"That's him, all right," Lula said. "Nasty little bastard."

Morelli was on his phone talking to his partner, feeding him the information, asking for more men.

Something was causing a disturbance on the opposite side of the field. We all craned our necks and stood tall to see what the noise and movement was about. People were parting in front of us, and suddenly a man burst out of the crowd. He was running for all he was worth, and Joyce was chasing him in her high-heeled boots.

"It's him," Lula said. "It's Dudley!"

They got even with our booth, and Joyce launched herself into the air and tackled Zito Dudley. Lula rushed in, pulled Joyce off Dudley, and grabbed his foot.

"He's mine," Lula said.

Joyce kicked Lula in the leg and wrestled Dudley away from her. Lula put a neck lock on Joyce, and they went down to the ground, kicking and clawing and cussing, taking Dudley with them. There was a gunshot, and Joyce yelped and flopped onto the ground, blood oozing from her red leather bustier.

Morelli had his gun drawn, but Dudley was on his feet, holding a gun to Lula's head.

"Drop your gun," Dudley said.

Connie, Grandma, Morelli, the guys next to us, and several passersby all dropped their guns.

"You won't get anywhere," Morelli said to Dudley. "There are police all over this park."

"I've got a hostage. And I'd be real happy to have one more excuse to shoot her. I've been trying to shoot her all week. And I would have done it, if I wasn't saddled with Marco the Moron."

"I thought he was a Maniac," Grandma said.

"I want a helicopter brought in," Dudley said. "And I want one unarmed pilot flying it."

"That only happens in the movies," Morelli said. "Trenton can't afford helicopters. We're lucky we're not all riding bicycles."

"Get the traffic report helicopter then. Get one from the beach patrol. Get one from NASCAR. You don't get me out of here in a helicopter, and I swear I'll kill my hostage."

Morelli went back to his cell phone. "I'll make some calls," he said to Dudley. "Maybe I can come up with something. Would National Guard be okay?"

Dudley looked at Joyce on the ground, bleeding.

"Get a medevac. I know you've got one of those."

"You got it," Morelli said. "I've got two paramedics here. I want you to allow them to treat her."

"Sure. Get her out of the way."

"This is confusing," Lula said. "What happens to the reward? How am I gonna get the reward from you if you're the one I caught?"

"It's my brother-in-law's reward. He's the owner of the company. I'm just a token vice president. He's the one who was the big Chipotle fan. Put his picture on all the sauce jars. I told him not to do it, but would he listen to me? Hell, no. Now see where that got us."

"Where'd it get you?" Grandma wanted to know.

"It got us nowhere. Chipotle refused to sign a new contract. He was screwing my brother-in-law's bimbo gold-digger wife. They were going to start their own company as soon as the divorce went through." Dudley looked over at Morelli. "Where's the helicopter?"

"It's on its way. You should hear it any minute."

"Some brother-in-law you've got," Connie said. "What did he do, go to the Chicago Mob and hire someone to whack Chipotle? And then send you along to babysit and make sure the job got done?"

"He would have been better to let me do it myself. He had this idea to get rid of Chipotle and turn it into a media frenzy. Get free publicity by chopping his head off. Chipotle never saw it coming. He was still drunk from the night before. Unfortunately, we had a witness who would have been safe, except she entered the contest."

Al Rochere ran over with his film crew and went in for an interview.

"Get him out of here," Dudley said. "I'll shoot her. Swear to God."

"Wait a minute," Lula said. "This could be my big break."

There was the unmistakable *wup wup wup* of a helicopter, and the medevac chopper flew low over us and landed in an empty area of the field.

Dudley still had the gun to Lula's head. "I'm taking her with me. I'll release her when we land."

"I don't like this," Lula said. "I don't like helicopters. I'm gonna get the runs."

"Shut up, and get walking."

"I don't feel so good," Lula said. And she farted.

Dudley stepped back and fanned the air with his gun. "Jeez, lady, what have you been eating?"

"Barbecue," Lula said. And she sucker punched him in the throat.

Dudley gagged and dropped his gun. And Morelli was on him.

"Is there still a reward?" Lula asked. "Does anybody know the ruling on that?"

A bunch of cops and security guards swarmed in, keeping the curious back. Morelli's partner cuffed Dudley and a couple uniforms moved in to help.

"My hero," I said to Morelli.

Morelli grinned. "Lula's the hero. She sucker punched him."

"And it was a pip of a fart, too," Grandma said.

I looked over at Joyce. The paramedics had her stable and ready to medevac out.

"How is she?" I asked one of them.

"Lost some blood, but I don't think anything critical was hit."

"I need to go downtown with Dudley," Morelli said to me. "Call me when you get things figured out."

I walked to our kitchen, where Grandma, Lula, and Connie were standing, staring at the blackened ribs and ashes spread across the ground.

"I don't suppose we're gonna win the contest, what with the grill falling apart and the ribs burning up," Grandma said.

"I'm tired of this whole barbecue thing, anyway," Connie said. "I could use a calzone."

"I'm in for a meatball sub," Lula said.

"And spaghetti," Grandma said. "Do you think we should stick around to see who wins the contest?"

"I don't care who wins the contest, since it's not me," Lula said.

Connie had her bag hiked up on her shoulder. "We can read about it in the paper tomorrow."

TWENTY

It was a little after six when I pulled into the Rangeman garage. Marco the Maniac and Zito Dudley were in jail. Joyce was being treated. Lula, Grandma, and Connie were at Pino's. I parked the cab next to the Buick and took the elevator to the seventh floor.

Ranger had called shortly after four o'clock and asked that I come in when the dust settled on the barbecue fiasco. I entered his apartment and found him in his office, at his computer.

"Come here," he said. "I want you to see something. This came in at four o'clock."

I looked over his shoulder at a grainy picture of a wall. A motion detector was fixed at the top of the wall, and alongside the motion detector was a small square box, the same size as the detector. A slim young man dressed in khakis and a white collared shirt came into the picture, looked around, fixed on the Rangeman camera for a moment, and left.

"Is that your break-in guy?" I asked Ranger.

"He fits the description, other than the uniform. I have Hal and Ramon watching the house, and they missed him. He drove up in a van from the client's pest control company."

"Was anyone home when he went in?"

"Mrs. Lazar, the homeowner. Her husband was still at work. She said she let someone in from pest control. We called the company, and they said he didn't belong to them. He was in and out before we could get the information to Hal and Ramon."

"So for some reason, he changed his routine. Maybe he saw Hector go into the house to install your camera."

"Or maybe he just decided it was time for a change."

"Now what?"

Ranger pushed back in his chair. "More of the same."

"I'm still driving my father's cab. Unless you have something for me to do, I'm going to run to the Starbucks on the corner, get him a couple of his favorite cookies as a thank-you, and return the cab."

"Sounds like a plan," Ranger said.

I took the elevator to the first floor and walked the half block to Starbucks. I ordered a coffee for myself and three cookies for my father. There were several people in line, buying a caffeine fix to get them through the night after a day in the office. Several people were hunkered down in the big leather armchairs, making use of the Internet connection. A guy sat alone at one of the small tables. He had a cup of coffee, and he was absorbed in a handheld electronic game. He was wearing loose-fitting jeans, a Cowboy Bebop T-shirt, and a baggy sweatshirt.

It was the guy in Ranger's surveillance video. I hadn't recognized him at first. He looked like everyone else at Starbucks. Except for the game. The game caught my attention.

I pulled my phone out of my pocket and dialed Ranger. "I think I've got him," I said. "You know how the break-in guy always took those little electronic games kids play? Well, I'm in Starbucks, and there's a guy who looks like the guy in your video, and he's sitting here playing with one of those games."

"Sit tight," Ranger said. And he disconnected.

The break-in guy stood and pocketed his game. He stretched and left the coffee shop, walking north on Myrtle Street. I left the pickup line and followed at a distance. I called Ranger and gave him the new directions. The break-in guy went into an ugly 1970s-style office building. Five floors of tinted glass and aquamarine panels interspersed with yellow brick.

I was able to see him through the revolving glass door. He crossed the small lobby and stepped into an elevator. I ran into the lobby and read through the list of tenants. Fourth floor: GOT GAME SECURITY. Bingo.

I was on the phone with Ranger again, and an instant later, three black Rangeman SUVs rolled to a stop outside the building.

I took the elevator with Ranger and Tank, Ramon and his partner took the stairs, Hal and his partner stayed in the lobby. We reached the fourth floor, and Ranger tried the door to Got Game Security. Locked. He rapped on the door. The door buzzed unlocked, and Ranger pushed the door open.

The break-in guy was at a ratty wooden desk. He looked at Ranger standing in his doorway and went pale.

"What?" he said. And then he jumped up and tried to make a run for an adjoining suite.

Ranger reached him in two strides, grabbed him by the shirt, and threw him against the wall. He hit with a *SPLAT* and slid down the wall like a sack of sand.

"Get him out of here," Ranger said to Tank.

There was nothing in the office other than the desk and a desk chair. No phone. No computer. Ranger pulled the top drawer open, and it was filled with handheld games.

The door to the adjoining suite opened, and a scrawny guy with a mop of curly red hair and freckled skin peeked out. "Oh shit!" he said. And he slammed the door shut.

Ranger opened the door, and we walked into a room crammed with all the stuff that had been stolen. The red-haired guy was pressed against the far wall, and I swear I could see his heart beating against his Final Fantasy T-shirt.

"Talk to me," Ranger said.

The red-haired guy opened his mouth and nodded his head, but no words came out. His eyes got glassy, and he slid down the wall and sat down hard on the floor. He looked to be about eighteen years old.

"Do we need medical?" Ramon asked, entering the room.

"Give him some time," Ranger said.

We stood around for a couple minutes, waiting for the kid's eyes to focus. When he looked like he had a thought in his head, Ranger pulled him to his feet.

"We wanted to be security guys," the kid said. "We wanted a job at Rangeman, but you wouldn't even talk to us. You wouldn't even take our applications. The guy at the desk said we were too young. So we figured we'd start our own security company."

"And?"

"And Toby thought it would be cool if we financed our company by robbing your accounts. Like we could make a game out of it. Toby is all into games. He had it all figured out. He had all these rules to keep it interesting. Toby's probably the smartest guy I know."

Ranger looked around. "Why have you got all the stolen property stacked up here?"

"We didn't know what to do with it. We figured we'd fence it, but we don't know anybody who does that. So we used the money to rent these offices while we looked for a fence."

"Turn them in," Ranger said to Ramon. "Let me know if there are problems."

Ramon took the kid out of the office, and his partner followed.

"You should be happy," I said to Ranger. "You solved your mystery."

"I was almost ruined by two goofy kids. I'm embarrassed."

"Whoa," I said. "That's an emotion."

"You think I don't have emotions?"

"I don't think you very often get embarrassed."

"It takes a lot," Ranger said.

"You brought me in to snoop around. Now that you've found your bad guys, does this mean I'm being terminated?"

Ranger looked at me. "That's your decision."

"I think I'll keep the job for a while longer, but I'll move out of your bed."

"That's the safe way to go," Ranger said. "But not the most satisfying. The job will get boring."

"But not your bed?"

"Not if we're in it together."

There was no doubt in my mind.

An hour later, I was in my father's cab with Rex on the seat next to me and a small stash of Rangeman uniforms in a bag on the backseat. I was on my way to my parents' house, but I took a detour and drove past Morelli's house just for the heck of it. Lights were on in his downstairs windows, and his SUV was parked curbside. I pulled in behind the SUV, went to Morelli's door, and knocked.

Morelli grinned when he saw me. "Couldn't resist my charms?"

"Couldn't resist your television. My father's going to be watching baseball, and the Rangers are playing the Devils tonight."

"I'm all set," Morelli said. "I've got chips and dip and beer."

I ran back to the cab and got Rex's cage. Rex wouldn't want to miss the Rangers playing, and he loved chips.

I put Rex on the coffee table, and I settled in on the couch, next to Bob.

"Have you heard anything about Joyce?"

"She's going to be okay."

"And what about the guy who owns the sauce company and hired Marco to whack Chipotle?"

Morelli scooped some dip onto a chip and fed it to me. He had to reach over Bob to do it. "They're looking for him, but haven't found him so far. He's probably in Venezuela."

"That was pretty scary at the cook-off. It took a lot of guts for Lula to punch that guy."

"I'm more impressed with the fart."

"Men."

"Hey, what can I say, men like farts."

I told him about finding the break-in guy and his friend, Morelli fed me another chip, and I drank some of his beer.

"Look at us," I said to Morelli. "We aren't arguing."

"That's because the game hasn't started," Morelli said. "Maybe we shouldn't watch the game. Maybe we should do something else. Are you still off men?"

"I think I'm off and on."

Morelli grinned at me. "Which night is this? Off or on?"

I smiled back at him. "There are some things a man should find out for himself."